JIM LAFLEUR

The Further Narrative of Arthur Gordon Pym

Contents

Foreword

When Edgar Allan Poe published *The Narrative of Arthur Gordon Pym of Nantucket* in 1838, readers were left suspended in a narrative as enigmatic as the uncharted southern seas it describes. The story ended abruptly, with Pym and his companion Peters at the mercy of strange forces, the true nature of their journey into the Antarctic unknown forever obscured by a veil of mystery. To this day, it remains one of the most haunting and unresolved tales in literature.

Poe's unfinished masterpiece captured my imagination in ways no other story has. The sense of wonder, fear, and the quest for the unknown that permeates every page of *Pym* lingers long after the final sentence fades. It is a book that speaks to our deepest fears—of what lies beyond the world we know, and the truths we may uncover if we dare to venture too far.

Yet, as much as I have cherished *The Narrative of Arthur Gordon Pym*, there has always been a part of me that longed to see its mysteries explored further. What fate befell Pym and Peters after they vanished into the void? What were the great revelations hinted at but never revealed? And what would be the consequences of traveling into the heart of the Earth itself, beyond the ice, into a world unseen by human eyes?

It is with these questions in mind that I undertook the task of continuing Poe's story. I do so with great respect for the original text and its themes of survival, sacrifice, and the unknown. But also with the desire to expand upon the journey in ways that Poe might have imagined, had he been given the chance to finish his tale. I seek not only to provide answers, but to delve deeper into the mysteries that haunted Pym and Peters, exploring the unseen worlds and civilizations that await beneath the surface of the Earth.

Writing this continuation has been both a tribute to Poe's genius and a personal journey. As a lifelong admirer of his work, I have always felt that *The Narrative of Arthur Gordon Pym* stood apart, its singularity resting in its unresolved conclusion. With this continuation, I hope to honor the original while adding new layers to its rich tapestry of themes—of human curiosity, hubris, and the natural world's unfathomable power.

It is with great humility that I present *The Further Narrative of Arthur Gordon Pym*. To those who, like myself, have been captivated by the questions left unanswered in Poe's tale, I offer this continuation not as an end, but as a new beginning. May you, dear reader, find as much wonder and terror in these pages as I have in writing them.

1

The Shrouded Figure

The Antarctic night lay upon us thick as oil, an endless expanse of silver-gray mist that swirled like the breath of a great beast, unseen yet palpably alive. Our canoe—more a splinter than a vessel—drifted aimlessly on the glassy water beneath the clinging shroud, a solitary leaf adrift on an ocean of nothing. The air held the sharp bite of salt and cold, clinging to our skin with a damp heaviness that numbed the senses. The paddle in my hand sliced through stillness, the water barely stirred—a calm so far removed from reason that I might've thought the sea beneath us frozen, save for its betraying, sibilant lap against the canoe.

Beside me, Dirk Peters sat hunched forward, his shoulders tense and broad in the narrowing silence. His fingers drummed mindlessly against the wood as if an unseen force dared him to move, to act. I watched him through a sideward glance, noting the way he leaned forward into the mist, narrowed eyes scanning a world he could not see. This was not an ocean, not anymore—this was purgatory, a place that lay somewhere between life and death. And Peters knew it, though he had not the words. His instincts spoke through his body—tension bristling like the hackles of a beast sensing some great, silent predator.

We'd been adrift for—how long? Minutes, hours…? Time had become a cruel joke since the mist had swallowed sky and sea alike. The Antarctic wastes offered no markers, no stars, only endless gray stretched across an ever-drifting horizon. Where were we? What were we drifting towards?

I loosened my tight grip on the paddle and resumed the rhythmic motion, feeling the faint resistance of water that seemed too sluggish, too thick. I frowned, but said nothing. If Peters had noticed, he gave no sign. His muttering had ceased minutes ago, replaced by a cold, watchful quiet.

What else is there... what else waits in the places we do not see?

The thought slithered unbidden through my mind, unsettling in its simplicity. I had spent the better half of my life exploring places unknown to most men—in jungles, in deserts, on oceans—but never had I known an environment that felt so actively hostile in its concealment. This fog-swathed sea did not merely obscure. It hid secrets—secrets I wasn't sure I wanted to uncover.

"We're cursed," Peters muttered, more to himself than to me. His voice, grating as it was, rasped with the tones of a man trying to reason with a force that defied reason. "I feel it… somethin' watches us… God won't even smell our bones once this sea takes us."

The chill from his words clung to the air, joining its natural dampness. I scoffed quietly, though even I failed to find humor in it. The mist was too all-encompassing, too overwhelming—it magnified every fear, squeezed every loose thread of doubt until one's mind began to turn mad with its weight.

"Nothing watches us, Peters. Only hallucinations form in fog such as this. Our eyes deceive with distance and unseen shapes," I said, though the certainty in my voice rang false even to my ears.

Peters did not turn his gaze from the horizon ahead, squinting into the distance as though it would give him something, anything, to latch onto. "Hallucination don't make the sea quiet itself. It's… thicker now. It ain't natural."

True enough, the surface no longer felt open, free. It resisted the stroke of the paddle. What had once been liquid now felt sluggish, near-treasonous. I caught the growing discomfort itching under my own skin. Peters' wariness had infected me, festered with the cold chill sneaking into my bones.

Yet, it was not fear, not yet. It was anticipation—*an expectation.* Some mindless part of me still clung to curiosity, determined to excavate truth from the unknown, even if that truth lay buried beneath things we should not see.

And then I saw it. Peters must have seen it too, for we both froze in synchronous halt, our paddles rising sluggishly from the water, dripping gleaming threads into the stillness. There, barely more than an impression in the mist—something vast and tall. Looming. Its size was monstrous, wrong in its proportions—a figure cast in shadow, so blurred, so imperceptible that I questioned its existence the moment it took shape.

At first, it was only a distortion, as if the fog played tricks on our eyes, warping distance. But no—it grew. A shape, tenuous but growing with each passing breath, emerged from that ghostly curtain. A mass of swirling gray rose higher and higher above our heads. There was no rationale to its dimensions—nothing on this barren sea should conjure such impossible height without revealing itself as mountain or berg or man-made colossus.

But it was none, neither solid island nor animal nor iceberg.

Nothing explained it.

Nothing should have.

"It watches," Peters' voice was brittle, barely a whisper now. His white-knuckled hands gripped the sides of the canoe. "Something waits out there."

"That's nonsense—" I began, but my words faltered, twisting in my throat when I saw it better.

There. Its eyes.

Far up in its form, two eyes, or something I'd call *eyes* by the nearest interpretation of human experience, glowed faintly where the vague outline of a face ought to be. Eyes like wide, hollow pits of black, but out-swirling, nebulous. Quietly… watching.

It had no expression. It showed no malice nor intent. And that frightened me more than anything.

I swallowed. My heart thundered in my ears, louder than the paddle's splash, drowning thought and rationality. This was not curiosity; this was primal fear—the kind that crawls when faced with things beyond man's understanding. I found myself frozen, not unlike an insect beneath glass, capable of watching but not of acting, mere prey beneath a god's indifferent gaze.

Peters was muttering rapid curses, edging toward panic, but he and I were alike in that moment—paralyzed by a comprehension we couldn't grasp and an instinct to run clawing its way into our minds.

"P-Pym…" His voice cracked—steeled—but faltering. "Get us outta here."

No response came from me, though I heard the demand fully.

The figure, immense and vaporous, did not approach. It had laws of reality we could not align with. A stray tendril of light or shadow shifted near its leg, uncoiling like something sentient—rippling through the water, arrested there only for a second before evaporating.

Suddenly, and too soon for my reality-starved mind, the figure contorted, twisting as if being torn at stiches. It began to flake apart. The edges blurred like insubstantial mist caught in strange light, unraveling piece-by-piece, disintegrating into the silvered air. One moment it hung like a monolith, too large, too still, and the next... it was simply gone, carried off on the wind in a way too silent to be real.

My breath caught; my heart failed to slow. That feeling, that awful, ever-spying gaze—it lingered in my chest, though my eyes strained to search the spot where no figure now stood.

We hadn't imagined it.

Something had been there.

Something vast.

Peters grunted, finally tearing his eyes away from the vanishing shadow. His fingers dug hard into the wood of the boat's edge, eyes wide and disbelieving.

"You saw it, right?" he asked, lips tight with suppressed fear. "It ain't just the mist?"

I hesitated. "I... I saw it."

For the first time, I felt the tremor in my own voice, the coiled fear that threatened to shake me. It was irrational. Yet telling him it was nothing—some atmospheric mirage—would be a lie that neither of our minds could afford.

***

The air turned electric before the water itself stirred. A sudden, eerie stillness passed over the sea—a breathless, suspended pause that froze time around us. The fog thickened, pressing in as though intent on choking us to a stop. And then, without warning, the surface of the water seemed to shudder underneath us, as if some unseen hand had brushed across its skin. No surge of wind, no warning clouds. Just the water, trembling beneath the canoe's hull, whispering promises I dared not try to comprehend.

A low murmur rose; too faint to determine its source, too constant to dismiss. The lake, I realized in a cold rush, was not still.

"Peters," I started, but the word had barely left my lips when the current seized us—an invisible force, powerful and unrelenting, like the pull of a great cosmic vacuum that could not be defied.

The water around the canoe began to churn, an insidious movement beneath a deceptively tranquil surface. Peters reacted first, his instincts honed far beyond mine when it came to the raw violence of nature.

"Grab the paddle!" he barked, his voice sharpened with fear

as he immediately dug his own paddle into the water, trying to push against the pull. His face, pale and taut beneath the shadow of his brow, showed no illusions of confidence, only the grim determination of a man well aware that survival was not guaranteed.

I fumbled momentarily, my fingers slipping on the wet, slick wood as I tried to grab my own paddle. The water's pull quickly accelerated, and a distant roar echoed from beneath us, a sound like a beast awakening from a long slumber—low, rumbling, and growing louder with each thundering second.

"Pym!" Peters shouted, digging fiercely into the rushing lake. His breaths had grown short and frantic, the veins in his neck standing taut as he strained to force our canoe free from the circling drag. The water was no longer placid; it swirled violently around us, pulling us ever inward to the center of something dangerous and unknown.

Something not meant for the world above.

I plunged my paddle into the water, but it was like pushing against the hands of a thousand grasping phantoms. The water resisted, thick now, like syrup turned cold. Every muscle in my arms screamed as I fought to hold our course steady, but it was in vain—the canoe lurched, tilting dangerously as the maelstrom beneath us expanded with terrifying speed.

The boat spun violently, the world tilting and spinning in dizzying equilibrium. My stomach dropped as we were yanked bodily toward a vortex that even now became visible ahead—a vast, churning maw in the center of the lake, growing in size with each breathless moment. Its mouth, a black hole, seemed eager to swallow anything that dared tread too close to its spiraling edge.

Peters growled, the sound almost primal. "We're gettin' dragged—paddling won't stop us now!"

"There's nothing we can do!" I shouted over the horrific symphony of crashing water and the unnatural hum booming beneath us. The atmosphere—dense and suffocating—pressed in, mingling with the electric tension in my nerves until my heart pounded so hard I could taste the beat in my throat. The water tenaciously pulled at us, the black eye of the whirlpool luring us closer, closer with relentless power.

Peters gave one last furious wrench with the paddle, but the vortex was already oblivious to our attempts, its pull too strong to deny. "Hold on, for God's sake!" he shouted. A few final strokes of the paddle—fruitless now, only an act of sheer desperation—before he abandoned it altogether. His hands grabbed onto the canoe's sides, his fingers digging so harshly into the waterlogged wood that they blanched with pressure.

I did the same as panic filled every fiber of my being. It barely felt real—we were caught in the grip of a force far older, far more powerful than any storm I'd ever encountered at sea. I had faced hurricanes, shipwrecks, and the vast, endless wrath of the ocean before, yet none of it had ever filled me with this kind of gnawing fear, this transcendent dread that spoke of something not entirely natural—but something primordial.

"Hold tight, Peters!" I gasped, fingers slick with the water that drenched the boat's edge. My heart drummed violently against the walls of my ribcage as I watched, helpless, while the whirlpool loomed ever nearer. There would be no escape if we went under, no return. What lay beyond that maelstrom was too far from salvation.

The canoe tilted at a vicious angle, throwing us hard against the bench seats. I managed to hold on by instinct alone, clinging as tightly as I could, though the slippery wood threatened to betray me with every second. Peters growled— a frustrated, feral noise—as the boat skidded, nearly vertical, through the water. "Damn it! DAMN IT!" His anger— unnerving as ever—only increased the terror of the moment, for even Peters, the unshakable anchor, seemed tossed adrift in this madness.

The whirlpool's center was only seconds away now. I tried, absurdly, to keep myself calm, to think logically as the world spun out of control. Beneath us was something monstrous, something vast… but what? What could have stirred beneath this hidden sea to create such a force?

Then the current took us fully.

The canoe pitched violently downward, and my stomach lurched as we fell, hurtling into the eye of the whirlpool with unimaginable speed. The roar of the water drowned out my attempts at speech—what could there possibly have been to say in such a hopeless moment? With an almighty crash, we plummeted into the towering walls of rushing water, careening forward toward the deep, yawning abyss.

And then we were no longer on the surface.

The world shifted and buckled beneath, around, and within. The cold drowned out sensation. The pressure around me felt like the sky collapsing inward. Peters let out a half-choked curse before he, too, was silent, both of us tumbling deeper into the water that spun, churned, and consumed everything in its path. The canoe... where was the canoe?

I blinked, but blackness swallowed my vision whole—like a great curtain, heavy and full of finality.

Strangely, I could still think. As we were pulled tight through the watery jaws of the abyss, my thoughts raced—disjointed, surreal fragments that were too quick to latch down into anything coherent. What had done this? What was this hidden pull beneath the water? No natural force, that was certain. But then, did I expect anything natural in this forsaken place?

The sound of the water—a raging behemoth bellowing its demands—grew distant, fell to something muted. It no longer pounded in my ears with the ferocity of its earlier wrath. There was... quiet.

Where...?

And then.

Light.

A pale glow, distant and muted at first, emerged from the dark—a sort of shimmering haze in the ink-black depth that surrounded us. Was it real? Or was it simply my mind's frantic attempt to make sense of the madness?

No, it was real.

The cold wasn't as suffocating now, either. Instead, there came warmth—a strange, unnatural warmth that grew with the faint, creeping glow from deep beneath our submerged prison. We were falling still, yes, into a world we could neither see nor anticipate. Yet the farther we dropped, the more the water's grip relaxed, no longer crushing, no longer unyieldingly frigid.

The light became brighter—an ethereal, bluish shimmer that lit the water in delicate ripples.

What in God's creation…?

I blinked, gasped for a breath I did not have. My limbs flailed weakly through the thick water, but my movements slowed. Darkness—cold, yet receding. The depth beneath us was infinite… stretching…

No, not infinite. Revealed.

The force of the vortex had lessened, though it still guided us down a smooth corridor of blue-black water with a single, inescapable current—a descent beyond the ice. The light became more distinct, flickering like an ambient fire kindled behind the walls of glass, its source obscured but somehow all-encompassing. Around me, shapes—large, nearly spectral—seemed to lie just beyond the edges of my perception. A city? No, that was madness. Some form of structure—unnatural still. The thought jittered madly in my head. Were we falling into some ancient ruin?

Finally, the descent slowed to a drifting weightlessness, my body buoyed by the supporting current. My lungs burned, the airless pressure tightening my chest. But still, there was no panic, for now the sense of otherworldly dread had become a kind of stunned awe—or denial. We could not survive this.

Telescoped ridges of ice, pale coral, perhaps? Bizarre formations—minds cannot hold contradicting truths—

Gasp.

Air surged into my lungs. The current shifted, surging us into open space again—breaking the water's surface with a suddenness that stole whatever battle-weary energy still clung to me.

I spluttered violently, instincts taking control as I grasped for something—anything—solid. My hand touched hard wood. The canoe.

Beside me, Peters' gasps filled the air as well, and I turned to see him clinging to the other end of the canoe, nearly overturned but miraculously unbroken. He spat out water and checked himself to ensure all his limbs remained attached.

"I—I thought—" he gulped, voice hoarse from the strain of survival. "I thought that was it."

His breath came in ragged bursts, his large frame visibly trembling under the familiar fatigue clawing at him now that fear and adrenaline had burned through.

I, for my part, stared blankly upward, barely managing to hold onto the lip of the boat with aching fingers.

"What… what is this?" I whispered, too drained to care if the words were received.

A strange silence followed. Then, softly, as though we had been swallowed whole by the Earth itself, the ethereal glow swelled all around us.

We'd emerged not into air—not into sky—but **another world**.

2

The Subterranean Tunnel

My lungs compressed, the air tightening in a desperate squeeze as I broke the surface of the water, panting. The oppressive warmth clung to my skin in thick waves, a humid embrace as uninviting as the turmoil that had swallowed us whole moments before. My arms ached, the muscles stiffening from exertion; hands, slack with exhaustion, dragged across the canoe's wooden lip as I struggled to grasp fully what had just transpired.

Above—no, around—me, a new world unfolded, an alien vastness that seemed both ethereal and unknowable in its breadth. Beneath the curling mist that clung low over the water's surface, faintly glowing patterns traced eerie lines across the cavern's walls. It was as though the subterranean ocean we had waded into had been engraved with some ancient design—glowing veins running through the rock face, pulsing ever so faintly in a rhythm I could almost feel against my skin. Seductive, mysterious, yet as terrible as a curse half-spoken into the darkness.

I shook off the vision momentarily and coughed up the water lingering in my throat, more aware now of Peters' ragged gasps to my right. He was gripping the side of the canoe with a fierce, almost desperate intensity, his breathing heavy but controlled. In the dim, otherworldly glow of the cavern, his wide eyes appeared to gleam with wonder and fear alike, though neither emotion seemed to claim full dominion.

"Warm…" Peters' voice was a rough whisper, escaping between labored breaths, as though the single syllable was guilt-ridden, an affront to the cold reality we had once known.

I nodded, my mind barely comprehending his observation. The warmth pressed in on us—unnatural, sticky heat coiling through every rivulet of water still clinging to our drenched clothes. My muscles, once rigid and stiff with cold, now relaxed under the oppressive balminess of the inner atmosphere, the paradox of the warmth compounded by the eerie glow that surrounded us. How had the frigid cold of the Antarctic above given way to this?

"This can't be real…" I muttered to myself, placing fingers—trembling slightly—from the edge of the canoe into the lapping water. The surface rippled, sluggish, carried by lazy undercurrents. Warm. The water itself was—against all reason—warmer than the air had been.

What madness had we fallen into?

I forced myself to sit straighter, trying to steel my nerves as the aftershock of the whirlpool and our tumultuous descent began to slowly ebb. My gaze lifted from the canoe's lip to the cavern ahead—a cavern so vast it felt boundless, narrowing into a series of sloping tunnels that burrowed impossibly deep into the Earth's bowels.

Walls rose on either side of us, smooth, featureless cliffs reaching so high overhead they disappeared into shadows—shadowed mist, ominous and impenetrable. Though there was no visible sky, a muted, bluish glow bathed everything in an odd twilight hue, emanating from the rock itself in places, as though the earth guarded secrets far older than man's brief existence on its surface.

And then there was the whisper—the faint hum that resonated through the stone around us, barely felt but inescapably present. It was a vibration, soft but persistent, as if the earth itself exhaled in measured intervals, alive with some deep-rooted, nameless energy—a breath both slow and patient.

A tremor rippled unbidden through my hand as I placed it against the canoe's worn surface, watching the water around us shimmer faintly in response. What *was* this place?

Peters groaned, drawing me back to present urgency. His eyes were still locked on the walls, his knuckles white where they gripped the canoe as if touch alone could wrest clarity from the surrealist canvas painted before us. "Unnatural…" he murmured, as though the word tasted bitter or wrong. "Whatever brought us 'ere, Pym, it sure as hell ain't no natural current. Ain't no earthly place."

I could not dispute the observation.

"We are… beneath," I ventured quietly, more to cement the truth in my own mind than to offer an answer. The hollow resonance of my voice echoed briefly within the belly of the stone chamber. "Deeper than—God knows how far beneath the surface… dragged past the ice shelf…"

I trailed off, the folly of even attempting to explain our situation taking hold. Beneath the ice. We had ventured, no—been dragged—into something far more encompassing, something entirely…below.

I glanced downward, my chest tightening with the creeping realization. The thought rose up like bile from the pit of my stomach: *we are no longer in a world meant for men.*

Peters shifted, finally sitting more upright, though his brow furrowed deeply with skepticism and fear coiled tight across his forehead. "Whatever took us, it ain't friendly. And we got no way up from here, unless you intend to climb back through that thing… and I ain't sure I have the strength left fer it."

He wasn't wrong. Despite the hum of life pulsing in the cavern, my body still felt limp, drained as though the very act of surviving had scrubbed away the vestiges of energy and will left in me. Too much lay ahead to think about escape, not when every step forward drew us deeper into the waiting jaws of this strange, underground beast.

Beneath us, the water rippled, and both our heads jerked downward in unprompted synchronicity. Peters, ever more guarded, let go of the canoe with one hand, his other slipping a knife out from his belt—a gesture both practical and futile. We had no longer anything akin to control over what would happen next.

A long shape, distant, darker than the water itself, slid out beneath us—a shadow formless but living, slipping with no sound beneath the static billows of the lake surface. The boat trembled the barest fraction, though whether from movement or our own raw nerves, I could not say.

"There's… something in the water," Peters' voice cracked under the dire weight of the admission. "Goddamn it, I told ya…"

"I know," I replied, voice strained as I reached without thinking for the paddle. My mind recoiled involuntarily, fragmenting away from the thought of what that shadow could belong to. I wasn't certain I *wanted* to know.

The cold, slick paddle barely gave purchase against the curdled water, but it spurred a motion all the same, a slow push forward while the thick ripples circled lazily around us. Peters read my intent, joining me by paddling as quietly as the heavy liquid allowed. Better perhaps to exit this expanse before whatever lay hidden beneath decided we were worth more than curiosity.

Ahead, the far shore offered a sloping stone ledge—small,

jagged, and untrustworthy, but more solid than the uncertainty stretching in every other direction. Pointing with the handle of his paddle, Peters muttered something about the nearest route, though his eyes were continuously drawn back toward the surface behind us. The lake's shadowy depths squirmed with intrusive possibilities—nothing certain, though everything too comprehensible.

"I don't like it here," Peters grunted, eyes ever-moving. "Too much wrong… too ancient."

I couldn't disagree. If anything, the only thing I *could* agree on was how alien this whole place felt, in the truest sense of the word. Alien in scope, in sensation, in history. Any scraps of rationality I had tried to cling to felt thin and frayed here, like the strings would snap if tugged too hard. What kind of world had we entered? A cavern beneath the ends of the Earth—an expanse of timeless **something** that had no name in any encyclopedic lexicon I knew.

"No one's ever mapped… or even imagined… this," I muttered, half to myself.

Peters glanced up. "Ain't to be mapped. Not a man's land, this," he growled, his paddle cutting through the water beneath mirrored glares of shadow.

Moments passed in strained silence as we paddled, our eyes drawn forever upward—scanning the towering walls, intricately layered with strange carvings. Symbols, etched perfectly in straight lines and curved spirals, dotted every surface of the rock, dimly glowing with latent energy—cyan fissures marking boundaries incomprehensible to us at that moment.

As we neared the jagged ledge of stone, my heart quickened its drumming, a nervous tension growing with every shift of water beneath the boat. The ledge stretched outward in a shallow curve, broadening and eventually tapering off far ahead into a tunneled path. The stone glistened in the blueish light, faintly damp from condensation or recent disturbance—somehow wetter than the deeper abyss around us.

Peters moved first, dragging himself with brute force onto the stone. His boots slipped momentarily against the slick rock, issuing a worried grunt but none of the usual curses he'd deploy in that moment. The weight of our surroundings swallowed such trivial personal reactions now—too much history caught in the air, in the beating stones that pressed omnipresently inward.

I followed, less graceful but equally quick. The canoe bobbed slightly in the motion, settling awkwardly behind us, now empty and half-forgotten, as though it belonged to a past fading further away while this strange present consumed us.

Standing, drenched and aching, upon the sloped stone, I gazed outward—following the carvings and shimmering etchings as they climbed impossibly high upon the smooth walls encircling the lake. Our world, once coated in fog and chaos, had transformed in the brief span of minutes into something so ancient that I felt as if we were trespassers in a tomb not meant for mortal eyes.

"We have to keep moving," I said quietly, an anxiety clawing at the back of my mind. Something in me stirred with a sensation that could only be described as paranoia—the sense that time itself shifted perilously here, that waiting too long in any one place would awake whatever lay just out of our line of sight.

Peters grunted his agreement, though his gaze remained transfixed on the peculiar symbols now marking out the expanse of rock ahead. He muttered reverently, perhaps even unknowingly, "Makes me wonder who mighta been here before..."

Who, indeed.

Or... what?

***

We sat on the edge of the rock ledge, bodies limp and aching, as if the very cavern itself sapped the strength from our bones with each passing minute. The wet ends of my clothes clung to skin too long submerged in icy water, but the strange warmth of this subterranean chamber had already begun to dry us—steam rising in lazy, curling wisps from our sleeves and collars. The air was thick and damp, oppressive like a blanket of feverish heat trying to lull us into uneasy stillness. I could feel the weight of exhaustion settling on my shoulders, as if every ounce of energy I possessed had bled out when we narrowly escaped the whirlpool's grip.

For a moment, I only held onto the sensation of breathing—deep but labored breaths—and let my limbs dangle loose atop the stone. My muscles throbbed in protest, less from strain than from the sheer shock of survival.

Peters sat beside me, hunched over, head held low but eyes flickering everywhere, as though even in this brief respite, he expected calamity to crawl out of the earth itself and swallow us whole. His broad chest rose and fell in ragged gasps, the echo of our pounding hearts seeming to reverberate through the cavern walls.

Though we said nothing, shared no words, the silence between us was full—weighted with the tension of all we had narrowly evaded out on that cursed sea above. And worse still was the knowledge that whatever had waited in the depths of the water below—well, we hadn't escaped it, not really. We'd passed through something. And where we now found ourselves—where it had taken us—was a question neither of us dared entertain aloud.

I could feel my mind lingering too long at the edge of unconscious thought, the buzz of exhaustion mixing fluently with the cavern's low, rhythmic hum. That feeling of oppressive vibration—it gnawed at the edges of my awareness much like an insect lingering persistently at the periphery of vision. A barely audible, almost imperceptible thrum moved through the rock beneath us, pulsing through my fingertips where they rested on the stone—constant, ever-present.

I wanted to ignore it; God knows I tried. But it buzzed under the surface of things, beneath every shallow breath, every murmured thought. Like the heartbeat of some vast, unseen creature slumbering deep beneath this new world.

Peters shifted then, straightening slowly, swiping the back of his hand across his wet brow. He exhaled sharply in frustration, shaking his head as if to clear the fog from his eyes. "We gotta keep moving," he muttered, voice low but insistent. His nostrils flared with what could have been a cautious breath, but it was more a measure of determination. "Can't sit here waiting to get swallowed by whatever's lurkin.'"

I nodded, though my own body felt slow to follow his urgency. The lethargy that hung upon us—thick, oppressive—seemed infectious, whispering dangerous thoughts: Sit. Rest. Linger. As though the air carried some invisible grip intent on rooting us to the stone where we had collapsed.

Yet still, when Peters rose and adjusted the knife strapped tightly to his waist, I forced myself upright. My legs wobbled slightly under the weight of half-despair, the other half— something like awe—pulling at the strands of my coherency.

My eyes traced the symbols etched into the rock walls around us, shimmering faintly in the dim, subterranean light. Their patterns were intricate, almost mesmerizing to look at too long. The longer I let my gaze drift over each line, each carving, the more hypnotic their presence became—an ancient language written in pulses and curls, as if the stone harbored memories not meant for mortal translation.

The sheer ancientness of it, the weight of history pressing under the surface of these caves, wrapped around us like air saturated with the remnants of millennia. Whatever languages these symbols had once formed, their meaning was far older than we could fathom. I almost laughed at myself, hearing the absurdity of every theory rising within me. Atlantis…? No, older than that. Older than any human history I had read.

I couldn't stop the small shiver that passed down my spine. Not from cold. No, the humidity clung too thick in the cavern for any chill to press into my skin. It was something else—an exhaled rush of air coming from deeper down the tunnel before us. The faintest howl whispered across the stone—a breath so delicate it barely rustled our soaked clothing yet carried with it a distinct sense of foreboding. It felt as if something unseen watched from just out of reach, inspecting us like foreign bodies in an ecosystem that had never known human touch.

Whatever it was, it did not want us there.

Peters grunted as he checked the durability of his belt, fingers absentmindedly touching the knife at his side. "Always be armed," he muttered, though I wasn't sure if it was more for my benefit or his own fragile sense of protection. "Not gonna be caught without it again."

I offered a silent nod of agreement and quickly set about gathering our scattered belongings. Not that much remained dry, if any of it at all. The small oil lamps we had carried—miraculously still functional—provided the faint promise of light, though each flicker felt half-hearted against the overwhelming shadow that loomed on every wall. The black leather bag with its few remaining dry provisions—if they could still be called "dry"—hung limply beside our canoe, dirty and scruffed from our rough trek through the torrent.

Peters's eyes never left the water, as if dreading some specter would emerge from its rippling surface, crawling toward us in silent hunger. His sharp, edge-bound focus unnerved me, though I had reason enough to feel the same unsettling tremors beneath my skin. I had seen the shadows beneath the water, the movements. Anything could be waiting there, waiting for us to turn our backs.

When all was ready, we slung what remained of our meager rations over our shoulders, and wordlessly—we left the canoe floating adrift, aimless now against the lip of the shore. A boat abandoned on a still lake with no future passengers, waiting only for time itself to erode it to nothing. Though we had entered this otherworldly place together, I could feel the pull ahead—it was calling us forward, leaving behind all else that had marked our lives before its dark introduction.

The floor beneath our feet shifted from a gradual sloping rise to a smoother, more uniform surface as we trekked further beyond the lake's shore. It didn't feel natural—nothing down here did. The stone weaved and arched inward over the tunnel, where our path though narrow, transformed bizarrely into what resembled a natural bridge cast over the waters we had escaped only minutes earlier. Not an actual construction—a freak occurrence, perhaps—but it stretched archlike between the walls of this subterranean sea with too much intention. It gave the unsettling impression of design, rather than accident.

The farther we walked, the wider the path grew under our feet. An ever-expanding stretch of crystalline, glowing rock formed beneath us, like walking on the surface of stars crystallized into hardened stone.

"Doesn't feel right…" Peters' voice, low and cautious, punctuated my own silent thoughts. His eyes never settled—each sound or echo in this space twisted under his scrutiny, as if expecting each shadow to bear a silent threat.

I kept my eyes ahead, fingers brushing occasionally against the surface of the cave wall. "It's…" I hesitated, trying to find some rational term to apply to what we walked upon. "It feels built."

"Built by what?" he mumbled, still not entirely invested in getting an answer. To him, the only concern remained whether it meant danger.

The hum returned stronger here. Every footfall against the stone sent small vibrations running under my boots, pulsating lightly through the floor and into my veins. The walls responded in kind—faint light trickling from places unseen, echoing that low, inevitable sound which had greeted us since our arrival in this lost world.

There was no vegetation. No sign of life. No fungi growing on damp walls as I'd expect from deep underground. Nothing alive crawled or clung to the surfaces we passed. No spores floated lazily through the thick air. There was only… nothing. The stone was its own presence—looming, dominant, but lifeless.

The further we walked, the louder the hum seemed to grow— an ever-present percussion beneath the silence. It crept into my mind like a gnawing irritation that would not be resolved, each step heightening the unbearable buzz. More than once, I felt it grow louder still, as if something enormous stirred beneath the ground itself. Something… waiting.

I shook off the thoughts and focused instead on the path ahead. The cave was a study in contrasts. Though it appeared to widen, the shadows ahead seemed to crowd in closer the farther we went. The light from the glowing veins in the walls dimmed, forcing us to rely more heavily on the oil lamps we had managed to salvage. Their flickers cast wavering halos in the darkness, casting strange allusions onto the walls—a twisted reflection of the reality surrounding us.

My breath quickened involuntarily. Each step we took seemed to descend farther into the earth. The air thickened, not with moisture but with the oppressive weight of enclosed space. It felt as though breathing became harder—labored as if the very air resisted filling my lungs. Peters too, I noticed, had begun to grunt occasionally between his steps, the fog closing in around us, both real and illusory.

Downward. Always downward.

Every instinct screamed at me to turn back—but there was no back. Only down.

Slowing our pace, I began to focus on the floor beneath us. The stone seemed different here. Less smooth, less unnatural. Deep, long cracks began to appear around our feet, as if the rocks had long ago caved inward, finally giving way to the weight of time's unrelenting decay. Whatever force had shaped this tunnel, it was older than any ancient civilization we could comprehend; older, perhaps, than the earth itself. The marks of chaos now lay beneath our very boots.

Still, we pressed onward, our feet moving mechanically while our senses remained on high alert, the strain ever-tighter on our nerves. Peters, uncharacteristically silent, kept stealing glances over his shoulder toward the shrinking sliver of light behind us—his instinctive bracing for danger heavier in the blossoming darkness.

Ahead, the tunnel sloped steeply, an incline pushing us deeper into what felt like a labyrinth of forgotten ruin. The patterns on the walls—those strange etchings—had become less regular, more… purposeful. There were shapes beginning to look familiar now, though my rational mind rebelled at identification. Very old… uncannily old.

"Pym," Peters grunted, snapping me free from my tangled thoughts. He'd halted quite suddenly and was staring intently at the walls ahead, the flickering oil light catching the sweat starting to drip from his brow. His eyes darted to mine, steady but full of tension. "Listen."

At first, I heard nothing outside of my own quickening pulse pounding accusingly in my ears. But a moment later, there it was.

Faint. Metallic.

It came from somewhere down the tunnel, a clattering sound—a sound that didn't belong in the stillness of stone. Cold dread licked up my spine.

The hum—a damnable hum—sputtered slightly in response, then revved harder, almost as if in mockery.

"We're not alone," Peters murmured, hand slipping once more to his knife. The heavy metallic echo faded, swallowed again by the ancient breath of the earth itself.

What had made that sound?

3

Emergence into the New World

We stepped gingerly from the water's edge, every motion deliberate, as though anticipating the ground itself might shift beneath us. My body trembled under the weight of fatigue—the accumulated strain from the whirlpool still made my legs feel loose, like lead barely melted away. Yet there was something else too, tightening around my chest as we cautiously progressed—an oppressive weight in the air, a pulse still faint but palpable underfoot. It didn't disappear with the watery descent we'd narrowly survived; it clung, almost as if some presence lurked beneath the floor, its pulse growing softer and fainter the farther we moved from the subterranean lake, yet never fully receding. It thrummed up through the stone, like a heartbeat too massive to fathom, buried somewhere deep within this ancient, hidden world.

With each step, our surroundings seemed to press closer in a way that couldn't merely be explained by the narrowing walls of the cavern. No—it was the atmosphere itself. The very air carried a density that felt almost suffocating. Every breath I took was filled with the sensation that something ancient, something foreboding, was watching us, its very presence saturating the stones.

Peters was silent, though his sharp intakes of breath betrayed his unease. His hands twitched every so often as if he was preparing for unseen dangers lurking just out of sight. I found myself quietly grateful for his presence. Despite the tension humming throughout the space—despite the foreboding—I knew Peters would still cleave through any threat with that rough, instinct-driven resilience that had kept him alive this long. But even Peters, hardened though he was, couldn't mask the wariness clouding his eyes.

As we moved deeper into the cavern, the vibrant glow casting eerie light against the walls began to recede slowly into shadows. The illumination sputtered and flickered at the edges, as though the energy that clung to the very bones of this subterranean world was shrinking away from us, unwilling to provide us the guidance we so desperately needed in our march forward.

With each wavering flicker from the stuttering lamp in my hand, shadows bloomed and grew on every surface, casting an array of grotesque shapes that rippled across the walls as if alive. Each long, spindly silhouette slid across the rocky surfaces, warping and shrinking with our every movement. They danced like mocking specters, twisting with a malevolent grace, never leaving our periphery. Every shadow I caught flickering just out of sight made the hair on my arms stand on end, and I swore I saw faces in the darkness—faces that evaporated the moment my gaze shifted to confront them.

It wasn't just the darkness, though. Sounds—faint, just out of reach—shifted around us, reverberating deep within the stone. It wasn't the sound of trickling water or the settling of earth. No, it was more... controlled, almost rhythmic. There was something about it that chilled me to the core. A hum—an otherworldly resonance—buried beneath the layer of silence, so soft you almost didn't notice it unless you were truly listening.

It enveloped us like a spell, draping around us, pulling us further inward. Neither of us spoke, though I sensed the tension in Peters increasing by the moment. His sharp exhales cut through the cavern air every so often, punctuating the oppressive quiet—but he, too, seemed drawn onward despite the growing unease knitting between us. We had gone too far to turn back.

Then, suddenly, the shadows loosened their grip. The walls seemed to pull away, opening wide. I squinted, trying to make sense of what I was seeing. The humid air grew softer, almost fragrant, and the darkness in front of us began to peel back like a curtain.

A vast opening revealed itself ahead—so wide and expansive that for a moment, I thought my weary eyes were playing tricks. The cavern had yawned open, its belly split to reveal what lay beyond its stone walls—a landscape both magnificent and impossible.

I slowed my pace, heart thudding against the cage of my ribs, its beat quickening as the reality of what lay before us began to come into focus.

The light—soft, warm, golden—filled the world ahead, as though mimicking sunlight but adorned with an almost sentient glow. It illuminated the behemoth trees towering beyond the cavern mouth. These trees… they weren't like anything I had ever seen, on any chart or in any textbook that had passed before my eyes. They twisted and shimmered, their trunks bathed in a strange, metallic sheen that shifted colors—a living kaleidoscope reflecting the light from some vast orb suspended high above, akin to a sun yet somehow utterly foreign.

"What… is this?" I breathed, the words spilling from me unbidden.

I took a deep breath, and the air—sweet and earthy and unlike anything I'd ever known—filled my lungs. There was life here, vibrancy, humidity that clung lightly to our skin, warm and yielding. It embraced us—the scent of blossoms, of damp soil, of nature so rich and primal, it felt almost sacred. Yet beneath that beauty, an urgency gnawed at my senses—a warning embedded within the heady perfume. As I exhaled, I felt the invisible boundary between the world we had left and the one we now entered begin to dissolve.

Beside me, Peters said nothing at first, his gaze wide as he absorbed the landscape. His breath came in long, measured inhales, though I could see the tension still brimming just beneath his skin. He took in the unfamiliar world with quick, calculating glances, his sharp instincts steering his assessment. His lips moved slightly, soundless for a moment until finally, in a low rumble, he muttered, "Beautiful... but dangerous too."

We stood at the boundary of two worlds—the heavy gloom of the cavern behind, and what lay before, this vast new land untouched by time. The flora stretched out in every direction, vast trees rising like sinewy pillars of some forgotten pantheon. Their trunks shimmered in hues that shifted and danced with an otherworldly electricity beneath the surface, reflecting the warm light that bathed the clearing. Their leaves—swirling and iridescent with luminous patterns—shifted and sighed in the soft, warm breeze, casting ethereal patches of light across the forest floor below.

I swallowed hard, my pulse racing in quick bursts. I reached out, barely aware of my own action, my curiosity too strong to hold back. My fingers brushed against the bark of the nearest tree, rougher than expected, yet vibrant beneath my fingertips—a faint, barely perceptible tremble in the wood, as though the tree was awake, aware of my touch. It thrummed.

"Incredible..." The word escaped my lips in a breathless murmur. I pulled my hand back, unsettled but fascinated. The life here, the power in it—it was almost tangible, a force that vibrated in harmony with the pulse of the stones beneath the earth.

Beside me, Peters cautiously edged forward, eyes continuously scanning the scene. He was a man of instinct, and those instincts were on full alert now. His gaze flicked from one corner of the clearing to the next, always watching, always ready. "We shouldn't be here," he muttered, his tone rigid. "I don't like it. Feels too alive… too unnatural. But it's too damn quiet."

And it was. There were no birds, no rustling beyond a strange, distant breeze… only the disquieting echo of our own presence.

That's when we heard it.

From the underbrush—a slight rustling, soft at first, subtle enough to be mistaken for the wind. Then it grew louder, closer, as something large and deliberate moved through the foliage, pushing aside the glowing vines with an indifferent strength.

Peters froze first, his instincts responding, and I followed just a fraction of a heartbeat later. Our senses heightened to the brink, our bodies tense as we locked eyes, reading the warning that passed unsaid between us.

We weren't alone.

The rustling grew louder—an impending presence barreling toward us through the densely knotted jungle. And then, from between the thick, towering trunks of the shimmering trees, the figure of a creature crashed through the underbrush—massive, breathtaking, and utterly alien.

It was almost dinosaurian in form, a relic seemingly plucked from another age. Its body was high-arched and muscular, with sinewy limbs that belied its sheer size. Scales shimmered across its back and sides, catching and refracting the pale light in vibrant hues. Its head—the most astonishing of all—appeared wide, adorned with strange bony ridges along its jaw and neck, almost avian in structure, though its size bested even the largest beasts recorded in texts of old–a mixture of the ancient and the primeval brought to sudden, terrible life.

My heart stuttered. I could do nothing but stare, transfixed in sheer awe as my brain struggled to reconcile this living relic of untold history standing there, gazing at us with eyes as intelligent as they were unknown.

Peters shifted nearer to me, his entire body humming with readiness, his fingers slowly twitching toward the hilt of his knife. "Get back," he breathed, barely audible, though the undercurrent of panic was unmistakable in his tone.

No. I couldn't move. It was impossible to look away—impossible not to marvel at this magnificent thing. My mind raced to process what my eyes took in, but it was drowned out by the overwhelming sense that we had crossed an invisible line, stepped immediately into something we couldn't possibly understand.

The creature—mercifully—seemed uninterested in aggression. Or rather, it regarded us with something almost akin to calculation—a cold, detached curiosity. Its enormous head tilted slightly, jaws parting to release a low, resonant bellow that vibrated through the trees, deep and reverberating but not menacing.

Its message was clear. We were seen. And then, just as suddenly as it had arrived, it turned, lumbering away with a fluid grace that defied its bulk, disappearing into the dense jungle expanse from which it had come.

Silence followed its exit—the tension in the air releasing in a long exhale neither Peters nor I had realized we were holding.

"We need to move," Peters murmured, his voice tight and barely masking his astonishment. He cast a quick glance at me before turning his attention back to the tangled underbrush. A flicker of disbelief shadowed his features, though it was gone almost as quickly as it had arrived— replaced by grim resolve. "We can't linger here."

With that, we plunged further into the jungle—the heartbeat of this ancient world pounding louder in my chest with each step.

****

We moved warily, each footstep soft, molded to the vibrating pulse of the jungle floor as it yielded beneath the weight of existence. It would have been easy, far too easy, to be swallowed entirely by the alien world around us—so dense, so alive with sounds foreign and impossibly vast. The soft hum of life embracing us tightly, winding through the creaks of towering trees and the shifting whispers of leaves, lured us ever deeper into the thick embrace of the jungle.

Strange insects, unseen yet constantly present, buzzed nearby, their wings beating harmoniously with the steady rhythm that still thrummed beneath our feet. Tiny vibrations, especially magnified in the weighty silence, hung in the air like a visible charge—scatterings of life barely known yet intensely felt. And then there was the undercurrent—a faint yet undeniable thudding of something moving… something large.

The jungle was never still. There were no true silences, only pockets of noise woven into the cloth of this place. Footfalls—other than our own—echoed like drums into the distance, third-party participants in a landscape brimming with shadows, lending the distinct sensation that we were not merely observers or foreigners in this world, but intruders.

Every snap and thrum struck at the frayed edges of my already taut mind, sending my pulse into a wild cadence that mirrored the jungle's own living beat. Even my breath—too harsh—became part of the jungle's symphony, each exhale taking on its own strange rhythm as it mingled with the world around us. Peters, beside me, moved with more deliberate ease, his every muscle visibly flexing with the coiled tension of someone waiting for an ambush that had yet to come.

The scent carried by the air shifted—turned sweet, earthy. My nostrils flared upon sensing it—a warm, intoxicating perfume wrapped in the scent of the soil. Soon after, we broke into a wide valley surrounded by towering flora, and before us, hanging from incredible heights, were fruits so vibrantly colored, they seemed to pulse with light. No groves back home, not even those nurtured in the most fertile soils, could boast such growth.

It felt like magic. But magic, in the end, was only science uncharted.

I inhaled deeply, taking in the odd combination of scents— the strange perfume mingled with the freshness of gleaming stone and earth. The fruit hung heavy, dense, from thick branches that reached out like fingers, as if waiting for hands to pluck them. Their outer skins glistened like freshly polished jewels, reflecting the jungle's warm glow back at us.

Peters froze mid-step beside me, his hand resting cautiously on his knife's hilt, eyes scanning the surroundings, always the pragmatist. "Too bright," he muttered, his voice nothing more than a growl under his breath. "Too bold for something that's harmless."

But I could not help myself. My curiosity hungered as heavily as the strange, shimmering fruit above us. I reached, fingers extending cautiously, my hand brushing against the soft surface of a particularly large, ruby-toned orb.

"I wouldn't," Peters warned, his voice fluctuating between scornful amusement and genuine anxiety as he held his ground, keeping his gaze on the trees and underbrush rather than the fruit. Still, his grip on the knife didn't slacken.

With careful deliberation, I plucked the fruit from the branch. A shiver passed through the tree, as though it mourned the severance, its gleaming leaves rustling delicately in response. I turned the fruit in my hands, mesmerized by the swirling colors that patterned its smooth, almost wax-like surface. It was unnervingly vivid—an irresistible mingling of scarlets and blush pink, flecked with hues of gold that seemed to shimmer beneath the membrane.

Without thinking, I lifted it closer to my nose, curious, inhaling deeply. The scent struck in waves—layers of sweetness, intense, like well-ripened berries mixed with something unfamiliar, some blend of unfamiliar spice woven into the air.

Peters made a noise of mock exasperation, shaking his head. "Don't go eatin' it. For God's sake, Pym, we don't know what's safe down here."

I nodded, though I felt the surge of temptation pressing at the edges of my self-restraint, urging me onward, deeper into that innate curiosity blazed by discovery. Such temptation came with a superior sense of intellect—an arrogant belief that I could decipher, test, and conquer anything nature, alien or not, might throw our way. But even I knew that obeying such instincts could prove fatal.

"We must test these things. The flora here... it's remarkable."

"And maybe poisonous," Peters shot back tersely, wetting his lips but still moving his eyes along the outline of the trees where shadows shuddered faintly in the far distance. "Don't become the guinea pig."

Just as the food in my hand began to tilt between my fingers, with me ready to further evaluate the unknown treasure, a percussive crack in the underbrush beyond us, followed by the distinctive snap of something heavy splintering against rock, jolted me from my thoughts. A sound unmistakably belonging to something large, and nearing.

Peters' hand tightened reflexively on the hilt of his knife. Without a word or signal, he lowered himself into a crouch, his movements as tense as they were fluid, honed by a thousand other dangers the world had thrown his way. That instinct of his had been our salvation on numerous occasions. It was the sole thing driving him now, keeping him sharp, alert.

"Keep it down," he whispered, eyes narrowed as they traced the line from which the noise had sprung. His posture was alive, electric, and every fiber of his being warned of peril behind every shifting leaf, every snap of twig.

I followed suit, lowering my body quietly to the jungle floor, soft ferns whispering against my arms and legs as I instinctively crouched beside him. Heart hammering in my chest, I strained to listen. My breath grew shallow, tension swelling between us—a silent, shared understanding that whatever approached could be far worse than curiosity had bargained for.

The crackling and rustling grew more pronounced with each second. Something was pushing its way through the thick underbrush with careless, unstoppable weight—a primal force indifferent to the foliage bending beneath its path.

Then it emerged.

A gigantic creature, its fur woven in long, luminescent strands colored with the same strange hues as the alien jungle—blue, violet, gold—almost as though it were wearing the jungle itself on its colossal form. The enormous beast towered over the surrounding undergrowth, moving with an unsettling grace that contradicted its apparent bulk. Its fur undulated with mirrored patterns—like living camouflage of pearlescent light as it basked in the golden rays filtering through the trees.

I exhaled slowly, though my breath caught halfway as the sight fully registered.

This was no simple herbivore, nothing like the lumbering dinosaur we had encountered. No, this creature was something predatory, something designed to thrive, hunt, dominate. Even in its subtlety, there was a coiled violence lingering within its frame, a quiet power waiting beneath the surface— ready to unleash if disturbed.

Peters shifted, his eyes darting across its limbs, his trained survivalist instinct analyzing every muscle twitch, gauging every detail for threat. The beast, however, seemed almost serene, unbothered by our presence as it moved fluidly through the underbrush, as if we were beneath its notice. Still, Peters remained motionless, knuckles pale with the strain of holding himself perfectly still.

For the briefest moment, I found myself unable to resist—a compulsion too strong. I fumbled for one of the oil lamps we had salvaged, shifting it subtly forward to better observe the creature in full. My hand shook as I adjusted the wick's flame. The flicker of light danced against the creature's rolling musculature, illuminating its form, casting an ethereal glow across it.

It noticed.

At that precise moment, the creature's massive head snapped toward us, its gaze locking onto mine. Its eyes—strange and reflective, twin pools of molten colors that shifted with the same rhythm as the jungle itself—stared, not with the mindless hunger of a simple predator, but with something keener. A living intelligence swirled there, a hovering question poised in its unreadable expression.

Time hung, suspended in the thread of that gaze, a razor-thin moment stretched to an eternity. My pulse stopped, stretched too tight; a dissonant drumbeat in my chest.

Then, the creature let out a deep roar, though not one of immediate threat—more of surprise, a surprise shared with us as it reared slightly before bounding away with astonishing speed, disappearing in long, graceful strides, blending once more with the jungle's endless maze.

Its absence left a vacuum around us—a terror vacuum like the aftershocks of an earthquake, brief and electric, threatening to return. Only after a long moment did I release the breath I hadn't realized I'd been holding.

Peters rose beside me in one cautious motion, his hand never leaving the still-ready hilt of his knife.

"This place is alive with danger," he muttered, clearly rattled, though his voice remained steady. "We need to keep moving. Now."

I couldn't argue. This jungle shifted too freely between beauty and threat, too eager to ensnare us in its mysteries—some deadly, others only lingering threats postponed. Without delay, we resumed our trek, moving deeper into the cautionary maze of tangled foliage, wary of the unseen predators lurking in every breath of wind, every rustling leaf.

Every step filled my mind with mounting questions—complicated questions that I couldn't yet answer. What had we truly stumbled upon? What world was this, with creatures both prehistoric and strangely intelligent prowling freely amid the glimmering flora? Why did it feel so resolutely... purposeful?

The land around us was not a wilderness in decay or accident.

No, this world breathed intent into its very air. **It wanted us here… didn't it?** The thought snagged uncomfortably in the back of my mind.

Then, just as the jungle in its dense layers threatened to swallow us once more whole—we broke free.

We stepped into an expansive clearing. Beneath our newly emerged feet, the jungle's tangled undergrowth gave way to a plush, soft vegetation—almost like moss, but far more supple and vibrant. The ground stretched outward like a massive, velvety carpet, meeting the vastness of the sky high above and casting warmth back outward.

In the center of the clearing stood a towering rock formation—a marvel silent, unmoving, yet utterly awe-inspiring. Carved by nature or the hands of some ancient race gone unknown was hard to say; jagged spires of multicolored stone rose into the sky, waving upward like a petrified surge of water suddenly frozen in time, swirling colors and lines embedded deep into its veins, curling with the intricacy of painted glass.

Peters stood speechless beside me, mouth slack with disbelief. His voice, when it came, was coarse with awe. "What is this place?"

I, too, felt the tension in my chest tighten, filled with the pulse of discovery. "I don't know," I murmured through a whispered breath. My hands shook faintly as I gripped the lamp, and my eyes took in the vastness of this new landscape.

"But… we need to… explore it."

I swallowed hard. History lay before us. Or something deeper yet—something more ancient. We had stumbled into a garden of answers, buried now beneath the pulse of time's oblivion. We **must** search it.

We exchanged a glance—an unspoken agreement, curiosity welded seamlessly with the strange instinct that had driven us this far.

Together, we stepped forward, drawn like moths to the flame of mystery. Discovery waited.

4

The Alien Landscape

We stepped away from the towering rock formation, our breath catching as the world beyond unfurled on silent hinges—a spectacle both surreal and impossibly beautiful. My heart pounded heavy against my chest as if it, too, had not yet fully recovered from the plunge through the watery abyss. Yet here we stood, staring breathless into a clearing that spoke more of dreams than reality, its vibrant colors shimmering under the lazy light of the glowing orb above.

The atmosphere felt thick, tangible almost, charged with an electric potential that sent soft prickles up along my skin. Each breath of air we drew in carried with it a warm sweetness, foreign yet intoxicating, laden with the unseen blooms scattered throughout the clearing. It clung to my lungs, heavier than any air I had exhaled before, curling its fragrance around my senses until every breath was imbued with life, with something almost euphoric in its simplicity. For a moment, I could lose myself in that scent—could let the tension between my weary shoulders melt away into the serenity before us.

Beside me, Peters exhaled a long breath, his shoulders sagging just slightly, though his eyes gleamed with a wariness that hadn't quite left him. It never did. I could almost hear his pulse quicken in tandem with my own, both of us caught in the breathtaking wonder of this place, yet neither able to bask in its beauty entirely. Not with the lingering weight of something… more—a potential that felt dangerous, even if unseen.

The ground beneath us had shifted from the cold and rough stone of the cave into something entirely unexpected—a soft, velvety carpet of vegetation that sprang back beneath our boots, yielding in gentle submission with every step forward. It wasn't like any surface I had encountered, not in all my travels through wildernesses both known and unknown. There was an almost dreamlike quality to it, as if the earth had softened beneath us to offer a more welcoming space.

But though it was soft and strangely inviting, I didn't trust it. Nothing in this place could be trusted.

Still, as my eyes swept out over the clearing, I couldn't help but marvel at the sheer tapestry of life spread before us—iridescent blues, yellows, and greens, dappled together in intricate patterns that rippled outward, shifting slightly whenever the ambient light from the orb above drifted across the landscape. The colors seemed to pulse, their brightness fluctuating in rhythm with the surrounding air, setting the scene aglow like some forgotten dreamscape half-remembered.

Yet, for all its foreign beauty, there was something unnerving in its stillness.

Peters, ever alert, continued to scan the environment, his sharp gaze flicking from one massive bloom to another, always searching for the faintest signs of movement. The trees—no, they were far more than trees—they towered over us, their trunks shimmering as if coated in molten metal, hues of copper and bronze gleaming beneath the glow. Broad leaves, wider than my outstretched arms, shifted gently above our heads in slow undulations, a rhythmic sway not unlike the waves of the sea. They projected a strange calm, casting shadows that danced in nearly hypnotic patterns on the ground.

The trees themselves seemed sentient somehow—alive in ways trees should not be.

I couldn't resist. My curiosity—overriding every rational thought—urged me closer to one of the colossal trunks. The skin of the tree was glossy, shimmered with subtle patterns that seemed to breathe with every shift of light. I held my breath as my fingers drew near, hovering just shy of its surface. Then, unable to help myself, I brushed my fingertips gently against it.

Warmth.

I recoiled slightly, not from pain but from surprise. The rough bark, which I had expected to feel cold and rigid, trembled beneath my touch, exuding an almost tender warmth that bled into my fingers. It pulse-throbbed lightly under the surface, as though the tree itself carried some internal heartbeat—a slow, methodical rhythm that mirrored the hum we had felt in the cavern earlier.

I traced the patterns along the bark. They swirled hypnotically, their spiraling designs catching the dim light from above and scattering it on the ground in unpredictable patterns that twisted across the landscape in strange, shifting arcs. For a fleeting moment, it appeared as though I was observing not just natural formation but design, intention. The ground beneath my feet swirled with the trees' projection like nature's own grandiose artwork.

"Careful," Peters grunted, stepping forward to nudge me out of my reverie. His voice was low, gruff, but it carried that edge—one I knew all too well, a protective instinct that frequently overtook him when the unknown brushed a little too close.

I looked up at him, noting the furrows creasing his brow. He was always on the defensive, always ready for danger to spring from the shadows, even on ground as seemingly soft and harmless as this. Our surroundings had done nothing to soften that primal awareness in him.

"Keep your wits about you," he added, his eyes casting upward, scanning the high canopy of leaves that loomed overhead, the broad tendrils swaying ever so slightly with the pulse of unseen winds. Peters' words snapped me temporarily back to the practicality of the situation—his pragmatism a sharp contrast to the wonder I still harbored deep within.

But that wonder stole its way back into my mind as my eyes wandered toward another tree, something high above near its crown—a couple of paces farther into the clearing now. From one of its boughs hung the most curious of fruits I had yet to see. It was plump, nearly the size of my outstretched hand, and it seemed to glow like a lantern, its surface shifting in color with each passing moment. Hues of aqua bled into violet, mingling with gold and back again in an ever-undercurrent of change.

Captivated, I stepped toward it.

"Look at that." My voice brimmed with childlike excitement, the words unbidden. I wasn't sure whether I was imploring Peters to share in my fascination or merely speaking to the spectacle itself, but I felt my heart leap with some primal, eager desire to investigate—through touch, through reason, through experience.

I stretched my arm upward, my fingers trembling slightly with anticipation as they neared the fruit. Something tingled within me, an awareness perhaps that I was crossing some invisible boundary, some line not meant to be traversed, but still—still I reached.

The smooth surface of the fruit connected with my fingers,

and instantly I understood. Warmth. Again, an inviting, almost human warmth thrummed through the vibrant skin of the fruit. It pulsed just as the bark of the tree had—alive, aware, something in it beckoning me closer, whispering to my sensibilities with a promise of sweetness, of sustenance.

Carefully, with an almost reverent motion, I grasped the fruit and plucked it from the branch. The sound it made was soft, a gentle—yielding—pop as it detached from the stem. The effect was immediate.

The clearing around us stilled, that subtle rhythmic sway of the leaves pausing as if—waiting.

I felt the tension return in Peters' posture immediately. His brow furrowed deeply as he watched me with an intensity reserved for moments of looming danger. The stillness crept back in around us once more. Even the sweetness in the air seemed to sour slightly beneath the new shift. "Careful, Pym," Peters muttered, his voice strained. "We don't know what that holds. It might be safe, or it might—"

He broke off, his sentence unfinished but the implication clear. He felt it too—the change. The jungle, previously alive with throbbing vibrancy, seemed to draw into itself. Peters' hand hovered close to his knife, every muscle of his broad figure humming with unease, waiting for something—for the jungle to react.

But I cared little for warnings as my curiosity drew stronger, emboldened. With care, I lifted the fruit to my nose and inhaled deeply. The scent flooded my senses instantly, overwhelming in sweetness and spice. Exotic aromas, layered and complex, invaded my lungs—the delicate sweetness of crushed berries blended with some unrecognizable spice that tugged gently at my mind, spinning me briefly into a trance of delight. I felt my body relax, the tension leaving my muscles as I spiraled downward into sensation after sensation, a cloud of seduction that numbed the edges of rationality.

It was wonder, pure and distilled.

For that moment, nothing else mattered. Peters' concerns were secondary, relegated to the background of my thoughts—whispers in a room where the walls vibrated with the music of discovery. I was lost in contemplation, in the potential of this alien world, the fascination overwhelming whatever warnings hounded at the recesses of my mind.

Then a strange urgency caught in my chest, and abruptly, like a man waking from a pleasant dream that had pushed too far into uncertainty, I stepped back. The reverie snapped, and reality crashed in again, too sharp and sudden.

I looked down at the fruit in my hand, suddenly aware of how foolish I had been to dismiss the dread lurking at the edges. Pocketing the fruit quickly, I straightened myself—determined to examine it later, to test it in a safer environment. A promise to myself to resist slipping back into intoxication for the sake of knowledge. Not yet anyway.

Peters, ever-watchful, remained rigid, scanning the ground

and sky toward the distant horizon, eyes slitting with new caution. His breath came shallow, almost feral now, though his instincts masked well the struggle to contain his trepidation. The soft rustling of leaves behind us swelled ever so gently in the air, many creatures unseen… but perhaps not unnoticed. It was as though the jungle waited; its breath, like ours, held.

Tension built upon itself, unseen cords tightening around the clearing. The vivid colors of the landscape seemed to shimmer just slightly sharper now, the atmosphere thickened in that silent stretch before some unspoken storm. Beautiful and strange as it was, with its sweetness carried warmly in the air—it felt dangerous again, treacherous beneath its charm.

This place was not our own.

And we were not alone.

***

A shift in the air was the only warning. Subtle at first, easily missed amid the vibrant hues and soft pulse of the alien jungle, but undeniable to those whose instincts had long been sharpened by the nearness of danger. Though my gaze had been drawn, inexorably, toward a cluster of brilliant flowers— each petal iridescent and sparking beneath the ambient glow overhead—the atmosphere curdled unexpectedly, the humidity thickening like unseen tendrils wrapping themselves around our lungs.

Then, came the rustling.

At first, it seemed little more than a breath of wind, a sigh from some distant thicket, inconsequential within the constant murmur of this living world. But this sound… it held a different timbre. Too purposeful. Too close. The brush and crunch of wet leaves torn from their perch, disturbed by something far more deliberate than a breeze.

Peters reacted before I could even fully register the change, his body shifting instinctively, instinct that trumped intellectual curiosity every time. With a grunt, he stepped back into my path, blocking me from moving any closer to the flowerbeds. His hand shot out, palm rigid, stopping just shy of my chest.

"Wait," he hissed under his breath, his every muscle taut as a coiled wire. His eyes darted side to side, scanning the periphery. The precision in his voice snared my runaway thoughts, yanking me back from my floral reverie.

"Pym, stop. We need to keep our guard up… Something's out there." His words, coarse with tension, resonated somewhere deep in my consciousness.

And just like that, the jungle itself fell quiet. A devouring hush, blanketing everything from the swaying foliage to the buzz of hidden insects. The oppressive silence closed around us, wrapping itself tightly across the clearing like a predator's gaze, assessing, waiting.

I swallowed hard, involuntarily. Nerves flickered to life within me, a staccato rhythm of unease building beneath my skin, replacing the fascination that had gripped me mere moments ago. My eyes, now alight with awareness, flicked to the edges of the clearing, scanning the shadowed fringes where light gave way to deeper darkness beneath the dense, undulating canopy. The leaves there flickered in the corners of my vision, lapping forward and back against some unseen force.

Do not move.

Every nerve in my body screamed caution, my senses tingling as the weight of Peters' warning sank into my gut, heavy and foreboding. The playful allure of the moment, the gentle pulse of this place, felt suddenly distant—receding behind a curtain of unseen tension. I peered through the haze of flowering vines and dappled light, fully expecting— no, feeling—that something crouched just beyond my sight. Something large… and hungry.

"Peters," I whispered, scarcely more than a breath. My voice was tight, unwilling to break the fragile equilibrium. "What do you think it is?"

The rasp of Peters' exhalation was loud against the stillness. He shifted his weight, muscles tightening in anticipation, and his hand instinctually eased toward the hilt of his blade—a silent testament to the danger he knew lingered. "Damn if I know," he muttered, his brow furrowing deeply, "but it's too quiet now. This is exactly how ambushes begin."

A growl—low, rumbling, melodic—rolled in from somewhere to our right. It thrummed with a primitive vibrato that set my heart into a dangerous race. This was no ordinary sound, no incidental stir of distant wildlife; this was a warning. A declaration of presence. It carried the menace of conscious awareness wrapped behind whatever intelligence moved cloaked in the underbrush.

The jungle floor crackled softly beneath unseen paws or feet, and the leaves whispered in alleys of disturbed air.

Peters swore under his breath, eyes snapping toward the source. "Stay close."

The growl came again, deeper this time, more resonant. It reverberated through the ground beneath my feet—an earthy, almost primal resonance—and my breath caught sharp in my throat. It was no longer just a threat; it held intent now. The steady sound of twigs snapping underfoot, slow and deliberate, suggested only calculation—a hunter biding his time. He was close.

The air around me felt electric, too thick even to swallow down fully. Sweat, cold and sticky, beaded along my spine. I became hyper-aware of the weight of my own limbs, the subtle tremor coursing through my fingertips as I pressed against the rough bark of one of the nearby trees for cover. It throbbed beneath my grip, part of the living rhythm of this place, and somehow that hum, comforting mere moments ago, now felt too loud—sickeningly intimate.

I held my breath, desperate not to draw the attention of whatever haunted us. My heart pounded frantically within the cage of my ribs, its insistent drumbeat the lone witness to the fear clawing its way through my rationality. But rationality, it seemed, had no words for what was approaching.

Peters, crouched low to the ground, began edging carefully toward the source of the noise, his body hunched as he moved in silence through the thick growth of vines and flowers. His fingers rested across his knife's grip, though I could tell his hesitation was calculated—not fear, but readiness. I followed his progression with my eyes, every muscle in my body tense, every breath measured, as he crept along the leafy perimeter, hoping to peer through the tangles of the jungle canopy.

The growling deepened once more, louder and raw with authority this time, its guttural echo threading through the stillness like a whispering leviathan stretching its limbs. The sound felt ancient. Feral.

It wrapped around us as if with an immortal hand, dragging our senses deeper into this predator's trap, where light itself seemed to fold under the weight of it. For the briefest of seconds, I thought I could taste it—the acrid tang of fear, metallic, resting on the air.

And that was when I saw it.

The leaves, thick and damp with life, parted as something large—a shadow at first—shifted noticeably through the dense greenery ahead of us. A vast shape, a silhouette too dark and too solid to be mistaken for some wind-tossed branch.

Limbs—large limbs—moved gracefully, swaying the foliage as they cut through the underbrush. The beast was nearly invisible at first, blending so effortlessly into the landscape that, for a heart-stopping moment, I doubted my own vision. But no—the sheer bulk of it soon emerged within the limits of my perception, solid, tangible. A weight that pressed on the air, announcing its presence without sound.

Peters, sharp as ever, hadn't waited for me to confirm it. He jerked backward in a startled motion that almost brought him into me. I met his wide, panicked eyes, my own heart ratcheting forward into a desperate cadence.

Not the beast from earlier.

No—this one was larger. Much larger. Its outline was bulky, defined with brute muscle and onyx fur that rippled tightly across its barrel-shaped chest and arms. Its head—it hunched low, neck thick with sinew, as it prowled through the shadows. From between the parted foliage, I caught the glint of teeth, glistening and sharp behind a maw far too dangerous to belong to anything docile.

For a split second, my rational mind failed me, my thoughts scattering like dry leaves beneath the sudden gale of terror. Its eyes met mine.

Two dark, intelligent pools—black as the deepest ocean depths—sharp with the electric glimmer of curiosity. Real curiosity, the sharp awareness tempered by prying intent. But this creature—unlike the peaceful dinosaur from earlier—it held no gentleness, no neutrality. It looked at us with the cold calculation of a predator surveying prey.

"Damn," Peters hissed, his voice choked with barely contained fear. His hand tightened around the hilt of his knife, but we both knew no blade would save us against this.

The beast grunted low, its growl beginning to morph into something stranger—an almost guttural chirrup that felt disturbingly wrong amid the vibrant beauty surrounding us. It ground its massive front paws against the earth, claws scraping in slow, deliberate focus. Whatever tension had brewed within it now materialized fully—a body primed for action.

Without warning, its nostrils flared, and with sickening speed, the creature lunged forward—wild-eyed and unblinking—crashing through the underbrush in a sudden burst of unimaginable speed. Time slowed, and for a brief eternity, all I could see was the dark blur of fur and teeth flung toward us with reckless haste. It was a deliberate force, a rising, inevitable crash that shattered the brittle silence around us and rendered everything meaningless.

"Move!" Peters' voice, raw with urgency, barely met my ears as I leaped aside, hurling myself down and to the right with the split-second reflexes of a man desperate for survival.

But it wasn't aiming for us. Not truly.

The beast barreled through the clearing, swerving as though toying with us, its wild gaze meeting ours once again, as if daring us to react, only to vanish with the same suddenness as it had come—disappearing into the distance with a final lunge, leaving in its wake the remnants of a shattered peace.

My breath came in ragged gasps. Peters, beside me, clutched his knife tightly, his hand visibly shaking for the first time as he, too, struggled to catch his breath. We exchanged fleeting glances, words unnecessary—my thoughts too wide-eyed and disbelieving to form.

We were lucky. Unbelievably, incomprehensibly lucky. We'd been spared, not by instinct, but by the creature's own whim.

No safety waited here amid the beauty of this jungle. This place might pulse with life, but it hummed with death in equal measure.

5

A Dance with Nightmares

The suffocating air thickened around us as if the jungle itself had grown sentient, aware of our invasive presence, and was now deciding how best to respond. Every beat of silence clung like a spider's web, each rustle amplified, reverberating like the beat of war drums through the pulsating foliage. I hesitated, body tense, the earlier unease twisting tighter in my gut. Peters remained low, silent, his breath controlled and shallow as his fingers, as always, flexed around the hilt of his knife, white-knuckled and ready. His broad frame trembled with anticipation, his instincts honed to the point of raw energy—ready to act at a moment's notice.

Blinking slowly, I felt the surreal beauty of the jungle around me—its otherworldly tranquility—grow darker, more oppressive. The soft glow from the canopy above shifted in hue as though the luminescent leaves themselves held conspiratorial knowledge, casting flashes of violet and teal across Peters' face in quick bursts.

A rustle snapped the hold of stillness. Not like an animal lazily picking its way through the foliage—instead, it was much heavier, a deliberate momentum behind each snap of broken branches. The kind of movement that could only mean something large was approaching, something unlike anything we had yet encountered in this strange world beneath our feet.

Peters' eyes flicked upward, his breath slowing into measured rhythm. The air around him quivered—muscles taut—yet his expression went unreadable, as though he'd tucked away emotion and now wore only vigilance as his armor.

"Stay low," he whispered through tight lips, the words barely carried through the thick air between us.

My pulse quickened. I strained to listen—to pinpoint the source. It was close, too close. The breath of the jungle seemed to narrow, choked by the proximity of some massive presence pressing toward us from within the depths of the thick undergrowth. My grip tightened on the fruit still clutched absentmindedly in my hand—the smooth warmth of it, once comforting, now felt alien, intrusive.

The rustling grew more intense. It wasn't the erratic stir of curiosity but rather the direct stride of something with intent—something grander, more significant in its movements. The jungle groaned around it, bending in obeisance to its will. I felt anticipation thicken with the quick shortening of my breaths, but curiosity—damnable curiosity—widened my eyes, freezing me in place.

Another snap—closer this time—and my mouth went dry. Beneath the wide, sheltering folds of an enormous tree, Peters and I crouched in the gnarled roots, our backs pressed against the bark that hummed faintly beneath us. It still bore its warm, vibrating rhythm, the same pulse that marked every living thing in this strange place. That pulse now felt too aligned with something larger, something hidden in the shadows creeping ever closer.

My throat constricted under the weight of tension, and I locked eyes with Peters. His expression screamed the same question that rang in my head: What could be so large?

A colossal shadow moved at last within sight, a dark blur that rendered the ferns insignificant in its wake. The leaves rippled in response as the creature—or thing—moved through them, each branch protesting with a muted crackling. There was no natural grace to it, no attempt to remain unnoticed—this was something that moved without fear.

I dared not move, my legs trembling but rooted to the ground beneath me. The storm of sounds in my head drowned out any coherent thought. Beside me, Peters leaned forward slightly, muscles taut, every fiber of his being fixated on the shadow as it loomed closer. His knuckles whitened around the knife's hilt but his posture remained unmoving—like an animal biding its time before deciding whether to strike or run.

Suddenly, the air was punctuated by a faint clicking—a foreign pattern carried through the dense air, underscored by a metallic scrape.

***

It came into view with terrifying grace—an enormous spider of such proportions that had it not emerged so quietly, I might have registered it as a myth rather than tangible horror. Its long legs moved in unison with an eerie precision, carrying its gleaming iridescent body through the underbrush with fluid, calculated elegance. Each step cast flickering shadows across the ground, distorting the already chaotic jungle floor, transforming it into a swirling mosaic of light and darkness.

Peters inhaled sharply, muffling a low gasp beneath his breath but making no effort to hide the shock plainly visible in his usually composed expression.

The creature's many legs clicked rhythmically against the earth, their jointed forms bending in odd, deliberate ways that sent cold shivers down my spine. It was beautiful in the most nightmarishly unsettling fashion—its reflective surface mirrored the glowing flora around us, casting prismatic shards of color as it shifted in place.

My heart pounded in disbelief as I stared. My mind tried to find some reference, some familiar shape or category to place this monstrous figure within, but there was nothing in all my studies—nothing in known or prehistoric record—that could have prepared me for this.

The spider's enormous body shimmered under the pale light

of the alien canopy, an articulate exoskeleton enveloped by patterns born of a world utterly foreign to anything that had walked above the surface. Its massive form was both intricate and terrifyingly delicate. Around its head were multifaceted eyes arrayed like glassy jewels, staring back at me with a predatory focus too rational, too calculating—swirling with hues of violet and gold that reflected the very essence of the jungle itself back toward us.

I swallowed hard, trying to force my erratic breathing to fall in line—but each inhale felt ragged and shallow, strangled by the enormity of what stood only a few paces away. Its legs— long, razor-thin instruments of movement—rose and fell in deliberate, near-surgical motion, carving shallow grooves into the earth beneath it. It was marvelously alien, and yet the threat it posed—there was no mistaking it—loomed as palpably as the air we breathed.

Peters' voice, raw, barely carried to my ears. "We gotta move."

The spider—in tune with every breath of wind around us— shifted forward. Each step brought it closer in a slow, horrible majesty. Its legs moved one after another, crossing over the glowing shrubbery as though weighing the very ground with each delicate tap. It had seen us—there was no doubt in that. Its shimmering eyes flickered from me to Peters with a lethal coldness, studying, calculating our movements.

Peters uttered a muted curse under his breath, his fingers twitching dangerously toward the knife. The grip on rationality between us weakened with every moment those unblinking eyes remained trained on us, and I felt my body respond not with logic but instinct.

I couldn't look away. Somewhere in the depths of my stunned mind, some part of me still craved the knowledge—still sought the understanding of how something like this could exist in our world, even this hidden one. But nausea lurked just behind the wonder, creeping in slowly as the spider crept ever closer.

Peters' voice again, demanding but softer, broke the trance. "Now."

My legs responded before my mind did—an explosion of motion, as though my body had mercifully bypassed rational thought and kicked survival into high gear. I sprang up from behind the tree, my heart pounding so loud it drowned out everything else, the thrum of adrenaline overriding the aching protests of my exhausted limbs.

I darted into the foliage, following Peters—my feet catching, stumbling, dragging through the thick undergrowth, but never stopping—never allowing the paralysis of fear to take full hold. The world narrowed into a singular focus: forward. Escape. Survive.

Abruptly, behind us, the spider hissed. Its long legs scissored through the dense vegetation with alarming speed, the elegant grace it had previously possessed shifting into something far more violent. The ground beneath shook ever so slightly as the creature pursued, its massive bulk scattering branches and vines like kindling.

Twisting urgently between the thick vines, Peters exploded ahead, carving a path forward with quick, slashing movements. His arm glistened faintly under the iridescent glow, streaks of violet dripping onto his sleeve where a glowing tree had pressed momentarily against him. He didn't stop moving—his blade cutting through every twisted root in his way, his breath now more growl than anything human.

I tried not to think. I tried not to look back. But my mind rebelled, compelling me to glance over my shoulder—just for a second.

What I saw turned my blood to ice.

The spider's legs flickered in the dim light—huge, blackened appendages covering distance with impossible speed, steadily drawing closer with each lurching stride. For all our effort, it was gaining rapidly, its many eyes locked onto us with a hungry intelligence that sent another raw spike of terror into my veins.

It would reach us soon.

Panic surged anew, crashing against rational thought. My breath came in sharp, ragged bursts now as the jungle seemed to close in on us from all sides. The trees and vines, once vibrant and awe-inspiring, now formed a labyrinth—a hostile, choking maze through which only survival dictated our path.

My heart thudded deafeningly as I felt the hot exhale of terror wrap around me. The beast was too close—too fast.

Following every footstep, shoving myself desperately forward through the thicket, I fought to stay upright even as the landscape conspired against us. Again, I stumbled, my foot catching on an unseen root, and my momentum faltered. But the urgency behind me pressed harder. The taste of copper filled my mouth as I surged forward, driven by fear.

With a final thrust of adrenaline-fueled desperation, Peters and I careened through a wall of dense foliage—tangled, glowing vines tearing at our skin and limbs—until, mercifully, we crashed into a narrow passage between gnarled jungle roots stretched outward like ancient fingers clawing from beneath the earth.

The massive limbs of the spider, reaching and searching, clawed at the vines just as we passed, grazing one of the twisted entrances we'd barely squeezed through in time, but not enough to follow.

We stood in stunned silence, lungs burning, senses heightened as the reality of our narrow escape caught up with us. In the dim confines of the root passage, the air cooled slightly. Though we had gained distance—momentary reprieve—the storm of chaotic energy coursing through my limbs refused to settle. I pressed my back against the bark, feeling the steady trembling of my pulse beneath the surface. We had no time to relax.

***

Peters' crouch remained rigid for a moment longer, eyes fixed on the tangled roots of the jungle that now shielded us from the nightmare in pursuit. His breath came in sharp, deliberate rasps, every exhale betraying a calculated tension ready to spring back into action. His eyes—dark and wild, yet clear-headed—kept traveling, searching through the shadows with the quiet intensity of prey that had yet to fully escape its hunter.

The jungle had resumed its clicking rhythm, vibrant as before, but now it pulsed with ambiguity. We might have been shielded, but we weren't safe. We never truly were.

"It's like this world's ready to kill us every step of the way," Peters growled between breaths, his voice thick with disbelief. "Even the beautiful things are deadly."

I nodded, though my mind still buzzed with confusion, grappling with the sudden shift between awe and terror. He wasn't wrong. Every shimmering leaf, every glowing branch—all seemed so otherworldly at first glance, enchanting almost, but underneath, they harbored a deadly lust for survival—and ours was not guaranteed.

Peters straightened, hesitating for just a moment longer. His hand still dug into the sheath of his knife, though the urgency had waned slightly now with the spider further behind. I, too, pressed harder against the vibrant bark, trying to rid my chest of the knotted tension that still hadn't fully released.

Slowly, the two of us dragged our exhausted bodies deeper through the claustrophobic space between the roots. Though tight and confining, there was a delicate safety to the passage now—a lull that held long enough for us to breathe without threat of calamity crashing into us like the waves of an unchecked tide.

But it was temporary. Already, the jungle flickered in warning.

Wiping the sweat from my face, I gripped the oil lamp in my hand with renewed determination. No words were necessary between Peters and me now—only the urgency of onward movement carried us through. Neither of us dared speculate aloud what waited next.

Together, we crawled through the twisting architecture of roots and foliage, the sounds of the jungle ever-present overhead yet quieter here, muffled by the weight of the earth surrounding us. The air grew musky and close, the tight confines of the passage offering little reprieve, but it was enough for now.

Finally, as if granted some reluctant permission, the walls of roots gradually parted, allowing us to step from the narrow confines into a more open space. The burst of color here— more vivid, more alive than in the earlier portions of the jungle—greeted us in a dizzying display. Bright swirls of light dashed through the trees, interweaving as they twirled in graceful arcs, casting long beams of flickering shade along the ground. It was mesmerizing, hypnotic even, as the florescent trail of colors chasing through the trees beckoned us forward.

Despite the lull, despite the beauty weaving its spell once more, my pulse still raced from the earlier encounter. It was a reminder—as though the jungle hadn't already given enough—that between every blooming tree and fallen leaf, danger still lurked, watching.

For a long moment, Peters and I stood, breath simultaneously slow and steady, reading the jungle for its truths, stripping back each layer of wonder for the shadows cast beneath them. Each rustle in the distance, each flutter of wind sweeping through the crooked branches heightened the tension already gripping us, yet beneath—deep beneath the caution and vigilance—we were drawn in. Called, pulled inward by the magnetic reality of this world we had fallen into.

"There'll be more where that came from," muttered Peters, his gaze scanning the bright expanse of trees. "I can feel it."

Despite every instinct railing against it, we stepped forward, drawn in by the glow of the ever-shifting colors that hummed a language only our instincts could interpret. Some deeper truth lay hidden here—some answer buried beneath the shimmering beauty waiting to unfold.

We'd escaped. This time. But the spider, the jungle itself—it whispered its threats, reminded us that we were never truly free of its reach.

6

Discovery of the Náiren

The dense underbrush crackled underfoot as we moved cautiously, our breath mingling with the thick, humid air clinging to every tree, every vine, every unseen predator hiding just beyond sight. The shimmering flora around us pulsed faintly, as though in response to the alien glow from above, casting ethereal projections along the trunks of the trees as if the branches themselves whispered of forgotten secrets.

Peters walked ahead, his movements precise, each step considered as though one misstep might awaken some unseen force beneath the soil. His broad shoulders were hunched slightly, the weight of his readiness bearing down on his strong frame. His knife gleamed faintly in his hand, still unsheathed from our earlier encounters. We had learned already that this jungle did not take kindly to intruders. It was Peters' job to make sure we didn't become another forgotten meal for what lurked beyond the canopy.

I, however, could not escape the lure of the unknown. Despite the danger, despite the chilling shadows bending and shifting beneath the vibrant beauty around us, my fascination pulsed stronger. It was undeniable—something in this place, this world far beneath the ice, stirred within me the kind of wonder that no man could easily resist. My scientific curiosity burned hotter with each new discovery.

So, while Peters was vigilant, my eyes wandered. I couldn't help but take in the iridescent flowers around us, their colors shifting in response to the glow from the strange orb above—an orb that served as a sun in this enclosed universe. Their beauty contrasted vividly with the muted danger that slithered through the air. Each petal seemed to pulse with life, soft tremors reacting to our very presence, as though they too were part of this predatory ecosystem. There were shapes within the flora I had no vocabulary for, no reference point. The plants gleamed, shimmered, reminding me that this was no ordinary jungle.

And yet, Peters' dark eyes kept drifting back, scanning the trail we had left behind us. His instincts were sharper than any blade he'd carried, honed from years of survival across oceans and deserts. He knew a predator when it was nearby and could sense it in ways I could not. Now, it was clear to me: the earlier encounter with that monstrous spider had not departed his mind as easily as it had mine. His gaze was wild, wary, fixed toward every shadow that moved too swiftly out of sight, every rustle that wasn't quite explained by the ambient wind.

"As quiet as it is," he muttered over his shoulder, "I don't trust that thing isn't still hunting us."

I said nothing in response—could say nothing that would ease his anxiety. After all, it may not have been pursuit that worried me, but the warnings the jungle had whispered in its own strange language. There was always something just out of sight here... always some shape that shifted in the shadows, evaluating us, waiting.

And then we stepped into a clearing.

Immediately, the air changed. The sounds of the jungle— the clicks, the rustles, the distant roars—fell away, muffled as if dampened behind a wall of anticipation. A stillness enveloped us, an unnatural tranquility hanging low over the landscape. My breath caught. Peters froze. His every muscle flexed at the sudden quiet as his fingers reflexively tightened on the hilt of his knife. That silence—the kind that fills the heart with dread for it knows what it precedes.

Our feet barely disturbed the thick moss-like vegetation beneath us, its softness matted by the lack of recent disturbance, as if this part of the jungle was forbidden ground. The faint whispers of wind, which had once rustled overhead, ceased altogether. Even the glow seemed muted here, an expectant pause as though the very light awaited what came next.

Then—there it was. A rustling sound, ever so faint, barely discernible but growing, unmistakable. Both of us froze, our eyes meeting briefly in a silent exchange. Tension crackled between us. The sound grew louder—consistent, deliberate, cutting through the thick quiet like a blade drawing near. Peters turned, bracing his posture defensively, lowering into a stance that might send him leaping into action at any moment.

The rustle came again, this time from higher up—a soft swaying of leaves disturbed by something, something moving toward us with intent. There was no menace in the carriage of the sound, but its regularity quickened my pulse in the same way the spider had. My chest clenched, breath halting as I turned fully and scanned the perimeter, following Peters' lead.

There—emerging from the dark green, from the shadowy depths of the underbrush—a figure. Taller than any of the creatures we had thus far stumbled upon, its silhouette was striking in its graceful stillness. What stepped into view was not the hulking form of an ancient predator but something altogether different—something that felt both familiar and unnerving in the same breath.

It was humanoid, tall and slender with alabaster skin that shimmered faintly in the soft light cast from the strange orb above. Its elongated limbs moved fluidly, impossibly delicate yet with a quiet strength beneath each motion—like wind bending the reeds of a riverbank, purposeful and ethereal. Dark, silver hair, or something akin to it, flowed like liquid moonlight over its shoulders, shifting softly with each breath it took. Its eyes—large, too large for a human visage—held a kind of glow within them, twin orbs of blue light that stared, unwavering, directly at us.

Instinctively, I tensed. Alien thoughts raced through my mind as I tried to comprehend what this being might be. It stood before us, roughly our height, yet everything about it radiated something alien and otherworldly—as though lives and thoughts danced beneath its skin, too ancient to understand.

Everything about the jungle seemed to hold its breath alongside us.

The creature—this, Náiren, though we knew not the name yet—paused in its tracks, its eyes widening slightly as it seemed to assess us. The way its head tilted, the fluidity with which its neck craned as it studied us silently—there was no malice, nothing threatening in the gesture. But there was something deliberate in the neutrality of its stillness, and it unnerved me in a way no predator's stare ever had.

Peters took a steady step back, his eyes never leaving the figure. His fingers unconsciously tightened around the hilt of his weapon, the quiet hiss of steel slipping further down an inch more audible than anything else in that moment. "What the hell…?" he muttered.

The figure's reaction was instantaneous.

The Náiren—this unearthly being—raised both of its hands slowly, cautiously, as though to assure us it meant no harm. Its fingers—long, slender and lightly glowing—were splayed openly, showing deference. And then, without moving its lips—without the need for any sound—the voice filled my mind.

"Do not fear..."

The words did not come like a normal voice. There was no vibration in the air, nothing tangible except the resonance left behind in the caverns of my mind. No, it was inside— words directly forming to thought, bypassing the limitations of verbal speech entirely. It was… melodic, spiritual, a kind of soft music that felt more like a part of the glowing air itself than the harsh realities of a voice. And yet, I understood it completely.

My heart raced—not from fear, though its fluttering had the makings of panic—but from an overwhelming weight of discovery. The need to understand—for answers to questions I hadn't yet formed—gripped every part of me. This creature—this being was of intelligence, of something deeper akin to reason, to purpose.

Peters' response was more grounded. His knuckles whitened further as his grip around the knife's hilt strengthened. He knew better than I did to trust anything here, even if words— mental or otherwise—offered peace. Whatever this was, it wasn't human, and Peters had survived long enough to know when an unfamiliar hand offered too much.

The Náiren looked at us both steadily—eyes glowing with a palpable calm—and then, in that same voice which never passed through the air, it spoke again.

"You are safe here. This is our land. You are visitors. Be at peace." For a moment, time hung suspended between breath and heartbeat. The Náiren's words lingered in my mind, not with the vagueness of a dream, but with crystalline clarity. I could feel the resonance of its voice, soft and deliberate, winding like a fine thread through the very core of my awareness. It offered reassurance, yet something about the way those words slipped into my consciousness felt almost too seamless—as though it knew just how to implant the right combination of thoughts to pacify me.

Peters, on the other hand, was not swayed so easily. His eyes narrowed, his body rigid and coiled with tension. He wasn't prepared to follow a voice simply because it came in the form of melody rather than menace. His survival instincts hummed like a taut bowstring drawn too close to breaking.

The tension in the silence between us thickened as the creature's gaze remained steady, its hands still raised in that gesture of non-violence. The pulse in my veins quickened as I glanced again at Peters, then back to the being before us. What was this? A messenger? A guardian? My mind raced with questions too numerous, too fragmentary to tackle all at once.

It waited, patient and serene, the soft light from the orb above casting a glowing halo around its pale form. There was a grace to the way it stood, its body loose and fluid, untroubled by the weapons clenched in our hands. I could feel my grip on rational fear loosening, bit by bit, under the weight of the wonder that threatened to overwhelm it.

Finally, taking a slow breath, I let my fingers relax around the handle of the oil lamp I still clutched. To my surprise, I found words spilling from my lips before I had fully formed the question in my mind.

"Who… are you?"

The moment the words escaped me, the Náiren regarded me with those wide, glowing eyes, unblinking yet full of something indefinable—a flicker of surprise, perhaps, but more likely an acknowledgment of a deeper, shared understanding.

"We are… the Náiren," it replied, the words once again sinking into my mind without ever passing through the air. "Descendants of those who once lived above. Many cycles have passed since we retreated here, to the deep. You are not the first from the surface. But few come as peacefully."

Its voice, if it could be called such, carried a weight that did not belong entirely to words. There was layers of history embedded into the meaning—a flood of understanding that pressed against the edges of my mind, as if reaching toward some forgotten truth. I could scarcely take it all in. Descendants…? Of the surface? The thought sent a shock through me, igniting my scientific mind with a thousand implausibilities, all tangled together.

I turned slightly toward Peters, whose rigid form remained

unyielding. His grip on his knife was as tight as ever, but there was a shift in his stance now—less crouched, though still wary. His eyes flicked from me to the Náiren, doubt plain in every line of his body.

"Doesn't mean we should trust it," Peters muttered, his rough voice cracking against the backdrop of the jungle's dying warmth. Yet, for all his distrust, he made no move to attack, no act of outright resistance. Perhaps his instincts, despite themselves, were recognizing the lack of immediate threat.

The Náiren must have sensed this tension in Peters, because it tilted its head slightly, the soft glow of its eyes flickering like a candle flame in a soft breeze. Slowly, with movements that seemed calculated to not provoke, the being gestured toward a path opposite the one we had taken into the clearing. There, just beyond the bordering trees, an intricately carved archway emerged from the foliage—made of the same crystalline material that shimmered in parts of the jungle floor. It looked almost as if it had grown naturally from the landscape, despite the craftsmanship evident in its ornate patterns.

"Follow. You will see," the Náiren spoke into my mind once more, as gently as before. This time, the weight behind the thought carried less mystery and more invitation—an openness, a peace offering.

I hesitated, but only for a breath. Rationality warred with curiosity, but in the end, my feet moved on their own, my body yielding to the unseen cord that now pulled me forward.

Peters followed, reluctantly at first, though his eyes stayed locked on the Náiren's movements, never fully releasing his suspicion.

As we passed through the archway, another shift overtook the atmosphere. The jungle's vibrant chaos, the swirling colors and shifting shadows, gave way to something calmer—a deep tranquility that settled over everything. The further we walked, the more beings I began to notice, emerging from the periphery like apparitions. At first, it was subtle—just a faint shimmer in the distance, a light-footed figure disappearing behind the trees.

But soon, as we entered the heart of what could only be described as their village, it became impossible to ignore the presence of other Náiren.

They moved with similar grace to the one that had first approached us, their pale forms gliding between crystalline structures that seemed almost woven from light itself. Each one greeted us with a quiet nod or a faint smile—a gesture that felt distinctly non-threatening but carried with it years of silence, as if we had invaded a sacred place of solitude.

Every step forward felt like peeling back a layer of mystery. My eyes could not drink in enough. They moved across each being—every gesture, every flicker of their ethereal gaze—searching for the connections, for the meaning hidden beneath their fluid forms. Their skin, though alabaster and delicate, radiated a softness that felt entirely natural in this setting, their movements blending with their environment as though they were an extension of the very world they inhabited. I marveled at their elongated limbs, their eyes always faintly glowing with that soft, secretive light.

My sense of time became tangled in the quiet wonder that danced through my mind, so powerful and overwhelming that I nearly forgot we were visitors here—foreign bodies walking among a species or civilization older than we could fathom.

As we reached the center of the enclave, my breath caught again in my throat. A sparkling fountain sat encircled by smooth stones, arranged in concentric rings with precision so immaculate that it could have only been wrought from centuries of practiced devotion. Above it hung a canopy of glowing vines, twined together in intricate patterns that flickered with faint blue light, casting a serene illumination over the entire gathering.

Peters stiffened beside me, ever-cautious, but even he could not hide the faint awe creeping into his expression. Guards were lowered in the face of such impossible beauty.

The others—the Náiren who had emerged from the shadows—gathered around us slowly, their faces full of wonder, though tempered with a calm camaraderie. I could feel it, almost taste it, in the warm air that lingered in the clearing: they did not see us as intruders. They saw us as guests.

The beings began to exchange glances—none of them speaking aloud, their words carried only in the soft whispers of thought that swirled beneath the surface of our consciousness. There was trust in their movements, gentleness in their motions, as though they believed nothing in this sacred space would ever harm them. Their wisdom and their understanding of the world—and perhaps ours—ran deep, far deeper than we had yet to discover.

For an instant—fleeting, but infinite in its impact—I felt connected. Not by words, not by language, but by some intangible thread that pulsed through the air. There existed an understanding here, one that transcended explanation or speech—a communion of sorts, woven together by centuries of existence, by knowledge not from books, but of experience, passed between them and now, ever so slightly, scratching at the edges of our understanding.

Peters, however, showed no such reaction. The hard lines in his face softened only slightly—not enough to betray outright trust. He would remain on guard, ever vigilant, until the answers we sought made themselves clear.

But I—my mind had already begun surrendering to the possibilities.

***

As we passed deeper into the heart of the Náiren village, a subtle change infused the air, as though the very environment welcomed us with open arms. The warm, humid atmosphere softened, and a gentle melody, barely perceptible at first, began to hum around us. It wasn't music—not in the way we understood—but a resonance woven into the very vibration of the earth, a sound that the rocks, the plants, even the stones beneath us seemed to breathe out in a soft chorus. It thrummed in harmony with the pulse of the land, blending effortlessly with the flickering glow of the strange, crystalline structures surrounding us.

It was peaceful—overwhelmingly so. Almost unnervingly so.

The Náiren moved through their village like shadows, their pale forms shifting in and out of the trees, their movements fluid and graceful, never disturbing the balance of the world around them. Their soft, melodic voices layered themselves into the hum, creating a symphony that resonated through our very bones.

Peters remained tense at my side, shadowed tension still gripping his body like a coiled spring. We stood together, side by side, at the edge of what felt like the nucleus of their village—a clearing where the plants gleamed with their own light, where vines twisted overhead, winding together in intricate patterns as though having grown with design, not chance. It was impossible not to feel the weight of the quiet as we stood there, watching the Náiren's silent, harmonious movements, their eyes filled with a deep, almost unsettling understanding that permeated the air.

Then, one of them stepped forward.

Where the others melted into their surroundings, this figure stood out—a presence commanding yet profoundly gentle. He was taller than the others, though not in any physical sense; rather, the space around him seemed to expand subtly with the weight he carried, as if he was not just a part of the environment but an embodiment of it.

This was Elys, I was certain—their leader. I could feel the deep resonance of his presence before even a single thought passed between us.

Without a word, Elys approached us, his steps noiseless, his silvery robes trailing like liquid light behind him. His gaze, those deep, almost glowing eyes, settled on Peters and me, taking in our forms with an air of serene curiosity, yet there was no mistaking the palpable depth in his expression. He surveyed us not merely as strangers, but as living beings— individuals with their own presence, their own weight in this world. It was as though he saw beyond the surface to the very core of who we were, without judgment, without fear.

Elys extended his hand in greeting, a faint but tangible glow radiating from his skin. His palms were open, fingers long and delicate, and the soft, pulsating light emanating from him matched the resonance felt in the hum that vibrated gently through the air, as though the rhythm of the land and the Náiren themselves were one and the same.

Without fully understanding why, I reached out in a gesture of instinct. My palm connected with his, and the moment I touched his hand, a wave of warmth traveled through me—this wasn't just a handshake. There was life flowing through that touch—like energy, like fire, but not burning. It was a warmth that seeped into my very core, a gentle and overwhelming surge of connection that somehow felt both natural and exhilarating. The energy flowed from his palm into mine in ripples like heat on the horizon, and I found myself momentarily dazed by the sensation.

It wasn't just warmth. It wasn't just contact.

It was life.

I withdrew my hand slowly, fighting the urge to linger in that ethereal tether. What had I just experienced? I scarcely had time to unpack it when Elys gestured softly, encouraging us forward toward a seating area constructed from stones arranged in exacting circles. The stones themselves hummed faintly with that same ambient energy, blending perfectly with the glowing foliage and the delicate fountain that lay at the center of the clearing. Without words, he invited us to sit among his people—and the mixture of unease and awe within me felt utterly disorienting.

Peters, too, seemed resolved, though he remained stiff, the tension in his arms and legs unyielding. His eyes darted toward me as though waiting for some signal that this was safe, that he could stand down from his post of caution—of readiness for violence. I could offer him none. My own mind was spinning too rapidly, unmoored from anything familiar.

A soft hum of voices grew around us as we sat; it was as though the village itself was awakening, each Náiren adding their own soft note to the chorus of melody that suffused the air. The harmony was gentle and inviting, but so personal it felt as though only we could hear it, that it was created for us, to calm our wayward spirits.

Elys' gaze fixed on me, his glowing blue eyes full of knowing compassion, then shifted briefly toward Peters, whose brow remained furrowed.

"Share," Elys spoke again, in that same voice devoid of sound but filled with presence. "Tell us of your journey, and the peril you faced above the surface. We listen. We understand."

There was something in the way he said it—"We understand"—that moved me to speak. Something deeper. A shared comprehension that transcended the simple boundaries of language.

So, we told them.

I recounted the whirlwind of events—the thick fog of the Antarctic sea, the haunting figure in the mist, the whirlpool that had snatched us beneath the ice, and the strange, violent current that had dragged us into this subterranean world. I spoke of the landscape and the creatures we'd encountered, the primal beauty laced with danger—dinosaurs, giant spiders—and the awe that followed us at every step through this unfamiliar realm. As I spoke, their glowing eyes remained fixed on us, unmoving, yet I felt the intensity of their listening. They seemed to absorb every word, every nuance of emotion behind the tale.

Peters, though initially reticent, eventually joined in, describing our harrowing escape from the giant spider—the close, choking moments when the beast had nearly overwhelmed us. His voice, though gruff and honed, held an unusual tremor—one of reverence for the unseen forces we had barely survived. Despite himself, even Peters seemed to succumb to the understanding present in the Náiren's gaze.

Through it all, they listened. There was no interruption, no judgment. Only a quiet, deep empathy radiating from the translucence of their eyes. The soft glow surrounding them seemed to pulse in rhythm with our words, as though they felt the story pass through us, sharing the weight of it.

When at last our words fell away, and the silence returned, I was left breathless by the unraveling of it all. The story, however surreal in its retelling, had united us—Peters and myself—a reminder of just how far we had come, how much we had endured… how much still remained unknown.

My curiosity flared into life then, burning hotter than the anxiety that had clouded my thoughts earlier. The questions—endless, teeming—swirled in my mind, desperate for release. And so, they spilled out of me uncontrollably, as if the need to understand this place trumped the caution still lingering in Peters' wary gaze.

"Who are you?" I asked, turning my attention to Elys. "How long have you lived here? What is this place really? And this… sun," I gestured, indicating the radiant orb that seemed to govern the entire ecosystem. "What does it power?"

Elys didn't blink, his glowing eyes deepening with something far older than curiosity—something more like knowing. Slowly, deliberately, he nodded, a faint sadness giving way to the air of authority carried in his graceful movements. "We are the Náiren, as we have said," he replied, his voice soft, laden with millennia beneath it. "We are descended from a world now lost to the surface. Once, we were not so dissimilar to you. The same air, the same elements breathed into us…"

He paused, and for a moment, his eyes softened with something akin to sorrow. "But many cycles ago—far longer than you can remember—cataclysm drove our people below. The fires of destruction on the surface consumed what was, and to survive… we retreated here. Into the depths of the Earth."

I exchanged a glance with Peters. He stared unblinking at Elys, but the tightness around his eyes betrayed the confusion and, perhaps, the disbelief simmering beneath.

Elys continued. "We found refuge here, sustained by the glow of the core itself, nurtured by what the land below provided. In that time, we have learned balance, harmony… how to listen to the world rather than seek its mastery. And we thrive—not by dominance, but by unity."

I blinked. Exiled beneath the Earth… Atlantis? No—no, that was folly. But something like it—a civilization lost and buried beneath the weight of the world above. The thought gnawed at me, clawing at the edges of logic.

Elys paused long enough to let us absorb the truth of it, then gestured around us toward the glittering structures that wove themselves seamlessly into the natural environment. Each appeared both organic and calculated, blending into the landscape with stunning precision. "This is what remains of our knowledge," he said softly. "These stones, these carvings—they tell our story. They preserve our past, even as we look toward the future. History engrained in every surface."

As he spoke, I could see the intricate patterns that adorned the structures—subtle, almost invisible until viewed in this light—each etched line illuminated softly by the energy pouring from the core of the world itself.

Peters' brow remained creased. He didn't fully trust it, likely never would. But even he couldn't keep the doubt entirely intact—there was a palpable, grounded truth to the way Elys spoke, a narrative passed not just through words but through existence itself.

For my part, I was utterly enraptured. The deeper realization began to take root within me, unshakable.

We had entered a world beyond our understanding—something far older than the dust we tread on, anchored not by conquest but by wisdom. My curiosity, every discovery unearthed with meticulous restraint, burned brighter now.

As the low sun hung softly in the sky, casting a final golden wash over the quiet village, Elys' soft voice cut through the air once more.

"Tonight," he offered, gesturing with gentle precision, "we will share our fruits with you. Taste the gifts this land has to offer. You are welcome in our world."

I hesitated, casting a glance at Peters. His jaw tightened, and I could tell he was still unsure, still cautious—but there was no evading the slight softening in his gaze, the way his eyes followed each movement of the Náiren carefully, trying to reconcile the harmony before us with the danger he had come to trust.

For my part… I surrendered.

"Let us see what you have to offer," I replied, my voice barely above a breath, feeling the warmth of camaraderie settle in.

The air shifted again, and for the first time since descending, I felt… peace.

7

Learning About the Náiren

T he path before us unfolded like a thread into a tapestry of wonder, each step revealing something more surreal, more breathtaking than the last. Elys led us deeper into the heart of the Náiren village, his pace deliberate, as though savoring the rhythm of the earth beneath our feet. The subtle anticipation that had brewed between us since our arrival in their world began to swell as we ventured further, and I found my senses overwhelmed by the depth of the Náiren's world—a depth so intricately weaved with purpose and intelligence that it stirred something deep within me.

At first, I had assumed the village a mere extension of the vibrant, otherworldly jungle—its buildings carved from luminous rock and crystal, capturing and reflecting the glow of the orb above. But as we moved further, the path shifted, transformed. The structures around us seemed to breathe, pulse even, with a life that transcended mere stone.

Glowing plants lined the walkway, their intricate tendrils curling and weaving like fingers reaching for something more. Their faint, bioluminescent glow pulsed rhythmically, casting soft hues of lavender and cerulean across the shadowy ground. Each pulse felt intentional, as though the plants themselves were guiding us, illuminating the way forward with a gentle, otherworldly beckoning. I could feel the energy thrumming beneath the surface—the earth alive in ways I had never imagined.

Peters walked beside me, though his movements were far less relaxed. His eyes jumped from shadow to structure, from one glowing figure to the next, shifting his weight with every step as though preparing himself to spring into action at the slightest provocation. There was something primal in his movements—a readiness to fight or flee ingrained in him from years of survival. Yet the stark beauty surrounding us seemed to slow even his instincts, as though the village itself compelled caution rather than aggression.

The buildings themselves possessed an elegance that defied explanation. No longer purely crystalline, they now appeared almost organic, as though they had grown from the earth itself rather than been built. Tall and arching, they rose from the ground with a fluidity that mimicked the natural forms within the jungle—their surfaces shimmering, impossible to discern where stone ended and the glowing flora around them began. Each surface reflected the golden light cascading from the orb above, casting overlapping layers of soft illumination that transformed the village into a living, radiant entity.

My eyes lingered on the patterns woven into the stone structures as we passed. There was an intelligence, a precision, to the designs—intricate symbols and geometric shapes that repeated with perfect symmetry along the curving walls. Something about them felt mathematical, as though the entire village was one grand, interconnected system— each line, each symbol humming with a silent energy that resonated in my bones. I couldn't help but trace their meanings with my eyes, my mind stirring with unspoken questions as I felt the growing urge to understand this world in its entirety.

Peters, on edge, caught my glance briefly before resuming his guarded surveillance. His eyes flicked constantly back to the Náiren who watched us with their quiet, graceful movements. Their figures glided effortlessly through the village, their tall forms blending seamlessly with the surroundings, their eyes glowing softly in acknowledgment of our presence, yet holding no malice. Still, Peters' distrust simmered—his instincts poised for the possibility of danger, though none seemed present.

We approached a large structure at the far end of the village, its open circular design inviting and vast. It stood apart from the others, its grand arches and wide stone steps leading down into a stunning amphitheater. The air around it thrummed with subtle energy—an undeniable pull guiding us forward into a space that radiated both beauty and wisdom.

As we stepped inside, the amphitheater stretched out before us in breathtaking symmetry. The floor was composed of smooth, overlapping stones, each gleaming like polished onyx beneath the soft light of the orb. The glow of the sun-like sphere overhead cascaded down in a delicate mosaic of colors, each one carefully reflected and scattered by the stones in a dance of nature's splendor and intelligent design.

The ambient hum of the jungle seemed to fade here, replaced by a deeper, more resonant energy that pulsed from the very ground we now stood upon. It was a sacred space—of that, I was certain. And with each step forward, the heavy weight of reverence settled further into my chest. I could feel it in my heartbeat, in the way my breath slowed, deliberate, attuned to the ancient rhythm vibrating subtly within the stones. It was as though every crack, every ridge, carried the memory of countless generations who had stood here before us.

We were not alone.

Náiren figures gathered instinctively around the amphitheater, their presence silent but profound. They moved in graceful arcs, forming a semi-circle around a shimmering fountain at the heart of the space. The water within the fountain flowed in slow, deliberate arcs—its movement guided by unseen forces, catching the last glimmers of light before gently disappearing into the polished basin below. There was peace in the way the water moved, each ripple an echo of something ancient, their flow unobstructed by time.

I couldn't tear my gaze away from the fountain. There was something alive, something sacred, about the way the water moved—not just a physical flow but a deep, whispered message carried on the currents, an unspoken history. I felt it, deeper than words—an understanding that settled in my bones and tugged at the edges of my senses. This place wasn't just where the Náiren gathered—it was where they had woven their knowledge, their memories, into the very fabric of space and time.

Elys stood beside me, his tall frame poised with a calm reverence. He said nothing, but his mere presence magnified the significance of the space around us. I could feel the weight of his gaze on me as I absorbed the magnitude of it all.

Then, from the gathered crowd, a few elder Náiren figures came forward. Their silver-tinged hair marked them as older, their faces lined not with age as we understood it but with wisdom—etched by years of knowledge rather than the ravages of time. Their presence exuded both authority and gentleness, a potent combination that infused the air with a sense of profound respect.

One figure, in particular, caught my eye. A female Náiren, her robes marked with intricate patterns of dark blue and silver, moved gracefully toward us. Her eyes—violet-hued and shimmering faintly—were wise beyond measure, and as she stepped into the center of the amphitheater, I felt my breath catch. This figure was different. She carried more than wisdom—there was something nurturing in her presence, something protective.

Elys took a step forward, bowing his head in deep respect before introducing her. "This is Lyra," he said softly, his voice a quiet echo that spread through my consciousness. "She is one of our scientists, a historian well-versed in the history of our people and the world above."

Lyra's gaze shifted to meet my own, her expression warm and inviting, though no words passed from her lips. Something about the subtle way her eyes glinted in the ambient light told me she already understood far more about me than I could ask. Peters, beside me, tensed visibly, his eyes flicking between Elys, Lyra, and me as though weighing her every movement, her every blink.

I could feel the distrust humming in Peters' body like a live wire. His muscles were taut, poised for action should anything—anything at all—seem amiss. But beneath his visible wariness, I sensed something deeper. He wasn't just suspicious of the Náiren, nor of the knowledge they promised to share. No, his tension carried something else— an instinctual need to protect me.

He watched with those sharp, calculating eyes of his, as though expecting at any moment that the weight of their wisdom might somehow crush or consume me. His duty to watch over me—to keep danger at bay—remained unyielding, a chain tethered to his every movement, every fraction of muscle beneath his weathered skin begging for release.

Lyra, meanwhile, seemed to sense this tension and responded not with force or persuasion, but with quiet understanding. She tilted her head slightly, her gaze softening, and moved delicately to sit near the fountain, her figure casting a long shadow over the shimmering water. The light played across her silvery robes, flickering like stars scattered across the dark. As she looked up at me, I saw within her eyes the vastness of time—the kind of knowledge only attained through centuries of existence.

There was a strength in her quiet, and it did something to quiet my mind too—its racing thoughts slowed, curiosity burning brighter.

And then, as before, her voice emerged not from her lips, but from her mind to ours, spreading like a calm wave across our thoughts.

"Rest," she offered without sound. "And I will share our history with you."

Her words—thoughts—flowed seamlessly, as though they were an extension of the very hum that wove through the jungle, reverberating with resonance. There was a quiet joy embedded deep inside her mind—a joy that blossomed in the sharing of their story, their past.

I sat at last, my mind spinning with questions, my body yielding to the sound of the water rippling through the fountain. Peters—still reluctant—finally took his place beside me, though his eyes continued to dart upward, unconsciously tracking the dizzying light patterns that swirled above us.

Lyra spoke then—not in words we could hear, but with feelings, shared across our minds like a current.

She told us first of the world above—of the destruction that had ravaged the surface and driven their ancestors below. Of the retreat into the earth, of the devastation they had witnessed, unable to stop the collapse of their civilization. Her words carried a weight that sunk deep into my heart, filling the space between sorrow and hope with a bittersweet truth.

As her thoughts sank further into my mind, Peters—though quieter now—narrowed his gaze ever so slightly. His skepticism hadn't vanished. No, if anything, it sharpened, more focused, as though picking apart every thought with the caution of a man searching for the cracks beneath the surface.

The word—"destruction"—hung in the air between us, deepening Peters' frown. His eyes darkened considerably, and I could see the doubt simmer like a low burn in his thoughts. I could sense the question swelling within him—was this the whole truth or just a carefully crafted story to mask darker secrets?

****

Lyra stepped forward, her silvery hair rippling like fluid moonlight as she gestured toward the finely etched carvings that adorned the amphitheater's glowing walls. My eyes, already entranced by the strange beauty of the Náiren, shifted to follow the slow, rhythmic movements of her hands. The carvings, subtle at first, appeared to dance under the pulse of light emanating from hidden veins within the stone itself, as if they too were a living part of this world—awake, responsive, alive.

Each carving glimmered, illuminated by a soft, almost ethereal glow that radiated with the same gentle warmth I had come to associate with the Náiren. Images of their ancestors swept across the walls, unmistakably echoing their own serene grace—their long, flowing limbs, high foreheads, and eyes heavy with millennia of understanding. Clad in robes of intricate design, these ethereal figures seemed to float through the carvings, bending and twisting as the light flickered in tune with Lyra's hushed tones.

"These," Lyra whispered, her voice matching the pulse of the glowing narratives, "are stories of our past. Stories we carry with us, through light and memory, so we may never forget the lives we once lived." The cadence of her tone, woven delicately, was hypnotic, painting each word with a brush dipped in reverence.

I leaned forward, transfixed. The carvings seemed to ripple as though they breathed—their static forms swirling into motion across time. My heart quickened as I followed the lines with my eyes, tracing the rise of a great civilization depicted in those sharp edges and flowing motifs.

Elys, standing tall beside Lyra, met my gaze and nodded solemnly, his luminous eyes reflecting the soft light. His hand hovered over the carvings almost reverently, mimicking the lines as if caressing a fragile truth long preserved.

"This is how we remember," Elys said, his voice low but

resonant, each word a weight, as though the very stones beneath us had formed to cradle his thought. "A city that once touched the stars. A place where minds sought not to possess the world… but understand it." He paused, the air trembling with the sadness embedded in his words. "The names of our lost homeland… we do not speak."

I felt a sudden shiver ripple through me, followed by an almost immediate and unbidden realization. Atlantis. He hadn't said it outright, but there it was—layered so deeply in the undertone that I nearly gasped aloud. The Atlantis of legend, the city that had once stood like a beacon of ancient knowledge, long thought swallowed by oceanic depths. Only now, it seemed it had not perished beneath the seas but had found refuge here, in this hidden realm beneath the Earth.

Peters, standing beside me, shifted uncomfortably. The gleam of the knife at his waist twitched, a barely perceptible motion but one that caught my eye. His fingers hovered near the haft, an instinctive response whenever the weight of the unknown pressed in on him. Though I could sense his unease returning, my own pulse thrummed with excitement.

Before I could ask more, Lyra's voice deepened, threading itself into the glowing images on the wall as though her words birthed the carvings anew.

"You see now," she continued, her eyes misted over with distant memories, "how our people thrived once. Towers of crystalline glass and stone stretched upward, attempting to grasp the very heavens from which we believed all wisdom flowed." As she spoke, a new shift occurred in the carvings. The images there—once so full of peace and prosperity—shuddered, and the stone figures began to collapse. The towers, their crystalline spires stretching high into the sky, trembled, splintering into thousands of irretrievable fragments.

I sucked in a breath as ancient structures I could only imagine twisted and crumbled beneath a darkened sky. The city—this ancient home, this place alive with wisdom, art, and purpose—fell. Lightning crackled at the edges of the engraved clouds. Thunder, though silent, rippled through the curves and etchings as cataclysmic forces worked their terrible power.

"And then," Lyra murmured, her tone low and filled with unspeakable grief, "came the fire."

Her words darkened the space in front of me. In my mind, an image formed—vivid and chilling—of a world consumed by chaos. From somewhere unseen, an oppressive heat washed over me, imaginary yet so real I could all but feel the blistering air tightening across my skin. The carving shifted again, depicting an all-consuming fire spreading with monstrous fury. Flames, forces unrestrained and wild, raced through their once-great civilization like living phantoms of destruction, their glowing tendrils twisting through the air. People—figures like the Náiren, those etched with perfect grace and harmony before—writhing in fearful escape, fled before it.

This had not been mere accident. This was destruction on a scale unfathomable. Whatever had triggered this inferno—whether it was the wrath of gods or something far more terrible in its design—it had ripped their civilization from the heights of glory and buried it beneath the Earth.

A lump, thick and heavy, formed in my throat as the weight of those images settled into my bones. These were not lost stories meant to remain embers in forgotten history… These were warnings. Lessons. Cataclysm, caused by hands too eager, too desperate. A heavy silence fell, broken only by the soft pulsing of light along the now-shifted carvings where the remnants of that once-great city smoldered beneath the telltale death of civilization.

I blinked rapidly, struggling to breathe against the oppressive weight choking the atmosphere, barely feeling the surface of the cold stone as I nervously pulled my knees toward my chest. I couldn't quite help it; my body reacted involuntarily, curling inward to shield myself from the all-encompassing destruction I felt was somehow nearing again.

Peters, meanwhile, fidgeted—restless. His fingers curled unconsciously toward the haft of his knife, brushing the hilt, a repetitive, reflexive gesture—a man accustomed to warding off threat. I could see the tension in his forehead, feel the electric hum of distrust that crackled beneath his skin. His every muscle seemed coiled with the need to act, to respond to imminent danger. His eyes slid toward mine, searching, and though he didn't say it aloud, the silent question lingered between us.

Was all this real? Could we afford to place our trust here?

Despite the skepticism in his gaze, Peters found himself rooted, too. The history pressing down upon us refused to allow any easy dismissal. Even Peters, who believed himself immune to emotional reach, couldn't ignore the grief embedded in this room.

I caught his gaze for a brief moment—flickers of doubt mirrored back at me—but before we could exchange words, Lyra's voice pulled us back to the carvings.

"The fire," she continued, biting the words through clenched teeth, the stoicism breaking slightly to reveal a deeper sorrow beneath, "was unnatural. It was a force that consumed without pause, leaving nothing in its path but ruin—a cataclysm out of control. We thought ourselves invincible. But the world is always hungry, always eager to balance what once grew too swift, too far." Her voice broke over the last words, barely perceptible.

The images swirled darker, showing figures trying— failing—to stave off the destruction. Cries etched into stone, heads bowed beneath mighty ruins. *Their towers cracked like bones beneath a weight they weren't built to bear.*

I felt pity stir alive within me—a sadness that ran too deep to name. I could see myself, see our world, reflected back in the broken towers and bowed spires. This was their Fate… But could it be a warning for *ours*?

My eyes traced the lines of the carving, watching the once-great cities bend, buckle, and collapse. That same fire—raging, greedy, consuming—licked at the base of the towers we, too, are so desperate to build. Even now.

Somewhere, under the grief, deep within my chest I felt a kinship form—an impossible bond to lives I never knew but whose tragedy now rippled into my own.

"But it's not only sadness," Lyra's voice broke gently through the melancholy still clinging to the space. Her gaze sparked ever so faintly, a light dancing behind her violet eyes, like a candle rekindled after a gust of wind. "You see the knowledge we still hold today."

She gestured lightly to the carvings nearest, where beneath the ruins, new scenes glowed softly against the dark shapes of the fallen towers. "We carry with us our remembrance, our failure. But we do so with purpose. You see the technology we used… technology we still use. Look here, the way we harvested the core's energy, using the natural forces of the Earth, maintaining harmony. We adapted, not through greed, but through balance."

The carvings brightened as different symbols appeared—figures manipulating light, guiding the energy of the Earth's core, a technology beyond comprehension. Energy flowed through their machines, not by imprisonment, but by catalyzing the raw forces already around them—powers renewed through syncretic balance. There was no exploitation, no drilling, no bleeding dry. Only peace.

Beside me, Peters gave a grunt, skepticism bleeding into his tone. "Ancient history, maybe," he muttered low, though his glare softened just enough, "but it doesn't mean we know everything yet."

Lyra caught the edge of Peters' doubt and turned her gaze to him, her tone softening as she replied. "There is much we have left unsaid… but time, in its wisdom, reveals all. You needn't fear us."

Elys, standing staid as ever, nodded gravely, his luminous gaze firm with that same unspoken promise.

And then, another of the Náiren approached us, a smaller figure but no less commanding. He—no, *it*—offered something small and delicate in its hands, a device no larger than clenched fingers, shimmering faintly with faint traces of energy still clinging to its surface. The device, though simple in appearance, was clearly one of great age, its curves and metallic sheen interlaced with patterns like those on the walls—a machine once used to amplify and store the energy of the core itself.

Peters leaned forward instinctively, brow furrowed as he inspected it closer. At first, his skeptical eyes flicked over the small object, doggedly searching for wires or tricks—some rational explanation. But then, something changed. The doubt in his expression, though still present, faltered. *This was different.* The simplicity of it didn't need grandeur or pretense. It hummed quietly in his hand, an undeniable pulse his mind couldn't explain.

"This," Lyra explained softly, "allowed us to channel the energies to power what you see. A reminder that harmony and survival have no need of destruction."

Pym's breath hitched. This wasn't myth anymore. This was *real*.

***

Elys moved with the same quiet grace he had wielded since first approaching us, his feet silent against the ground as though he was a part of it—grown from the very earth, like the crystalline structures that now loomed into full view. In the fading light from the glowing orb above, the village unfolded itself in ways I hadn't anticipated, revealing layers upon layers of architectural brilliance that seemed to defy both logic and nature. Yet, as had often been the case during our time beneath the Antarctic ice, the lines between the two blurred into an indistinguishable amalgam of incredible, incomprehensible beauty.

As we followed him deeper into the village, I realized these buildings—these radiant structures—were not constructed in any traditional sense, but rather grown, coaxed into being by some unseen force that mirrored the organic pulse of the world around us. They did not cut sharply against the landscape; they emerged from it, weaving between the foliage with the same effortless harmony that suffused everything in this place. The expression of nature here was unlike anything I had witnessed on the surface—the lines of the buildings echoed the vines, the roots, the branches of the jungle. They glinted in the same soft light, reflecting it back in strange iridescent hues, alive yet static in the stillness of the village.

Peters, still at my side but ever-so-slightly behind, stiffened with each new step. I could feel the tension rolling off him—unfamiliar to these surroundings and suspicious of Elys' serenity. Even though the landscape of the village appeared to hold no immediate threat, a chill ran through me subtly, reminding me that here, even the most beautiful things could harbor dark secrets.

I noticed how Peters' eyes flicked toward his belt again, toward the knife he carried—the older blade that had seen everything else and trusted nothing. He had survived too long in dangerous worlds to let allure mislead him. But for now, he stayed quiet, waiting, watching.

We came to a stop in front of a building—if it could so be called—that stood taller than the rest. The light from the glowing orb above stretched over its surface, casting it in a golden hue. Here, the intertwining forms had grown into something grander, more deliberate, though still as effortless as if they had been woven from the jungle itself rather than shaped by Náiren hands. The organic structure reached upward, its crystalline surface cutting smoothly into the backdrop of glowing flora and descending light. Even from the outside, I could feel it—an ancient presence humming from within, whispering of histories I had yet to comprehend.

Elys turned to face us, his expression calm as always, though his eyes—glowing faintly in the dim light—held something deeper, something more weighty. His gaze locked onto ours for a moment, then drifted along the surface of the hall behind him. The light shimmered slightly in response, casting shifting shadows that seemed to flicker in time with the soft hum that always thrummed through the air here.

"Here," Elys said softly, his voice almost a breath, yet it carried the kind of certainty that made you pause, made you listen. "This is where you may best understand us. Knowledge has been preserved here—our triumphs, our peace... and our mistakes." He hesitated for a moment, eyes flickering briefly with something like regret before continuing. "Preserved so they may never be repeated."

I glanced briefly at Peters. His expression was guarded, dark eyes narrowed as he subtly assessed what stood before us. There was no mistaking the skepticism in his tight-lipped silence. Knowledge, unity, all those lofty words meant little without the history behind them, without the recognition that such unity came at cost. Peters knew better than anyone that behind every peace lay remnants of conflict long past.

Elys turned toward the entrance, and with a slow, deliberate motion, he lifted his hand. The doorway responded instantly, its edges flaring briefly in sudden brightness before folding open like a petal uncurling in the morning light. The illumination from within cast a soft glow along the ground, as though bidding us to step forward and, perhaps, offer ourselves to the knowledge stored within.

Without fully understanding why, I felt a pull—not just

curiosity, but something more primal. My heart skipped at the prospect of what lay ahead, at hearing and seeing the world through the lens of those who had long ago retreated from its surface. What bleak revelation had led them here to build in such secrecy?

As we entered the Hall of Memory, I was hit not with the grandeur of architecture but rather with something quieter, more intimate—an air so thick with presence, it felt as if the very stones around us were conscious, watching us with the quiet weight of ages. The walls were etched with glyphs, carvings that twisted and curved with mathematical precision, forming circles within circles that shimmered as the light caught them. As I approached, the symbols themselves appeared to shift, responding to our presence, the faint glow flickering in and out as though adjusting with each footfall.

Immediately, my rational mind took hold, seeking patterns within the symbols, trying to unearth some logic in their arrangement. But there was something more nuanced hiding here, more intricate than interpretation allowed for. These were not mere words written in stone; no, they were something living, pulsing. I could almost feel the energy vibrating through them with a gentle rhythm that spoke of knowledge passed silently from form to form, creation to creation.

The light ebbed and flowed, responding cryptically to the space we took up within it. Each flicker seemed to shift my perspective, offering me brief glimpses not just of history, but of something deeper—a living connection to time, as though the timelines of the Náiren all spiraled back into this one place. A million stories told all at once, not through voice or written script, but through creation itself.

Beside me, Peters let out a sharp breath, his suspicion still unshakable, despite the beauty of what unfolded around us. His eyes followed mine as I approached the closest wall, hand hovering inches from the intricate carvings. I longed to understand, to know what had driven the Náiren to retreat so far beneath the surface of the Earth—and more importantly, how they had survived, how they had thrived in a place so hostile and ancient.

Elys came to my side, his presence always quiet yet imposing, and his voice—without sound—slipped into my mind once again. "These carvings," he began softly, "are more than records. They are lessons, carried forward so that each generation may learn what must be known, and what must be remembered."

I gazed deeply into the glyphs, the complexity of their lines unfolding before me as I desperately tried to grasp their meaning. They were not mere symbols etched haphazardly— every curve, every loop was precise, as though designed with a purpose far beyond what the surface world could comprehend. A fine balance of art and science, intertwined and inseparable—timelines depicted not in words but in cycles, signaling key moments of decision, survival, conflict. Patterns that both mesmerized and overwhelmed me.

Elys moved his hand over one of the carvings, and as he did, the light flowing beneath the ridges pulsed in unison with his motion. "Here, in this section, you see how we harnessed the energy of the land itself for our existence. But here"—he gestured toward a smaller, more intricate set of patterns—"this is where we nearly lost what was dear to us. The mistakes remind us that even peace has its costs. Survival always comes with choices."

Without thinking, I placed my hand gently against the stone. Warmth bled into my fingertips. It was not a residual heat, but something alive in its vibration—warm and tactile as if the stone itself recognized my presence. I could feel it pulse underneath, the same heartbeat that had intertwined every layer of this world, every thought of the Náiren, their fears, their successes. I could feel it all, laid bare beneath the stone, bound not by words but by something more elemental.

The silence in the sacred hall only deepened that connection. It was not the silence of death, but stillness—a quiet hum that reverberated through the glyphs like the exhalation of the Earth itself. Time here had not stopped; it flowed in currents beneath the surface, woven into every symbol, every ripple. As I traced the curves and lines with my hand, I was struck by an overwhelming feeling—that I was not just observing history, but that I was part of it.

Behind me, Peters lingered near the doorway, eyes narrow, the knife ever at his side. He didn't trust any of it. Not the light. Not the symbols. Certainly not the peace they claimed. His eyes, dark and unyielding, watched everything cautiously, not eluding to any shared fascination with what unfolded before us.

"Too perfect," he muttered quietly, his voice nearly drowned beneath the soft hum of the hall. "Too peaceful. Where's the hardship? The enemies?"

Elys seemed to sense the tension in Peters, the suspicion that never wavered, and turned toward him, his expression as soft as it had been from the beginning. Yet his eyes carried a weight now, a sadness that sank deeply beneath his ageless form.

"Our people have faced challenges, Dirk Peters," he said, speaking directly to him with the same quiet reverence. "We know hardship. We have lost and gained and fought for what we have now." He gestured toward another section of the wall, and as I turned, my eyes met a different set of glyphs. These were darker in both color and complexity. The patterns disjointed, marked by angular shapes rather than the flowing curves from before.

Lyra, having approached silently, gestured to it, her voice gentle yet filled with the weight of a leader's wisdom. "After the cataclysm, our people did not find unity easily. There were conflicts—decisions to be made that threatened to unmake us. But through understanding, through harmony with the Earth itself, we found our survival."

Peters narrowed his eyes. "And your enemies?"

Elys' sigh was quiet, filled with a deeper truth, one he had perhaps known for far too long. "Enemies always arrive, in some form or another. Even here." His tone shifted, darker now, and I couldn't help but feel the tension return.

I stared again at the glyphs—heavy, intricate, and intertwined. Here lay the stories of the Náiren's struggles—their triumphs, yes—but also their scars.

As the silence expanded once more, the weight of what was held behind those walls, those lives, settled in the space between us.

We were only half in the light. Half in a truth not yet fully spoken aloud.

8

The Hidden Threat

We set out from the Náiren village with a slow, tentative pace—more out of reluctance than any outward sign of fear, but the weight of the unknown pressed heavily between my shoulders. Peters walked ahead, as always, eyes scanning the thick underbrush, every step full of deliberate caution. His breath came sharp now and then through flaring nostrils, a sure sign that his instincts were prodding him, telling him something wasn't quite right. I could almost hear the hum of those survival-driven senses, sharper here beyond the reach of the Náiren's tranquility, as though the air carried an unseen warning.

The jungle whispered faintly around us—tendrils of sound woven through the vines, soft sighs from creatures unseen. That strange luminescence still hung in the air, cloaking the landscape in hues of blue and violet, but it no longer felt as comforting as it had when we sat among the Náiren, listening to their quiet, peaceful words. No, this part of the jungle, as we ventured outward, carried something different, and the tension that clung to the thick humidity seemed to increase with every step.

"The quiet," I muttered, mostly to fill the unnerving silence. "The jungle's… quieting."

Peters cut me a quick glance over his shoulder, not bothering to respond. He didn't need to. The crease deepening between his brows spoke all the words necessary. He, too, had noticed the change. That ineffable something—a stillness where moments ago, life had thrummed under every leaf and shadow—now made the atmosphere impossibly thick, cloying, wrapping around our senses in an impatient grip. Both of us walked silently for another stretch, our earlier hope for further discoveries dampened slightly by the sense of isolation creeping up behind us like a shadow slipping back into its own void.

The terrain itself seemed to shift beneath our feet. Where once massive trees gathered dense and cloistered overhead, leaving only thin beams of light to penetrate the canopy's embrace, now the foliage thinned. The trunks of towering trees appeared less often, giving way to open patches of rugged ground. The landscape, still foreign, still vibrantly alive, held fewer visible traces of that otherworldly warmth we had come to associate with the Náiren presence. It felt exposed here. Bare. Vulnerable under a yawning sky. And the further we moved from the village, the more pronounced the shift became.

Peters slowed abruptly, eyes narrowing as he scanned the

horizon—thoughts still vivid behind the darkness of his gaze. His every muscle, honed over years of careful survival, betrayed his growing unease. The warmth of the Náiren village was too far behind us now for comfort, leaving Peters visibly tense in ways that even I could detect. He'd always been the wary one. The one who trusted what lived beyond the fringes of any light—not the safety of the circle itself. There was no comfort for him, not in these expanses where the wild things had again taken root.

"It's too quiet," he growled low, dragging his fingers along the edge of his belt where his knife rested still, wrapping and unwrapping them in a nervous rhythm. He shifted his weight, turned to me fully, and lifted his chin slightly in that way he had when checking for final confirmation. I knew what the gesture meant—**Are we wrong to keep going?**

For an instant, I wavered. I couldn't deny the slow tension winding itself tighter around my chest, an all-too-familiar sensation akin to being watched. The jungle wasn't speaking to us anymore—it was listening. But, despite the rise in my own pulse, the curiosity that churned in place of silence refused outright retreat. Not yet.

We pressed on a few paces more until—against the shimmer of faint vines, laced deep into the earth—a glint caught my eye. At first, it was barely a flicker, a metallic sheen that winked shyly from within the creeping underbrush. But once detected, such things didn't escape my notice. I stopped, nudging Peters' arm to draw his attention to the anomaly. He froze instantly, his eyes zeroing in on it before my finger could even point.

"Up ahead," I muttered. "There's something… not natural."

True to form, Peters' instincts took over immediately. I watched the subtle tightening of his grip on the hilt of his knife, heard the slow exhale through his nose as he surveyed the exact spot I had indicated. There was no hesitation in him, no pause in calculating the threat. And yet even he, despite the wariness he wore like a cloak, was curious once I pointed out the sheen breaking through that tangle of flora.

We pushed forward, crouching as we neared the anomaly, our movements cautious yet deliberate. Vines of spiraling green and violet swamped the unfamiliar shape peeking through, drawing us closer, entangling us in something foreign to this natural world. I could feel it now—that pulse of electricity weaving through the foliage like threads barely bound to their origin.

There it was. Woven clumsily into the vine-laden earth— a glint of metal, exposed after years of slow decay. As we approached, the creeping sensation of wrongness settled heavier in my gut. Where the world of the Náiren had been flawlessly synchronized, seamlessly blending life with its surroundings, this thing… this **intrusion** seemed out of place, unsettling in its irregularity.

The shapes revealed themselves as we got nearer. **Man-made.** At first mere suggestions in the tangle, but soon clear— suddenly too clear—as their harsh lines glared against the soft backdrop. Thick, rectangular frames of rusted machinery half-buried in the earth, their surfaces stubbornly resisting the jungle's slow embrace but helpless against time's decay.

Peters' face darkened. He crouched further, frowning before he even touched the cold, abandoned machines. "This… this isn't natural," he breathed, the disdain dripping with a suspicion that curled around him like fog over the tundra. His knuckles tightened until pale against the handle of his knife as he catalogued the evidence before us—the shapes, the angles, the iron bars twisted where nature refused to swallow them. His expression became a grim acknowledgment of something already familiar in the worst way.

My brow furrowed. I knelt beside one of the rusted pieces of machinery, studying its weathered surface in the low light. It was still warm to the touch, though the jungle around us barely allowed for the cold anyway. There was something wrong in the feel of it—the parts were too foreign, too disconnected from the thriving world of the Náiren and their flowing, harmonious systems. This was harsh. Brutal. It spoke of manipulation rather than synergy, of forged metal meant to break rather than nurture. And the lines, those cold, rigid lines, were so **jarringly** out of place here—where life twisted and curled with fluidity.

Peters' stance shifted again, and he gestured roughly toward a piece of the structure splayed against flattened vines— something that might have tumbled ages ago but was now almost obscured through erosion and growth. From here, though dusty and partially buried, something stood out against the rubble: **Words. Letters. Symbols of a language long forgotten in this place.**

My breath caught. German. And beneath that—a **symbol.**

Dark memories surfaced like a buried wound.

I swallowed hard against the rise in my throat, my pulse quickening with realization. Peters saw it too, stepping closer to the piece of debris as his eyes narrowed. "This…" he muttered, voice rough with pronounced anger, "**isn't right.**"

A chill crawled up my spine—one not attributable to the humid air clinging to my skin. The sight before me, so terribly foreign against the lush backdrop of alien vegetation and glittering skies, drove home a message I had been unwilling to accept until now. Something **human**—something **dark**—had found its way into this untouched world once before. And nothing about it felt connected to peace.

We both knelt, more methodically now, picking through the clutter around us. The overgrowth had done a surprisingly fair job of submerging the evidence—metals, plastics, fractured tablets—all pieces of objects whose purpose escaped us entirely but whose reckless, authoritarian presence was impossible to ignore.

Moments passed in heavy silence as I carefully sifted through handfuls of grime and torn foliage. Reams of scattered papers turned to ash as they brushed the air around them—dried, brittle folk-wisdoms once stored as **blueprints**, now long abandoned by their authors. Beside me, Peters ran his fingers along the fractured surfaces of what once might have been **machinery**, but whose purpose and origin had clearly darkened with age. His frown deepened further as his hand brushed the charred remains of something faintly mechanical—though precise in its weight and shape.

"They've been here a while," Peters muttered darkly, picking up a fragment of what looked like some form of a futuristic element, its body matte black, marred only by faint scorch marks.

My throat tightened.

Among the collection of rusted parts, my hand found something smooth—a small metallic object awkwardly embedded within the tangle of vines. I pried it loose, staring down at its peculiarly sleek shape. Its surface gleamed faintly but gave no outward indication of its purpose. Some kind of advanced technology. Yet it didn't remind me of anything we'd seen with the Náiren or any remnants of our own machinery from above. I turned it over in my hand, feeling the disquiet stir deeper within. This—**this** was beyond what we could comprehend. **Beyond anything from our world.**

Peters looked to me, eyes narrowing in that perceptive way of his—his gaze drawn to the object in my palm. He didn't speak, but his expression mirrored my concern. We weren't alone.

And then, suddenly, it all became clear.

A weapons cache lay scattered nearby—a brutal contradiction to the beauty we had only just witnessed among the Náiren. Rough metal implements, tangled under thorny creclusion. Designs both savage and efficient in their barbarity lay before us. I could hear the blood pounding in my ears, hear the wind returning with a sharp hiss through the trees around us. Something… something was **wrong. Something—**

"We need to get back," Peters murmured. His voice carried no pretense, only the protective instinct that had always been his closest companion. His rough hands hovered, blade exposed now, in a silent promise to guard us against whatever had risen from **this.**

A shiver crawled over my skin. I stood there beside him—a body ravaged by curiosity and dread, caught between mystery and devastation—for my mind still reeled from what lay in my palm, what knowledge rusted beneath our feet.

There were darker things in this world waiting for us to discover.

***

The strange, metallic object still cold in my hand, I stood there—silent—the weight of our discovery sinking like stone into a deep well. Peters crouched nearby, his fingers lightly skimming over the charred surface of what had been some form of mechanical device. Our thoughts were entwined by the unnatural wrongness of it. This was human-made, or something bearing the scars of history neither of us had seen.

I startled, nearly dropping the object. Panic prickled through my chest as I straightened, my breath catching in my throat. Peters rose slowly beside me, his knife sliding smoothly into his palm—instinct taking hold. His gaze, sharp as the blade he clutched, darted toward the noise. Every muscle in his frame tensed in preparation, eyes narrowed, calculating. It was as if the very air contracted with him, coiling tighter before a strike.

Another rustle. This time, closer.

"Stay quiet," Peters whispered, leaning forward slightly, his whole body poised like a predator, aligning instinct with readiness.

From behind the thickest of the vines bordering the clearing, figures emerged. Tall. Commanding. Grim-faced. They stepped into the clearing with deliberate caution, their boots pressing silently against the overgrowth—armed men, clad in the unmistakable severity of military uniforms. The sight of their grim faces, half-obscured by shadows cast from the surrounding flora, sent ice-cold dread snaking down my spine.

I instinctively took a single step back, feeling the pulse of the jungle shift—tightening, now holding its breath along with me.

Peters did not move. His stance was ground into the earth by years of experience, his hand steady on his blade. His eyes locked onto the men, calculating every possibility in mere seconds, his body primed to deflect danger. But even I knew he wasn't used to this—men in uniforms, trained to kill in the coldest, most efficient ways possible. We had stumbled into a battle zone. The enemy here wasn't just nature; it was fellow man.

The air thickened with tension as we froze, caught between instincts that battled within us—fight or flight, both screaming for dominance in the face of this sudden, unmistakable threat. Each glance, each breath, carried the promise of violence tempered only by the thin barrier of silence.

It broke with a voice—sharp, commanding, reverberating harshly against the heavy hum of the jungle.

"Identify yourselves!" One of the soldiers barked, his voice punching through the stillness like a shotgun blast. The authority embedded in it left no room for hesitation.

We stiffened, our limbs rigid, caught like cornered animals. I could feel their eyes on us even before I properly dared to meet their gaze—metallic, gleaming in the fractured light, carrying about them a disciplined sharpness I recognized only in men drilled ruthlessly for one purpose: conflict.

For a painful moment, I couldn't speak—my voice strangled in the vise of fear and realization. But the silence felt worse, threatening to strangle us both before anything else had a chance. Forcing moisture into my throat, I swallowed hard before speaking, dragging the words up from the pit of my chest.

"We… we're merely explorers," I managed, though my voice wavered, betraying the weight of disbelief I barely had time to wrestle with. "We mean no harm!"

It was feeble at best and I knew instantly it hadn't made the impact I'd hoped for.

The leader of the group—tall, sharp-featured, with fierce, cutting eyes—took a calculating step forward. His presence was magnetic in the worst way, his gaze stripping away any remaining illusion of isolation we had clung to since descending beneath the ice. He measured us in an instant, our worth, our threat, and whatever meager defense we might offer.

"Explorers?" He scoffed, the word slithering between his teeth like sour venom. His lips curled slightly in disdain before a cold chuckle escaped. "You've stumbled into our territory." His voice maintained a dismissive edge, his posture stiff and intimidating. "Do you even know who we are?"

Panic clawed at my insides as I struggled to keep my mind sharp, to grasp at the sheer horror we were now drowning in. Peters, though silent, shifted imperceptibly beside me, his fingers now gripping his blade tighter—not through nervous energy but with the grim readiness of a man who would make his stand if pushed.

Peters' protective instincts flared like lightning, crackling visibly as the men inched closer. His stance shifted subtly, a feral energy rolling through his limbs. "Back off, or you'll regret it," he growled, the rasp in his voice carrying both warning and promise. Strangely, the controlled viciousness in his tone made me feel less alone, even as terror curled tighter around my mind.

The leader's gaze flicked toward Peters, assessing the danger with a mild, almost dismissive sense of amusement. He and the others exchanged glances of mutual understanding, their demeanor hardened with a blend of arrogance and impatience—the posture of men who believed themselves unanswerable to anyone.

As my eyes moved between them—Peters standing defiant against their encroachment—something clicked violently in my mind. My breath came short, ragged; the puzzle that had been forming since we stumbled upon this equipment snapped painfully together. We were not just facing soldiers or another desperate antagonist bent on survival.

These men were unmistakably human—more than that— they were relics of conflicts long past, remnants of a violent history we could not yet name. Their uniforms, insignias, and weapons were alien in both design and intent. Though I could not decipher the language stitched into their patches or the symbols that adorned their gear, the air around them was thick with the threat of something far darker than what we had yet encountered in this strange, hidden world. It was as if these men carried the weight of an unknown war—one from a time after our own—full of horrors we could barely imagine.

For a fleeting moment, I desperately tried to shake the realization, refusing to believe it should have been possible. But then, one of the men—the one still standing off to the side—stepped forward, his eyes glittering with malice and, somehow, pride. His movements were slow, deliberate, and as he grew closer, a symbol, stitched to his uniform, came fully into view.

The insignia stopped my breath short. My stomach lurched violently, though I couldn't immediately grasp why.

"Yes… now you see," the leader murmured darkly, following my gaze, pushing forward through the space between us. He leaned closer than I thought possible, given the tension in the air—the malice practically oozing from his every movement. His eyes held a glint of malevolent satisfaction— like a predator toying with its cornered prey. Then, with a deliberate pause and the shadow of a smirk playing behind his eyes, he spoke the final words that confirmed a dawning truth I hadn't yet fully comprehended. "We are men of the Reich."

The words hung there, thick and alien. My heart pounded once, hard enough to echo in my skull. The term wasn't one I recognized, but the venom with which it was spoken cut into me nonetheless. There was a weight to that name— a darkness, as if history itself was etched into the syllables. Unforgiving. Purposeful. Something terrible, buried beneath those clipped consonants, found resonance deep within me, even as comprehension evaded me.

Peters, standing tense at my side, mirrored my confusion. He wasn't a man of books, nor someone to waste time grappling with abstract ideas—but like me, he could feel it. The wrongness. The sickness within those words.

"You've stumbled into something greater than you know," the leader continued, clearly reveling in our confusion. "This land and its treasures will serve a higher cause," he spoke slowly now, eyes flicking between us, carefully watching every movement, every breath. "And with the power hidden here, our Reich will rise… and take back what was lost."

He gestured conspicuously toward the wrecked devices scattered at our feet.

"A higher cause?" I sputtered. "What in God's name are you talking about?" I knew better than to expect a straightforward answer, but I hoped my desperation might rattle something from his poised, smug stance.

The leader sneered, stepping closer, his cold eyes gleaming darkly as though fueled by the secrets he carried. "The Reich is an order beyond your understanding—a power the world will remember, a power the world will fear again. These skies, these resources," he gestured broadly around him, as if the entire subterranean world beneath our feet were but a prize to be won, "are ours to command."

A shiver passed through me—not for the words themselves, but for the evil lurking beneath them. Whatever power he sought, it was for no good purpose. I could feel it in my bones.

Peters, though less concerned with words than I, stepped forward, bristling like a cornered wolf. His body tensed—as though moments away from lunging. "You need to watch your step," he growled, voice low and dangerous. "You ain't taking anything."

For the briefest moment, the air thickened unbearably—the space between us a tight wire ready to snap, our breaths shallow and measured. The jungle seemed to amplify the tension. Gone was the earlier sense of awe and discovery. Now, even the very earth beneath us seemed to recoil.

Despite Peters' challenge—or perhaps because of it—the leader only laughed, a cold, mirthless noise that set my teeth on edge. "You think you can stand against us? You don't even know who we are." He leveled his gaze at Peters, and for the first time, I saw genuine menace there.

Peters didn't yield, though the muscles in his arm flexed, his fingers twitching near the hilt of his knife. "I don't care who you are," Peters spat. "You don't belong here."

The other men—the same soldiers who loomed just behind their leader—seemed to tense as well, reacting to the rise in tone, fingers inching toward their weapons. The threat of violence hovered over us like a thick cloud, its weight stifling, inevitable.

The leader dipped his head ever so slightly, a predator

savoring the moment before pouncing. "You have two options," he began, speaking as though explaining something to a child. "You can either join our cause, or you can stay out of our way. But make no mistake…" His eyes narrowed, his voice dropping to a slithering hiss, "We will take what we came for."

I glanced again at the strange symbol on his uniform. There was something horrifying in its design, something far more than pompous militarism. A sense of dread looped through me—a dread tied to what he was referring to, a darkness too terrible to name, something we hadn't yet seen.

And yet, despite my terror, my instinct for self-preservation might as well have been screaming in my chest. "No." The word came out stronger than I intended, my voice shaking but laden with certainty. "We will not be a part of whatever madness you're weaving here. This world is not yours!" The weight of history and lives far older than this man meant more to me than whatever sinister agenda he served.

The leader's sneer hardened into a cold, calculating expression. The smug satisfaction drained from his face, replaced by icy resolve. His eyes, reflecting nothing but darkness, now bore into me with the force of someone who had long since stopped listening to reason.

"You have no idea what you're rejecting," he said, leaning forward, his voice brimming with thinly veiled hatred. "Soon enough, you will come to understand. Know this: we will reshape the world. And you, with your naive idealism, will be swept away by the current."

A fresh surge of fear ran through me. My gaze flickered to Peters, who was still locked in a defensive crouch, ready to spring if the situation demanded it. "You think you control everything," Peters growled softly, his voice deadly now. "But you don't control us."

The tension erupted. For a moment, it seemed we were on the very verge of a clash. Peters' muscles coiled like a wound spring, every fiber of his being poised for battle. The soldiers, too, seemed half a breath away from drawing their weapons.

But, in a sudden motion, the leader took several calculated steps back. His face twisted into a cold grin—one that sent a fresh wave of nausea through me. "You have no idea of the world beneath your feet," he hissed. "But I will leave you with this warning: Be wise about your next move. We will win."

Then, without another word, he turned, his soldiers following closely at his heels. The jungle seemed to swallow them whole, the oppressive quiet settling like a shroud over what remained of their presence.

I let out a long breath, the tightness in my chest spilling out with each exhale, but the terror hadn't left—it lingered just beneath my ribs, creeping and building with every moment I stood there in the suffocating, humid air.

Peters stood beside me, his eyes fixed on the last spot where the enemy had vanished, his stance still rigid, fingers splayed near his weapon. Slowly, he relaxed his posture, but his face remained dark with the weight of realization.

A realization that settled harshly over us both.

"We need to get back," Peters said, his voice rough with a gravity that hadn't left him. His eyes flickered toward me, shadowed and weary, but unmistakably focused. "We can't let them get there first."

I nodded slowly, feeling a similar weight pressing on my shoulders. The world beneath our feet—the world of the Náiren—was not the sanctuary we'd once believed it to be. Darkness from above had already seeped into its ancient, peaceful roots.

We were no longer just explorers in this hidden world. Something far more dangerous had arrived.

9

The Nazis' Plan

The clearing was suffocating, though not with humidity or the otherworldly flora that surrounded us. No, it felt as if something far more dangerous now clung to the air itself, thick and hostile, a force we couldn't see but that pressed down on us with the weight of unreleased dread. My pulse, which hadn't fully settled since the encounter, thrummed heavily in my ears. Across from me, Peters stood rigid, his body humming with barely contained tension while his sharp eyes darted along the fringes of the forest, expecting the Nazi soldiers to emerge at any moment. He hadn't moved more than an inch since the men had disappeared into the tangled undergrowth, and when he did, it was only to let out a slow, deliberate breath through his nostrils.

With a grunt, he finally slid his knife back into its sheath but kept his fingers resting near its hilt as though wary of sheathing it entirely. His free hand, still trembling faintly from the surge of adrenaline, dragged across the sheen of sweat gathered on his brow. He cast a wary glance toward me, eyes narrowed. His voice, when it came, was a low tremor, vibrating with barely restrained anger. "We've gotta warn the Náiren."

I heard his words, but I couldn't immediately respond. I was lost somewhere—caught in a snare of my own thoughts, turning over the events that had just unfolded. The strange device I held in my palm—small, sleek, and unfamiliar—dragged my focus again and again, as if I expected its cold metal surface to provide some answer to the storm inside my head. The insignia burned into my memory pulsed darkly at the edges of my vision, clinging with a shadowy persistence. *Reich.* The word bled out into tributaries of questions and dread, boiling and festering in the corners of my mind until all other reasoning seemed to falter.

How? How could they be here? In this pristine, untouched world? A world isolated from the violent wars of men? The past, one I'd thought surely left behind, had clawed its way into the very depths of the Earth.

Peters let out a curse, his patience evaporating. He seized my shoulders, his knuckles brushing the edges of the device I still clutched. He gave me a hard shake, forcing my gaze to snap up and meet his, breaking me from the spiral of questioning confusion that had locked my mind in place.

"Arthur, *move*," he spat, his voice cutting sharply through the fog in my head. His eyes, dark and gleaming with fury, drilled into mine. That fire of his—the one that led him through storms and shipwrecks, through endless danger without so much as a step miscalculated—burned hot. And with it came the urgency I had momentarily lost. "They know we're here. They won't wait for long."

I blinked, the madness in my mind dimming, though the horror lingered just under the surface. My heart pounded furiously against my ribs, as if trying to push me forward where my mind had failed. With a quick nod, I stowed the device into my jacket pocket, feeling the weight of its alien cold pressing into my side. The sensation grounded me, though it did little to ease the horrible tension gnawing at my gut.

"Let's go," I managed, though my voice felt fractured, weaker than I'd hoped. I cast one final, reluctant glance toward the underbrush where the men had slithered away like shadows retreating into the dark. The jungle felt different—wrong now. Where once its mystery and otherworldly beauty had wrapped around us with potent allure, there was menace in every quiet rustle beneath the vines. As if what had once lived here, harmoniously entangled with earth and sky, had become infected—violated—by this unexpected intrusion.

Side by side, we started moving, our pace brisk. Each step was hurried, the eerie silence behind us urging us forward. The once alluring jungle now felt hostile, and every sound, every flicker of movement in the shadows only heightened my dread. Peters, as ever, took the lead, his motion determined, purposeful, his eyes scanning every patch of undergrowth with the sharp precision of a hunter watching for predators unseen. His muscles remained tense—as though caught in an endless stance of readiness—while his nostrils flared slightly with every stray noise the jungle spat back at us. He was deep in the moment, while my thoughts, chaotic and scattered, raced back to the encampment and the cold, merciless eyes of the men who had found us.

The jungle pressed tightly around us—you could feel it, the vines tugging ever so slightly at our limbs; the bioluminescent leaves fluttered, but any sense of peace had long since vanished. Now, every passing shift of the foliage forced me to flinch inwardly, as though expecting our pursuers to burst from whatever darkness still existed within this treacherous beauty.

The device in my jacket pocket stayed with me, heavy and cold against my chest. Every move I made seemed to jostle it, and with each shift, it reminded me—this world… radiant, harmonious, thriving—now had something foreign embedded inside its heart. The sharp contrast between the peace I'd thought we found here and the cold, ruthless ambition that had found its way in sickened me. I could feel a coil of frustration rising somewhere behind my sternum. How had they arrived here? *Why?*

Peters stayed several steps ahead, though he shot the occasional glance over his shoulder toward me, his lips tight, his gaze swimming with silent determination. There was an unspoken yet powerful understanding that crackled between us. He didn't need to articulate what I already knew: time was slipping away from us, chased by something far darker than the jungle shadows.

As we moved, the vegetation began to shift as well. What were once towering trees—glimmering pillars of foreign life—gave way to familiar shapes. The outlines of the crystalline structures began to shimmer faintly in the distance through the twisting flora. The place I once viewed as sanctuary, unbreakable… it appeared vulnerable now, fragile in a way that made my heart hammer harder against my ribs. What had been beautiful and serene now seemed a flickering dream, one poised on the edge of destruction. Peters seemed to sense my hesitation, though he slowed only enough to ensure I hadn't fallen too far behind.

Ahead, the soft, golden glow of Náiren life shimmered faintly at the borders of the village, casting overlapping halos of light across the jungle floor. Usually, the sight of it brought with it a sense of calm—of deep, undeniable peace that existed far from the chaos of man.

But now, cloakless and unshielded, I saw it differently. Fragile. Almost ethereal… as if the village might shatter under the weight of what was coming. Perhaps it wouldn't happen immediately—perhaps the men we'd encountered would head elsewhere for a time—but they would be back. And when they returned… the devastation would follow. I could feel nothing else now.

We slowed as we approached the village center, our hearts still racing though the sounds of the jungle dimmed, replaced by the soft hum of Náiren life. For one disorienting moment, as I inhaled the warm air of their world—the scent of sweet earth and glowing vines—I felt the briefest pull of denial, as though the beauty had the power to sweep everything else away. As though the threat looming just beyond the borders of this place did not and could not exist. But it wasn't true. Not anymore.

I paused, catching my breath, letting my hands settle into nervous fists at my sides. Peters, his jaw locked in an unyielding resolve, stopped only when I did. His presence beside me flared with the kind of determination that accompanies grim foreknowledge.

At that moment, I heard the faintest sound of footfalls, though delicate, quiet—barely an intruder on the air. From the center of the village, Elys and Lyra emerged from behind one of the radiant crystalline structures, their figures bathed in soft, gentle light. Their faces were as they always were—tranquil, patient, calm—but that only deepened the disquiet in my chest. How could such peace continue, unbroken, when the storm was already upon them?

Elys moved with his usual grace, gliding toward us with that familiar, implacable serenity. His pale blue eyes rested upon ours, curious yet without alarm. He approached slowly, Lyra at his side, her violet gaze filled with welcoming warmth. There was no sense of urgency in their movements—no reflection of the explosiveness I felt tightening under my skin.

Elys was the first to speak—though of course, he used no

words. His mind reached out. The gentle, soothing hum of his thoughts entered mine like a river running through smooth rock. "You return in haste." He tilted his head slightly, his expression almost querying. "What troubles you?"

For an impossible second, no words would come. My throat tightened with the enormity of what we'd discovered, the tension knotting my chest and locking my voice. The tranquil setting of the village clashed so violently with the terror that had wrapped itself in every corner of my mind. These people… these radiant, peaceful people… *did not know what they were about to face.*

"They—they're dangerous," I stammered, barely containing the frenzy in my voice. "We found others. Nazis."

Peters stepped forward before I could continue, too driven by anger to let the words stumble over each other. His voice growled low, fierce. "They call themselves Nazis. Escaped Nazis in your world… and they aren't here by accident. They're here for a reason, and it isn't good."

At the harshness of his tone, the Náiren stiffened—not visibly to the untrained eye, but subtly, as though their auras rippled for an instant with a discomfort so brief it could barely be perceived. But I saw it. Lyra's placid expression faltered just so, her smooth brow wrinkling with confusion.

"Nazis?" she asked aloud, almost like tasting the word was foreign, the syllables leaden on her tongue, heavy with unspoken questions.

I cast a quick glance at Peters and then back to Elys. "They want your resources. Your technology. They want to… exploit this world." I swallowed hard, my voice breaking slightly. "They intend to use everything—the knowledge, the power at the core—to rebuild their empire. They won't care what they destroy."

Disbelief fluttered softly among the gathered Náiren, a quiet ripple that rippled out like a stone dropped into the wide serenade of their calm lives. One of the younger ones stepped forward, shaking his head faintly. "Exploit?" His voice resonated with sheer confusion. "That is not… how things work here. You cannot."

"They will," Peters cut in, his usual gruff manner hardening entirely as he took another menacing step forward. "Believe me. These aren't men who care about rules. They're already here, machines, equipment—the whole lot. They'll turn this place upside down. They'll drill into your core, harvest your power, gut the land if it means getting what they want."

The words seemed to suck the air from around us.

Destroy echoed through the space, clashing brightly against the gentle hum of peace that had always hung in the air of their village. Elys, his ever-serene eyes now flooding with uncertainty, took a measured step forward. He turned to me, locking his gaze with mine. "This energy of which they speak… this violence… they plan to harness it—corrupt it? Use the energy of the Earth itself?"

With a nervous swallow, I nodded, the enormity sinking deeper within me. I could imagine it—a nightmare scene of war machines, weapons arrayed under the gentle light of the central glowing sun, all of it bent to a force of twisted ambition beneath a strange, angular cross. The image battled for space in my mind, swirling through my thoughts.

"They'll rip this world apart," Peters added, his tone growing darker, more disgusted with every breath. "They'll use your power for their destruction. They don't care what gets in their way."

The silence that followed was terrible. The Náiren, for all their wisdom, all their harmony, now grappled internally with concepts they had long believed left behind—violence, destruction.

Lyra's bright violet eyes darkened, her humanity surfacing amidst the alien grace with which she normally carried herself. She spoke, her voice low, burdened now with the weight of knowledge she had not foreseen. "This is… grave."

Elys, stoic as ever, yet visibly conflicted, turned toward his people, his face unreadable and pained. He knew now that what we spoke of was not fantasy, not some distant threat.

It had found them. And it was real. Unknowable violence, once thought to belong solely to the world above, had already seeped into the heart of their sanctuary. The weight of it pressed down on all of us, a force too heavy to ignore, an anticipation of the inevitable devastation that loomed ahead.

I could see it in Elys' eyes—the quiet shift as his own understanding deepened. His serene expression remained, but beneath the delicate surface, a sea of internal conflict churned. The peaceful veneer of his society, built on millennia of isolation, balanced now on the edge of a blade neither he nor his people had ever anticipated encountering. His luminous gaze flicked briefly to the fountain at the village square, as if drawing strength—or, perhaps, one last semblance of normalcy—from the glowing, spiraling water.

But that unshaken calm—despite his inherent grace—now felt strained, and I could sense his hesitation.

I swallowed against the dryness in my throat, feeling the enormity of the moment. "They will try to harness the energy that sustains your very existence," I added softly, my voice laced with unspoken fear. "They came here for it. They think they can control it. They will corrupt everything in their path to get it."

Elys let his gaze linger on the water for a moment longer before turning back to us, his voice quiet yet resolute as it unfurled in our minds. "This… cannot happen. The energy of the core is life itself. Any attempt to weaponize it would…"

He didn't finish. He didn't need to. The nightmare thought bled into all of us unspoken—the desecration of their world, their peace, their light turned into a weapon of destruction so complete it would raze everything and everyone beneath its radiant power.

Lyra, standing beside him, had grown visibly pale. Her violet eyes flickered with uncertainty, the soft light playing across her angular features, casting shadows there I hadn't glimpsed before. "This is beyond grave," she murmured, her words dipped in heavy disbelief. "Do you truly believe they will go so far?"

Peters stepped forward once more, his posture hard, unflinching. "I know they will." His voice was cold, steely. "They've done it before. Wars, worlds burning… their empire died once, and now they've crawled into this place to bring it back to life. They're determined. And they'll destroy everything in the process if they have to."

The words hung in the air, thick like a storm threatening to break. For a long moment, no one spoke. The quiet that lingered around us was no longer the serenity of before—it was a growing storm, a tension that bound the air too tightly, holding my lungs like a vise.

The Náiren—who had once radiated with such peace, such easy presence—now felt different. And though they still carried themselves with the elegance of their centuries-old existence, the weight of our words had reached them, pierced through the layer of calm that had always surrounded them like a shroud.

Elys, ever the stoic leader, raised his head and allowed his eyes to meet mine directly. The earlier flickers of doubt and confusion settled into a clarity—foreknowledge, even—that what had been so lovingly protected here for ages was under a very present, very real threat.

"This energy was never meant for such destruction," he said slowly, his voice carrying a kind of sorrow I hadn't noticed before. "Even we do not wield it with total understanding. It holds creation, life itself… and yet, if twisted, it could…" He trailed off again, as if the words were too difficult to form.

I could feel the chill settling deeper within my chest. This wasn't just a matter of saving the Náiren—it was about saving something far larger. And if we didn't act—and act soon—the destruction that would follow would be far worse than any of us could comprehend.

Elys straightened, his eyes flicking briefly to Lyra, who nodded—it seemed they had already made an unspoken agreement. Then he turned back to us, his voice soft but resolute.

"We will prepare."

***

The sacred gathering point of the Náiren village spread out before us, a beautiful, serene space that seemed an impossible place to contain the gravity of what was about to unfold. The soft hum of energy pulsed beneath the soles of my boots, gentle yet steady, vibrating up through the stonework like a heartbeat. There was something alive in the ground beneath us, as if the very earth hummed in tune with the people connected to it, in perfect harmony with the world around them.

But now, that pulse seemed strained, like a breath caught in a throat—unsure of whether to exhale fully or remain suspended in petrified anticipation. The Náiren elders, all of them poised with the quiet grace and dignity they had always carried, circled the meeting space. Their serene faces reflected the glow from the crystal-laden center of the assembly, casting soft, ethereal light that did little to soften the tension now thickening the air.

From where I stood, beside Peters, the scene felt unreal. We were intruding on something ancient—something sacred—but time no longer had the luxury to bow in reverence. The threat that now loomed over the Náiren was too present, too urgent. And while they displayed no outward sign of panic, there was no denying the weight of anxiety that swirled among them now.

Peters' fingers twitched near the hilt of his knife again, his eyes scanning the slow procession of the elders as they met each other's gazes, wordlessly sharing grief, confusion—fear, even. But there was no time left to deliberate in silence. Every moment we lingered in this stillness, the danger growing beyond the village's borders crept closer. Time, once so soft and infinite here, had now become an enemy unto itself.

Elys was the first to break the spell of quiet that clung to the gathering. He stepped forward, his figure tall, graceful, though I couldn't help but notice the tension curling around his pale blue eyes. For all his outward calmness, I could sense the internal war brewing beneath the surface—the weight of leadership pressing down on an outsider to the very concept of violence.

His voice, always soft, resonated with more depth now, echoing in a way that grounded the conversation in the realm of necessity. "The core has long been the source of our life here," he began, his words measured, deliberate, heavy. The assembled Náiren leaned in subtly, their stillness accentuating every syllable. "Its energy flows through all things, binding us to this world. To use this power as you describe," he hesitated, as though choking on the very words he now had to utter, "for war—for domination—it would rupture the balance we have maintained for centuries."

I watched his face as he spoke, saw the faint tremor of ancient conflict in his expression. The weight of the words he had to speak, the reality he was now forced to confront, tore at him. Elys had lived a life—and led a people—dedicated to peace, unity, balance. His reluctance was not from indecision but from the fundamental shift that was about to reshape the future of his world. His thoughts washed through my mind, distant, weathered by sorrow.

Beside him, Lyra stood as stoically as always, yet her usually bright violet eyes now held a different light. She glanced uneasily toward the gathered elders, who shifted subtly, the movement breaking the perfect serenity that had once characterized every gathering. They were not accustomed to this. To being uncertain.

"We have always lived in peace," Lyra's voice echoed within our minds, her telepathic tone still as graceful as ever, though now tinged with conflict. The very concept of war seemed to tremble at the edges of her communication, permeating the serene calm she projected. *"Never in all our generations have we raised arms against any who would enter our world... But what you speak of... it is chaos. It is..."* She hesitated, the weight of her thoughts hanging heavily in the space between us. The next word emerged slowly, as though it carried far more than its surface meaning, burdened with a fear she had never before entertained. *"...destruction."*

The final word seemed to echo unpleasantly in the space, lingering where it should never have existed. Destruction. Something too harsh, too raw, for the delicate balance they had sustained here for eons. In their eyes, it was as if existence and destruction couldn't coexist—they had kept both the world and themselves in a state of harmony for so long, that these new words we thrust upon them felt heavy, clumsy, unwieldy.

The light around us dimmed for a moment. Two of the elder Náiren, faces etched with a serenity that likely had never been disrupted in their lifetimes, exchanged startled, worried glances. They moved with subtle gestures, their hands brushing against the soft fabric of their robes, silent questions whispered without words.

From just beyond us, a Náiren scientist, her hands trembling slightly with an emotion I had never seen cross even a flicker of these people's expressions before—fear—spoke, her voice low and filled with the deep sorrow of something she had never imagined would come to pass. "Are we to lower ourselves into conflict as they wish?" Her voice broke with the final word, her hands clasping together in a vain attempt to suppress the tremor in her chest. "We have thrived without violence. Must that change now?"

The sorrow embedded in her words settled heavily over the gathering like a dark storm cloud, ready to break. The concept of violence was a weight they weren't prepared for, and even I could feel the deep conflict in my own heart. How could we ask a people who had spent so long distancing themselves from brutality to now take it up in their defense?

My hands clenched into fists at my sides. My teeth ground together as tension continued to build inside me. I could not allow them to hesitate. If the Náiren refused to act, if they resisted this call to fight, then the Nazis would proceed unchecked. They would corrupt this place, turn its beauty into a monstrosity—and there would be nothing left afterward.

I swallowed hard, forcing my voice to remain steady, though my heart pounded violently in my chest. "I understand your reluctance," I said, stepping forward slightly to meet the eyes of Elys and the other elders. "But this is not a threat you can peacefully ask to leave. They are ruthless. They won't listen to reason… they won't care about your balance or harmony. They are coming whether you want to face them or not."

A soft murmur spread through the gathered Náiren at my

words—a wave of shock and disbelief that came and went like a passing cloud over the sea. The world they had so carefully built, so fiercely maintained, seemed on the verge of crumbling under the weight of pure violence. And I was the one asking them to confront a storm they had fought so long to avoid. It weighed heavily on me—deep sympathy for their plight mingling with the urgency to survive.

Peters, never one to mince words, pushed past me, his boots making decisive contact with the pulsing stone beneath our feet. He strode into their midst with a confidence that only a seasoned survivor could possess—a man who had faced death, stared hardship in the eye, and come back the victor, time and time again.

"You're not soldiers," Peters growled, his voice gruff but laced with an appeal to their survival. His eyes burned as he moved toward the center of the gathering, standing resolute before them. "I can see that." He exhaled sharply. "But if you don't stop 'em now, they'll wipe this place clean. Peace won't do a damn thing when someone's pointing a gun."

His words cut through the anxious murmur, silencing it in place. His tone was harsh, direct, but it carried the solemn truth these people needed to hear. There had been a time when I might have objected to how bluntly Peters approached delicate conversations like this, but now, increasingly, I realized just how essential his pragmatism was. The Náiren wouldn't listen to gentler words. What they needed was the severity of reality, and Peters knew just how to deliver it.

An elder Náiren, his features marked by centuries of wisdom and understanding, slowly rose from where he had been seated. His long-fingered hand pressed delicately against the stone floor, carrying with it the weight of his people's history. When he spoke, his voice was broken, careful—a pained murmur that felt like the softest wind against ancient trees. "We have lived too long in peace to now raise weapons in defense," he said quietly, though his words reverberated through the gathering. "To do so would strip us of what we hold dear… The unity of life."

I saw his hands trembling as he lowered them again. The words were laden with grief. For a moment, I saw not just a wise leader, but a being looking at the long, peaceful history of his people and feeling it unravel before his eyes. He wasn't simply reluctant; he was mourning.

Elys, his form now more rigid, his aura visibly darker with the sorrow of the decision looming ahead, nodded at the elder's words. His face, glimmering in the soft glow of light, now carried a subtle but unmistakable frown. He turned toward Peters and me, his focus intense, the weight of his people's future tightening the space between his words."We do not know this… war," Elys's voice resonated in my mind, each word woven directly into my thoughts. His face remained serene, but there was a heaviness in the telepathic echo of his words—a weight that bent beneath the simple acknowledgment. "It is foreign to us."

I could sense the struggle in his thoughts, each one pulling against an ancient, deeply-rooted refusal to consider violence.

His mind was a maelstrom of conflicting emotions — a storm that, even in the silence of his telepathic voice, rippled with a tension all too palpable, tugging at the foundations of his peaceful resolve.

"But," he hesitated, his eyes cool but full of an internal storm of conflict, "perhaps now… we must… learn."

The declaration—though soft, unsure, unwilling—rippled through the gathered Náiren. It was the first step toward understanding that their world, their way of life, was no longer safe from the threat imposing on them. And I felt it in my chest—the burden Elys now carried, the burden of forcing his people to confront something they had worked so hard to distance themselves from. It stirred deeply within me, pulling at a sympathy I didn't want to face, but could not deny.

Lyra, her expression painted with inner conflict, took a step forward. Her movements, once fluid and confident, now appeared subdued—weighted by the enormity of what was to come. She met Elys' gaze briefly before speaking, her words soft but laden with the dread of a decision they had never thought to make. "We… we have never wielded weapons in this way before," she said, her voice straining to meet the unfamiliarity of the thought. "Our defenses are born of energy and nature… not instruments of war. We are unprepared."

The admission left the air still once more, the final phrase echoing in the silence.

"We are unprepared."

I could see it—simmering in their eyes. They were unprepared, unwilling. But they would have to be. I could sense the deliberation still circulating through their quiet, peaceful souls, unraveling everything they had built.

And that burden—preparing them, teaching them—was now ours to bear.

Peters let out a rough exhale, the tension in his shoulders easing slightly as awareness settled upon him like a cloak—a weight he, too, understood all too well. "That's where we come in." His voice, though quieter now, held the same unbreakable tone he always used when facing a task he could not shift but instead had to shoulder alone. "We've seen this before. Faced it before." He gave a hard nod in Lyra's direction, then to Elys. "We'll show you how to fight. How to stop them."

Elys' eyes dimmed slightly, sorrow curving along his soft brow, but he nodded. The acceptance of what had to come, though it came reluctantly, was impossible to avoid.

Quiet murmurs spread through the Náiren elders now, a final sound of contemplation before they turned gut-wrenching decision into action. Lyra exchanged brief words with another elder nearby, questions floating back and forth about what food or resources they might need if it came to war—not just defense, but war. They had never thought of these things before. They had never needed to.

Elys turned back toward Peters and me, his eyes solemn but resigned. "Teach us," he said softly, his voice cool yet filled with reluctant authority. "Teach us so that we may defend what we have built. It will tear at the threads of our harmony. But it must be done."

And just like that, in the soft light of their gathering place, the wheels of fate set into motion.

10

The Brewing Conflict

The once-breathing jungle felt strangled now, suffocated by the intrusion of something monstrous. I crouched low beneath the thick canopy of leaves, dense foliage obscuring the dull glow of iridescent spores drifting lazily from the massive vines overhead. But the beauty of this hidden world—its untouched splendor—had wilted. Where once the air felt alive with color and sound, now there hung only the sick scent of oil and smoke. Hydrogenous fumes rolled over us like a stifling fog, replacing the once-pristine fragrance of the earth. The noise of clanging metal, distant yet oppressive, filled the void, tugging at the edges of the jungle's fading serenity.

Beside me, Peters shifted slightly, his posture tense, his hand raised in a sharp motion for me to stay low. I watched as instinct bled into his movements, arms steadying in perfect stillness, eyes sharp as a hawk's as they scanned through the gaps in the foliage. Nudging aside a vine, his lips tightened into a harsh line as the scene unfolded before us.

The land beyond our cover had been stripped bare. What was once part of the vibrant Náiren jungle—an ecosystem that shimmered and writhed with life—now lay gutted, hollowed. The chaos was evident. Where lush foliage once towered, jagged scars of soil and stone bit uneven into the ground—deformed heaps of earth cast aside by brutal, monstrous machines that dominated the landscape.

Machines—imposing, terrifying things—hauled endlessly at the earth's surface. And my God, they were unlike anything our time had ever conceived. Large, hulking devices with armored exteriors and bulging, pulsating metal limbs sank their teeth into the land. Their garish shapes offended the eye, brutal and mechanical in their movements, each one adorned with jagged edges that shredded nature without hesitation. I could barely comprehend the sheer size of them—larger than any ship or industrial contraption I had ever seen—steam rising from vents in their underbellies, their exhalations thick and churning the sky until the once-clear atmosphere turned into a gray, rotting pall of stench.

At intervals, the metallic groan of hydraulic presses echoed down into the jungle. It reverberated deep in the earth, a sound more animal than machine, vibrating the ground under our knees. They weren't just excavating—they were devouring.

Peters turned toward me, his face shadowed under the canopy, but I caught the snarl rippling beneath his breath. His words came out in a growl, each syllable biting with anger barely restrained. "Look at this." He swept his weathered hand broadly to the nightmare tableau just beyond, eyes fixing on the massive drills carving away layers of soil like it was nothing but butter under a hot blade.

"They're not wastin' time," he muttered. His jaw was tight, eyes cold.

I swallowed thickly, feeling my chest tighten. It was a scene of desecration. The harmony I had once admired between nature and the ancient technology of the Náiren—the fluid way the earth seemed to blend with the architecture of their world—had been utterly ripped apart. This was not a land of wonder anymore. It was a battlefield. And the soldiers' war wasn't against us—not yet—but against the land itself.

"They're mining…" I croaked, my voice thin, stolen away by that same crushing sense of violation. "Mining toward the core," I whispered.

The realization felt heavier with each second. This ruined space—this odd crossroads of machinery and devastation—wasn't just an assault on the jungle's natural beauty. It was a direct, cold attack on the very life-source of this world. The machines gouged deeply into the landscape. Massive cables snaked across the bare earth, black tendrils burrowing grotesque scars back toward the hulking engines that drove power into the drills. They throbbed and pulsed like veins, pumping sickly energy into the hungry jaws of machines, leaving nothing but churned, broken soil in their wake. Swarms of debris littered the place—silent testaments to the furious speed at which these people worked.

They weren't here to buy time or explore. They were here to strip it bare, leaving nothing for anyone or anything.

The jungle had turned on itself beneath the weight of such violence, leaves trembling as the great trees—those ancient, luminescent giants—collapsed with a thundering roar, their once-dignified presence shattered. The sound was gut-wrenching—loud cracks followed by mournful groans as titanic limbs bent, and broken trunks crushed to the earth. Vibrant leaves, shimmering with unearthly light, scattered like glass, shattering into iridescent splinters that once looked delicate but now lay twisted, broken.

These were no longer trees. They were corpses.

Peters cursed beneath his breath, the low growl still coiled tight behind his teeth, his eyes flicking to the group of soldiers standing off to the side. They barked orders, jagged voices rough-spoken and miserable, cutting cruelly across the mechanical noise. Their speech, harsh and impossible to fully grasp from where we crouched, carried with it all the hallmarks of command, sharpened into authority. I strained to listen, catching fragments of their guttural tones.

They spoke of the core. Whatever reverence existed in the mentions of that source was absent here, replaced by cold, calculated efficiency. Each word spat out as clinical as the machinery they slaved under. No consciousness of what they were defiling. No understanding of life humming beneath the ground, the sacredness inherent in the core they wished to tap. To them, it was a resource. A limitless source of energy to exploit. Nothing more.

"We've seen it before," Peters muttered, voice low and full of bitter resignation, the weight of what he'd witnessed before haunting him like a specter. "Greed like this doesn't stop till everyone's dead."

I nodded faintly, though my chest constricted painfully, my breath coming in short, rapid huffs. Every inhalation filled my lungs with the stench of acrid smoke and oil, as though the very act of breathing had become a fight against the corrosion now spreading through the land. "If they reach the core… " My voice wavered. "If they access it… there's no telling what they'll unleash. This entire world—perhaps not just this one—the surface… all of it could be affected."

Peters' narrowed eyes slid toward me, his lips pulling into a bitter sneer. "They won't stop till they've razed every inch of soil between here and hell. We need to do more than sit and wait." His words were guttural, full of rage masked behind his trademark hardened resolve. Even then, though, I noticed the edge of desperation breaking through his usual ruthless calm.

"What do we do?" The question sounded childish even as I said it, a sudden weariness rising in me. My mind spun relentlessly, slipping between possibilities. Was there another solution? Any route we hadn't yet explored? Some diplomatic means to halt this madness before confrontation became inevitable?

But those ideals—those familiar hopes—hung by a fraying thread, unraveling the longer we watched this scene unfold. The rational part of me that still clung to something purer, to the idea that reason alone might suffice, was slowly withering. I forced myself to glance up at the brutal contraptions cutting deeper into the earth each passing second. The harsh scrape of metal against stone etched an unshakable dread beneath my ribs.

A nearby explosion tore through the landscape, shaking the ground where we knelt. The force surged through the soil, a shuddering wave that sent jagged sprays of dirt and fragmented leaves into the air. I flinched instinctively, feeling the pulse of the blast through the soles of my feet, through my hands braced on the now-wavering ground.

Peters hardly reacted, though his narrowed gaze had already returned to the machines. He followed a group of figures nearby—silhouettes among the rubble—his focus tracing their movements, catching where they drove thick stakes into the ground, laying cables across the freshly gouged earth.

"Sabotage..." Peters muttered darkly, speaking to the trees, to the wind—to himself more than me. "When night falls..." His voice trailed off, his thoughts sharpening, "...we cut the lines. It'll slow 'em down."

I didn't argue. I knew by the tone in his voice he had already resigned himself to what needed to be done. His pragmatism—his calculating survival instincts—were more necessary now than ever. Sabotage, resistance. There wasn't much more left to do. The machines would keep eating away, whatever we did—the earth would continue to be stripped bare inch by inch, regardless of our efforts. The end stretched before me like a cliff approaching fast—there was no avoiding it. No denying it.

I kept watching—frozen, transfixed by the cold brutality of this mechanized assault on a world we had barely begun to understand. The land was their prey. And soon, we would be too.

****

The lanterns flickered weakly in the gathering dusk, their soft glow casting long, wavering shadows across the hillside, giving the Náiren outpost an almost ethereal quality. Tiny beads of light danced amongst the silhouettes of gently swaying trees, but the peace, now, felt hollow—fragile. Within each shimmer, I sensed the presence of something dark lurking just out of sight, something that did not belong to the serenity so carefully woven into the life of this hidden world.

Peters crouched beside me, both of us nestled beneath a tangle of low-hanging branches that obscured our figures in shadow. My pulse quickened in the dark, the weight of anticipation pressing down on my ribs, almost suffocating. This place should have felt like a sanctuary, an oasis removed from the frenzy of violence that churned beyond it, but now, as we watched the Náiren move quietly about the perimeter—unknowing, unaware—I couldn't help but feel the thick fog of dread creeping in around my thoughts.

"They don't know," I whispered, more to myself than to Peters. The Náiren moved with the same deliberate grace they always possessed, tending to their tasks in the flowing, harmonious rhythm of a people untouched by the brutal machinations of war. Their glances toward the lanterns were calm, placid, as though the world hadn't begun to crumble around them.

But Peters—he knew better.

Peters shifted beside me, his face a sculpture of tension. His fingers curled tightly around the hilt of his knife, knuckles pale, like white stones jutting from the murky shadows. I saw it in the sharpness of his gaze, the narrowing of his eyes as they traced the perimeter of the outpost. Deep inside him, something coiled—an unease, a readiness perfected over years of confronting dangers. Surviving them. His instincts told him what mine only sensed desperately—that the storm was far too close, the threat was all around us, looming, wrong.

"They're too close," he growled softly, his voice low, tight with the weight of what was coming. The words scraped harsh against the otherwise quiet air, a sound that didn't belong but felt right. His eyes narrowed as they moved carefully over the Náiren, who continued in their unhurried tasks, their world steeped in a peace that refused to acknowledge the danger hovering just beyond the trees.

"They'll come for them next," Peters bit out.

I nodded uncertainly and gripped at the rough bark of the tree beside me, feeling its ancient ridges dig into my palm. My breath was shallow, ragged. I fought to steady it, but dread continued to creep low in my gut, tightening with every passing moment. The lanterns' light fluttered, but it did not warm my skin—it did nothing to push away the cold that had begun crawling through me from the inside.

Could we still save them? Could we do something? My mind raced with possibilities. **Surely. Surely they hadn't been discovered yet.** There must be time still to evacuate, to gather everyone and retreat into the deep places of this world before the terrible viper finally struck. Surely there was time.

Before I could give voice to the desperate scramble of thoughts in my head, a sharp noise sliced through the night. It came without warning—a sound like the crack of a whip, violent, unnatural—and a second later, its meaning registered in my mind. A gunshot. The air went still and heavy in its aftermath, and that stillness was broken only by the guttural yell that tore free from the darkness beyond the treeline.

Peters stiffened beside me, his entire body snapping to alertness, every muscle wound tight as a bowstring. His acute instincts flared with a sickening synchronicity, ready to spring into action. The subtle motion of his arm brushed against mine. I could almost hear the rapid pounding of his heart that surely mirrored my own as we ducked lower into the shadows, our forms pressed harder against the damp earth.

Then it began. Chaos.

From the distant treeline, armed men poured forth like a wave of malice, their boots thundering against the earth, their weapons glinting malevolently under the weak light of the lanterns. They moved with methodical precision, sweeping through the outpost with a ruthlessness that crushed the fragile peace underfoot. Their heavy, dark figures silhouetted against the softly glowing horizon were monstrous, inescapable—an avalanche of power unstoppable in its descent.

An overwhelming sense of helplessness flooded through me. My hands shook as I watched the violence spread—watched as the peaceful Náiren, caught entirely unawares, were forced to their knees under the brutal command of their captors. Cold, barked orders reverberated through the clearing, and in seconds, the warriors of this otherworld, these men of distant horrors, had reduced the serene outpost to a scene of desperate submission.

Peters, always resolute, cursed bitterly under his breath. His eyes burned with a cold fury that I knew well—he had seen this, lived it. The weight of the truths he carried about the nature of man—truths I had always hesitated to believe— now bore down on him with a savage clarity. And through that cold fury, he watched, sharp and calculating, but the dissonance in his expression made it clear this tragedy was no less bitter for its familiarity.

I swallowed hard, my throat dry despite the humidity weighing down on us. It was madness—the way it could happen so fast. Ancient lives—peaceful lives—upturned in mere seconds. As I stared through the gloom, I could do nothing but watch, rooted to the spot like the tree against which I pressed. Every breath ached, and slowly, a cold, nauseating weight twisted in my stomach, climbing up my throat like bile.

"Pym…" Peters' voice was barely a whisper now but sharp-edged, a quiet rasp that drilled its way through the cloud of fear circling in my mind. His words seared against my skull alongside the scene unfolding under the weak light, forcing me to focus. "This is what they do."

His tone—hollow with long-buried resignation—sent a deeper chill through me. **This is what they do.**

This wasn't violence born of desperation, of survival. This was methodical, mechanical, a deliberate disassembly of peace. Peters wasn't new to it, and even now, as each pulse of time stretched unbearably long, I began to understand something I hadn't before. **This is what they do.**

I could barely manage a reply—barely manage any thought beyond the horror playing out before me. **Was this what we had come all this way for? Was this the collapse of hope that awaited us—this descent into cruelty unchecked, into violence we couldn't stop?**

The distant sound of clanking metal reached my ears, low and rhythmic, as some of the soldiers began rummaging through the small outpost. I watched in growing horror, every breath a battle as they upturned the simple structures, their dark figures delivering heavy, punishing blows to anything that stood upright. Tools, equipment—anything they could find— were dragged, overturned, examined with a cold detachment that hung thickly in the night air. Pained gazes of the Náiren shimmered faintly in the torchlight, their quiet desperation plain on their glowing faces. **This wasn't just an attack— this was desecration.**

I flinched as one of the soldiers—an enormous figure with a low, brutish brow—seized one of the Náiren by the arm, yanking him roughly from his knees. Repressed screams jolted through me, trapped somewhere between my chest and throat. The soldier barked something unintelligible, pointing harshly toward a strange, intricate apparatus standing against the edge of the outpost—Náiren technology.

Panic surged in my chest, tangling with the helplessness. My mind spun with the terrifying realization of what was unfolding. **They're after the technology.** They're seeking to understand it—to replicate it. These soldiers—if they got their hands on such power... if they understood... if they harnessed it...

I inhaled sharply, the world around me spinning under the weight of that thought.

Beside me, Peters was vibrating with tension now. His breathing was shallow, ragged. I could see the fight building in him—the burning urge to do more, to act, to stop this before it spiraled further out of control. Beneath the cold fury in his gaze lay the embers of a more primal urge—to protect, to fight back. But ever pragmatic, he held himself back, muscles coiled tight, ready, but restrained.

There was no way we could simply storm in. There were too many of them.

Another gunshot cracked through the heavy air. This one tore through the night, a sound so final and sickening that it left me motionless, heart hammering wildly in my throat.

And there, near the center of the outpost, a Náiren fell.

A young one. Silent. His lithe form cradled his side, where a dark stain began to spread against his pale skin.

Something inside me shattered—no, **cracked**. A visceral burst of anger shot through me, something deep and primal clawing its way out from beneath the hopelessness that had tried to suffocate me earlier. I couldn't understand it. Couldn't stop it.

Was this all that awaited us? Had we journeyed all this way through darkness, through worlds unknown beneath the skin of the Earth's crust, only to witness peace snuffed out by such cold, methodical cruelty?

An image of the bragging Nazi leader flashed through my mind. His boasting words, his condescending sneer. How could we let something so vile twist the beauty of what we'd found—pervert it into ruin?

My chest tightened, anger choking out despair. This was not how it was supposed to end.

I jerked forward without thinking, every muscle in my body straining for action. But at the last moment, Peters' hand lashed out, gripping my sleeve and pulling me back sharply, his teeth gritted as he hissed through clenched lips. "Not yet," he spat. His eyes bore into mine, warning, thrumming with raw intensity. "We'll only get ourselves killed if we don't keep our heads on straight."

I met his glare, feeling the fire within me swell… then dim. He was right. I could feel the weight of his hand grounding me, pulling me back from the brink of reckless desperation.

But my pulse refused to calm. It thudded fiercely in my ears, drowning out rational thought. The sight of the Náiren—so peaceful, so vulnerable—broke against my tortured morality. **How could we sit by and watch? How could we do nothing?**

The truth crashed into me, violent and cold. This was no longer a choice. Conflict had already begun, with or without us. We couldn't hope to stop it now. War had found us whether we wanted it or not.

Steeling myself, I forced my breath to steady and turned my focus sharply toward Peters. "We have to act." My voice emerged low, ferocious. I could feel my body trembling, anger pulsing through every nerve. There was no avoiding it now. No more hiding behind ideals or desperation. "There's no turning back."

Peters' nostrils flared as he watched another soldier strike a kneeling Náiren, but there was the smallest flicker of understanding in his otherwise rigid expression. Slowly, he nodded, his form dark and imposing in the low light. The shared understanding settled between us like the final weight atop a mountain. We had no choice.

More soldiers flooded into the outpost, their faces locked in tight, mechanical expressions, their movements sharp and efficient. The noise swelled—the sounds of suffering, of orders barked, of the clank and clash of metal unsettling the once-serene earth.

I swallowed back the bile threatening to rise in my throat. My body was cold with shock, but beneath it, a shift was taking place. Slowly, steadily, fury was rising from somewhere deep within me, overpowering despair, hopelessness, everything rational. This was never going to be a battle of words, of intellect, of hope. It had taken a much darker, uglier turn, and there was no retreat now.

Peters looked at me one final time—caution still flickering in his sharp gaze, but softened now with steady determination. We were already embroiled in this conflict, and now there was no more watching from the shadows.

Without another word shared between us, we withdrew from

the clearing, motioning silently through the thick shadows of the trees.

The sounds of suffering echoed behind us as we moved, nothing but grim purpose propelling us forward into the night.

We would resist.

11

Forming the Alliance

The crystalline walls of the Náiren council hall shimmered in the soft glow of the subterranean sun, golden light filtering through the translucent structure in ripples, as if mimicking the play of sunlight over water. The grand space, always a place of profound peace and wisdom, now felt curiously muted, its usual serenity tainted by the weight of words yet unspoken. As I stood before the high archways, so delicately carved despite the immense strength they possessed, I felt the pressure of history looming overhead, as tangible and heavy as the crystalline columns holding this place together.

It was a beauty I had admired once—a reflection of the Náiren themselves: graceful, timeless, untouched by the corruptions that marred the surface world above. When we had first arrived, I had been in awe of it, drawn into the tranquility this place effortlessly exuded. Now, however, the shimmering light seemed like a distant memory of a peace that was about to shatter. The air inside the hall felt thick, not with dust or heat, but with an invisible pull—tension, fear, confusion. Gone were the tranquil conversations that usually filled the space. Now, the Náiren elders stood in subdued clusters beneath the towering ceilings, their serene features marred by faint lines of doubt that had no place in the faces of an ageless race.

The hum of ancient energy, which had always been present, vibrating through the air like a soft lullaby from the depths of the earth, now seemed distant, retreating. The village itself had become quieter—the hum still there, but more hollow, as though the evil approaching their world threatened even the core of their being.

I felt a breath catch in my throat, my heart knocking against my ribcage as Peters followed just behind me, his heavy footsteps an intrusion to the still sanctity of the space. His silence was worlds apart from mine. Where I was left contemplating the gravity of what lay ahead, he strode with utter purpose, eyes calculating, hardened by years of survival. His time on the sea and his brushes with death had afforded him a colder kind of wisdom. While I grappled with how to present what needed to be said, Peters had already accepted the inevitable battle. He would fight and die, if need be, but there was no question that action was the course to be taken.

Elys, the quiet leader of the Náiren, stepped forward with the slow, deliberate grace of one who had lived several lifetimes and carried them all tenderly upon his shoulders. His pale, glowing eyes met mine, and I could see it there— a flicker of trepidation that hadn't belonged to him before.

He had always radiated an implacable calm, an effortless authority, but now the slightest crease marred his alabaster brow. The ghost of concern moved behind those pale-blue irises, swirling like mist caught in the golden light cast by the sun above. Weighed down by the impending conflict, his movements were uncharacteristically slow, hesitant even.

He turned his head toward the gathered elders, motioning for them to focus their attention on us. His hand gestured, soft but filled with purpose, as he signaled Peters and me to address the council, though the fluidity that often marked his motions seemed to drag, burdened by the haunting knowledge of what he would soon have to counsel his people toward.

I took a deep breath, my mind running in frantic circles despite my outward calm. Convincing these people—who had woven pacifism into the very fabric of their existence—that violence now loomed as their only means of survival filled me with a dread I could scarcely manage. An almost paralyzing weight settled squarely on my shoulders, compressing my chest. I was no soldier—how was it my place to tear apart something they'd nurtured for who knew how long, to thrust them from peace into some form of war?

And yet, I knew what awaited if the Nazis were allowed to continue unchecked. Their machines already clawed their way toward the life-source of this world—blind to all but their need to conquer and control. I'd seen the outpost fall. I had witnessed their treachery firsthand. They would tear this world apart, rip the very heart from these people's sanctuary if we did not act. There was no room for hesitation anymore.

Every eye was on us now. The swirling light patterns on the walls flickered across the floor, refracting against the faces of the Náiren elders. Whatever peace once existed in this hall was hanging on by the thinnest thread.

"Your way of life is threatened like never before," I began, my tone low but urgent. My heart hammered harder as I forced myself forward, searching the eyes of each elder, willing them to understand the gravity of the situation. "I know it's not in your nature to raise arms, to fight," I continued, aware of how alien my words must have sounded to them. "But you must understand… inaction will only bring ruin to this world."

The words carried the force of undeniable truth, but they echoed back at me in the pause that followed—uncomfortable. The weight of the forthcoming fight pressed heavily against the atmosphere itself, magnified by the telepathic murmurs that began to ripple quietly through the chamber. No voices were raised, yet I felt the hum of quiet discomfort, the buzz of thoughts uncertain as they passed between them. The room seemed to darken, the walls closing in with a tangible sense of dread. Faces that were usually composed and full of serene wisdom now bore faint creases of doubt, confusion.

An elder, one I had come to recognize as Ralos—a figure of immense reverence even among the Náiren—stepped forward, his expression heavy and sorrowful. His long, silver hair gleamed in the glow of the council hall's light, but there was something in the way his shoulders sagged underneath the flowing robes that underscored the weight of centuries, perhaps millennia, of peace now on the verge of collapse.

"For eons," Ralos began telepathically, filling the room with his soft, mournful tone that seemed to settle like a weight on every spine. "We have survived without ever turning toward violence. To do this would be to abandon what we hold most dear." His gaze swept the room as sorrow colored each word. His hands, ethereal and long-fingered, folded against his chest, as if holding something fragile and sacred. His plea hung in the air, like a pendulum caught mid-swing, straining against the call of reality.

I could feel the quiet crumbling of hope in the room, saw it reflected in the eyes of each elder gathered, in the faint tremble of Ralos' brow. This world was so far removed from violence. How could they be expected to understand the urgency of what must follow?

Peters moved abruptly, his presence a coarseness that shattered the room's delicate energy into jagged fragments. He crossed his broad arms tightly over his chest, his frustration filling the hall like the scrape of a blade dragged against a stone floor. "I understand. You wanna protect your peace," he barked, his words harsh, uncompromising. "But your enemies don't care about peace." His voice dripped with cold reality, cut through with a hint of bitterness. "They're coming regardless, and if you don't defend yourselves..." He let the threat hang, unsaid but vivid, and as it settled, the weight of his words brought a kind of visceral dread that spread in a slow wave through the elders.

Their faces tightened at the abrupt force of Peters' statement. I could almost feel their discomfort stirring the air, a ripple of resistance much like that which passed between us and Peters on the beach so many months ago, when we faced early mutinies aboard the Grampus. The elders, still locked in their peaceful ideals, tried to push against the pragmatism of his words. What Peters spoke of—a need for defense through force—it went against every fiber of their existence. I saw it in their darkening gazes, felt it in the sudden downcast turn of a dozen pairs of eyes. They weren't ready to make the leap toward conflict, nor could they envision what that conflict truly entailed.

I stepped forward quickly, sensing the need to temper Peters' sharpness. His words, while true, couldn't stand alone here. I wouldn't let them. "This… isn't about destroying what you've built," I added, tone softer, more pleading. "It's about defending it. You must adapt to the circumstances. Fight not for the sake of war, but for the sake of your survival."

There was a long pause that followed—a silence that landed heavier than the one before, thick, weighted in the air like a great stone hanging just above the earth, preparing to drop. The platitudes of peace were clashing with the brutal inevitability of violence.

From where I stood, I watched as Elys' gaze drifted away from the assembly, his eyes trailing along the shimmering crystal walls, their flowing iridescence doing nothing to soothe the storm roiling beneath the surface. His glowing eyes, so often filled with certainty and calm, now seemed distant, as though searching the patterns of light for an answer that did not exist.

Finally, Lyra, who had remained silent until now, shifted. Her usually brilliant, inquisitive gaze was dimmer, her violet eyes darkened as she stepped forward quietly from her place beside Elys. She moved as if caught between two worlds—one of stone-carved pacifism and another of sudden, violent necessity. "Adapting does not mean forgetting who we are," she said softly. Her voice flickered between telepathy and speech, as though she herself struggled to reconcile this fracture between words and thought. "We can change. But we cannot allow this change to undo us."

Lyra's eyes—once full of curiosity and clear brightness—turned toward me, a quiet apprehension reflecting within them. "What... exactly do you propose we do?"

I glanced at Peters. His nod was sharp, terse—a signal. The weight that had pressed down on me earlier began to ease, replaced by the clarity of purpose I'd lacked before. This was the moment. There was no turning it back now. They needed direction, and I had to give it. I was no leader, but in this instance, I could not afford to refuse the role.

I took a deep breath, turning once more to face the room, my eyes scanning each elder who continued to listen, bracing themselves for what they didn't want to hear, but would have to accept.

"We propose… forming a defense," I said finally. The words felt heavier than they should have, hanging in the crystalline air like black smoke. But I continued, drawing out the weight of it. "It won't be like the wars I know. You don't need to destroy. But you must protect what's yours." I glanced toward Elys, his still figure like a marble statue caught mid-thought, but the depth of his wisdom pulled at me, pushing me onward. "You have knowledge… technology—things the Nazis could never understand. Combine that with your abilities, your spirit, and we can build a resistance without losing who you are."

The murmur that followed was more intense this time. A shift was happening, even if only subtle for now. I watched as some nodded—hesitant, yes—but considering the inevitability looming over their world. Others still shied away, clutching deeply onto their ideals of nonviolence, as though even discussing a defense would fracture that sacred bond. It was difficult to tell which would win out—the pragmatists or the idealists. For now, they seemed perfectly divided.

The debate reached an uneasy lull as Ralos, the elder who had spoken earlier, took a step forward once more. His expression was pained, filled with sorrow weighed down by centuries of peaceful counsel now teetering toward a decision that gutted him. "We cannot jeopardize all that we hold sacred," he murmured, hands slightly trembling at his sides. "But… perhaps you are right." He closed his eyes momentarily, struggling under the unbearable gravity of his own words. "If this enemy is as relentless as you say, we have no choice."

Concession filled the room now, no longer whispered objections. What was faced was too vast, too real to deny. The inevitable tug of survival had festered within, replacing the slow pull of ancient serenity.

Elys exhaled deeply, his telepathic voice buzzing faintly in my mind. I could feel the quiet hum of tentative acceptance. "Then we shall unite our people. We will learn… to defend, whether we wish to or not."

And with those words, the first breach in their peace was made. A victory, even if small.

The tension in me unraveled ever so slightly. I allowed myself to shoot a glance toward Peters. His expression softened just the faintest bit—a shared satisfaction passing between us like a solitary breath, quiet and fleeting but undeniable.

Victory, for now.

***

Elys led the way with a soft step, his ethereal form gliding across the ground like a shadow cast by the glowing orb that floated high above their world. The pathway beneath our feet was a living thing—smooth stone that seemed to blend seamlessly with the earth itself, its surface softened by the warmth of centuries of peace. Yet, as we descended deeper into the village's core, it felt as if we were entering the innards of something vast and organic, something that knew far more than it let on. Even the air changed; it thickened around us the closer we came to our destination, the air itself humming faintly, vibrating with energy that neither Peters nor I could fully comprehend. The sensation was less like walking and more like being gently guided, like a leaf carried on a delicate breeze, ushered toward a force too great to resist but too graceful to fear.

The entrance to the armory loomed before us, though "armory" felt like the wrong word for it. This wasn't a fortress of weapons, no grim chamber cluttered with the iron implements of war. Instead, the walls seemed to have risen—grown—from the earth itself, as if the ground had come alive under some unseen force. It felt almost wrong to think of what lay inside as tools for violence. The truth rippled just beneath the surface—this was a place of power, not destruction. Of potential, not devastation. The structure before us shimmered like the trunk of some ancient tree from the jungle outside. Only here, the crystalline substance was perfectly smooth—with no indication of tool or hammer, no interruption in its natural progression upward.

The moment we stepped through the threshold, I felt it. Tingling at the edges of my skin—a low hum like the moment just before lightning strikes. Energy, potent and alive, flickered through the walls. The air buzzed faintly, thickening as it surrounded us, like static building before a storm. Each breath tasted different, subtly metallic, yet not unpleasant—more like an electric charge left hanging in the damp evening air. Light slashed through the space in gentle waves, casting patterned shadows that rippled across the crystalline walls in elegant, mesmerizing swirls. There was a rhythm to it, too—something intangible yet palpable. My heart, still unsettled by the calamity we'd come to orchestrate, skipped in time to the pulse. It was as if we'd entered the very veins of this world and could feel its heartbeat coursing through us.

At first glance, the armory wasn't filled with swords or shields, or anything resembling the tools of war that we might have anticipated. Instead, while crystalline shelves stretched up to the edges of the ceiling high above, they held what appeared to be relics. Each one glimmered faintly in the low light of the chamber. They hummed with barely concealed power, whispering secrets I could barely begin to imagine. These weren't crude inventions of violence— they were far beyond such primitive conceptions. The air around a particular artifact seemed to shift slightly, as though reacting to our presence, as if alive.

Lyra joined us, her presence as quiet and graceful as always, yet today there was a glint in her large violet eyes that I hadn't seen before—curiosity mixing with something else, something heavier, more solemn. No longer were her steps merely the tread of a serene scholar, but that of one shouldering a new burden—a burden she had not wanted but accepted nonetheless.

"These," she began softly, her voice carrying the weight of both awe and melancholy as it slipped into our minds like a ribbon weaving through thick air, "are ancient designs." Lyra's fingertips barely brushed a small device—some fragment of crystal, small enough to fit in her hand, yet glowing faintly with an inner light far greater than its size suggested. She studied it for a moment, her gaze distant.

"Primordial knowledge from our ancestors who first came to this place. They allowed us stability and peace, but their use here now…"

Her thoughts paused, a wave of regret coloring her features before she whispered, "Their use will now change."

I stepped closer, drawn irresistibly to a larger crystalline structure mounted on a central pedestal. It radiated warmth—though not heat—and presented itself as something spiritual. Approaching cautiously, the hum seemed to grow stronger the nearer I came, an almost hypnotic pull guiding me to it. I reached out, my fingers hovering just above its surface. The pulse that emanated from its center wasn't violent or scattered—it was rhythmic, purposeful, controlled.

"This is unlike anything I've ever seen," I murmured, my words almost lost to the low hum enveloping the room. I let my fingers skim its glassy surface, and instantly, I could feel the shift—an immediate awareness that whatever power lay dormant within this device, it had been alive far longer than I had been on this earth. Warmth surged beneath my fingertips—flowing like a river beneath the crystalline surface—rising, retreating, almost as though the thing was breathing.

Lyra, still beside me, looked down at the device with some-thing akin to reverence. "We draw energy," she began, speaking slowly, choosing each word carefully, as though to break the wrong one would fracture the nature of the device altogether, casting it into something darker. "Not for destruction. But for harnessing the natural flow around us—what breathes life into this world." She blinked softly, her long lashes lowering over those lilac eyes for a moment. "It was never meant for defense…" She trailed off, her voice catching in an unheard sadness that burrowed into me. "It goes against the very nature of these devices."

Her fingers skimmed across the surface of another relic. I could see the sorrow in her movements, as though merely touching these devices now sullied them, tainted them with the knowledge of what they might soon be used for—what they were never meant to become. She stood there, silent for a moment, letting the weight of what she had already sacrificed settle over her.

Peters, meanwhile, shifted closer. His movements, unlike Lyra's delicate grace, were grounded and deliberate. The low humming in the air didn't unsettle him the way it did me. Instead, he regarded the devices with a sharpness in his eyes that signaled his mind was already at work. Skeptical always, but now—fascinated. His fingers extended, hovering close to the same large energy-lined structure I had touched moments before. For the briefest second, his face softened, brow furrowing with curiosity. His fingertips ran along the pulse of the device—his touch nowhere near as soft as mine, but instead full of a trusting familiarity, like someone appraising the strength of a sword before battle.

"If we can figure out how to use this…" Peters' voice emerged from the silence, a slow murmur punctuated by the shifting of light around us. He nodded, turning the thought over in his mind. "Combined with what I know about defense… We might have a chance."

Lyra glanced up, studying Peters carefully, as his eyes roved the room, thoughts clicking into place like tools falling in line. I could tell—he was already running through strategy, figuring out.

"What do you have in mind?" I asked, stepping back slightly from the glowing pedestal that pulsed like a living heart below my fingertips. It was an involuntary question, one that spoke more to my need for understanding than anything else—an attempt to draw the shape of a plan from the fog surrounding us. In my mind, the fate of this world bounded uneasily between what technology might accomplish and what was even possible when faced with the spreading sickness of war above.

For a moment, Peters was silent, calculating, his intense gaze trained on the shimmering devices in the room around us. His eyes, darkened by years of surviving conflict, didn't linger long on the beauty of the artifacts. They processed instead what they could be—what they may have to become.

He turned to Lyra, his voice firm yet tempered with a quiet respect for the power she herself was only now understanding in a new light. "The surface world… it's all about brute force. Firearms. Explosions. If… if we can channel this energy into something different," he paused, letting the thought turn over in his head before continuing, "into shields—something to protect yourselves, rather than trying to fight them head-on—you can keep your people safe without becoming like them."

Lyra's eyes flickered, her delicate features holding still while the gears in her mind turned over. Her brow furrowed slightly, intent, and for what seemed like several long breaths, she ruminated on his words. The stillness stretched like a thin thread, one filled with potential but dangled over the abyss of uncertainty.

Finally, she gave a slight nod. "Perhaps," she said, though her voice carried with it a sense of reluctant revelation. "We must adapt. But teaching this will not be easy. We know only peace."

There was something beautiful in that—tragic, too. That the instruments of power now placed in her hands had been created to sustain life, to nurture, and now they must be bent toward defense.

Peters spoke softly then, his voice steadily reassuring—but never unrealistic. "You have the technology," he said. "You have the knowledge. You only need a new perspective—one that comes not from choice, but from necessity. You'll learn. And so will they."

His words landed heavily on all of us, the finality that laced them settling deep into the armory's surrounding silence. We weren't embarking on this lightly, but the reality had become clear. Defense wasn't just an option—it had become survival.

My own voice found its place beside Peters'. "This is about survival. Let us guide you." I breathed carefully, eyes flicking over the intricate devices surrounding us—each one of them capable of far more than I could ever imagine. "We'll find a way."

What followed was not resignation but a solemn acceptance. The hours that stretched beyond that tense moment were long and filled with quiet collaboration. Together—humans and Náiren—we worked, bending fragile theories into strategies that would allow them to protect their world. It began with small, almost imperceptible changes—training in evasion rather than brute force, integrating their natural agility into self-defense techniques. Every piece revolved around protection, never aggression.

Peters led the effort to visualize their environment as part of their strategy, blending seamlessly into its moving parts, demonstrating fluid gestures that matched the contours of their native landscape. He showed them how to evade attacks without meeting an enemy head-on—how to focus on outmaneuvering aggressors rather than direct confrontation. It was the very essence of defense born from knowledge, from instinct. His role as a protector solidified—it became tangible, personal, a mantle that he wore now as naturally as breathing.

Even as fatigue began to pull at us, the Náiren's natural

abilities shined. Their agility and finesse allowed them to catch on quickly despite their initial reluctance. Their connection to the environment made them nimble, their movements flowing like gentle waves reflecting the rhythm of the jungle that cradled their lives.

But I couldn't ignore the growing weight within my chest—the thought, gnawing at me as night wore on, of these gentle beings resorting to combat. They moved with precision and grace, yes, but watching them prepare for something as ugly as conflict sent the smallest tremor through me. I could feel the turning of time, the shattering of what I had hoped could remain untouched.

They didn't have a choice. None of us did.

When it was finally done, the group stood, sweating and spent, but together. Peters crossed his arms, surveying the tired warriors before him, eyes narrowed with grim satisfaction. It was a start—a meaningful one—but I could see in his demeanor the same doubt that gripped me. This would not be enough.

As the final lingering Náiren filtered out one by one, amid flickers of farewells spoken not in joy, but determination, Peters turned toward me. He brushed dust off his shirt, eyes shadowed, lips tight.

"It's a start," he muttered, in that low, gruff tone of his. "But it won't be enough."

I nodded silently, the familiar pang of doubt settling in my gut. He was right. What we'd done—it was something. But in the face of what was coming, it still felt far too little. Not enough to turn the tide of violence that was already spreading across the land.

As Peters narrowed his gaze toward the horizon now darkening beyond the open doorway, I caught the barest sense of hope struggling to surface despite everything. The Náiren had at least chosen to fight, to defend themselves. That—for today—was something.

12

Training and Preparation

The Náiren council hall resonated with a faint, almost imperceptible hum—a sound that had always hovered just beneath the surface, like the distant memory of a once-whispered song. That soft, old energy was constant, thrumming through the crystalline walls, binding this sacred place together. But now, I felt it: the shift, the subtle change pressing down on us all, thick with the weight of uncertainty.

The light of the false sun filtered weakly through the translucent ceiling, casting pale ripples over the gathered elders. It should have been beautiful, comforting even, but today the light seemed diminished, darker. Heavier. Its warmth, which once flowed through the space like the drain of honey from a jar, now hung limply in the air, as though even the rays themselves hesitated, aware of the immense decision awaiting those who stood beneath it.

Peters and I stood at the forefront, side by side, a partnership newly minted from the fires of survival. The Náiren—formidable in their tranquility—gathered before us, their tall frames still, their glimmering eyes soft with the remnants of serenity they had always known. But beneath that soft glow, I could sense their burgeoning unease. The air around them vibrated faintly with half-whispered telepathic hums, brushing against my awareness like the flutter of moths' wings. In each mind, the same questions played, repeated, overlapped like discordant tones of a song yet to find harmony.

Curiosity. Fear. Reluctance.

I swallowed hard, feeling the weight of the moment settle over my shoulders. The impulse to order my thoughts, to find some rational anchor in this sea of foreign uncertainty, threatened to pull me under. But rationality wasn't enough here—words weren't enough. These were not people I could sway with eloquence alone. What stood before them—machines, destruction, violence—was not something they had been trained to face. And even now, with the truth pressing on the borders of their world, they could not grasp it fully.

"We've all seen the threats we now face," I began, my voice thicker than I intended but rising in confidence as the gravity of my words took hold. "The machines, the destruction, the violence. It is not something we had prepared for." As I spoke, my gaze moved from face to face, each one reflecting the same quiet, questioning uncertainty I felt within myself. The words clawed their way out, steady, resolute, but it took every ounce of willpower not to falter. "But they are coming regardless."

Each word landed like a stone being dropped into a still pond. The ripples spread, almost visible in the way their postures shifted. Eyes that had remained placid began to flicker—unease bristled through the room like an invisible wind caught between walls. Their deep-rooted pacifism held strong, but I could feel the first cracks quivering beneath the surface, waiting to split open when confronted with undeniable truth.

Elys stood slightly behind me, his tall, regal figure ever a beacon of grace and calm. But even he was not immune to the tremors coursing through the room. His pale-blue eyes, always shimmering with soft, iridescent light, dimmed slightly. There was a tightness in his jaw, a hard awareness pulling at the corners of his composure. I saw it, though he did not speak of it. His head, typically held high, dipped almost imperceptibly, nodding for me to continue.

I inhaled sharply, wary of what indignities my next words might provoke but knowing they were necessary all the same. "I'm… not asking you to become soldiers," I said carefully, gently. I wanted to temper what was to come, to make the burden of this new reality land softer on their hearts. My gaze swept the room again, watching as Náiren faces, still ruled by their vestiges of serenity, softened slightly. "But we can't stand by while they tear apart your world—our world— without defending what matters." My words gained strength as the reality of the threat lashed against my own fears. "Not when they'll leave nothing behind when they're done."

The murmurs grew. Telepathic vibrations buzzed through the space, flicking at the edges of my thoughts without fully claiming them. Some of the Náiren folded their long, slender arms across their chests, defensively drawing themselves inward. Others shifted subtly, as though leaning away from the group, seeking refuge behind reluctance. A few stood perfectly still, but the tension in their stance betrayed reluctance. They had survived centuries—millennia even—on the principles of peace. Peace lived within the very bones of their society. Now, I was asking them to cast it aside. But I knew that words alone wouldn't break through the deep roots that had grown around their pacifism.

Beside me, I felt Peters take a deep breath. His irritation—the tension packed into the iron resolve of his muscles—was palpable. While I struggled to appeal to their reason, I knew that Peters would not concern himself with such subtleties. He had always been a man of action—a man whose life, like mine, had been shaped not by ideals but by the brutal reality of survival.

He stepped forward, his frame solid, immovable. In his eyes burned the truth he already accepted—truth I had been slower to embrace. His voice, when it came, was stripped of pleasantries, a cold and biting realism cutting the air like a knife. "You've been peaceful for… who knows how long. Good for you," he sneered slightly, his rough tones resonating with that hard, practical edge I had come to expect from him. "But this ain't peace anymore. Not when you've got death on your doorstep."

The room stiffened. The air itself seemed to contract under the weight of those words. I saw the shadows in their eyes darken, the faint glow dimming as they digested what he had said. Peters' voice carried the cold bite of salt and iron—it was not the diplomatic plea I had laid before them. It was raw, abrasive, and uncompromising.

The dissonance grew. I noticed it first in the younger Náiren gathered near the back—their eyes wide, brows furrowing in quiet disbelief. They bristled, their psychic murmurings temporarily flaring with surprise, discomfort, and something else—betrayal, perhaps? The world Peters described lay so far removed from anything they had ever experienced. His words felt like an attack on what they believed in what they held dear. And in their defense, perhaps they were.

They believed in peace—that was their world, their doctrine. I had seen its beauty myself. But here was Peters, leaning into the ugly necessity of violence, of self-defense, of what we humans, even in our most enlightened moments, always seemed required to face.

"I'm not askin' you to go slaughterin' left and right," Peters growled, his sharp gaze locking with theirs. I could see the frustration in his tight-lipped expression, but some part of him also softened, recognizing the unease his point was breeding. "But if you wait for them to come to you, you'll be kneeling at their feet." His eyes hardened—clear, uncompromising—daring anyone present to look away, to pretend they didn't understand the consequences of inaction. "And believe me, they don't care about peace when they've got your neck under their boots."

I felt it then—the weight of his words settling over the space like dark fog creeping into every corner, every heart. The faint hums faded, replaced by tense, physical silence. The soundless tension in the room vibrated, magnified by a truth they didn't want to face.

But it was a truth nonetheless.

My back straightened instinctively beside Peters, knowing that the sudden heightening of tension could rupture if left unchecked. Diplomatic as I liked to think I was, even I couldn't ignore Peters' words. Rationality demanded I meet them halfway. I raised my hands in a gentle motion, forcing calm into my limbs as though it could carry through the air and settle over the room. "We combine your technology with new ways of thinking," I said in a calmer tone. The words flowed, guided now by a mixture of reassurance and practicality. "They don't expect innovation from you. They believe you're defenseless. We will use that to our advantage."

Lyra, who had been standing close to Elys, nodded slowly, though the apprehension dancing in her luminous violet eyes was clear. The wave of mixed feelings—confusion, fear, even a glimmer of understanding—rippled from her as her fingers grazed her arms, tightening around herself as though physically holding in the whirlwind of thoughts. I felt her before I fully looked at her—her internal conviction rising beyond the waves of doubt Peters had stirred.

"But we've never—" Lyra paused for only half a second, searching for the words to express her thoughts. Her eyes finally met mine, her mind brushing against mine like the gentlest of winds stirring autumn leaves into cold waters. I felt the burn behind her gaze, the frustration and fear swirling in unison, but she understood. "How do we fight… without losing who we are?"

Her question, so simple but so weighted, landed heavily in the room. Elys turned his head to her, his posture weary but his light still steady.

Peters' jaw clenched almost imperceptibly, but when he spoke, his tone softened—only just. "By survivin'," he rasped. "That's who you are. You survive, and you protect what's important by standin' your ground. Doesn't mean you become what you hate."

His words, though blunt and iron-tipped, carried a strange sympathy now—something I hadn't realized he could express. They hung in the chamber, melding with the quiet hum that lingered in the walls, deep in the foundations.

A rare silence fell over the room—not due to ignorance, nor resistance. It was the deep, contemplative silence brought about by inevitable change.

Slowly, hesitantly, the shifting eyes that had dug into their own reluctance began to ease. I saw it first in the smallest movements—a tilt of the head here, the relaxing of tense, rigid arms there. The silence now vibrated with something else—resolve, perhaps tentative, but there. The truth had descended. It had arrived. That same soft telepathic murmur began again, but not one of protest or fear. Instead…

Elys' head, which had bowed in near-meditation moments before, lifted slowly. His eyes, glowing with ancient wisdom, found mine and held fast. His very presence, once imposing in its ethereal stillness, flickered with hope. From him spread a calming aura, gentle but firm, brushing against the hall like wind through a still meadow. "Perhaps…" Elys began, his telepathic hum strong now. His voice felt reassuring, pulling gently at the atmosphere, guiding it toward steadiness.

"We must… learn."

His pause was deliberate, each thought weighed and measured before spilling into the space. He gazed those thousand lifetimes ahead of him, seeing every consequence yet relying on none. "Perhaps, we must evolve… one last time."

For the first time that day, I felt the subtle loosening of tension in my chest. His words—we must learn—could not have been faintly whispered or stemmed by reluctance. They carried the resonance of acknowledgment, action.

I exhaled slowly, letting the weight of the exchange settle into the chambers of my heart. Hope, though fragile, stirred and budded quietly through me, though it was far from a brilliant bloom.

As if reading my own thoughts, Lyra stepped forward with urgency, no longer questioning the morality of change but eager to participate in it. She turned first to me, then to Peters, violet eyes gleaming with muted urgency. "We must move quickly." She said it as an undeniable truth. "Before they act once more. Show us—teach us—what we need to know."

The gears of action, though slow to begin turning, had now started in earnest. The time for hesitation had passed.

Though reluctant, they were ready.

***

The Náiren armory greeted us not with the tranquil hum that had defined it in its most peaceful moments, but with a mounting tension, something palpable in the air, like the gathering storm clouds of a coming tempest. The once-familiar glow of the warm crystals was still present, casting its soft, faint light across the hall's radiant walls, but its quality had changed. Much like the Náiren themselves had changed. The light flickered now, hesitant, mirroring the uncertainty pulsing throughout the room.

Clusters of tired but determined Náiren gathered in huddles, each group small, each figure noticeably more unsettled than they'd been earlier. Their quiet, almost imperceptible murmurings still played through the air, brushing against the edges of my mind. But if before they had stood in this place out of curiosity—drawn to these beautiful weapons of power by the novelty of necessity—now they gathered with something far more akin to grim purpose. The weight of their decisions, their recent knowledge of what was happening just beyond the protective shroud of their hidden jungle, had settled over them like a melancholy fog.

Peters drew in a long, deep breath as we stepped further into the armory, allowing his gaze to sweep across the radiant, pulsing structures before him, his eyes taking in the strange, unfamiliar contraptions with the same tight-lipped intensity I had seen in him when confronted with dangers on the sea.

From our time together, I understood the way he evaluated threats, calculated risk against reward with cold precision. But here, in this foreign world of flowing silver light and humming, mysterious powers, I could see the awe. Even Peters, normally one to scoff at anything he didn't fully understand, didn't sneer at these devices. They were unfamiliar, perhaps—alien, even—but they represented potential. If anything, that was enough for a man with survival imprinted thoroughly in his being. And now, that primal instinct wasn't solely for himself. There was a greater responsibility to protect.

"Alright," Peters began, his rough voice finally breaking the quiet tension that hung in the room. The gathered Náiren, many of them standing in small, anxious ranks, turned to face him, their luminous eyes blinking slowly in his direction. "We're not lookin' to turn this into a battlefield." His tone wasn't as harsh as before, but the weight behind it was still unmistakeable. He paused, gesturing toward one of the shimmering devices mounted carefully on the walls, a soft, pulsing apparatus that seemed to glow with periodic flashes, like rhythmic heartbeats. "But we're lookin' to keep folks alive."

The emphasis was heavy, punctuating the unspoken truth: they weren't warriors, and Peters wasn't about to change that. This was about survival, pure and simple.

At the far side of the hall, Lyra stood quietly near a younger group, assisting them as they handled the strange devices scattered throughout the armory. Her hands moved gently, guiding them through without inexperience, though even her own fingers trembled slightly under the weight of their new task. The crystals, hovering gently beneath the Náiren's soft hands, began to pulse faintly. Every time the young ones fumbled, nerves shaking through their slender fingers, the devices shifted, rippling with light, sending delicate pulses of energy sizzling faintly into the dense air around them.

Peters' voice droned on, but I couldn't help but falter for a moment as I watched them, each figure far too young to be handling any instrument of war, no matter how otherworldly. I saw their uncalloused hands gliding over the smooth surfaces of the powerful relics. Their pale, alien skin shimmered with the energy that radiated quietly from the devices beneath them, and despite the elegance with which they moved, their apprehension screamed louder than any words could have.

My breath hitched. These were not creatures equipped for

survival in the way Peters and I had come to understand it. We had asked these people—these beings who had rarely, if ever, touched such tools of conflict—to take up an impossible task. To fight an enemy they did not fully understand, whose weapons and methods were so utterly different from anything the Náiren had ever encountered. And yet… here they were, hands trembling as they sought to learn the unlearnable.

"We'll start easy," Peters' voice softened—surprisingly gentle but still firm. I could see that he understood their reluctance, much as I did. But where I would have hesitated, he knew better. There wasn't time to indulge their fear. Smoothly, he stepped towards a nearby mount, fingers grazing one of the small devices, detaching it with the kind of care reserved only for things of great power.

The machines seemed fragile in his grasp, even though they pulsed with energy far greater than any rifle or cannon he might've held in years past. The structure of the crystal was smooth and warm to the touch, its soft glow reflecting the tension in the room. He held it delicately, as though acknowledging its weight—both physical and otherwise.

"What you've got here," he said, glancing toward the gathered group, "is the best way to keep people from gettin' laid out."

I could see the ripple of uncertainty in their pale expressions. There was something raw about the way the Náiren fluctuated between fear and curiosity. They weren't naïve. They had never needed much physical force before, but they were quick learners. That, at least, was clear.

Peters moved toward one of the taller males, his pale skin glowing faintly under the somewhat dim light of the armory. The newcomer flinched ever so slightly—the result of a lifetime of knowing how to listen without the dull noises of human dialogue. Perhaps he was unaccustomed to any contact in this regard, but still, the tremor that passed through his limbs was unmistakable.

Peters lifted one of the devices high—allowing the shimmering blue-green light to catch the edges of the male's tentative fingers, and pressed it firmly into the space between his hands. "Here," he said with surprising patience. "We'll work through it."

He offered a small smile.

Then, stepping back, he motioned toward the group, his strong voice carrying with a cadence meant for instruction. "These aren't swords or anything meant to kill someone," Peters stated clearly. His rough, practical demeanor did not waver. "And that's the good news." He looked around, caught the hesitant eyes fixed on the glowing tools now clutched in pale Náiren hands. "You may not be the aggressors, but if you can defend properly, well…" He glanced toward the male holding the device. "They'll walk right into their own mistakes."

Beside me, Elys observed carefully. His keen eyes moved between Peters and the group, not missing a single gesture, a single flinch. But for all the weight of what was brewing around him, his luminance remained muted, serene even. In his posture, I felt no resistance—only acceptance. Admiration might have been too strong a word, but there was something to the way Elys regarded Peters. The man was brutish, yes. Emotionless, even. But in recognition of the Náiren's limits, Peters had found something Elys understood all too well—the need for protection without forsaking principles.

I stepped forward, pushing the steady pulse of unease still throbbing within my chest to the side. "We will teach you to protect, to move quickly," I said, my voice striving for a quiet command. "To survive in this storm, without becoming the eye of it."

The younger Náiren fumbled at first, pale fingers gripping the crystalline tools far too delicately, afraid to impose on them anything resembling force. Their bodies were not used to holding anything akin to weapons—though these, if anything, more resembled shards of illuminated beauty than weaponry we'd ever known. They were tools of protection, not of destruction. Peters coaxed them into basic movements— simple blocks, evasions as he called them—each one gentle, almost rudimentary.

But as the minutes lingered on, their movements grew more natural, fluid. The hesitation that had marked their initial attempts retreated. The grace that came so naturally to them began to show in the turns of their wrists, the lightness of their steps. It was as though the land itself was guiding their bodies into place. Their breath evened, their figures moving less like reluctant apprentices and more like those whose very blood, very limbs were tuned into the protective nature of the world around them.

"Good," Peters called out, his voice less military now, more solid. "Keep it light. Stay quick. Think like the land—you know it better than they ever could." His words resonated in ways I doubted even he fully understood then.

Before us, the Náiren began working themselves into a slow rhythm, the glowing relics pulsing in unison as they moved. There was something beautiful about the way their collective movements, though delicate, focused on the shifting patterns of light reflecting from the devices in their hands. Each pulse, each shift in breath, felt aligned now.

Lyra had moved quietly to the greater part of the group, pausing beside one or two as they worked. For a moment, her thin lips turned upward in a faint smile—pleased, if not entirely comfortable with the changes. I watched as her own pale fingers lifted one of the smaller crystal relics, a shield not meant to instigate but to protect—all too befitting for someone like Lyra. She lifted it beside Peters, its soft glow melding into the air between them, a faint pulse radiating outward anytime she moved her arm.

The silent flicker of respect between them did not go unnoticed.

"You're admirin' the tech as much as the fight," Peters added quietly, his words still rough and earnest amidst the strange rhythm of training.

Lyra looked up, caught off guard, though her expression was soft. A wry, unreadable smile began to etch its way across Peters' weary features. "That your way of survivin'?"

Lyra opened her lips slightly, but instead of responding, she tilted her head, her soft gaze conveying what words failed to articulate. "I suppose it is…" The briefest of pauses settled between them, the glow of their shared moment flickering through the room. "Learning is the only way through any storm."

The drills continued, their quiet hum filling the room for hours after dusk began to fall outside. Slowly, ever so slowly, the rhythm of reluctance was replaced by one of unified effort. Watching from one side of the room, I saw what should have filled me with dread but settled differently along my bones— an understanding I couldn't suppress. The Náiren were fighters, after all. Even in their defense, they were becoming something more.

But Peters remained right.

It wouldn't be enough.

Exhaustion settled firmly over the Náiren as the final hours of drills concluded. They began to retreat from the room in droves, their figures slower, hunched from the unfamiliarity of the work. The sky above had begun to darken, the twilight hours settling over the village in soft golds and light pinks.

I turned to Peters, watching as the last of the group filtered out, Lyra exchanging soft words with the braver few who lingered.

"They're gettin' there," Peters muttered under his breath, his voice low, not quite resigned but not resting in satisfaction either. His eyes followed each figure disappearing into the dimming horizon. "Still ain't enough. But it's gettin' started."

I nodded, feeling the weight of his words bearing against me once again—wisdom born of practical experience.

It wasn't victory. Not yet.

But the fight—

The fight had begun.

13

The First Skirmish

The jungle loomed around us, a dense pocket of ancient life seething with both beauty and menace. Every step we took was met by the gentle protest of moss and leaves beneath our boots, the earth soft as a dream, yet charged with the waking nightmare of the world we had stumbled into. The towering trees, their bark shimmering faintly with the strange bioluminescence unique to this hidden domain, cast long shadows that seemed to waver and dance, as if alive with secrets. Even now, after all we had seen, the mystical hues—green flickers over blue-tinted vines, spidery golden veins running up thick trunks—remained alien to me. Familiar in their constancy, yet forever foreign.

The air clung to our skin like a sickly second coat, the humidity oppressive, rolling over us time and again like the warm, fetid breath of some unseen beast lying in wait beneath the canopy's tangled limbs. My shirt, already soaked through, stuck to me uncomfortably, and I could hear Peters breathing heavily beside me, though it was not exhaustion that filled us but the raw anticipation of imminent danger. Since our descent into this hostile Eden, survival had become second nature—our senses constantly trained for the telltale signs of threat, even in moments of quiet. Especially in moments of quiet.

That infernal hum floated through the stillness again, as it had been since we passed into the deeper reaches of the jungle— the low, almost imperceptible drone of distant machinery gnawing at the edges of reality, like a dark echo lurking beneath the natural symphony of the wild.

Peters' fingers snapped up, making a sharp, deliberate flick through the air. I froze instantly, body tense, my breath halting in my throat. He dropped into a crouch, boots sinking softly into the earth, and I followed suit, settling beside him. The lingering silence, for a brief moment—a moment too long—felt absolute. The sound of machinery pressed faintly into my ears again, like the distant pull of a nightmare you only half-remember upon waking.

Beads of sweat ran from my brow, trailing over the crevices of my dirt-flecked face and settling at my lips, the moisture thick and unpleasant. There was something deeply unsettling about knowing you were being hunted but having no clear image of the predator. In that moment, the predator could have been anything—the machines, the jungle itself, or more immediately… the men we knew lurked just beyond.

My heartbeat was a steady drum against the humid fabric

clinging to me, chest tight with anticipation. Every muscle in my body stood on edge, my eyes darting past the bioluminescent flashes flickering around us, trying to see through the foliage to whatever lay ahead—or worse, what might lie behind.

I peered through the thick, knotted leaves and dense underbrush, and there, just beyond the forest's threshold, a clearing opened up—wide enough that I could make out the movements at its edges. A soft blue light flickered intermittently on the other side. Náiren figures. Their slender forms moved with a fluidity that seemed as woven with their surroundings as the very vines they worked beneath. They worked quickly, aligning delicate, shimmering shields in elegant arcs, their movements rhythmic, the flow practiced yet charged with urgency. As the faint gleam danced across their tools, I could feel the pulse of energy coursing through the air—the pulse that ran through this strange land, that sustained its bizarre beauty.

But even the sight of them—their artful, elegant preparation— did little to shake the dread. The hum was growing louder. Closer.

Then, a sharp snap cut through the wood. A twig perhaps. Or the crumpling of leaves beneath heavy boots.

Too loud. Too close. A breathless stillness followed.

Peters reacted with the precision of a man who had survived terrors beyond imagination. His hand shot to the hilt of his knife, body coiled, his eyes narrowing and focusing on the source of the sound—a primal urge to protect sharpening every one of his senses. I mirrored his movement instinctively, though my own hand trembled. My head snapped toward the direction of the disturbance, mind racing.

And then the forest erupted.

The voice came first—harsh, guttural, cutting through the stillness like a blade dragged across rusted metal. *Achtung.* The shout rippled with command, tearing the breath from my lungs as if the word itself had snared and strangled me. The accent, twisted by aggression, was unmistakably German.

Half a dozen men, uniforms disheveled but eyes gleaming with cold, brutal determination, emerged from the thick greenery. Rifles raised, faces twisted into primal masks of menace—they moved as one unit, military precision honed by the taste of blood and conquest. The jungle, which had moments earlier enveloped us in a near surreal calm, now bristled with the sharp crackle of danger. My throat felt tight, my heart banging hard against my chest.

I had seen them before—seen what they did at the outposts, seen their ruthlessness. Now they'd emerged from the jungle itself, as if the earth had spawned them, hell-bent on tearing apart the beauty before them.

The flickering light from the Náiren shields glowed once more, only this time it was framed against those pale, angular faces twisted in sudden shock. For a second—the barest inhalation of breath—it was as if time itself stopped, as though the jungle reached out and stilled the frenetic breath of all those within its midst. Two groups, divided by worlds they could never understand, stared across the clearing at one another. Weapons poised—but hearts gripped only by the terror of the unknown.

And then—

The gunshot. A crack as loud as thunder resounded through the chaos, the report echoing off the towering trees and reverberating through the pit of my stomach. My world collapsed into that singular sound—sharp and final.

I saw the Náiren stumble back before I had even registered what had happened. Blood, bright and unnatural in its shimmer, arced like a ribbon, slicing through the air, catching the bioluminescence as it spilled. The form crumpled, pale limbs folding under the sheer weight of the wound, sinking with an elegance that should never accompany death.

Reality fractured, and chaos exploded.

Peters moved before my mind could keep pace. He became a force, pure instinct detonating within him. Without waiting—hesitation foreign to his very existence—he barreled toward one of the soldiers, the ferocity in his movement doing more damage than his knife ever could have. He collided with the man, a brutal mass of muscle, slamming into the enemy with such force they both tumbled into the thick mud, the very earth beneath them rising to swallow their struggle.

Panic surged up my spine, locking me in place for one, agonizing second. It felt as though everything around me were spiraling in slow motion—the sounds of combat dulled by the overwhelming shock drowning out my senses. A blur of sights, sounds, movement—worlds colliding. Elongated bodies, untouched by violence for who knew how long, thrown into the fray by men from a distorted, damaged sphere of existence.

A soldier, seemingly materializing from the thicket of underbrush, surged forward, his rifle raised—a wicked bayonet poised at its tip. He was moving toward one of the Náiren, and I—I could see it, but my body, rooted in the thick mire of disbelief, refused to respond. A silent scream formed in my mind—a desperate plea to move—but my limbs remained frozen, disconnected from the terror unfolding before me.

Move.

Peters. His voice roared across the battlefield like a blast of cannon fire, reverberating through my skull. "Move, damn it!" His eyes flashed, fierce and wild even as he wrestled with his own assailant in the mud. The sound of his command shattered the paralysis that held me in place.

I moved.

Somewhere, beneath the scrambled mess of fear and inertia, my body remembered how. In a rush, I hurled myself toward the nearest soldier, reckless, desperate, caring little for form or strategy. The sheer weight of my body collided with his, and we tumbled hard into the earth. For a brief, confused moment, there was nothing but the sharp tang of musk and grit in the air around me, our twin breaths harsh and wild, mixing with the sudden burst of violence between us.

The soldier's rifle slipped from his grasp, clattering against the jungle floor—a grotesque symphony somehow quieter than the rifle cracks that kissed the air.

Nearby, one of the Náiren's shimmering shields flared in sudden brilliance, absorbing a rapid volley of bullets. The power coursing through it reverberated like thunder behind glass, soaking the world in splintered light. The shield held, the light swelling briefly before warping around them in cascading waves, leaving those within securely protected from the chaos just beyond.

The tangle of limbs and broken breath between myself and the soldier on the ground snared my attention once more. Hands searching for purchase, desperate to outmaneuver the struggle beneath me—his grip firm, brutal, sinking into the meat of my arms. Fear spiked through me like a knife to the belly. He was younger than I had realized. His face pale beneath dust and grime, his eyes wide with panic—but a panic born of training, not faltering.

His fist connected squarely with my jaw—a wet crunch resonating through my skull as I reeled back, teeth grinding in pain. My vision blurred momentarily, stars dancing at the periphery, but I did not fall back. Could not. The fear—the adrenaline—drove me forward, deeper into the fight. My hand, numb and aching, clawed forward, searching for something—anything—solid.

I found the pommel of a discarded weapon in the thick mud beneath us. Blindly, I gripped it tight and swung. The blunt impact reverberated up my arm as the edge connected with his temple. I felt, rather than saw, the way his body slumped immediately beneath mine—the nauseating finality of it settling over me like a shroud.

A scream cut through the chaos—younger, softer. My head snapped to the side, my breath stuttering in my chest as I saw another Náiren crumple into the dirt, blood slick against the viridescent leaves. It stained the fluorescent flora in gory iridescence. A soldier loomed over them, rifle still hot from the shot, mindlessly reloading for those who remained.

Peters, locked in his own battle, spun with vicious purpose and drove his knife into the side of another soldier as they grappled. The sound of tearing flesh and the man's gasping cry filled the air for a moment before the jungle seemed to swallow it, leaving only the retreating moans of the dying.

Just then, some scrap of static-laced German barked from a soldier's radio—and the remaining men fell back, crashing and stumbling in retreat toward the trees. Bullets flew wildly into the brush, chaotic, unsighted. The edge of the jungle lit with distant flickers of light, but two Náiren brought their shields forward just in time to protect us in flashing bursts of brilliant energy.

The sounds of war faded. The violence ebbed.

And then—stillness.

Peters stood nearby, mud-splattered and breathing heavily. His eyes were sharp, scanning the jungle's edge for any further signs of threat as the soldiers' forms vanished into shadow, their retreating figures merging with the infinite dark of the wild.

I, too, stood—but my legs trembled beneath me. Distantly, across the battlefield, I could see the broken silhouette of the soldier I'd downed. The weight of it—the weight of what we had done—settled deep in my chest. I could not disentangle myself from the writhing confusion, the sickening clarity that came with knowing I had taken a life. My hands shook uncontrollably, my mouth dry, dread pooling in my belly like oil threatening to ignite.

None of this was supposed to be real.

But it was.

***

The jungle had fallen into a harrowing lull. Where earlier the hum of life and vibrant energy had coursed through, painting each leaf, every vine, with an animated pulse—now only silence reigned. The symphony of the wild had doused itself;

the only sound left was the ragged breathing of survivors. I could feel it—the absolute stillness of death clotting the space around us.

The scent of gunpowder clung to the air in stark contrast to the natural fragrances that once dominated this forbidden paradise. It mingled with the earthy musk of crushed leaves and torn branches, a foreign intrusion into this living world. And blood. That scent was unmistakable now too. Its coppery tang lingered in my nostrils, acidic in the way it gnawed at my throat, making it impossible to forget what had transpired only moments ago.

The battlefield lay around us, strewn with bodies like discarded dolls, limbs twisted and frozen in unnatural poses. Some lay partially submerged in the dense undergrowth, while others were sprawled openly in the clearing, framed in the soft, fading light that flickered in uneasy rhythms through the trees. It was an eerie dance that nature tried to reclaim, as though the jungle itself didn't understand the intrusion of such raw violence and sought, in its way, to cover it with the shroud of ordinary life.

But there was nothing ordinary about it. And nothing could cover this.

Bodies. So many bodies. Fallen Nazis with their helmets gleaming ever so slightly beneath the shifting shards of light filtering through the canopy. Their blood smeared the rich earth, a crimson black against the vibrant greens, the once-lush undergrowth now trampled, torn—transformed into a desolate battlefield where violence had birthed permanent scars.

Peters stood next to me, tall and unmoving. His shirt was torn at the collar, splattered with mud and streaked with the telltale signs of brutal combat. His knuckles bore the dark stains of blood—both friend and foe—as they hung stiffly at his sides. His breath had slowed from the feverish panting earlier, but there remained a tension in every quivering muscle. Peters was always coiled, always prepared for the next fight, as if battle had etched itself into the very marrow of his bones. Always anticipating, like a man who'd never known true peace—but only the pauses between conflicts.

I glanced at him, but his eyes, though watchful, were distant. He was still here—but already far-flung, beyond this place, fingers of his mind curled around the future, thinking of what lay ahead. After all, for Peters, violence like this was a fact of life—a language older than any spoken word. One he had long since learned to speak fluently.

But for me, standing amidst the wreckage of this battle— it was different. The bloodshed, the senselessness of it— something in me recoiled with every breath I forced into my lungs. My hands still trembled from the fight that had ended less than an eternity ago, though it felt as if lifetimes now rested between then and now.

I couldn't help but focus on a fallen Náiren lying just at the edge of the skirmish's wake. His form had gone unnoticed in the rush of retreat, his pale, delicate frame now slumped awkwardly against the earth, crumpled like a leaf that had fallen too soon from its branch. He lay there, unmarred by bullets or blades, but the unnatural twist in his body spoke enough cruelty. The life that had thrummed through him only moments ago—gone. It was at once dignified and grotesque, a casualty of violence that did not belong to his people. The very fabric of his world had been ripped apart, not by monsters, but by men.

My heart hammered in my ears—the fading echoes of gunfire still ringing within me like some cursed bell that refused to stop. *How had it come to this?*

The flaming question ricocheted inside my skull, pricking and burning every doubt I hadn't yet had the courage to voice. What had we done? Brought these people to war? The line between right and necessary had begun to blur, and in that gray fog, despair clawed at the edges of my reason.

"You did what you had to," Peters muttered beside me, his voice thick and grating, laden more with acceptance than comfort. There wasn't judgment in his words, but there was no need for it either. His eyes flicked toward mine, meeting them briefly—long enough to convey understanding, but not long enough to linger in the horror of it all.

For Peters, there was nothing in this scene that would give him pause. This—the violence, the bloodshed, the waste of life—was routine. It was a cycle he had navigated countless times before, a grim pageantry of cause and consequence. His face, though hardened by years of witnessing death, betrayed nothing resembling shock or dismay. *Violence,* it seemed to say, *was a constant companion.*

But for me, it was unexpected—unnatural in the way it had cut through everything, even the bright beauty of this world. I nodded, not trusting my voice to speak. Not trusting myself to voice the shattered thoughts scrambling for coherence in my mind.

The silence that stretched between us was both a relief and a weight. Peters, standing still but forever vigilant, could sense my inner turmoil. There was no need to say more. He knew—he knew exactly what this fight had cost me, even if I couldn't bring myself to admit all that had been torn asunder.

Shifting uncomfortably, I dragged my eyes away from the lifeless form of the Náiren and scanned the landscape—the devastation around me sinking deeper into my chest. The broken bodies of the soldiers lay lifeless, awkwardly draped across the roots of trees, their once-imposing figures now hollow shells of twisted metal, cloth, and flesh. Though we had won the skirmish, the hollow ache in my chest refused to dissipate. This… this wasn't victory. It felt like nothing more than a temporary reprieve against a greater shadow looming ever closer.

Far worse waited beyond.

Peters, undeterred by the aftermath, knelt next to one of the fallen soldiers and began rifling through his belongings with the same cold efficiency that had kept him alive all these years.

There was no reverence in the movement—only practicality. His hands moved with purpose, tugging at the fabric of the soldier's uniform, searching. His brow remained furrowed, not with guilt, but with focus. "They're better equipped than I thought," he grunted, his voice measured but grim. "They're not gonna stop at this."

The words didn't surprise me. I had known—they would come back. That this was but one encounter with many more awaiting. "This is only one group," Peters continued, his weathered hands now pulling free a crumpled set of papers and staring briefly at their contents. His frown deepened. "Where there's more of them, there's more machines. We'll need to be ready—their reach isn't just here."

I clenched my jaw. My gaze slid without meaning to the fallen Náiren still lying motionless in the dirt. The grief that rose up to strangle me was a monstrosity that held no sound. The reality had set in: lives were being torn away from this strange, beautiful world—lives that had previously lived in peace, never knowing the brutality of war. We'd brought it to them.

Everything in me screamed for respite, to wrench myself away from this horrific scene, to leave behind the destruction and the blood, the trauma of it settling deeper than I had anticipated. Yet, something in me, something deeper and more terrible, forced me to keep looking.

There would be no rest now. Not until the invaders had been pushed back to whatever abyss from which they had slithered. The cost of that would be steep—unbearably so. But the price… the price of doing nothing, of standing aside and allowing the devastation to spread unchecked… that would dwarf even the greatest tragedies.

My mind, though still rattled by the violence, began to harden.

With great effort, I stepped toward Peters' position, willing my body to move, to act—anything to escape the weight of guilt pressing heavily on my shoulders. Together, we rifled through the last of the fallen soldiers' belongings with a grim efficiency, though each item I touched sent fresh tremors through my fingers. Maps, crumpled instructions— all evidence of how meticulously the Nazis had planned their invasion of this world. The once vibrant, wild beauty of the jungle seemed a distant memory now. All I could feel as I looked at the horizon was the darkness creeping ever closer—not from nature, but from man.

The silence between us was thick, swollen like the storm before lightning breaks through the clouds. Neither of us needed to speak aloud the thoughts that simmered beneath our shared glances. Where words failed, the aftermath of the battle spoke louder than anything I could ever say. An understanding passed between us, unspoken but undeniable.

Peters stood at last, slinging a rifle over his broad shoulder— scavenged from one of the fallen soldiers with the same emotionless efficiency that had marked all his movements since the skirmish ended. He stared into the dense trees ringing the horizon, his jaw set. "Better get used to it," he murmured, his voice lower now, grating with the weight of the truth. One of experience, one of survival. His eyes, sharp but distant, flickered with the knowledge of what lay ahead. "This ain't over."

I nodded, the sick ache in my gut tightening, though my mind solidified further with a growing resolve. I could feel it— the voice that had once been barely a whisper now growing louder. The truth was as apparent as the blood soaked into the earth around us. There may be no end to this war, but we would be part of it, for better or worse. There was no stepping away. No returning to the peace we had once known. Not now.

My eyes traced the battered landscape one last time. The bodies, the darkened blood seeping into the cracked earth, into the jungle's rich dirt like spilt ink, remained. I would not forget it. I could *not* forget it.

And so, with that dark knowledge festering in us both, Peters and I turned. Together, we walked toward what remained of our makeshift defense line—the smoke coiling low over the trees, the broken remnants of machinery scattered across the torn jungle path. It was a glaring prelude to something far worse. Something bloodier than either of us had prepared for.

14

Discovering the Nazis' Base

The Náiren council hall was dim. What little light filled the room came from the crystalline walls, their surfaces gently glowing, flickering like the dying embers of a once-great fire. It was a far cry from the lush brilliance we had grown accustomed to seeing in this world, a kind of strange, heavenly beauty that normally saturated the air. But now, the air felt thinner—heavier—as though it was absorbing the tension radiating from the gathered Náiren. Even the soft shimmer of the crystals above seemed dulled, barely able to cast the shifting reflections that danced weakly over the floor beneath our feet.

Peters and I stood at the center, surrounded by the elders whose expressions—normally serene and distant—were tight with unease. The neutrality, the passive calm they'd always worn, had slipped. Here, before the reality of the things we prepared to face, their tranquillity faltered, allowing a sliver of trepidation to seep through. It was unsettling to see their mystical grace bruised by the human reality of fear, but in a sense, it reassured me, too. This world, for all its distance from mine, was not so invulnerable as I once thought. Even here, faced with something as vile as war, harmony could break down.

Beside me, a short distance away, Elys cast a tall shadow against the delicate mosaic of light on the floor. His ethereal form—a wisp of silver-white hair floating down over his alabaster skin, long slender limbs standing unnaturally still—seemed completely at odds with the figures gathered at his feet. I could barely see the soft flicker of his pale-blue eyes, shimmering faintly as they caught the glow of the walls. Yet, his stillness was deceptive. I could feel his mind working—could feel the delicate tension hanging about him, like silent breaths drawn just short of speech. He was always deliberate, always considerate of the arcane balance he and his people had cultivated. His collected presence did little, though, to diminish the unmistakable hum of concern weaving between the elders.

At the center of the room, projected onto the smooth crystalline surface, was the enemy. The Nazi base.

It was little more than an outline, flickering intermittently like an insidious ghost—called from Lyra's device, the image wavered at the edges, lines shimmering, then solidifying enough to give an impression of space, fortified walls, and cold, harsh angles. A momentary chill settled beneath my skin at the sight. The hardened geometry of the compound clashed so violently with the organic beauty of everything else in this world that it felt almost profane to even look at it.

Peters leaned forward, his left hand braced on the side of the table, his right finger tracing a rough arc over the projected landscape map. "The base is here," he growled, his voice a thick, low rasp that reverberated briefly in the silence of the room. He tapped the edge of a dense patch of jungle on the map. His rough fingertip, stiff with callouses, thudded softly against the image, but each tap seemed to pulse with a foreboding weight. His expression was set, a grim scowl carved into the stern planes of his face. "They're deeper in than we thought—nestled tight." There was a heaviness in those words, their dull finality unspoken but ever present.

I shifted beside him, my gaze locked onto the projection. It shimmered faintly as though resisting clarity, but I could see enough. Just enough to understand the enormity of what lay ahead. My breath caught slightly in my chest, the air thick and unforgiving in my throat. My mind raced, trying to grasp the full scale of what we needed to do.

Reconnaissance. Find out where they were stationed. How many soldiers they had. What machines they were using to tear into this world. Our mission was simple in concept, yet felt impossible in execution. One wrong turn. One small misstep, and it'd all be over—there'd be no returning. Not for us. Not for the Náiren.

A sense of dread spread through me, tightening around my spine. I forced myself to remain steady, my hands balling into fists at my sides. As my mind jumped ahead, I couldn't help but feel like we were steps behind an invisible enemy, already entrenched, already destroying the fragile core of this place.

Lyra, her delicate form stepping out of the shadows near Peters, moved forward, her long silver hair trailing behind her like liquid moonlight. Her deep violet eyes, normally soft with curiosity, now gleamed with something sharper—an intensity that I hadn't seen in her before. She stood on the other side of the projection, eyes scanning the flickering map for any details that might have been overlooked.

"What you plan—this reconnaissance—it must be swift," she said quietly. Her voice, normally so light I could barely hear it, cut clear through the tension in the room. It carried a weight now, each word deliberate, firm. "Every hour they extract more from the earth. Every hour the damage grows." She paused, blinking once. When she set her gaze on me, it sent a quiet chill through my bones. There was no question about it—time was not on our side.

Peters grunted in acknowledgment, his gaze darkening. He straightened up slightly, pulling his hand away from the table. His posture shifted ever so subtly, the weight of his presence grounding the gathering with a new purpose. He had already embraced this role fully, I realized. Peters no longer saw himself as just a protector of me, of us. He had taken on the mantle of strategist—his mind carefully ordering tactics, weighing risks, determining the best course forward. I could all but see the mental calculations playing out behind his eyes. He muttered aloud, pacing a step to the left. "We'll go under cover of night." A pause. "Small group. Quick in and out."

He glanced at Elys and Lyra, the light catching his rough features, hardening them into something almost unreadable. "We gather intel—who's guardin' what, what machinery they got… then we get back here." His voice hardened. "No risky stunts. We don't engage unless we have to."

He turned back to face me, and I could feel his dark eyes on me, waiting for something. My nails dug slightly into the palm of my hands.

I raked my hands through my sweat-dampened hair, anxiety swirling beneath my skin like a cold wind trapped in my chest. Despite everything we had seen, despite everything we had done, I still felt out of my depth. These kinds of missions were meant for men like Peters—for those who had survived years of calculated risks, of battle, of close-call decisions that pulled them back from the brink. I was no soldier. I was no covert strategist. And yet—

"We need to know the full scale of what they're planning. The damage they're doing…" I let out slowly, trailing off. The words hung heavy in the air for a moment before I gathered myself. "I'll go with you."

Silence. I could feel the tension in the room shift slightly— a ripple of telepathic murmurs brushed through my mind, their soft concerns barely reaching me before fading away. The vibrations felt like tiny waves of conflicting thought.

Peters shot me a sidelong glance, his weathered brow lifting faintly. Despite everything, there was a flash of something between us in that moment—something like respect, or perhaps just mutual understanding. His lips curled into the faintest of smirks. "Thought you'd say that, partner." There was no hesitation left in him, just a steady acceptance of what needed to be done. "You ready for this?"

I held his gaze for a long beat, the flickering projection casting strange shadows across his rough features. Slowly, I nodded. Fear still thrummed beneath my ribs—I couldn't deny that. But it was sharper now, forged into something harder, something more focused. This hidden world, fragile and delicate, had become ours to protect. For both of us. There would be no turning back now. Only forward.

Elys turned toward us, his eyes distant, far off into thoughts this world had known long before either of us set foot in it. He remained silent for a long moment, his brow furrowing slightly as if considering the weight of everything that had just been said. His posture was tall, but there was something weary about it, the knowledge of what must be done settling over him like a heavy shroud. "Pym and Peters will be accompanied by a small group of our scouts," Elys said softly, his voice thick in the air. His telepathic hum was filled with soft authority now, carrying the unspoken weight of his leadership, of his approval. "Those trained to move undetected through the wilderness. They will guide and protect you as much as possible." The thought lingered in my mind as his psychic presence brushed up against mine. This was as much as he could offer—an extension of trust, though fraught with the risks still looming on the horizon.

Lyra stepped toward me, her fingers brushing against my arm with a fleeting, feather-light movement. Her presence was a quiet whisper—a voice that curled around the words she did not say aloud. "Stay focused," she murmured telepathically into my thoughts, her voice like the faint wind stirring leaves in the distance. "Avoid detection at all costs. This plan cannot be rushed, though I know urgency weighs on you."

Her hand slipped away before I could respond, but her eyes remained locked on mine—sharp, intelligent, but shadowed with the same worry I felt creeping up from the pit of my stomach. I nodded in acknowledgment, turning to face Peters again, his sharp glare catching the subtle message. Detection was everything. If we were spotted, the mission would be for nothing.

Peters didn't speak, only nodded in silence, but I saw the tension flickering through him—a subtle, subconscious twitch in the way his broad fingers flexed for a moment by his side, grasping at memories he quickly shut down. Whatever thoughts of past military operations were needle-pricking at his mind, he knew there would be no room for error here. Not like before.

I exhaled slowly, feeling the weight of it settle deeper.

"May the energy of this world protect those who go forth." Elys' voice, full of conviction, hummed quietly, vibrating through the now still air, resonating softly in the bones of the gathering. When he spoke, it was as though the very crystals in the walls reverberated with him. "Return safely and we will be ready for what comes next."

For what comes next.

The weight of that settled over us both as the chamber dissolved into soft murmurs, the unified hum of shared concentration palpable. Lyra gave me one last look in passing before turning to follow Elys into the fading shadows, the light growing dimmer as the projection vanished, leaving only the chilling memory of the threat still out there.

Peters caught my eye, his expression unreadable save for the slightest rise of his brows. We shared one last glance. It was all that either of us needed to continue forward—side by side into what waited ahead.

The weight of what was to be done coiled tightly in our chests.

****

The air hung thick with tension, each breath like dragging oil through our lungs. Around me, the muffled rustling of ferns and heavy jungle flora clung to the silence, brushing against our sweat-slicked skin with every cautious step. Even the soft currents of wind, which occasionally stirred the oppressive night, did little to alleviate the weight pressing down on us. Instead, they seemed to only drive the wet heat further into my bones. My shirt was already drenched, the cool night air doing nothing to relieve the anxious sweat that soaked through the fabric.

Stillness was a weapon now—one just as sharp and perilous as the steel Peters kept at his side. We navigated the pitch-black jungle night as if walking a tightrope, the smallest step potentially sending us hurtling into oblivion. Above and around us, the jungle walls, already dense beyond measure, tightened with every step. The natural barriers contorted like a beast, each branch, each vine reaching out with malicious intent. Here, we were concealed just as surely as we were exposed. My heart hammered loud in my chest, each beat a muffled scream of urgency tempered only by the terror that one wrong move could end it all.

Beneath my feet, the soil was soft—too soft—almost sponge-like in texture. Every delicate shift of my weight seemed to be felt by the Earth itself. I could feel the pull, the drag of the rich humus absorbing my footfalls—an unmistakable reminder of the inescapable pull beneath everything here, as if even the ground sought to swallow us whole.

The light was almost non-existent now—only faint tendrils of moonlight broke through the tangled web of twisted branches far above, casting pale threads across the already-dark foliage. Even the ever-present bioluminescence that had guided so many of our earlier paths seemed to fade beneath the oppressive weight of the night. We were truly alone, swallowed by this crawling darkness.

Without warning, Peters' fist shot up—a silent command, decisive as a rifle shot in the void. The entire group froze, movement halting mid-motion. I felt the air grow taut, every breath silenced as we became statues amidst the living world.

My muscles stiffened, and I held the breath already trapped in my chest, afraid to release it.

I strained my ears, pushing all conscious thought aside, focusing only on what little sound had reached us. Peters' senses were honed like a wild animal's, and he must have heard something. In the distance—somewhere hidden within that interminable darkness—came the faintest murmur of voices. Muffled, but sharp with intent. I tilted my head, leaning into the sound, straining—and then I caught it, too. The inflections of harsh, clipped syllables. German.

A flash of cold swept through me, an icy draft skittering over my skin despite the stifling humidity. Though we couldn't comprehend the exact words, the unmistakable cadence and intonation of the voices bit through the humid air like the promise of thunder before a storm. They were too close. Closer than we had hoped.

Peters turned his head, his eyes locking onto mine, and I saw the glint of confirmation—a silent understanding passing between us. Yes, the enemy was near—uncomfortably near—and the margin for error was steadily shrinking.

He jerked his head forward, a signal I immediately understood. We had to keep moving.

Our movement resumed, slower now, each step a lesson in quiet desperation. The jungle, which had once seemed so vast and impassive, felt as though it was watching us, holding its breath to see if we would survive. Every scrape of a leg through low-hanging vines sent a cascading ripple of motion through the dark green underbrush. The thickness of the air seemed to choke every whisper of sound, forcing us to cling tighter to the shadows cast by the towering trees and ferns. Here, the jungle acted as both a prison and protection. We slipped through its fingers like hunted animals, hoping the dark would make us invisible to the wolves wearing uniforms just beyond.

The jungle, unwilling to be ignored for much longer, began to reveal what we had been dreading: the faint light from the Nazi base lulled into view just beyond the break in the wild vegetation.

The flickering light of torches and electric lanterns traced the rough outline of the enemy camp, conjuring silhouettes of twisted metal and imposing watchtowers. The beacon of that artificial glow broke the primal bond the jungle had on us in an instant, casting the alien presence of human invaders against the natural beauty of this hidden oasis. Dark metal, harsh and gleaming beneath the distant moon, rose from the ground, the defensive wall puncturing the earth, a cruel reminder of their occupation. It was a scar, a ruin in the making, erected in defiance of the alien harmony that should have enveloped us.

I felt my breath catch in my throat, the visceral shock of it squeezing every nerve in my body. The sight of it… it was far larger than I had anticipated. Far more dangerous. The base seemed to stretch on and on, with machinery—great hulking behemoths scraping against the horizon—rising from the ground like twisting titans. Even from here I could feel the dull thrum that vibrated beneath us, the relentless pulse of the mining apparatuses.

Each thud, each heavy rotation of metal tore into the earth, violently extracting its secrets. The sensation reached our hiding place, swaying the tall grasses beneath my legs. Every instinct in me screamed at the sight. Whatever the Nazis were doing here, it wasn't just industrial mining. This was something larger. They were after more than just valuable minerals—they were tearing directly into the veins of the earth itself.

"They're gutting it..." Peters' voice barely rose above a whisper, his teeth clenched tightly against the building fury I knew surged within him. His eyes narrowed as they scanned the inner workings of the compound, locking onto the strange, seamless dance of crude mechanical force and something far more intricate, far more dangerous than I had expected. I watched helplessly as his gaze fell upon the mix of advanced engineering and crude cruelty. Whatever possessed these men, whatever unholy knowledge they had seized, it allowed them to blend the ruthlessness of strategy with technology's raw power.

Peters motioned for the Náiren scouts to close the gap. Their bodies hugged the underbrush, vanishing into the thick greenery as though the forest itself had absorbed them. They moved like shadows, slipping between tree trunks and moon-dappled brambles effortlessly, their form melding with the wilderness in ways that defied expectation. Though I had admired their grace silently over the past few days, it was here in this perilous proximity that I found myself in awe. Stealth in their movements came not from training but from a deeper connection to the land—a place where their understanding of the world intertwined perfectly with existence itself. Stealth in this sense was alive, palpable.

The guards appeared ahead of us. Human figures moving against the forbearing walls—a pair of them, their rifles slung casually over their backs, unaware, it seemed, of what lay in the thick tree line just beyond their sight. Their movements were slow yet deliberate, clearly part of their usual, regimented rounds. The cold efficiency with which they paced, showing neither fatigue nor hesitation, was unsettling. The rifles on their backs looked foreign, almost monstrous in the moonlight.

My heart skipped a beat, and I ducked lower, instinct pulling at me to remain unseen. Desperate whispers passed between our group, mere flickers of sound carried through trembling breaths. We could feel the tension rising, scraping at the backs of our spines.

My eyes darted to the center of the compound.

A massive drill.

It was a grotesque beast, its body harnessed by chains, the steel structure plunging into the earth with relentless force. Every slow, methodical rotation of that machine pushed it deeper into the ground—seeking something hidden within.

More strange cylindrical machines flanked it, shimmering faintly in the moonlight—a disgusting blend of unnatural and divine. The sickening realization spiraled through me like venom. They weren't just looking for resources.

"They're… they're going straight for the core," I whispered into the thick night air, the words pulling themselves from a sense of dread I hadn't allowed myself to acknowledge until now.

Peters stayed silent, jaw set hard against the weight of it all. His eyes did not waver as he took in the meaning of the sight before him.

He motioned for us to move forward, suppressing the rising fury in his gut. There would be time for anger later. Now, we needed to keep unseen. Together, we crept toward a low drop in the wall's perimeter—toward an area where the cold metal met the earth in an almost organic decay. There, a mound of broken dirt and cracked stone provided cover. This blind spot would allow us to press ourselves against the looming structure without detection.

Each breath was painstaking, pressed thin and shallow as though oxygen itself had to be rationed.

As the hum of machinery grew louder, the darkness seemed to grow deeper around us, pulling us deeper into its bosom, welcoming us into the fold with knowing hands. Something in that noise—industrial but rhythmic—moved almost like blood through arteries. It thrummed within us, vibrating the very air. A deep pulse, as though the world was coming alive.

I tasted iron. Fear locked in my throat.

One false move, and it would all be over.

We halted just beneath the shadow of the outer wall. The rocks and earth were rough beneath our hands as we crouched low, hidden in the jagged recesses between the sharp beams of metal. My chest constricted, holding in every breath, my fingers curling tightly against the jagged edges, counting the rhythms of the unseen threat pacing above.

The faintest rustle rustled near Peters' head.

I glanced toward the sound, heart leaping into my throat. A split-second instinct rooted me to the spot. Any wrong step, any subtle movement divorced from the perfection of silence, and we would be dead.

They'd waste no time firing.

Peters narrowed his eyes, signaling us to press tighter. He inched along the length of the wall, his calloused hand gripping against it for balance. Behind him, the Náiren tucked themselves tightly into shadows, blending with the structure as though nature itself cloaked them. We weren't just avoiding sight now. We were avoiding death.

Up ahead, where the wall grew darker, the wooden beams had begun to rot. Peters gestured toward the small entry—a space where time had chewed through the structure, leaving a slight gap beneath the decaying latticework.

One of the scouts, a slim figure with limbs fluid as water, dropped to his knees and slipped through the gap first. He barely made a sound as his body threaded through the small space like a shadow sliding through cracks in the earth.

Then, Peters motioned me forward.

The damp earth clung to my shirt as I crawled beneath the weakened beams. My heart pounded ferociously inside my chest—each beat loud in the still air, but loudest to my ears alone. The sharp edges of dirt scraped against my side, rough splinters grazing my shirt sleeve as I forced my way through the gap. I dared not make a sound, even as loose clumps of soil pressed into my skin.

Once inside the base, everything felt different—closer, hotter, as though the air itself had changed in the smell of oil and metal. Death lived in this place.

The base pulsed with a dull, mechanical energy—more alive than anything we had yet seen. The slow, rhythmic thrum of engines and machinery submerged the space, a relentless assault on the heart of the land beneath. No matter where I looked, the twisted anatomy of the base hummed with a deep, uncaring energy, as though thirsting for more. Energy plowed into the metal contraptions, cogs turning, earth churning—it was endless. The soldiers—stoic figures wrapped in shadows—moved briskly between buildings, their terse orders barked in harsh German clipped through the air like sharp bites, slicing through the droning hum of the machines.

I could hardly catch my breath.

We slipped silently past patrols, every nerve on fire, to a nearby supply depot nestled in the shadows.

Peters halted, crouching near some stacked crates. I followed, my lungs burning with the effort of restrained movement. My eyes widened when I spotted the insignia painted on the side of the boxes. The same grim symbol. Dark crosses etched into wooden surfaces. My heart skipped, my blood cold.

But worse still was what I found among the discarded items strewn about the depot floor.

A blueprint.

No—several.

Hastily scrawled diagrams, strange drawings, machinery— machines they had yet to build. I knelt, my fingers trembling as I grabbed at the papers. "We have to get this back," I muttered breathlessly, my voice so low I scarcely recognized it.

Peters glanced at the blueprints, eyes narrowing. His jaw set in grim fury. He nodded.

Torchlight flashed nearby. The faint sound of boots crunching over gravel reached us. I froze; time stretching painfully thin.

I dared not move.

For a terrifying heartbeat, I held my breath. No one moved.

Then—

The boots moved past.

Peters turned to me, eyes hard but furious. His whispered command cracked through the tension like a gunshot. "We need to move. Now."

Hollow, cold relief washed over me. I exchanged hurried looks with Peters and the scouts, then we withdrew back through the gap—one by one, breaths shallow, limbs trembling from the tension.

We moved through the gap in the wall once again, finding safety in the depths of the jungle. Only then, in the thick embrace of the wilderness, did I let myself breathe.

Wiping the sweat from my face, my pulse still hammering, I met Peters' hard eyes.

"We have what we need," I whispered, barely believing it.

Peters cast one final look back at the Nazi camp. In that brief moment, I saw the weight of their threat shift inside him, as though he now understood more than ever the enormity of what lay ahead. The victory was only partial.

"Yeah," he said, his voice gruff and hoarse. "For now."

15

The Reconnaissance Mission

The acrid scent of grease hung thick in the air. It oozed from the metal crates we crouched behind, mixing with the oily residue that clung to every surface, seeping into the fabric of our clothes, into our pores. It was a smell that would have been oppressive anywhere—but here, in the midst of this amalgamation of flesh, steel, and unholy machinery, it felt suffocating. Every breath I took was heavy with the ghosts of construction, industry, and—somehow—destruction.

The air itself seemed to buzz, as though the static of electricity coursing through the machines around us were alive, infusing everything with a barely-restrained kind of energy ready to arc out in thin blue streaks of violence. Somewhere nearby, probably no more than a hundred paces by my estimation, the massive drilling apparatus continued its relentless work, tunneling deeper into the earth. I could feel it, distantly, in the soles of my boots—its endlessly monotonous hum—a dull but constant vibration that traveled up through my legs as though it had been designed not only to burrow downward into the planet, but to dig into the very flesh of those who trespassed too close. Each pulse, gentle but unyielding, was a reminder: There was power here, immense and unforgiving.

The ground beneath us trembled slightly in rhythm with the drilling, a small but tangible quiver that moved through the earth, through the cold metal crates pressed hard against our backs, through Peters' tense posture beside me—the whole world seemed alive with this malignant hum. From time to time, I could feel my bones vibrate beneath my skin, as though the machine's insistent churning was rattling something deep inside me.

Suddenly, a soft clang—metal striking metal. The sound folded itself into the incessant hum of the base's mechanical core, distorted yet unmistakable. It echoed louder in the tight air where we stood frozen behind the crates, my heart lurching painfully in response, a quick stab of panic climbing up my spine before settling back into its cold nest in my chest.

Immediately, both Peters and I went rigid, instincts firing in unison. My breath caught, suspended halfway between exhale and nowhere, and I felt my heartbeat hammer violently in my throat. That short metallic note had ricocheted through the overbearing tension thick between us—like the toll of an invisible bell cracking through a funerary silence.

My hand, as if no longer entirely my own, instinctively darted inside my jacket. The blueprints—folded, precious, damning—were tucked neatly against my chest, their paper edges crinkling beneath my trembling fingers. Even though I already knew they were in place, I had to confirm it again, my mind operating on base impulses: **Safeguard your evidence. Keep your proof. Keep moving.** A ludicrous thought flashed briefly through my mind: Was this fear or belief jittering my muscles into action? Was it the knowledge of what they'd found, or the terror of what might happen if we were discovered?

Beside me, Peters was still. But it was the stillness of a predator—not calm, no, never calm—the taut anticipation of something about to spring. His eyes—narrowed, sharp, filled with that steely quality forged in battle—remained locked on the nearest guard, a young soldier pacing listlessly by a pile of discarded equipment. The soldier's boots scuffed lightly over the dirt and metal plates beneath him, a sound amplified by the silence now lodged in our heads. He moved with an uneasy precision, his eyes haunted by some imagined threat only half-renounced in his chest—a fear that, like a parasite, had borrowed beneath his skin. That banal, repetitive motion: a walk designed to make a man feel in control when in truth, none of them were in control here— not of themselves, not of their world.

The soldier's gaze swept the area, passing over the crates, barely missing the narrow slits of darkness where the cold metal created hiding places deep enough for two men desper- ate not to be seen. Peters' hand wrapped tightly around the handle of his knife. I could see his knuckles turning white, twisting against worn leather, ready to sink the blade into the guard's jugular if the man paused just a second too long.

The soldier's footsteps echoed again, fading. We waited—Peters' body poised high with that familiar energy, ready to pounce daggers-first should the soldier's head crane back toward us. Though we remained hidden, every muffled noise felt magnified. My chest constricted to the point where breathing felt like an act of defiance.

Only once the echo of distant boots had merged with the ambient noise of the base, did I allow myself to chance a slow, shallow breath. It came out ragged—quiet, but to my mind, painfully obvious. I caught the sharp metallic tang that hung heavy in the air, tainted by electricity, scorched rubber, oil, and iron. All at odds with everything this world had been before.

My eyes flicked toward the center of the compound. Massive drills. Cold. Relentless. Their whirring and churning stretched endlessly into the ether as the harsh gears, fitted with blades too precise and too monstrous to be man's alone, gnawed deep into the belly of the Earth. But that wasn't what gnawed at **me**—it was the stolen technology festooned across the compound, entirely out of place here, like plucked feathers glued haphazardly to a corpse. Half-completed projects. Strange sigils carved on the sides of metal scaffolding, blazing faintly, and languages that even I, in all my learned travels, had never encountered.

Marks… like Náiren symbols.

My stomach roiled at the half-intelligible realization. The base—this abomination of unfathomable design—had begun to utilize the infrastructure, the systems of this world, twisting them into mechanical perversions. Begrudgingly, I had accepted that the conflict before us was already raging, and now… now, the evidence sat glaring all around me. They weren't just stripping the land. They were mining **it**—in a way that seeks to burrow deeper than soil or rock, to unearth something far more ancient and powerful than we could comprehend.

Panic pressed against my chest, stifling my breath once more. I'd seen them before—those symbols gleaming innocuously in the technology the Náiren used for knowledge, growth, and society. Now, though, they were… changed, mutilated by the hands that sought to desecrate this world. And the knowledge that those same hands sought **more** left me cold.

A cluster of Nazi scientists stood to the left, huddled around a large control apparatus lit by sickly glowing blue screens. They spoke in sharp, clipped tones, their German dulled by the hum of machinery but still distinct. Cold faces, devoid of everything but the grim fascination of men studying some grotesque aberration. One scientist had his attention fixed on a fluctuating dial atop the control apparatus, murmuring something to his colleague. The other—a gaunt man with hollowed cheekbones—nodded, adjusting readings on the instrumentation beside him without ever pausing to glance at the unfolding spectacle around them.

I edged forward slightly, straining to hear. German words I hadn't heard in years slipped through the static-filled air, fragments of jargon trying to knit together in my mind like some impossible puzzle. "… **burrowing deeper**… *the core…* **harnessing…**"

I blinked, my mind grappling with the technicalities. Fragments danced. Conjecture pieced together bit by bit.

Something about "…the core… providing **unimaginable energy reserves…**"

I opened my mouth—to breathe, perhaps—to whisper something to Peters—but Peters' elbow jabbed sharply into my ribs, snapping me back to the present. He had heard it too, but his senses were already tuned to something more immediate— something brutally real. He twisted toward me, eyes flashing in warning.

A sentry's boots scraped against the cold ground nearby, stirring up dirt and dust as they ground across the cobbled earth, the metallic ring of his gear—not exactly foreign, but almost mechanical—struck the tension once more like a hammer. Then, a crackled burst of static broke the airwaves, accompanied by the shrieking bark of an officer's order through the sentry's handheld radio. The noise carried across the compound, flitting around like an electric ghost before vanishing as quickly as it had appeared.

Dozens of trained instinct snarled at me in that moment. The guard rounded the corner.

His flashlight flickered, a long tongue of cold white light washing over discarded parts, forgotten gearing mechanisms, and the cold backs of the crates where we now huddled to **become** shadows. Both Peters and I flattened ourselves against the ground, soft mud oozing beneath me, the filthy scent mingling with the grease-soaked air. I could feel the vibration of the crates pressing into my spine, the pulse of electricity and machinery humming through the metal, crawling beneath my skin. The tepid thrum below my ribs mirrored in my head.

My breath stuck halfway down my throat. **Do not move.**

I held it, the plea barely escaping the confines of my thoughts. The heavy thud of the guard's boots reverberated through the cold ground, the weight of his footfalls betraying every thick moment he spent closer, each beat dragging impossibly long as I lay trembling in the dark.

Peters' knife hovered near his belt, his hand still taut and vicious in preparation—each knuckle visibly strained beneath the white skin. His body told me everything before his words could. One movement in the wrong direction, and we would see blood.

The invisible arc of the sentry's flashlight danced above us. Too close.

His boots stopped.

I squeezed my eyes shut, clutching the blueprint inside my jacket, feeling the fragile paper crinkle beneath my grasp. **He's found us.** The light burned faintly overhead. My lungs screamed to release the tension suffocating them.

But then—

Another officer's bark shot through the night.

The sentry paused, glancing toward a distant section of the compound—his mind already working to obey the command lodged in his ear. His attention shifted elsewhere. He turned.

He moved.

Sharp, obedient like a good blade in motion, retreating with the tension trailing behind him, folding invisibly into the low droning hum of the compound.

Peters exhaled a long-simmering breath, his eyes remaining narrow, but his hand finally dropped from the knife handle. He turned slightly, motioning sharply at me. "We stay too long here, we're dead," he muttered hoarsely. "Let's get out."

I nodded automatically, though the weight on my chest hadn't lifted. If anything, it had only deepened—every breath wrapped tighter around the truth. A silent scream clawed at the back of my throat, a revelation made real in the flickering flash of disturbed machinery behind us. My eyes drifted back toward the drills, the visages of excavators gnashing away at the earth. **This—they aren't just tearing into the land…** Something else… something older… unseen. **This isn't about power at all. It's about unlocking something catastrophic.**

As we crouched, poised to retreat, I caught one of the scientists murmuring a final phrase to his companions, his voice cold and distant, not allowing for emotion's intrusion. Almost bored, despite the magnitude of what he said: "**The energy from the core... it will make us unstoppable.**"

My blood turned ice-cold.

This wasn't just about fuel or control. This was about dominance. It was about turning whatever ancient unknowable force lay dormant beneath us into a weapon—one that could destroy **everything.**

I turned sharply to Peters, my breath shallow, my voice broken with the cold truth in my gut. "We need to move. Now." My voice came out hoarse, matching the urgency in his eyes. My curiosity, the awe that had kept me suspended all this time, solidified now into one hard certainty: We had to stop this, whatever it took.

With that, we slipped back into the shadows lining the edge of the perimeter, keeping low against the debris, weaving through the scattered crates and forgotten parts. Our footsteps became whispers, skirting patrols like wraiths pulled tight between life and death. With calculated agility, we moved away from the epicenter of the chaos, retreating beyond the threat, eyes trained on the darkening path ahead.

By the time we vanished into the thick jungle beyond, the relentless mechanical hum of the base faded into the distance. But the image of the drills gnawing deeper into the planet's core… the dangerous inevitability of it all… stayed imprinted in the cracks of my mind.

We had escaped. But the reckoning was far from over.

****

The twilight draped the village in a serene, soft glow, like the very last breath of a dream that refused to concede to morning. Around us, the warmth radiating from the smooth, crystalline structures cast pools of faint light that shimmered with a celestial presence, their colors shifting softly between gold and pale blue, as though in gentle, private conversation with the sky. It was a world built on peace, a peace that hummed through the very air, enveloping the village and its inhabitants in a shared tranquility. And yet, despite the familiar beauty, there was something new here— an undercurrent that prickled the skin, invisible but palpable. Tension.

The Náiren village, for all its natural grandeur and stillness, had changed. It had accepted silence in place of harmony— in place of the hum of life that usually coursed through its very stones. The weight of everything we'd witnessed— everything we'd dragged from the bowels of that wretched camp—clung to us like the shadows stretched long across the ground. Peters and I emerged from the thick jungle like specters, feeling as though we carried the damnation of the world with us, bundled in the worn, crumpled papers hidden inside my jacket. The knowledge we had gained felt toxic, unraveling my very soul as we walked, each step weighed down with the grim future we brought back with us.

Somewhere deep within the village, the crystalline structures murmured, casting light over the smooth marble paths that wound between sleeping alcoves, gardens adorned with delicate iridescent flowers, and streams that drifted lazily through the air without needing an earthly bed of water. The golden luster caught the ridges of my weathered face, illuminating every deep line carved over the course of our endless journey. Even in this moment, surrounded by all the village's lush, otherworldly life, the vibrancy felt muted by what we were about to reveal. Would this place ever look the same once the words left our mouths?

Peters moved next to me in silence, his broad shoulders taut beneath the damp fabric of his jacket, his eyes darting across the sleeping village with the sharp awareness of a man who had spent his life in battle. Every sound was a potential whisper of danger. Every shift of light his body reacted to with fierce, understated calm. His was a presence marked by the kind of tension that came before violence, the point just before a break. He moved quickly, fluidly but deliberately, the worn leather of his boots barely making a sound against the smooth, luminescent ground.

"Feels like the calm before a storm," Peters muttered, though his gaze stayed fixed ahead.

I didn't respond, but I could feel the same tightening in my gut. The village was calm, undoubtedly. But it wasn't peaceful—not anymore. That subtle but ever-present hum that had always flickered in the atmosphere, beneath the leaves, inside the walls of every structure—the pulse of Náiren life—had faltered. It was waiting. Watching.

We passed the sleeping alcoves, winding through the heart of the village where all life had found solace in quietude. The pale marble beneath our boots gave way to soft, verdant grass that spiraled up, creating walls and domes that glowed faintly under the twilight. Still, despite the village's beauty, my perception was dominated by the cold metal compound we had just fled, and the silhouette of the unholy machines that tore into the earth. The scent of oil still clung stubbornly inside my nose, a metallic miasma that refused to leave my thoughts.

The central hall came into view—a towering structure, its arched ceilings constructed from veins of crystal that ran through the earth itself, glowing faintly in the deep, ambrosial darkness of pre-dawn. The soft light radiating from within cast long, delicate shadows over the pathways, flickering faint with every dappled breath that passed through the air.

At the entrance stood Elys.

His pale form, sharp and effortlessly elegant as always, loomed in the golden-blue twilight. He was a man known for his ability to beckon peace, even in silence, to radiate authority where words might fail. And yet, as Peters and I drew nearer, I could see the subtle shift in his expression—the rigid posture of his body, the tension clinging to the stillness around him. His figure remained tall, yet something about the way his hands twisted within the folds of his gown—fingers weaved together, betraying the quiet uncertainty lurking beneath his calm exterior—gave him away.

His eyes, glowing with the faint, violet luminescence common to his kind, caught my gaze and held it with a finality that felt almost unnatural. Behind them, I saw the same darkness I felt creeping through my own thoughts—a knowing. There was only one possible conclusion to our hurried return.

A wordless understanding passed between us as we stopped before him, the humid air pressing gently against us, wrapping itself around the space. Elys did not speak aloud, his presence strong yet restrained. Instead, his telepathic command brushed softly against my consciousness, allowing us passage. The great crystalline doors behind him opened soundlessly, followed by a gentle, subterranean sigh of air moving from deep within the hall. We stepped inside.

The moment we crossed into the council chamber, my heart became acutely aware of how far everything had fallen. Inside the great domed hall, the elders of the Náiren waited, seated in silent, poised elegance—serene but watchful. Their eyes, each shining with that same faint glow, were fixed upon us the moment we entered, casting an eerie light that barely touched the soft lines of their faces. Tension, palpable and ancient, pressed into the room, each breath finding us a little heavier than the last.

The council didn't shift, didn't bristle, didn't speak. They merely watched—tall, silent, their silver hair falling silently past their shoulders, robes folded like smoke over their slender forms. It was incongruous, jarring, to witness such composed, perfect elegance in contrast to the storm now swelling inside my chest.

I forced myself to meet their gazes as Peters and I made our way to the center of the chamber, where the light from the ceiling filtered down onto us like some heavenly judgment come to earth. If not for the immediate weight of the information we carried, I might've been struck again by how alien—how incredibly otherworldly—this place still felt, even now. The tranquility that radiated from the structures, the walls, the plants hanging from the glowing ceiling, was nearly unbearable in its contrast to what we were about to ask of them.

Lyra stepped forward then—her form emerging from the shadows of the back alcove like a thought becoming real. Her eyes fixed on me, shining with curiosity and concern as time stretched unbearably inward.

"What did you find?" Her voice was as measured as it had been before—the almost-breath that clung to each syllable—but now, beneath it, there was something more. A tremor.

Peters gave her a grim look, his face hardened from the long, brutal night and the horrors we'd seen within the Nazi base. He shifted uneasily, his voice rough and worn as he finally spoke into the silence that threatened to drown us all. His words seemed to hang in the air, weighted down by the dense reality of what we had uncovered.

"They're not just mining. They're digging straight for the core..." he rasped, his gravelly voice barely audible but all too clear.

The air shifted, cool against the rising flush on my skin.

For the first time, the silence of the elders broke. It was not a physical sound, but the ripple of their collective minds as if a great pulse had surged through their telepathic bond, brushing faintly against the edges of my consciousness. I felt the wave of disbelief—felt the shock vibrate between their thoughts.

Lyra's brows furrowed slightly as she processed what Peters said, but I could see the flicker of disturbed thought in her eyes. The idea of accessing the very heart of the planet, of tearing past the natural barriers that had kept the core untouched for millennia, was unthinkable. Madness.

And yet...

"They can't be so foolish," a faint thought whispered from one of the elders. It was quickly quieted by another sharp spike in the telepathic hum of the gathered council.

Peters' jaw tensed, his hands still balled into fists. Every fiber of his being was taut—a man who no longer had room for doubt in what we had witnessed. Nothing could have prepared him for this world, just as nothing could silence the voice of war already beating through him.

Elys stepped forward, his calm presence snaking its way close to me, his gaze piercing mine in the dim light. His telepathic projection pressed lightly against my thoughts, searching for verification of Peters' words—an answer to the silent question none of them could bring themselves to ask aloud.

"The core has been untouched for millennia," Elys whispered, though his voice reverberated through the room with its timbreless cadence. "What do they seek to unlock?"

It was a question filled with an eerie weight, filled with something darker than curiosity.

I felt the pressure. I took a breath.

"They believe they can harness it," I answered, though my throat strained against the words. "The energy source beneath us… it's not just a source of power. It's something far more."

Elys' presence, though cold and distant as ever, pierced through me more sharply than before—his mind wrapping itself around mine as though pulling the truth out of my bones. His violet eyes narrowed, fixed on mine, willing me to continue, despite my uncertainty.

I hesitated, grappling with the staggering reality of the information I was about to offer, trying to wrangle the scope of it into language. I didn't have all the answers, but what I did have was enough to send a spike of terror through me. "I'm still trying to understand all of it myself," I continued, my voice tighter now. "But… whatever they're after, it could give them control—far beyond what anyone on the surface comprehends."

Lyra's glow dimmed faintly as she processed my words, her face drawing into a tight frown. The telepathic tides swirling through us grew heavier. "If what you say is true…" she said slowly, her tone cracking with the weight of it, "then they intend to destabilize everything we've built. The Earth. Our harmony."

Peters, eyes hard, nodded gravely. His voice was flat yet undercut with the kind of urgency that demanded attention. "If they keep digging, they'll rupture something uncontainable. Once they tap into that energy, it won't just stop here. It'll spread. They'll have the power to destroy the surface. The entire world."

His words fell into a silence thicker than I expected. The sheer stillness that followed was deafening—deafening even against the backdrop of soft, shifting light from the walls. Despite the outer calm, I felt the writhing storm suffocating the air within the council chamber. Unseen but all too present.

The elders' pale eyes shifted among one another, nearly imperceptible gestures, though I could feel the churn of their thoughts. Worry clung to the walls now, swirling faintly over the crystal-strewn ceiling. The delicate beauty around us contrasted with the horrific calculus we had laid before them.

Everything—their world, their beliefs, their peace—was now balanced on the knife's edge of that conversation.

My pulse quickened again, the words tearing at the inside of my throat, desperate to escape before it was too late. Time had stretched, dragged tenuously between the realms of the peaceful day-to-day life they had known and the coming oblivion prowling just outside. We needed to move. We needed to act.

"Every second we wait," I said, my voice gaining strength, "they dig deeper. They're growing closer to their goal by the moment. We can't wait to act—we can't afford to hesitate. By the time we do, it'll be too late to stop them."

The room remained still—heavy silence shifting between us once more. The air swirled around my neck, warm and stifling.

Elys stood perfectly still, his frame rigid, though I could see the flicker of something darker cross his face now. His voice remained soft, but just beneath it lay the smallest tremor of something else—something beyond the calm he so effectively maintained.

"We are not a people of violence, Pym," he said, his gaze unmoving. "But if we do not act—if we wait too long—we will be complicit in the ruin of this world. We must… consider more drastic measures."

The thought of it seemed foreign coming from him—

undermined somehow by the quiet resolve beneath his voice. A people of peace considering war.

War.

Lyra hesitated, her voice barely above a murmur now, but its weight was unmistakable. "A preemptive strike, then."

Her words hung heavy in the chamber—filled with the solemnity of the moment, violent in their implications.

"We cannot let them destroy everything sacred here," she whispered, her mind reaching across to mine with the same tremor I felt in my own heart. "We have no choice. We must act first."

For a second, the air between us hummed with expectation, all of us feeling the swell of inevitability pushing closer. Pushing us toward war—for the first time in Náiren history.

Peters and I exchanged a glance across the room. The taut line of fear pressed hard against us both, but under that pressure lay something else. A grim understanding. There was no returning to the peace we had known before. Silence now meant only one thing.

War had already begun.

"We stand at the edge of something larger than this world," I said softly, lifting my chin with renewed determination. My voice carried the same weight of resolution I saw glowing in Peters' eyes. "This doesn't just end here—it won't. This war will spill over to the surface—to everything we know, everything we've fought to preserve. We need everyone prepared for what's coming—no matter what it takes."

Elys' eyes flickered once more, processing something deeper than words.

He turned, his gaze sweeping through the silent assembly of elders, his telepathic presence feeding into them, waiting for the gravity of the decision to settle in their ancient bones. For a moment, the silence was coiled—packed tightly into the smallest corner of thought, ready to snap.

Then—

"We will defend our home," he said. His words carried the weight of finality. "We will not allow them to ravage this world."

With that, the council meeting was over.

Our message had delivered us full circle to the only conclusion that remained: war.

The elders rose as one, their pale features drawn with resolute understanding, their silent gazes rippling through the empty space between us all in unison as they departed into the dim morning light. It was a strange, delicate dismissal, but no less deafening for its quietness. The need for immediate action pulsed through the council chamber, curling with the warmth of the early dawn just brushing past the horizon. I could feel the air shift with it, no longer heavy with stoic calculations, but now more… marked. The Náiren—their entire existence forged in the body of peace—would march toward a war they had never wished to know.

In that quiet, Peters and I made our way back toward the entrance, exhaling the shared weight of everything that was still yet to come. The morning still lingered sleepy, and the village beyond had begun to stir with life—the light sounds of Náiren voices finding one another in gentle conversation somewhere beyond the hall. But all this, peaceful and idyllic as it may have appeared, was a fragile illusion now. Beneath the surface, this village, this entire world, poised itself on the edge of chaos.

And we marched toward the storm.

Peters walked in step beside me, his eyes sharp as they watched the villagers begin to stir around us. We left the hall behind, our bootfalls muted against the delicate landscape. Neither of us needed to speak. We knew.

There was no turning back.

The war had begun.

16

The Climax Approaches

The once vibrant village of the Náiren—their tranquil halls and walkways that had, only days before, pulsed gently with the undulating rhythms of a people in balance with their world—now felt transformed. Tense, hurried energy surged through the air, carried not on the soft hum of life, but on the hard edges of impending conflict. Where the hallways had sung with quiet beauty, where each arch of the crystalline structures had shimmered with the soft translucence of peace, all had paled to an anxious, anticipatory light. As I walked, my footfalls muffled by the lush grass beneath me, I couldn't avoid the weight now hanging over everything.

On the outskirts, the village had erected defenses—makeshift barricades of iridescent crystal panels that, under any other circumstances, would have drawn admiration for their beauty. Now, they were interlaced with thick, organic materials, hastily gathered from the nearest trees and woven tight like braided sinew. Their once-pristine transparency was marred, dulled under the strain of its new purpose. This was no monument to elegance, but to survival. Even the light passing through it did so in fractured shards, not unlike the hearts of the Náiren warriors who stood, now tense, beside them.

I watched them—tall, silver-haired sentinels—dart between points of defense, their movements graceful even as the frenetic energy between one task and the next threatened to steal this natural elegance from them. There was fear in their eyes, though few would admit it, and fewer still would voice it aloud. The weight of an enemy as unyielding and vicious as the force the Nazis represented was inconceivable to many of them—and yet here they stood, readying themselves for a battle they had never expected to fight.

I let my gaze drift away, unable to stand too long in reverie, as my eyes sought out Peters—his familiar frame unmistakable amidst the alien figures. He stood just beyond the first barricade, his broad figure a rough-hewn slab amidst the delicate shapes of the Náiren, his voice gruff and barking orders that cut through the tense buzz of quiet conversation. Though he commanded a group who could communicate telepathically, Peters had no tolerance for such subtleties. Instead, his grating tone rang across the clearing, crisp orders bending formality to practicality. The language barrier might as well have been such noise before now, but something in Peters' bearing uprooted such concerns. Every bark, every tersely spoken command, carried meaning beyond words: confidence dredged from experience, a certainty that came not from theory, but from the countless hours spent breathing in the acrid stench of war.

"Move that, now," he growled, pointing a thick finger toward a cluster of lithe Náiren warriors struggling to properly brace one of the crystal barriers. His voice commanded such authority that even those more comfortable with telepathic communication snapped to attention. "That position won't hold when they come hard." His scathing eyes swept over the group, his brow tight with frustration. "You need natural cover—move it over to that outcrop," he motioned, pointing toward a small rise of rock part-hidden by dense foliage.

For a fraction of a moment, hesitance spread across the group—perhaps confusion, too. None knew war the way Peters knew it, none understood yet the brutal calculus that soldiers understood—that what seemed cohesive to the eye rarely remained intact beneath the onslaught of gunfire and cannon blasts. The moment hesitated on the edge of silence, but only for a beat. Then, Peters stepped forward, his hands moving to demonstrate as much as his voice explained. The warriors followed quickly, moving the barricades into position with a speed that belied their unease.

I stepped forward, closer now, observing each delicate gesture from the Náiren—a reminder that every movement, every bracing of their weapons, every footfall with their translucent tools—all of it felt hopelessly out of place. Here was technology—living, humming, shimmering as it pulsed beneath the soft light—that was designed for nurturing, for symbiosis with the world. And yet here it was, being wielded in preparation for war. One warrior, no taller than

I, came forward carrying a long staff of vibrant, shimmering crystal. Its core pulsed with a faint glow, flickering like the dying breath of some great cosmic entity. Peters paused in his instructions, watching with a mixture of wariness and curiosity.

"Here," Peters said, grabbing the staff and positioning it against a natural groove in the rocky terrain. "Like this." His weathered hands held the elegant weapon with a clarity born of necessity, though it was clear the smooth feel of it unsettled him. Despite its beauty, this was no ceremonial staff. It hummed beneath his fingers, faint whispers of energy brimming beneath the surface. He passed it back to the warrior, who took it in an almost reverent motion. The contrast was hard to ignore—the strange beauty of the Náiren's ancient armaments and the grim intent now forced upon them.

Watching him, I couldn't help but draw in a slow breath of my own. Peters had absorbed himself completely in the preparations, a force unto himself, honed and edge-sharp in his authority. In contrast, I felt… brittle, misplaced. The air here—the soft, vibrating warmth from the crystalline ground all around—felt strange beneath my feet. This should have been no place for war, and yet, here we were, twisting the very nature of what was meant to flourish into what would now destroy.

I moved past the formation, almost without intention, and to one of the many weapon caches already in place. There, nestled among shimmering shields and staves, was a glowing panel I hesitantly reached out to touch. My fingers hovered just over the surface of the device, and almost reflexively, it responded, humming to life, pulsing soft energy that seemed alive beneath my fingertips. I traced the edge lightly, wondering at its craftsmanship—everything about it felt fluid, seamless, like it belonged not only in the world but to the world.

Yet, there I stood, preparing to send it into the path of destruction.

My heart clenched tightly in my chest as my fingers brushed the smooth, cool surface of the shield. It seemed too… gentle, too elegant, for what it was about to be used for. My fingers followed the contours on instinct, the faint glow just barely visible under the shine of dewy light that formed along its edge. This was meant to protect, but I knew—deeply, viscerally—that it couldn't protect everything. Nothing could protect everything. Not now.

"You see these shields?" A soft voice echoed faintly within my mind. I turned my head almost before I recognized the sensation, and found Lyra standing beside me. Her presence felt both immediate and distant, like a cool breeze threading through a midnight shadow. Her eyes were soft, wide, and filled with something I hadn't seen in her since we first met— something unguarded.

"We've never had to use them like this," she said softly, her voice filling my mind like a whispered thought more than a sound. She glanced toward the shield in my hands, touching it as I did, and gave a faint nod. "It's never easy to stand at the edge, knowing this moment will decide the fate of everything."

Her hand lingered on my arm for a moment—brief, almost imperceptible—an attempt at reassurance. But it didn't have the power I think she wished it had. I could feel the faint tremor in her fingers. She too felt the gravity of the battle ahead. Everything about her radiated uncertainty, though she kept it tightly under control—for now. I swallowed hard, my own frustration muted. What could she say that would change what we knew had to happen next?

I turned from her, about to respond, but Peters' usual gruff voice cut through the air like gravel on stone, shattering the delicate mindfulness around us.

"Stop overthinking it, Pym," he barked, his eyes narrowing as he gestured over his shoulder toward the distant horizon. His breath hitched once before he steadied himself. "We've seen what they're capable of—don't f—don't romanticize this." His voice dropped, quiet but sharp as he motioned to the weapons scattered before the two of us. "This is about survival— ours and theirs." He stopped, his rough finger pointing toward the natural curve of the horizon where machinery hid, where preparations for war churned on beyond our sight. His eyes, which held no room for whimsy or doubt, lingered. Then, there it was—the faintest flicker of something deeper, something behind that ironclad certainty—a sliver of uncertainty, even fear.

I wanted to say something—to give voice to the creeping dread that had, for days now, threatened to drown us all—but Peters wouldn't allow it. There was no room for it. No time.

We marched, side by side, toward the central node of the defenses—a clearing at the edge of the village where Náiren tacticians huddled over a projected hologram of the surrounding area. Glowing symbols, delicate and alien, floated above the map. Indicators of enemy movements, projected supply lines—machinations and predictions I recognized too well.

I watched as Peters leaned forward into the conversation, drilling the gathered commanders on their defensive lines—his grim tone unyielding. There was no real barrier between them now, not even language. Only strategy.

"No shame in surviving to fight again," I heard him mutter, fixing his gaze on one of the tacticians as though daring them to contradict. They didn't.

A distant rumble shook the ground before I could process what came next. We all turned, eyes snapping toward the sound.

It was coming.

Tomorrow.

Or sooner.

***

The jungle felt alive in a way that only those doomed to battle could sense—each leaf, each shifting vine seemed to hold its breath along with us, waiting. The dense foliage blurred the line between shadow and substance, and even the normally glowing, pulsing plants that surrounded the Náiren village had dimmed to a whisper, as though nature itself had quieted for the monsters approaching in the distance. I could barely hear the hum of the low-frequency resonance from the crystalline structures behind us. They, too, seemed weak tonight—muted in the face of what was to come.

Peters and I stood at the edge, where the trees thickened enough to form a natural barrier. The jungle canopy above rustled ever so faintly, the branches scraping together softly like brittle bones. The open plain stretched out beneath it, a no-man's land waiting to become a site of blood and fire. The darkness was palpable, oppressive—less a lack of light and more a substance that pushed against us. It clung to our skin, to the edges of our minds, refusing to be shaken off.

I let out a shaky breath, the air rushing from my lungs like a man surfacing from the depths, clawing for the surface of reason. I hadn't even realized I'd been holding it. Somewhere overhead, the faint rustle of leaves responded with a shudder, as if the world was reminding me to keep quiet, to not disturb this fragile peace.

I hated this waiting. It felt wrong—out of sync with the very nature of anticipation itself. And yet, there was something inevitable about it, too. Something about the night that whispered of a storm building in the distance, of thunder rumbling low just beyond hearing. It was as if the fabric of the world itself trembled, knowing it was on the cusp of being torn apart. A fragile illusion, this stillness, one that could break with the smallest breath of wind, the barest sound of a boot scraping against loose stones.

I clenched my fingers tighter around the edge of my jacket, the leather cold and stiff beneath my touch. How had it come to this? How did something that had begun so innocently—a voyage into the unknown, a pursuit of discovery, knowledge—how had that naïve dream warped so, and become a fight for survival?

I knew the answer, of course. You don't venture into the abyss expecting to come out unchanged. But still, I wasn't a man designed for war. Not like Peters. Not like the soldiers of this world—they had been forged by it, hardened in the fires of conflict. I was a relic, desperately clinging to some hope that reason would prevail. That discovery—truth—would be enough to stem the tide of destruction. But beneath the surface, beneath my stubborn refusal to let go of that hope, I knew. There's no place for rationality here.

Beside me, Peters stood, his thick arms crossed over his chest, staring into the black expanse before us with that familiar, unperturbed grimness. Even now, in this moment, his breath was slow—steady. His body was coiled, wound tight not with panic, but with focus—he was cataloging, calculating, as reliable and cold as any machine could hope to be. Every shift of the leaves, every distant thump of movement beneath the ground, was another addition to his mental list of threats: another potential hazard, another thing to survive.

And yet, for all his outward stillness, there was something distant in his gaze tonight. Like part of his soul, too tired to live only in the present, had retreated backward—slipped away into some distant memory long before all this had started.

"What are you thinking?" I asked, my voice a whisper in the night air, almost afraid to disturb him.

The silence stretched between us, long and purposeful. For a moment, I thought he wouldn't respond. Perhaps he was lost—too far into those thoughts to hear me at all. But then, without turning his head, without shifting an inch:

"I'm thinking about Maryland," he said at last, his voice coming in a low grumble, rough around the edges. "About cigarettes and rain... about all the things I shouldn't be remembering."

The words hit me in a way I hadn't expected—strangely nostalgic, tinged with something like sorrow. A man like Peters didn't often indulge in thoughts of the past. In all our time together, he hadn't once mentioned home, not with more than a passing reference. But the way he said it now— with that faint edge of bitterness—there was something deeper beneath it. Regret. Or maybe just resignation. I wasn't sure.

He paused, shifting slightly where he stood, tension easing from his neck. "But mostly, Pym… I'm thinking we're not getting out of this clean. You understand that, don't you?"

I hesitated. His words, though typical of him, held more weight than I was comfortable with. Of course I understood. How could I not? But there was still a part of me—some deeply buried, childish hope that refused to accept it fully, that wanted to believe we could still survive this by virtue of something else—by understanding, by outwitting them. There had to be an answer beyond brute force, beyond bloodshed.

"We have the technology on our side," I offered quietly, my voice lacking the confidence I tried to project. "They're primitive compared to us—they can't possibly comprehend what we've got."

Peters laughed, low and bitter, a sound that rippled out into the jungle like a growl. "You think that matters? Doesn't matter what you've got, or what they can't comprehend. Those things don't win wars. You wanna know what does?"

I didn't, really. But I remained silent, waiting for him to tell me anyway.

"War isn't won by machines or by geniuses," he continued, his voice barely above a murmur now, as though his words weren't intended for me, but for himself. "It's won by who can keep fightin' the longest."

I glanced at him, his face cast in shadow, obscuring the usually sharp lines of his expression. For a fleeting moment, the overwhelming cynicism in his voice stung. It was... raw. And it cut through whatever thin layer of hope I'd still been clutching like a brittle shield.

"But haven't we survived impossible odds already?" I asked, desperate to grasp at something—anything—to pull us back from his pessimism. The weight of what we'd already faced surged through me, the memories of uncharted worlds, impossible creatures, ancient secrets. Despite everything, we had endured. "... maybe... maybe, we can survive this too."

Peters was quiet for a long stretch, the jungle swallowing up the silence between us.

Finally, he turned to face me fully, his broad frame casting a dense shadow, almost blotting out the faint light of the jungle's bioluminescent flora. His features were half-hidden in the darkness, yet there was no mistaking the steel in his eyes. "Listen—no matter what happens out there, no matter how it plays out—the men who survive this kinda thing..." His voice was softer now, rougher somehow. "... they leave parts of themselves behind."

The words sank into me, heavy and crushing. I didn't know if they were meant to offer comfort or a warning. Probably both. But deep down, I knew the truth of them. I looked down at my hands, at the dirt embedded under my nails, at the cuts and scrapes and stains—the rawness of palms rubbed raw from handling gear I'd never been skilled at using. Almost unrecognizable now. I had already changed in ways so profound, so irreversibly. And if we made it past this… if we stood at the end of it all, who would I be then?

The weight of the unknown loomed large and unspeakable.

A low howl echoed far off in the jungle, dragging us both out of our thoughts, breaking whatever delicate moment had passed between us. Somewhere, amidst the deep shadows and twisted branches, something stirred—an ancient creature, perhaps, or something worse. Peters was the first to react, tensing beside me, an almost imperceptible change in posture, his mission-driven focus back in place. I followed suit, my own heartbeat quickening once more, my senses straining in the quiet. The heaviness in the air grew thicker, less like anticipation now, and more like the oppressive weight that heralded an incoming storm. Peters scanned the darkness before us, every muscle taught.

It was time.

Without a word, we turned back toward the village, toward the warm glow of the crystalline walls. Their light no longer comforted me. Instead, it only seemed to reflect the stark reality of everything awaiting us at dawn. The battle, the bloodshed—it loomed just ahead, like a wall of violence ready to topple over us all.

We walked in silence, side by side now, the tension between us quiet but palpable. It felt oddly intimate—an understanding formed between two very different men, bound not by anything native to our personalities, but by what we'd had to become. The jungle around us hummed with life, but to me, it suddenly felt strangely far away, like I was walking through a memory instead of a place. The village gates loomed before us before I realized how far we had walked. The guards, Náiren sentinels, were already in position—silent and vigilant. They offered us only the faintest nods as we passed through.

Peters stopped just before we crossed the threshold and turned to meet my gaze once again. For a moment, he hesitated. "You're a good man, Pym," he muttered, his eyes still hard but softer than I had seen them before. "Don't get lost in the booze when this is over."

And, without waiting for a response, he disappeared into the ranks of warriors preparing for war.

17

The Battle Begins

The wind howled through the narrow jungle paths, carrying with it a taste of cold, metallic air. It was as if the very breath of war was winding its way toward us, slipping through the dense foliage and wrapping icy tendrils around my neck. I shifted my weight, crouched low beneath the sprawling roots of an ancient tree, my breath coming in shallow, uneven bursts. Beside me, Peters stood like a sentinel—rigid, unmoving, his eyes locked on the distant Nazi base. The dim glow of twilight silhouetted the massive drilling machines. Enormous, skeletal, their metallic arms stretched heavenward like giants frozen in time, waiting for the moment to awaken and tear the earth apart.

The tension was pronounced, hanging in the air like a thick fog. It prickled my skin, pulling the cool sweat from my pores down in sticky trails along the collar of my shirt. My heart thumped wildly, a steady drumbeat against my ribcage, each pulse answering the quiet crackle of latent energy that flickered through the shield mechanism cradled in my hands. My fingers fumbled with the smooth control interface, checking and rechecking the damn thing even though I had already gone through the motions multiple times. Beneath my fingertips, the surface was warm, almost alive, humming in delicate syncopation with the pulse of the jungle around me.

I glanced up. Just ahead of us, a group of Náiren warriors—faces pale against the backdrop of gathering night—moved soundlessly through the undergrowth. Their silver hair glinted under the thin beams of moonlight, their movements impossibly light, as if they barely disturbed the ground beneath their feet. They led the way with an eerie grace, navigating through the twisted branches and low-hanging vines with a precision I could only admire in silence.

Peters lifted his hand in a crisp gesture, two fingers slicing the air. It was the signal. My breath caught in my throat, every muscle tightening reflexively. The Náiren archers—their tall, lithe forms momentarily disappearing into the thick underbrush—shifted forward in perfect unison like shadows stepping through the veil of twilight. Their bows were drawn, each archer nocking an arrow glowing faintly with an otherworldly pulsing energy. I saw their hands tremble faintly, but only faintly. They were unaccustomed to this, but they were ready. We were all ready.

The soft click of radio static caught our ears. I held my breath. Peters froze like a spring wound tight, every sinew in his body taut with anticipation. A German guard ambled out from one of the outposts to the southeast, his flashlight flicking back and forth lazily as he neared the edge of the base's perimeter. We stayed rooted, hidden in the shadows, watching him—every fiber of me screaming for him to stay oblivious, to keep moving.

The seconds hung in a cruel, unbearable limbo. The battle teetered on the edge of a knife. And then…

The guard turned, the beam of his flashlight sweeping the opposite direction.

Peters gritted his teeth and snapped his fingers in a quick, decisive motion. His grit held the pressure of a dam waiting to burst. The time for subtlety was gone.

The hiss of arrows sliced through the jungle air, their luminous tips streaking toward the outposts like falling stars, radiant and deadly. They struck with unerring precision, exploding in bursts of brilliant light that cascaded across the landscape. The southeast perimeter of the Nazi base erupted in chaos. Guard towers flared as white-hot sparks rained down in magnificent arcs, lighting the jungle with an ethereal glow. One of the guards barely had time to scream before an arrow embedded itself into his chest, his silhouette reduced to little more than drifting smoke as the energy from the weapon consumed him.

The moment of calm shattered instantly. Shouts of alarm echoed across the base, guttural cries carrying through the clatter of boots as Nazi soldiers darted from their sleepy watch posts. The metallic clang of machinery stirred to life, gears grinding as the once-idle drills groaned against their restraints. It was as though all of creation had been on pause for a single breath, and now the universe had snapped back into frantic motion.

"Hit 'em now!" Peters roared, his voice sharp, cracking like a whip over the rising clamor. His hand shot out, making an insistent motion toward me, his eyes locking onto mine with that familiar, unyielding intensity. "Go!"

There was no hesitation. I slammed my fist down onto the small, shimmering panel strapped to my arm. The energy shield flared to life, radiant and protective, casting a warm, golden glow across my chest. I barely had time to steady myself before I charged forward, diving headlong toward the fray. Around me, the air filled with the rattle of gunfire—the harsh, guttural staccato of submachine guns spitting bursts of fire into the darkness.

The Nazis were frantic, their initial shots wide and clumsy, scattered into the humid night air. Bullets tore through the trees, stripping the jungle floor of its verdant undergrowth as the soldiers struggled to compose themselves amidst the chaos detonating across their encampment. But they were gaining momentum, their fire increasing in accuracy with every heartbeat, the sharp clang of steel and concrete ringing out as the guards scrambled into defensive positions.

I pressed forward, my legs burning as I charged toward the front lines, the shield gleaming with bright intensity as bullets ricocheted off its surface. I could feel the heat of them, each impact sending ripples of energy up my arm, but the shield withstood every strike. Peters had drilled into my head exactly what we needed to focus on—keep moving, keep advancing, don't flinch. I didn't dare let my mind dwell on possibilities: the errant bullet, the misstep, the sudden jolt of failure. There was only motion.

At the front, Peters stood like an unstoppable force, barking orders to the Náiren archers who remained cool as ice even in the thick of their first real battle. Their energy-charged arrows found critical weak spots with pinpoint accuracy. I watched as a volley of arrows tore through a line of gas tanks left exposed near supply tents. The explosion bathed the clearing with orange light, sending a shockwave through the air that vibrated in my core. The blast peeled away part of the perimeter wall, leaving jagged, twisted metal silhouetted against the firelight. Another arrow struck a nearby ammunition cache, and the tower behind it collapsed in a shower of flame and debris, its frame crumbling into the ground with the sound of screeching metal.

Another explosion sent tremors through the base. I turned just in time to see one of the lead Náiren warriors raise a shimmering staff high over their head. The ground shook as the warrior slammed the staff down, a wave of energy exploding outward in a brilliant flare of blue light. The barrier it created rippled, forming a crackling, translucent bubble that shimmered between the warriors and the advancing German soldiers. Bullets pelted the barrier in rapid bursts, but each one was deflected harmlessly, ricocheting off into the distance.

I could hardly believe it. The lead warrior moved fluidly within the barrier, twisting and bending in ways that seemed almost alien—every motion understated, deliberate. Their staff crackled with energy, every turn of their wrist commanding another fragment of the shield's power, the graceful deflections weaving a protection that seemed alive, sentient, almost as if the warrior was communing directly with the energy that now surrounded them. Their body glowed faintly in the dim light, the fading moon above casting their figure in ghostly silhouette.

Then—an ominous rumble. This one felt different. It wasn't the sudden jolt of machines turning on, nor the quake of an errant explosion. This tremble was a deep, guttural resonance—starting low, barely perceivable, but growing, building from somewhere deep within the earth.

At first, I thought it was just the drilling again, crushing deeper and deeper into the planet's core. But no—it wasn't the machine. This was...something else.

Then I felt it.

The growl—a low, primal sound—vibrating up through the soles of my boots.

Before I could process what it meant, the night erupted into chaos once more. From behind the far barricades, a rumbling roar cut through the smoke and fire, a noise so deafening that it pushed the gunfire into the background. My gut twisted. Something massive was moving—more than one thing, bodies so large that their sheer weight caused the ground to shake beneath them. I blinked, heart racing, and peered through the smoke.

And then I saw the hulking shadows emerge.

They lumbered into view—massive, scaled forms that looked like something pulled straight from nightmares. Dinosaurs— not the creatures of my books or illustrations, but something far more feral, primal. They were hybrids, monstrous fusions of reptilian behemoths, their forms strapped with leather harnesses and thick steel reinforcements. Their eyes glinted ominously, reflecting the cold white moonlight in the midst of the chaos.

My breath hitched. I couldn't move, couldn't think.

There were no legends that could have prepared me for this.

The leader of the creatures—a gargantuan beast with a neck as thick as a tree trunk, its arms stretched wide and tipped in razor-sharp claws—tore through the jungle brush. Nazi handlers, perched on a platform fastened to the beast's back, brandished long spears crackling with electricity. The handlers stabbed their weapons toward the battlefield, sending high-pitched signals into the air, controlling the roaring creature like some sinister conductor leading an orchestra of destruction.

"They're using them as battering rams…" I muttered, half to myself, half to the unbearable noise around me. The realization hit with cold finality. The Nazis had turned them into living weapons.

Peters snarled next to me, slashing with brutal precision at a German officer who tried to blindside him. "Keep those prehistoric bastards away from the walls!" he bellowed, barely sparing a glance before hurling his attacker to the ground. He turned to face me, his expression fierce. "They're using command signals—take out the handlers!"

Above us, the roar of the approaching beast grew louder. I flinched as its massive frame barreled forward, claws tearing deep into the earth. I barely had time to lift my shield before a massive chunk of crystalline barricade was hurled into the air, sent flying by the beast's charge. The debris struck my shield with thunderous force, nearly sending me skidding backward into the dirt.

"We have to stop them!" I shouted, scrambling to my feet as the creature rampaged closer. The battlefield was falling into disarray, our barricades crumbling under the constant onslaught of fire, claws, and chaos. The technicolor brilliance of the jungle gave way to the cold glow of deadly efficiency, the fires spreading faster than I could comprehend.

Peters had already moved, diving through the fray. His form, half-shrouded in the firelight, pressed toward the center of the battle zone—his target clear. I watched in awe as he cut through German soldiers like a man possessed, each strike measured and deadly, his focus narrowed with a clarity that seemed inhuman. He was heading toward the handlers. If he could take them out, we might have a chance to turn the tide.

Yet amidst the roar of dinosaurs, crackling blasts of energy, and the gnashing of steel against earth—I could feel the ground trembling once again. This battle was far from finished.

The mechanical drone of the drills pulsated louder, filling the night air with an almost palpable thrum. It was like a rhythmic hammer, beating relentlessly into the earth—a sound that reverberated through the ground, up through my feet, into my marrow. Every second that passed, I imagined the tremors spreading deeper into the planet's crust, forcing their way into the very bones of this hidden world, like a malignancy eating through vital organs.

I crouched low, gasping for breath, my body hunched behind a half-collapsed barricade of twisted metal and shrapnel. My muscles screamed for rest, but I couldn't give in to the exhaustion clinging to my limbs. I forced myself to look out over the wreckage, my eyes following the grotesque silhouette of the drilling machine stabbing deeper into the ground—a giant metallic locust gnawing at the earth's core. Huge mechanical arms twisted and groaned as they stretched downward, driving their sharpened drills further and further into the shattered crust. Sparks erupted in violent showers at irregular intervals, spraying across the compound and lighting up the haze of smoke that swallowed the jungle.

Each spark was a promise—no, a warning—of the devastation that awaited us if the Nazis succeeded.

I gulped in burning air, filled with the acrid stench of oil, as Peter's voice sliced through the tumult. "Pym!" His bellow was garbled, nearly lost amid the clanging of machinery and sporadic bursts of gunfire. "Pym! Get back!"

Before I could even register his words, a harsh whirring noise gripped the sky, like gears catching in some massive wheel—a foreign, unnatural noise that sent an electric shudder down my spine. I winced instinctively, looking up, searching the fractured skies above the battlefield for its source.

And then I saw them.

Metallic discs, shimmering under the pallor of the wounded moon, hovered soundlessly over the compound. Four... No. Five of them. Each gleamed like a blade, lethal and flawless, hanging ominously in the smoke-choked air. They drifted just out of reach, casting down their eerie, razor-thin beams of energy—a perversion of light that glanced off the cave walls and flickered across the battlefield like the wandering beams of searching eyes.

Instinctively, my stomach lurched. Flying machines. Airborne discs, perfectly circular and alien in design, floated over us with chilling precision. The thought hit me like a hammer blow: The Nazis had fused their barbarism with Náiren technology. They had taken the ancient, untouched mechanisms that preserved this world—and twisted them into something unspeakably grotesque.

It was abominable.

There was no pause. As if the air itself commanded them, the metallic saucers tilted forward—and fired.

Blinding yellow beams lanced out across the compound, splitting the night wide open. Each shot hissed through the air, searing, deadly arcs carving through trees and barricades with terrifying speed and efficiency. Defenses, carefully erected just hours ago, exploded into rubble and debris, upended in the blink of an eye. A spray of energy cut through a row of Náiren archers, the glow of their luminescent arrows briefly visible before they were vaporized—reduced to nothing more than smoke.

An upturned tree cracked with a thunderous groan and collapsed beside me, nearly crushing my legs. I scrambled backward, barely keeping my balance as another round of energy blasts tore through the foliage. The tides… they were shifting fast.

Peters, already a blur of motion, yelled something incomprehensible, diving behind a thick stone wall just as one of the flying discs let out a high-pitched whine. It swiveled on its axis, releasing a concentrated blast of molten energy that scythed through the battlefield. The beam hissed, glowing with a terrifying intensity, and as it passed, trees turned to ash and soldiers… soldiers were reduced to smoldering nothingness, their bodies collapsing mid-run, like burning silhouettes before disintegrating into the earth.

A scream caught in my throat, the breath freezing inside my chest as panic clawed up my spine. I stumbled backward, tripping over debris, and crashed bodily against a mound of overturned supplies, my head spinning. I could barely think—barely feel anything but the pounding terror thundering in my ears. All around me, the earth burned, rippling under the onslaught of inescapable energy beams, and in that moment, I knew…

We were losing.

I had no right to feel disbelief. Hadn't Peters warned me? Hadn't he looked me in the eye, told me war wasn't about things you could predict? About things you could understand? But some part of me had always held on… some laughable, distant strand of hope that reason might still win the day.

But there was no reason here.

Only destruction.

Falling stars were what those damned saucers looked like—fire raining down in shimmering arcs, devastating everything in their reach. I turned to Peters, choking back the screams that rattled at the walls of my chest. "We have to get to the core!" I shouted, the words a mangled gasp. "They're getting too close! If they—if they reach the core—"

There was no time to say the rest. Peters had already moved. He lunged forward, ducking through fire as cables and wires snapped, showering debris across the battlefield. The monstrous dinosaurs—harnessed and corralled just moments ago—now reared back into the fray. One of the creatures flung its massive head sideways, barreling through what was left of the barricades, the last defenses crumbling under the monstrous blows.

Peters spun, evading a direct blast from one of the discs, his eyes widening with grim understanding as we hit the tipping point. There was no pulling away from this blaze. We had to end it, here and now, or everything would be lost.

A blast of crackling energy split through the chaos—this time from the Nazi forces. I turned instinctively, my stomach dropping as I saw one of the lead handlers, crouched near the core machine, holding a strange, handheld device. His body wracked with the pulses of energy he channeled. He'd aimed it straight into the drill's core-tapping structure.

The bluish-white arc of energy erupted from his device, skating across the metallic arms of the colossal drill, wrapping the core in an unnatural, shimmering light that hissed and buzzed with a menacing fury.

"They're overcharging it!" Peters roared, his voice clear despite the chaos. His body moved instinctively, positioning himself to avoid the spew of molten fire cascading in all directions. The core was going to blow—if we didn't stop it, now.

I swallowed hard, bile rising unbidden to the back of my throat. The horror of the situation finally sunk in, settling in the pit of my stomach like lead. They were trying to overflow the energy output—to force the core to rupture, to unleash uncontrolled amounts of power so great that not only the base, but the entire hidden world, would collapse.

"We need—" I gasped, staggering forward, my legs barely obeying my mind's commands. "We need to disarm it! We have to turn it off!"

My words ripped through the din of everything around me, aimed squarely at Peters, but the solution was nowhere. My feet carried me, stumbling and half-falling across the uneven ground, my arms throwing open debris with the desperate hope that something—anything—would help disarm the death we had dived headlong into.

The ground gave way beneath me again as the drill began to spin faster, wider, shaking the entire compound with sharp, metallic screeches. I pressed further into what remained of the scattered defenses, my mind racing, every thought a chaotic scramble between fragmented possibilities and outright terror.

At last—there it was. The controls.

An exposed panel lay just ahead, wires jutting out, crackling with static arcs. It appeared to be some sort of control panel—covered in strange buttons and levers, positioned at the heart of the mechanism. My breath hitched, and I pushed myself toward it, ducking past streaks of fire and dodging chunks of debris.

My hands moved before my mind could.

The wires buzzed beneath my fingers—snarling, alive, dangerous. But I didn't care. I wrestled them into place, my hands trembling as I fought to shut down the core. The faint, sickening hum of energy traveled up my arm, but I barely registered it. Sparks exploded beside me, lighting the dark sky with burning flashes, but my mind was somewhere else—focused on this single task.

It had to work.

I couldn't breathe.

One wrong move would destroy us all.

Sparks shot around me—the drill screeched again—its engines wailing louder—louder—

18

Turning the Tide

Peters and I crouched behind the warped metal of a destroyed barricade, our breath ragged and mingling with the thick, acrid air. The battle above us raged on, a cacophony of distant screams, the rattle of gunfire, and the constant, pulsating hum of drilling machines. It was a hellscape, absolute chaos, and worst of all, it was clear we were losing. The graceful tactics of the Náiren, the elegance of their precision, were no match for the brute, unfeeling force of the Nazi war machine.

For every strategic assault we managed to launch, the Nazis countered with overwhelming force. And the air—the very air we breathed—was heavy with the scent of burning foliage and toxic fumes, a thick cloud settling over everything.

"We can't win like this," I gasped, more to myself than to Peters. Sweat trickled down my neck, and my heart slammed against my chest as the reality of our situation set in. "They're getting closer to the core; if this keeps going…"

Peters was quiet, his face locked in that unreadable mask of determination he wore whenever things went completely sideways. His eyes were on the horizon, on the soaring drones shooting down brilliant beams of plasma, cutting through barricades, through men, through everything we'd built. All that remained between us and oblivion was the hope that somehow, someway, we could shut down the core-tapping machine before it was too late.

He didn't even look at me when he finally spoke. "We're going in."

I swallowed hard, my pulse quickening. "What?"

"We can't keep holding the lines. It's already collapsing," he said, his already gravelly voice rougher than usual. "If we don't stop that drill, there'll be nothing left to defend."

I stared at him for a moment, the weight of his words sinking in. He was right, of course. He always was when it came to things like this. There was no time to quibble or doubt. The machine was drilling closer to the Earth's core every second, and once it reached critical depth—the thought alone made my stomach turn.

I nodded, my throat constricting tightly with fear, and Peters turned on his heel, already moving silently toward the collapsed remains of one of the jungle's natural outcroppings. There was a tunnel—one we'd discovered earlier during one of our failed reconnaissance missions—leading directly into the heart of the Nazi base… and into the belly of the infernal machine.

✱✱✱

The air was oppressive in every way imaginable. It clung to us, thick with the iron tang of metal, sweat, and fear, and filled that small alcove beneath the Nazi base. Each breath was like dragging fire into my lungs—short, sharp bursts that stung and never really satisfied. I crouched low, my back pressed hard against the cold stone wall as the rhythmic thrumming of the core-tapping machine vibrated up from deep below, rattling my teeth with every pulse. Overhead, muffled shouts echoed down the tunnel system—a dissonant chorus of voices barking orders and the dull, bone-shaking explosions rippling across the battlefield. Somewhere up there, the war still raged on without us, but here in the dark, time seemed to move differently, expanding and collapsing on itself with every breath held and every breath released.

Beside me, Peters crouched with deadly focus, his jaw set in lines so tight they seemed carved from stone. He shot a glance at me, his eyes narrowing to slits just visible under the rim of his helmet, and then jerked his chin toward the small hatch a few feet ahead of us. Shadows clung thick around it, but I could make out enough—steel bars cast in harsh, angular lines against the dim glow of hanging wires swaying gently overhead. Peters' fingers tapped twice against the barrel of his rifle in a deliberate rhythm I'd come to recognize as the signal that it was go time. His body was coiled tightly with raw energy, ready to spring, always sharp and poised for action.

I, however, felt a tremor in my hands I couldn't fully control. Whether it was the fear or the pressing weight of seconds ticking away, it didn't matter. The small spaces between each of my pulses closed tighter, and the more I tried to will them apart, the more suffocating they became. Each inhalation was shallow, rattling deep within my ribcage like a trapped bird thrashing against the bars of its cage. Above us, the Nazi machine continued to hum—relentless, all-consuming.

Dark splotches of burnt oil and the metallic scrape of machinery accompanied the faint flickering of exposed wiring that snaked down the tunnel walls, casting weak, sterile light over our faces. Every now and then, a spasm of sparks jumped from a loose wire, briefly illuminating the alcove in a flash of sickly yellow. In those moments, I could see Peters' grim expression more clearly—darker than the shadows gathering around him. His unspoken message weighed heavy between us: move now or lose everything.

A dozen thoughts flitted through my head—possibilities, contingencies... failures. I shook them off. A glance toward Peters told me all I needed to know. His silence, his steady gaze—it was enough. We do this, or it's over. We hit that hatch, and we don't look back.

A small wave of static crackled from above, followed by the faint thundering echoes of footsteps rushing past our position. I winced, gritting my teeth to fight against the wild urge to spring up and run. The footsteps grew louder, then abruptly stopped. Silence. Then more footsteps, more Nazis—engineers or soldiers, it didn't matter anymore. Their guttural voices, sharp and rushed, cut through the stillness as they barked hurried orders, their boots scuffing over dirt and rubble. We exchanged a glance again, but this time it wasn't question or doubt. Just grim resignation. Time—our enemy, pressed with cruel indifference against the steel walls around us.

Peters moved first.

His hand reached forward deliberately, gripping the tunnel grate hovering just above the ground. With a slow, deliberate motion, he wrenched it open. The metal creaked loudly, too loudly, as if even the tunnel itself was working against us. My breath hitched. Every sound felt like a signal, like a beacon drawing attention with its awful vibration, its screech that echoed unforgivingly in the narrow passage. But Peters didn't flinch—he slipped into the opening with his usual, predatory elegance, vanishing before I even had a chance to wince at the noise.

I followed quickly, taking only a half-second to glance behind us. Shadows spilled into the space we'd left behind as I pulled the rusty grate half-shut, tentatively easing it into place. The tunnel beyond was nothing but a gaping maw of darkness. There was no room for trust—just instincts and an ever-present awareness that the tide of war could crash down, swallowing us whole. The core machine's relentless hum vibrated through the walls, pressing into my skull with a weight that made my head feel like it might explode if I thought too deeply.

As we moved through the tunnel, it began to shift—each step pushing us further from the natural, earthen walls of the outer caverns and deeper into the cold, mechanical heart of the Nazi base. The transformation was not subtle. The walls morphed from rough-hewn stone and dirt to jagged, artificial metal, each surface slick with a strange sheen that seemed unnatural against the cave's damp breaths. A shudder ran through me. Veins of synthetic material stretched up along the ceiling and floor, crisscrossing wherever they pleased, pulsing faintly with sickly green light—like the base had decided to grow its own mutations in the form of iron and wire. It felt alive.

It was hideous.

My stomach twisted in knots. The closer we got, the more grotesque it all seemed. This—this was what they were doing with the core? Twisting something as magnificent as the heart of a world into a perverse tool of industrial carnage. I could hardly bear the sight one more second. Peters led the way, pushing forward through the narrowing corridor, his face a mask of grim determination.

And as we descended further, the tunnel shrank. At first it was barely noticeable—a shift here, an errant pressure there—but by the time we'd walked another fifty feet, the passage had constricted so tightly that Peters had to crouch to press ahead. His broad shoulders scraped against the cold, unforgiving metal with each step, and I could hear the rasp of strained breath from his chest. But he pressed on. He always did. Every step was a testament to that strength—a predator closing on his prey.

I swallowed hard, trying to focus on keeping mind and body in sync. Don't think. Don't lose it. My mind raced—panic feeding upon itself, a violent spiral threatening to consume me from the inside out. I forced my legs to keep moving. **It's just a machine.** But my heart wasn't paying attention. The fear kept growing. With every step, I felt another part of myself slipping, as though the passage was shrinking not just physically, but metaphorically—binding me closer to an impossible choice I wasn't ready to make.

Then, a sound. A faint rush of footfalls behind us. I froze, my senses flaring. Far behind—the hurried step of more Nazi engineers, or perhaps soldiers—moving swiftly through the passages behind us. I couldn't see them yet, but it didn't matter. My veins turned to ice. Any second now, they'd be on us. The orders barked between them grew louder, clearer, and I heard the delicate clink of metal with each shuffle of supplies. If they found us—

"Stop," Peters hissed, his voice barely above a whisper, his hand pressing firmly to my chest. He flattened himself against the cold, jagged wall, his figure blending into the shadows streaked by taut wires snaking along the passage. Instinctively, I followed suit, pushing myself against the opposite wall, my entire body tense to the point of pain. My hand gripped my jacket so tightly that my knuckles turned white as my body merged with the cold steel, trying to make as little noise as possible.

The drill's incessant mechanical whine grew louder as we stood waiting, swallowing all other sounds. Above, the war pressed on, explosions and blaster fire fading into a distant echo, like a storm raging just beneath the surface. I squeezed my eyes shut for a brief moment and steadied my breath—so weak, so infinitesimally quieter than the roar in my chest. I meant nothing here. Just another man, waiting for the unknown.

Peters moved first. He always did. Like a black phantom, he shifted around the corner, sliding along the walls with silent, predatory grace. There it was—the next turn. The next crawl. The moment between decisions. He nodded once to me, so brief I could've imagined it. We were close now. Just a few more feet. Just a sealed hatch and what, maybe fifty feet of reinforced steel, between us and the machine.

His voice met my ears—hard and sharp—but barely above a whisper. "We bypass those patrols," he murmured, his words soft, calculated. "Then we hit the main control apparatus. Don't screw this up."

A small, humorless laugh almost escaped my lips, but I held back. **Don't screw this up.** As if I hadn't been telling myself that since the moment the battle started—that somehow, I would find the answers, ensure we would survive and—the crawl wasn't over.

We reached the hatch, our breath coming in shallow gasps now, but still controlled. I watched—entranced and horrified—as Peters knelt down by the sealed door and, with the deft precision of a seasoned hand, pried it open just enough to peer through. The mechanical hum of the core was strong on the other side. I could feel it vibrating in my knees as I crouched, this immense cosmic force lurking inches below us.

I felt like an ant crawling over the back of a sleeping giant.

This was it.

One foot ahead. No turning back.

Peters glanced at me once, his face grim but resolute, and nodded.

We slipped through the door, side by side—silent, hopeful, doomed—moving step by step closer to the heart of oblivion.

***

The second we stepped into the chamber, the air shifted. It was different—heavier. As though the weight of everything—the war, the machine, the tension—was woven into the space itself. Each breath I took felt denser, thick with the unspoken menace that hung in the room like a thick fog, clinging to my skin, to my lungs. The chamber was vast, a near-perfect circle with walls that hummed faintly as if alive, tinged with the eerie glow of panels dripping with unfamiliar symbols and glyphs.

Directly in the center of it all, suspended between interlocking metal arms, was the core-tapping machine.

It hovered there like some twisted version of a beating heart, its contours slick and smooth, glowing faintly beneath the sharp steel scaffolding caging it. Blues and reds danced across its surface, pulsing weakly in faint rhythms, almost as if it were breathing, as if it lived. But despite its fragile appearance, there was nothing weak about it. The energy radiating from that machine was immense, unfathomable— the kind of power that didn't care where it came from, only that it could be wielded. It made the hair on the back of my neck stand on end and buzzed up through the soles of my boots, the vibration filling every nerve.

I couldn't move for a moment, just stood there, staring. My breath hitched slightly, my thoughts crashing into each other in panicked waves. This was it. *This* was what the Nazis had been after all along—the key to untapping unlimited energy from the Earth, harnessing the very core of our planet for their own twisted ends. The culmination of an entire world's history wrapped into a single, awful device.

"Damn," Peters breathed softly beside me. It wasn't often I heard awe in his voice, but there it was—tinged with a discomfort that matched my own. His eyes locked onto the machine, tracing the arcs of energy as they coiled and unwound across its structure, brilliant and terrifying. He seemed transfixed for a moment, watching how those electric tendrils flickered like serpents, each twist sending ripples of raw heat into the air.

I tore my gaze away from him, trying to force down the chill crawling up my spine, the dread that thickened and hardened in my stomach. This was the tipping point. I knew it in every fiber of my being, even if I wasn't ready to face it. If we didn't move quickly—if we didn't do what we came here to do—then we'd lose everything. But even acknowledging that, the idea of destroying this machine, of dismantling something so monumental, it…

It turned my stomach.

Every step forward screamed at me, rebelled against the violence of it. The control stick in my pack pressed against me like a constant reminder, but I damn near wanted to fling it away, to leave this place untouched. This machine—it could've changed the world. No, *it would've* changed it. It *was* changing it. How many lifetimes of knowledge were embedded in those mechanisms? How many secrets of the Earth's inner workings—things we'd never even dreamed were possible—would now be lost forever because we were about to shut it all down? The sheer potential brimming inside that device… it gnawed at me.

But there was no other way.

"We need to move," I whispered. My voice felt too small, trembling against the overwhelming reality of what we were about to do. Peters didn't wait for me to continue. He never did.

He was always the first to push forward when I hesitated,

every step forward a testament to his readiness to protect, to fight—to burn down whatever stood in our way if it meant survival. He wasn't interested in the machine's potential. The only thing Peters saw was a threat. And now, he circled the perimeter, assessing the mechanical behemoth with methodical precision, studying it like a chessboard where each wire, each panel, was another piece waiting to be exploited.

His movements were quick and quiet, but they carried an urgency I couldn't ignore. I followed stiffly, my eyes flicking over the alien glyphs and symbols projected into the air around us, columns of data that must have meant something—something extraordinary. But all I could feel was a gnawing sense of guilt tightening around my chest like a vise. This machine could have been… should have been so much more.

It was wrong. Wrong to just end it like this, to tear apart something so brilliant. Knowledge like this didn't come around often, and yet here we were preparing to destroy it. It felt like a betrayal—not of myself, but of something far deeper. Of everything I had ever believed in.

I bit back the nausea. If we lost this battle, there'd be no future left for knowledge—no world left to study. Peters' logic, as brutal as it was, held more truth than I was willing to admit. So, with a final, shaky breath, I followed him toward the core-tapping control apparatus.

The massive structure hummed softly, its energy discharges

mingling with the low thrum of the machine at its center, crackling with ominous pulses and humming with what felt like anticipation. I flinched as a particularly bright flash of light flared before my eyes, forcing me to squint and shield my face. I blinked twice to clear my vision and saw... that moment we'd been waiting for—our window. It was brief, just enough.

"Now," Peters ordered, his voice cutting through the static in my head as he moved forward. No hesitation. He was a blur, weaving between the spitting wires and connections as he reached for the sabotage device in his pocket—a small, iridescent orb given to him by the Náiren before we descended into the tunnels. Though he had no knowledge of the technology itself, they had shown him how to activate it. Inscribed with their ancient glyphs, the device hummed faintly in his hand, its internal mechanisms far beyond our understanding but designed for a single, clear purpose: to overload and neutralize energy systems. It was so small— almost absurdly simple compared to the sprawling web of energy that surrounded us. He bent low, his wide figure disappearing into the mass of conduits and columns. The disruption device clicked into place at one of the primary junction points, where cables extended from the ceiling like the gnarled roots of some twisted tree, branching into the core's structure. The grotesque beauty of it all made me dizzy.

Peters barked, "Go for the controls!" and jerked his head toward the far side of the room. Instinct took over, and my legs sprang into motion even though my hands still shook under the weight of it all.

His usual grimace faded into raw determination. I could sense, even then, that there was no room left for hesitation. Stopping now wasn't an option. Thinking through the enormity of what we were doing only made it worse—there was no time to reflect, no time to measure what the cost would be. I ducked low, weaving through the mangled remains of wires and shattered stone as another brilliant flash of energy exploded from the machine. The air grew tense, as if the very walls could barely contain the energy gnashing its way across the room, twisting and writhing like the tendrils of some horrible beast.

Keep going. Not much farther now.

My feet skidded, nearly losing purchase on the slick ground beneath me. Shards of broken stone and molten fragments snapped underfoot, burning my boots. My breaths came hard and uneven, each inhale raspy and rough like drawing in smoke from a fire. The device—I knew it had to be somewhere near the heart of this wretched thing. My hands fumbled across the smooth surface of what looked like some kind of control point, a large slab covered in strange, pulsing lines. The surface was alien to me—the tools from a time far beyond my own understanding.

I pressed forward, nearly dizzy with the mounting tension. There—they'd sealed something here.

One last breath. One last flicker of doubt.

Then…

I shoved the disruptor into place.

A blast echoed deep inside the machine—a shrill hiss of static crawling up from the base of the core and shooting into every surface as if every wire, every conduit had screamed to life at once. My vision flashed white. Then—

A rumbling whine.

The air beneath my feet warped, trembling with the sharp, erratic pulse of the machine as it bucked violently against the walls. The very room seemed as if it would tear itself apart. Electricity sizzled, angry arcs of light spidering across the floor, glowing like veins drawn from molten silver. I stumbled back, choking on my breath as another wave of dizziness crashed over me.

It worked—Peters' device worked. God help us, it was working.

But for one agonizing second, as sparks rained around me, I doubted whether we'd make it out alive. The machine roared like a wounded animal, every ligament of its metallic body buckling, collapsing inward. Sparks exploded from the ceiling, jagged bolts of energy flailing without purpose. The air thrummed with the ugly sound of metal warping and wires burning, as strange conduits burst with energy, discharging in wild arcs under the intense pressure of the sabotage. The machine's pulse grew weaker, strained, and then…

Silence.

The power that had drained this world—had stabbed its way into the planet's core—shuddered, then screeched to a halt.

Everything went dark.

The glowing limbs of the core-tapper—those horrible, brilliant mechanisms—dimmed, shrinking into themselves until nothing remained but smoke and the twisted metal of failure. The Nazi base—once so alive with chaotic, methodical fire and noise—now sputtered, a dying ember.

I collapsed against the nearest wall, my body spent. My heart pounded inside my skull, the world turning in sickly circles beneath me. But it was done. And through the stillness, I felt it—the core beneath our feet breathed, relieved, for the first time since this nightmare began.

Slowly, Peters leaned against a pillar, his shoulders heavy with exhaustion and something deeper… something closer to grief than triumph.

"I—" I began, but Peters cut me off, his face hardened by the fight, his voice coarse.

"Doesn't matter," he rasped. "It's done." He pushed himself upright, his eyes already scanning the room for the next threat.

And then I heard it—the sound of boots. Heavy, deliberate. Footsteps, marching rapidly in the distance.

We weren't done.

19

The Nazis' Last Stand

The narrow passageway pressed in around us, the jagged walls vibrating with each tremor as explosions thudded in the distance. My lungs burned as I drew in sharp breaths, the high, thin air scraping against my throat like sandpaper. I could feel each pounding footfall reverberating in my chest, pressing down like the weight of the cavern itself. Peter's shadow moved ahead of me with terrifying speed, his silent determination manifest in every step.

Behind, the Náiren warriors followed, their footsteps as imperceptible as the shifting of shadows. They held their weapons close—their bows glowing faintly in the dim light of the passage—as the world around us shuddered. Those same explosions that once sounded distant were now closer, sharper, echoing against the cramped rock walls.

The further we ran, the hotter it grew.

The heat was insidious, creeping up gradually until it felt like I was running headlong into the mouth of a blasted furnace. Sweat lined my palms, but the rock seemed to absorb every drop of moisture, leaving the air arid, heavy with the oppressive scent of ozone and burning metal.

As we rounded a corner, I staggered, almost slipping on loose debris scattered across the tunnel floor. A low, unnatural glow began filtering through the cracks in the rock, casting flickering shadows against the walls. And then—I felt it.

The heat.

More searing now than before. It wasn't just the stale air or the remnants of broken lava tubes beneath the earth. It was radiating through the stone itself, a deep, suffocating heat that felt alive—growing thicker with each step.

Ahead, the passage widened slightly, and for the first time, I could see glimpses of the chamber that lay beyond—flickers of light, the erratic glow of something vast and terrifying flickering and charging the very air around it with raw energy. My stomach twisted. There was no mistaking it. We were close—the core, the heart of the Earth itself, was just ahead.

The ground shook again, harder this time, and I flinched as rubble crumbled from above, pelting down in fine dust and pebbles that grated against my skin. But there was no stopping now. I could see Peters silhouetted as he rounded the next corner, his broad shoulders blocking out the source of the light.

We burst from the tunnel into the core chamber.

My legs stuttered. The breath left my lungs in a rush. Nothing could have prepared me for the sight that unraveled before my eyes.

The cavern opened up before us on a scale that defied reason. It was a place born from myth—unfathomably vast, stretching upward toward a ceiling that vanished into shadow. And there, right at its center—suspended impossibly above the floor—was the Earth's core.

No... not quite a core—not in the way I had imagined. This wasn't the infernal incandescence of molten rock and fiery plasma that I had feared. Instead, a massive, pulsing sphere of raw energy hovered in midair, radiating vibrant, intoxicating light. It was alive with motion, churning waves of orange-red light rippling out like waves on a storm-tossed sea. Each pulse felt like a heartbeat, thrumming through the floor beneath our feet, deep and ethereal—ancient beyond reckoning.

At first, I could only stare at it. It was—it was beautiful. A scientific wonder wholly beyond anything I had dared to encounter. I blinked up at it in awe, the light washing over me, warming me, calling me toward it. It was like looking into the very soul of the Earth.

But as I stared at it, the awe began to twist, souring into something closer to terror. I could feel it, even from this distance. Energy. Unstable, raw, and endless. It was power beyond what anyone should have touched, let alone controlled. It wasn't meant to be tampered with.

Around it, I could see the twisted shape of the Nazi scaffolding—massive iron beams rammed into the rock and suspended over bottomless chasms—all forming a crude network, like black iron webs wrapping around some leviathan caught in their snare. Cables—thick black coils of rubber and steel—stretched from the scaffolds all the way to Nazi power converters stationed at the edges of the cavern. There, standing like metal beasts in waiting, machines rumbled and groaned as engineers scrambled around them, frantic, fueled by raw desperation as they tried to tap into the core's radiant energy.

Peters swallowed the scene in one glance, his sharp eyes sweeping across the room, cataloging everything—the soldiers guarding the perimeter, the engineers working feverishly at the central stations, their hands deep in intricate machinery, their movements frenetic, hurried. The sweat gleamed on their brows as they barked orders to each other, frantic to finish whatever twisted plan they'd set into motion.

I couldn't move. I couldn't even breathe. My brain warred with itself. Part of me recognized what had to be done— this infernal thing needed to be stopped before it tore the Earth apart, but the other part—God, the other part of me recoiled at the thought. This wasn't destruction—it was— was achievement. Science. Monumental. A discovery that hundreds of lifetimes could spend studying.

Peters nudged me—more like a shove—and growled under his breath. "Now's not the time, Pym. We're too late for doubt. They won't stop until this place is a smoldering crater. Think fast!"

The sharpness of his voice cut through the haze, snapping me back to reality just as the shrill clang of boots against metal rang through the chamber. On the opposite side, from beyond a high section of scaffolding, a new wave of soldiers poured into position, taking up defensive perches along railings and catwalks. The light from the core flickered over their slicked uniforms, their movements methodical and precise. Rifles lifted toward us, motions as orderly as clockwork.

The moment crystallized, sharp and final. This was it.

The Náiren warriors moved with professional elegance. Their bows slid from their backs as their free hands traced the curves of the luminous, vibrating arrows they held aloft. And then—smooth as liquid silver—those arrows flew. Shimmering projectiles shot out from beneath the cover of rock, their translucent shafts sparking as they collided with dripping steel walls. Each arrow burst with luminous energy, rupturing the metal barricades the Germans had erected.

Screams rang out as the arrows hit their marks—Nazi soldiers thrown backward by the pure force of impact, their forms struggling against the glowing sear of the energy. A group collapsed along the eastern platform, convulsing and curling into themselves, their weapons falling useless from their hands as their bodies smoldered.

Peters was already moving—cutting low through the debris-strewn passage, his eyes flitting between the towering machinery and the creeping lines of engineers working feverishly to reroute energy around the core. The tension in his movements was electric—almost animal—his every instinct tuned to survival. His twin blades flashed briefly under the core's glow, the serration glinting just once before he melted into the darkness.

I could barely keep track of him—could barely make sense of the chaos unraveling around me. Bullet sprays ricocheted off steel beams, tracing jagged metallic scars over the floor. Whatever arrogance the Nazis had begun with was being stripped away, replaced with raw desperation. And I knew why. They were running out of time. Just like us. They wouldn't—couldn't—back down. This was their final stand, the culmination of whatever dark fantasy they had concocted.

I flung myself behind a stanchion, gasping as stray bullets sang overhead. My hand clenched around the Náiren disruptor device strapped to my waist and I scrambled to reset the controls—a small, rectangular pad emblazoned with delicate, foreign symbols. My fingers worked through sheer habit, shaking so badly that at one point I nearly dropped it. The heat of the core was oppressive now—it came in waves, cascading across the room, bending the air and twisting it into a shimmering mirage of light. And somewhere, in the haze of that glow, I knew we couldn't stop.

On the platform ahead, the Nazi engineers toiled, utterly engrossed in their work. Their hands flew over the central control apparatus, ripping wires free, their faces bathed in the sickly yellow of blinking lights. One of them snarled something, and all at once, the core was suddenly bathed in an angry, orange light as power flowed directly into its thumping heart.

Behind them, perched slightly higher, two Nazi officers lurked. One shouted orders, his mouth twisted with ferocity. The other, quiet, stood with a calm, calculating demeanor. His eyes. Those cold, soulless eyes—locked on the core, focused, as though time barely registered. He knew what was coming.

Peters slinked closer, his eyes locked on the engineers with brutal intent. "They're rigging the core to blow," he snarled, his voice low but throbbing with urgency. His electrified blades sparked faintly in the dim light as he ducked beneath a swirl of bullets. "If we don't shut this down—everything's gone."

The entire cavern shuddered again, light spilling from above in dangerous waves. The core's thrumming pulse grew stronger, each burst a warning, rippling out with shivering energy. My chest tightened against the weight of it. It was unstable— so volatile I could feel it through the soles of my boots.

Everything was motion now—motion and heat and chaos— the world contracting inside this cursed cavern. My eyes locked on the core, thrashing between conflicting thoughts. Could I stop it? Or was this our end?

We were out of time.

The moment closed in around us as another terrifying sound rent through the chamber—a deep, otherworldly growl. Massive doors, their outlines previously hidden in shadow, began to close. Huge slabs of steel dropped like guillotine blades, sealing off our final means of escape. The sound echoed through the chamber like an executioner raising his axe.

"They're locking us inside," I gasped.

Peters' head jerked toward me, his face splitting into a tight grimace. "No more running, Pym." He gripped his blade tighter, his eyes glinting with fierce determination. "This is it."

Somewhere under the noise, under the roar of the pulsating core—I felt the Earth quaking beneath us.

The core chamber roared with a thunderous cacophony as raw energy crackled across the towering columns lining the perimeter, illuminating the hellish battlefield in bursts of blinding light. Heat radiated in waves from the core—a searing, almost sentient force that pressed against my skin, filling the air with the scent of ozone and burning oil. The cavern trembled with each pulse of energy, massive groans vibrating through the scaffolding as its fragile construction threatened to collapse at any moment.

Ahead of me, Peters moved like a beast set free—a whirlwind of violence and survival instinct, his figure an indistinct blur amidst the flashing fires and sparks. He ducked low and surged forward, his twin blades slicing cleanly through the chaos. Two Nazi guards never even had the chance to scream before their bodies hit the ground, their lifeless forms bathed in the flickering glow of collapsing machinery. Each step Peters took left a trail of ruin in his wake, his body driven not by strategy, but necessity. He was fighting for more than just victory—this was survival, pure and unflinching.

But we were running out of time. I could feel it in every nerve, every frantic beat of my heart. The core pulsed again, its radiance flaring violently, sending arcane bolts of energy searing through the chamber, scorching everything they touched. The mechanical arms of the core's rigging apparatus groaned in protest, buckling under the weight of the immense power they strained to contain.

I ducked instinctively behind a collapsed scaffolding, barely evading a crackling whip of electricity as it snapped across the open ground. "We've got to shut it down—now!" The words came out hoarse, torn from my throat by the effort of moving, fighting, and staying upright amidst the quakes of the rumbling floor.

From the heart of the Nazi line, the commander stood, his imposing form draped in the stark black of the Nazi elite, his face twisted in grim determination. Flanked by two heavily armed officers, he barked something in German, his voice drowned by the mayhem. He pointed toward the core, and his troops shifted, firing desperately, futilely, to protect the final fragile steps of their twisted plan.

I yanked the disruptor from my belt, feeling the gentle hum of its energy beneath my fingertips—a small comfort against the chaos surrounding me. The device thrummed with purpose, the strange energy from the Náiren technology giving me hope. Somewhere deep inside, I held onto the belief that it could stop this. That it had to.

My target was clear: a massive, elaborate control apparatus perched high at the far end of the chamber, where Nazi engineers scrambled with frantic desperation. Their hands flew over strange wheels, levers, and glowing panels covered in unfamiliar symbols. They frantically pulled at the handles and twisted devices, trying to quell the core's erratic pulses of energy, but the sheer urgency in their movements told me that even they struggled to keep the wild power at bay. They were driving it perilously close to a catastrophic collapse, the madness of their plan laid bare before us. But I knew, instinctively, I wouldn't make it across the open ground without cover. The space between me and the control apparatus was a deathtrap, crisscrossed with whipping metal cables and errant blasts of directed energy.

Then—without warning—the core surged again. The air itself seemed to ripple as the temperature within the chamber spiked sharply. The beams holding the drilling apparatus crackled as metallic veins of energy lit up the room in violent, jagged arcs. Cables snapped loose, writhing like serpents freed from their constraints, screeching through the air like whipping tendrils thirsty for destruction.

"Peters!" I yelled, diving to the side as one of the cables shattered the ground where I had been seconds before. The force of the energy surged through the floor, sending a wave of heat and static up my spine. I hit the ground hard, a painful jolt shooting through my limbs as debris scraped against my clothes and skin. Peters dove alongside me, narrowly avoiding another lethal lash of loose wiring as it crackled and hissed like a beast trying desperately to break its chain.

He groaned in frustration, pushing himself upright with a snarl. There was no retreating now. The commander stood before us, statuesque in his zealot's determination, barking commands at his remaining troops, even as molten metal from exploding machinery rained down around him. His face was pale, stretched taut with mad defiance, as though he'd sooner die in this chamber than see his twisted vision fail.

Peters wiped the blood from his jaw—whether his or some-one else's, I couldn't tell. "No more," he growled, rising to his feet in a singular fluid motion, turning toward the commander's position like a predator scenting weakness. Before I could say a word, he was moving again—charging forward like a force of nature—a hurricane of fists and fury. Two guards raised their weapons to fire but were too slow. Peters lunged, his blades carving a brutal path through the first soldier's chest, the second barely raising his rifle before he was brought down with a crushing elbow to the temple.

Somewhere behind us, a crackling explosion ripped through the air. I turned just in time to see one of the core's secondary nodes flare to life, spitting wild flashes of light. Sparks showered the chamber as two Nazi engineers were violently hurled backward across the floor, their twisted forms lying still, lifeless before they even hit the ground. The control apparatus overloaded in a brilliant flash of energy, debris and shards of metal raining down as the entire northern section of the chamber buckled under the strain.

"We've got to disarm it, now!" I screamed, my voice raw and desperate. Without thinking, I hurled the disruptor I had been holding toward the largest, most visibly active section of the machinery. It flew through the air, spinning wildly, before colliding with a tangle of cables and metal pulsing with energy. The device latched on with a magnetic clink, and for a brief moment, everything seemed to slow—time freezing as sparks flew from the control apparatus in bright, erratic bursts.

The core—God, the core—hesitated. The entire world around me seemed suspended in that breathless instant, the pulsing radiance flickering as though it were deciding whether to stabilize or detonate. I held my breath—watching, waiting—as everything around us teetered precariously between salvation and destruction.

Then, the light from the core dimmed—it flickered weakly, its once-blinding radiance closer now to the glow of a dying ember. I could feel my heart in my throat, the pulse of it thudding dully in time with the faint pulses of the core. Relief surged through me like a wave of cold, pure clarity.

But almost as quickly, that relief was shattered.

From the corner of my eye, I saw it—a sudden movement. I turned, eyes wide, to see the Nazi commander with a twisted grin plastered across his gaunt face. From his belt, he pulled a small, black device—bearing a likeness to a device of infernal design. It had a short metal rod sticking out, flashing ominously in the dim light.

A dead man's trigger.

If he couldn't have the core, no one would.

His thumb hovered over a red button on the black device, that sick smile still playing on his lips as if daring us to stop him.

Without hesitation, Peters launched himself forward, his body hurtling toward the commander like a hammer striking steel. They collided with a sickening thud, crashing into a mass of wires and machinery, sending pieces flying in all directions. They grappled violently, their bodies intertwined in a vicious struggle for control. Each blow from Peters landed with brutal force, but the commander fought back with crazed ferocity, his every counter filled with raw, burning madness.

Amidst their violent struggle, the core surged again, shaking the entire chamber. The glow flared wildly as it fought the chaotic energy surging through its labyrinthine structure, the once-sporadic pulses growing stronger with each second. It was going to explode. My mind raced, frantically searching for something—anything—that could still stop this madness.

I stumbled toward the unfamiliar set of controls, my hands fumbling over the assortment of levers and panels, desperate to find some way—any way—to sever the black device's connection to the core. The strange machinery before me was a mess of wires, glowing dials, and flickering lights, all completely alien to me. I had no idea what I was looking at, let alone how to disable it, but I couldn't stop. My heart hammered in my chest, urging me to act. I clawed at switches, pressing buttons that did nothing but ignite feeble sparks.

"Forget the control apparatus!" Peters shouted, his voice hoarse, strained. He was still wrestling over the black device, his arms locked around the commander in a deadly embrace. "Stop him!"

My heart leapt into my throat, adrenaline surging hot and thick in my veins. I leaped over the debris-strewn ground, sprinting toward them faster than I ever thought possible.

The commander's thumb bore down on the switch just as Peters twisted his body, locking both arms around his torso and yanking the madman backward. Their movement was fluid—terrifying—as Peters bodily threw the commander to the cold floor.

I reached down, desperation clawing at my chest, and snatched the black device from the commander's outstretched hand just before his fingers could curl around it again. Without thinking, I hurled it to the ground, stomping down hard, crushing it beneath my boot. The small device let out a broken whine before crumpling under my foot.

And then—

The core, almost as if responding to the destruction of the switch, pulsed one last time—then stilled. Its wild, erratic light dimmed to a simmering, soft glow, the deadly energy receding.

Silence fell.

For a moment, nothing moved. Nothing dared to move.

The tremors ceased. The air cooled. The tension that had gripped my chest for what felt like an eternity finally released.

Across the chamber, the remaining Nazi soldiers faltered, their eyes filled with sudden, dawning terror as the truth of their defeat washed over them. Several began to drop their weapons, the rifles clattering to the floor with muted thuds, their hands raised shakily above their heads.

The Náiren warriors, moving with disciplined grace, closed in swiftly. More arrows, crackling with energy, cut through the air, slamming into the few remaining stubborn Nazis who refused surrender. Those who weren't felled by the glowing bolts soon knelt in surrender, their forms still, broken, awaiting whatever judgment came next.

My hands shook violently. I stared at the central control apparatus, disbelieving, unable to fully process what had just happened. The core's energy levels were finally dropping, the inferno we had fought so desperately to contain ebbing into a steady, almost peaceful pulse.

Behind me, Peters stood over the unconscious body of the Nazi commander, his face bloodied but unbroken. He staggered slightly, his breath labored. But when our eyes met, all I saw was exhaustion—something deeper than physical. He gave me a single, slow nod.

The battle was over.

The glowing core now hovered peacefully at the center of the chamber, its once-vicious light calm for the first time. We had won.

And yet, as I stood there, breathing the heavy, stifling air, I found no sense of celebration, no joy in the victory. We were alive. But something—something was lost.

Peters turned away from the fallen Nazis, his voice hoarse, hollow. "Let's hope it's over."

The chamber fell into silence—a silence filled not with victory, but with the quiet weight of all we'd sacrificed.

20

The Aftermath

The core chamber finally fell into an uneasy silence. Thick clouds of smoke and debris swirled around us like malevolent ghosts over a battlefield littered with wreckage. Peters and I stood among the aftermath, our bodies trembling, still heaving to catch our breath as the last tremors from the great core's convulsions rolled across the floor. The oppressive heat was now muted but still clung to us like an invisible blanket, pressing against our burnt skin, demanding that we remember the searing power we had just faced down.

The Earth's core, once flaring with apocalyptic brilliance, now glowed faintly above us—a dwindling ember at the heart of a world that had nearly torn itself apart. The light it cast was gentle now, a rhythmic pulse far removed from the wrath that had threatened to consume everything in its grasp just moments ago.

All around us, Náiren warriors moved like shades as they

quietly, almost reverently, rounded up the remaining Nazi soldiers. Silent but efficient, there was something both comforting and eerie in their graceful movements. The Nazis, by contrast, were anything but composed. Some thrashed violently in their bonds, their faces curled in snarled sneers of defeat, their eyes uncertain yet burning with a fanaticism not easily extinguished. Others slumped against the cold walls, energy sapped from their bones as the hopeless realization of their failure set in. The sounds of their chains—formed from those luminous cords that seemed to hum with their own life—echoed eerily in the chamber. The scene was a bizarre juxtaposition of victory and despondency, life and death entwined once more in the struggle for dominance.

Peters wiped the sweat from his brow with a grimy hand, streaking blood and dirt across his already weathered face. He scanned the room with that vigilant gaze of his, sharp as a hawk's. Even in this moment of uneasy calm, he never let his guard down. His eyes darted from corner to corner, tracing every shadow that clung to the walls, every crevice that could hide an ambush or lingering threat. His broad shoulders tensed at each small sound—whether it was the sputtering of broken machinery or the faint rasp of voices echoing from the heavily injured Nazis still restrained by the Náiren.

"It's quiet," I remarked, my voice hoarse and shallow, though the observation felt absurd as soon as I'd spoken it.

Peters gave a curt nod but kept his eyes trained on the scene before him. "Too quiet." His words were taut—coiled like the tension still coursing through his muscles. Years of battle had trained him to expect the unexpected, to never trust the stillness that came after. I felt it too, though in a different way—a different fear. Everything here still felt foreign, as though the battle we'd just survived was only part of a larger, darker unknown waiting to reveal itself.

My heart still thudded in my chest, adrenaline tapering into shaky exhaustion. As I wiped the dust and sweat from my face, something caught my eye. Through the haze and smoke, my gaze snagged on the far end of the chamber, past the shredded scaffolding and the haphazard wreckage of cables and machinery. There, beneath a twisted metal column, was something subtle, easy to miss—a faint shimmer against the ashen rock surface. It wasn't like the reflective sheen of metal or the natural imperfections in the stone. This was deliberate. A seam. A boundary between surfaces that shouldn't have met naturally.

I squinted, leaning forward, my instincts prickling to life. The seam shimmered faintly under the dimmed light from the core, now pulsing in lazy rhythms. Its outlines glowed with soft, ethereal light, stark against the chaos surrounding it, a subtle invitation blended into the fabric of time.

I gestured wordlessly to Peters, pointing toward it with a hasty motion. "There," I said.

His gaze snapped to the location, his expression darkening for a second as he followed the line my finger traced. For a moment, I could see that curious flicker rise to the surface of his otherwise controlled demeanor, though it quickly gave way to the tense wariness he always assumed when danger could be lurking ahead.

We moved toward the far wall, careful in our steps as we picked through the debris, our boots crunching against stone and glass, every noise small but amplified by the otherwise oppressive quiet. The heat seemed to grow cooler as we neared the seam, the stifling air giving way to something slightly fresher—more untouched. Since our arrival, every part of this venture had reeked of human interference, but here… there was something older. Something…organic.

The seam wasn't part of the Nazi installation, that much was clear the closer we drew. It curved just too perfectly, too fluid as it cut across the rock's façade. Up close, I could see it was unlike any of the other thick, steel doors or hatches the Nazis had embedded into the wall. No cranks or locks. It almost seemed to flow out of the stone itself, an extension of the environment, as if the rock itself held a secret it had yet to reveal.

Peters raised a brow, darting a glance at me. "This isn't part of their operation." He gestured to the seam, his voice lower now. "Too precise. Too… concealed."

"Atlantean?" I whispered as my fingers hovered just above the faintly glowing line.

Peters didn't reply—his silence an unspoken confirmation. Neither of us needed words to acknowledge how oddly deliberate this appeared. And yet, even as I stared at it, I felt that thrill beginning to beat once again inside my chest. It was the same feeling that had driven me from one impossible discovery to the next throughout my life—a compulsion to move forward, to unravel the mysteries poised before me, no matter how dangerous the path.

Without thinking, I let my hand rest against the seam. The surface was cool, a welcome reprieve from the heat that lingered in the rest of the chamber. As my fingers glided over the surface, something hummed deep within—not with violence but with a quiet, rhythmic pulse, almost like a living thing. The wall beneath me gave a slow, groaning shift as if suddenly allowing itself to recognize my presence. I felt it slide inward, soft and near-magnetic in motion. It opened, smooth and deliberate, revealing a dark, narrow passageway behind.

I shot a glance at Peters, and he gave a stiff nod. His hand immediately rested on his sidearm, fingers curling around the hilt, though the tension in his brow suggested he wasn't feeling imminent danger—yet. "Be ready for anything," he warned. His voice was barely more than a whisper, but in the echoing stillness, it felt louder, heavier with its weight.

Without exchanging another word, we stepped into the narrow passage. The air was notably cooler, almost still, as though we had crossed some threshold out of time itself. The oppressive heat from the core now completely dissipated in this space, and the war outside the walls of this hidden chamber felt suddenly far away. Every sound—the soft brush of our clothes against the narrow rock walls, the steady rasp of our breathing—was muffled, almost as if the space had swallowed all interference, allowing nothing to disturb whatever was concealed ahead.

The farther we moved into the tunnel, the more certain I became that this discovery, this hidden chamber, had nothing to do with the Nazi operation. No, this place stretched back centuries—millennia, perhaps. Each step brought with it a deeper sense of reverence, a dawning realization of the significance of what we were approaching.

Finally, the passage opened—not into another cramped tunnel, but into a wide, breathless space of architectural splendor. I stumbled forward, my eyes widening as they adjusted to the sight laid before me.

We had entered a chamber, its size dwarfed by nowhere near that of the enormous core chamber, but there was something singular about the atmosphere here—more intimate, more profound. The walls were lined with intricately carved pillars that rose luminously from floor to ceiling. The space was bathed in soft, warm light, though its source seemed impossible to trace. And on those pillars—etched in with such precision they appeared almost alive—were markings, glyphs, and strange murals that screamed with a familiar presence: Atlantean.

My heart stuttered in my chest, then began to race as I took in the sheer majesty of what stretched out before us. Glyphs. Structures. Arches carefully aligned in geometric patterns I couldn't even comprehend fully in my state of awe.

Peters remained at the entrance, scanning with his usual cautious attention, his fingers resting lightly on his weapon still. Yet, even his watchful eyes softened ever so slightly as they took in the strange space. He could feel it too—that ancient calm, that hidden grandeur concealed in every delicate line carved into the perimeter. His guard remained up, but for a brief moment, even he couldn't tarry within his curiosity.

I could barely breathe. My eyes drifted to the far wall, where a table made of dark marble was laden with what appeared to be relics. Artifacts so old, so alien, yet pulsing with energy that immediately called to me. My hands trembled as I crossed to them in hesitant steps, each movement drawn by that inexplicable hunger for discovery. There, resting atop the marble, was an obelisk, carved with strange, flowing symbols and diagrams.

"Atlantean," I murmured, my voice reverent as my fingertips brushed softly over the surface. The faint pulse beneath the stone seemed to vibrate in response to my touch, alive with memory, with history. My heart raced under my ribs, the excitement, the sheer wonder surging back through me—unstoppable.

Yet, a shadow loomed at the corner of my periphery. Peters' voice broke through the haze. "It's all well and good," he murmured, his tone measured. "But this still seems far too convenient." He stood cautioned against the rising tide of my fascination, his brow drawn into a tense frown. "We're not done yet."

He was right, of course. But I could barely hear him—the allure of the space overwhelmed me. The whispers of Atlantean history etched into the stone told stories and themes my mind had longed to glimpse, a migration of an ancient, lost people, converging on familiar iconography. A connection that… that…

Náiren.

Atlantis.

***

The air was dense with anticipation, still and expectant, as though the chamber itself held its breath. That eternal hum, faint and rhythmic, tapped against my senses like the pulse of a slumbering giant—slow, steady, and ancient beyond comprehension. As I moved deeper toward the center of the room, my hand came to rest above a glyph—a symbol curved in tight spirals, pulsing with a light that tugged like gravity.

The warm glow from the walls—that gentle, ever-present light—responded subtly as my palm hovered closer. And when my fingertip finally brushed the smooth panel, a slight vibration shot through the stone beneath me, humming faintly against my touch. The light around us shifted, growing more intense, almost eager, as if the chamber had been waiting. The glyphs rippled with renewed energy, one line after another lighting up in sequence, casting faint shadows that danced across the stone floor. I could feel it in my bones—the chamber was waking up.

My breath caught, but the sensation wasn't fear—it was awe. I wasn't just gazing at history. I was *touching* it, activating it. This place, this ancient repository, had been waiting for someone, for this moment—waiting to relay a story buried so deep within the Earth that it had almost escaped time itself. It hummed louder now, the glow intensifying, casting warm hues of red and gold deeper into the corners of the room. Each glyph seemed to be breathing, pulsing in unison with my racing heart.

Confident enough that I wasn't in immediate danger—at least, not yet—I set my eyes on what lay directly in front of me. A moderately sized brass tablet, mounted carefully on a pedestal near the center of the room, beckoned my attention. It was distinct from the rest of the artifacts. Its edges gleamed brighter than the worn relics surrounding it—positioned just so, as if it held significance unlike the others.

I approached cautiously, holding my breath without intending to. The moment my fingers wrapped around the cool brass, a dull thrum radiated from within—a subtle hum of recognition, like the feeling of grasping the handle of a well-worn tool. Beneath my hand, the brass was smooth, polished over millennia, yet the engravings were sharp, unweathered by time. Intricate lines of glyphs spiraled inward, moving concentrically from the edges toward an unseen center buried beneath layers of symbology. My chest tightened, as though the closer I examined it, the more weight pressed on my lungs.

I lifted the tablet—carefully, reverently—and the glow from the chamber surged. A long arc of energy leapt from the nearest wall, skittering across the air like a dancer poised upon invisible strings, curling toward the tablet with a deliberate grace that stilled my breath. I jerked my gaze toward it as more streams of light laced themselves through the air, each ripple of energy bending and twisting toward the brass plate in my grasp, as if drawn to it by whispered command.

The room... came *alive*.

Stray arcs of soft yellow, blue, and purple light poured from the walls, creating a web of energy just above us—beautiful, like nebulae coalescing in a perfect storm. Pulsing waves crackled through the air, forming interweaving, holographic projections. Images—celestial bodies—all of them danced across the energy signatures, intricately connected lines trailing from one constellation to the next in a hypnotic display. Stars, planets, moons—all unfamiliar—hovered just above us, spinning in synchronicity with the relic's hum. Shells of alien ships appeared, their shapes foreign, immense, yet almost familiar within the strange narrative weaving itself before my eyes.

"It's...like a map," I whispered, awestruck, as the constellation shifted and twisted in the air, seamlessly integrating the stars into a bigger picture—something far grander than the individual pieces. I was no stranger to the concept of cosmic charts—a passion buried in my earliest studies—but this… this was beyond anything Earth's telescopes had ever glimpsed. Beyond anything I dared believe.

Peters, driven by his survival instincts as always, stiffened beside me. His muscles, coiled for immediate action, tensed as the energy cascaded around us. He took a step forward, his broad shoulders drawn taut, hands hovering over the hilts of his blades in case the air *itself* dared attack—but I held a hand up, shaking my head to reassure him. No danger. Just awe.

"This is…" My voice trailed off, lost to the incomprehensible wonder flickering before me. The projections interlaced, moving seamlessly, liquid-like, into a twisting narrative. There, in those images cleaving through the soft, glowing air, I recognized Atlanteans. Beings—with pale skin, slender features, so much like the Náiren—began to take shape.

"They weren't just descendants of Atlantis," I said, each word a revelation bursting forth, widening the narrative before me. "They… they came from beyond."

The mural that lined the chamber wall came to life in the air, visuals swirling and entwining with histories long forgotten. What was once thought to be Atlantis—this hidden world beneath the Earth—was no mere ancient sect of humanity. These beings… they had not only fled from some catastrophe. They had journeyed **from the stars**.

I took a shuddering breath, my hands gripping the tablet tighter as more images streamed before me. Starships, glittering like jewels, arced through strange planets and nebulas. Alien landscapes shimmered under suns I had never seen before—and there, always there, were the Atlanteans. Shimmering in the heat of some incomprehensible past, the starlight casting shadows across their pale features as they spread out across—*throughout time.* My hands began trembling violently as the full weight of the revelation pressed on me with unbearable intensity.

"This is bigger than us, Pym..." Peters' voice rang lowly beside me. He didn't sound amazed—he sounded... terrified, his usual edge dulled, wariness softened by a fear rarely seen in him. As he stepped into the path of the swirling projections, his shoulders shook slightly beneath the weight of this knowledge. "If those Nazis... *God*, if they'd gotten their hands on this..."

His voice, rougher now, fell into something between disbelief and rage. The maps swirled like a cosmos, and for a moment, Peters stood before it as if to block the cosmic knowledge with the breadth of his frame, as if shielding the truth might somehow change the implications that fell upon us like stones.

The images blurred and shifted, honing in on one particular visual—a glowing orb, spewing life, encased within a grand starship. The starship groaned against invisible forces, pulled like a meteor from its heavens, spiraling down toward the surface of a lush, unfamiliar Earth. Primitive, green, untouched Earth. The image zoomed out slowly, carefully exaggerating the moment. The orb—the core—embedded itself into the heart of our planet, striking deep beneath the earliest oceans, energy bleeding into the planet's veins slowly over eons.

The breath left my lungs in one violent exhale. "It wasn't… it was never natural," I whispered, feeling the weight, the gravity, the *truth* settle onto my chest like a glaring, impossible fact that I couldn't bear. "The core… the core we thought we were protecting—was never part of Earth. It was… was…" words failed me as the image lingered of that initial impact with such finality it twisted in my mind, punctuated by that ancient silence only burdened by time.

Earth's most precious resource…its precious, untapped core had never been the molten heart of the planet itself—it was an alien energy source. Extraterrestrial. Náiren.

I was nearly overwhelmed. The world I had known, everything I had studied, shifted beneath my feet as if time itself had crumbled to dust. History—our history—was not simply the stories of kings and conquerors, the battles of men against empire. No… Earth's history had always been shared with the stars. The uncanny heat from the core chamber overhead pulsed quietly now, as though acknowledging its cosmic origin… a long-forgotten being without a home. My knees weakened, but I remained standing, frozen in time against the magnitude of such revelation.

Beside me, Peters flexed his fingers, staring intently at the projection but with eyes hard and slick like stone. He was already past the awe…past what this discovery meant for men like us. A light snarl furrowed his brow as he looked to me.

"We can't let anyone else find this," he rasped, voice dark and twisted with understanding. "The kind of power… the greed… it'll destroy the world." His hand clenched into tightly bundled fists as he regarded the empty space above us. Every muscle trembled—not with excitement for discovery but with that familiar dread I had seen in battle. A fear of impending doom driven not by known enemies, but by the unintended consequences of what we had just uncovered.

His fear was justified. "If any more of them found this…" His voice lifted, thick with anger. "We already almost lost everything. This—" He gestured sharply to the whirling projections around us. "This was too close. Too…*real*."

I swallowed hard, still trying to untangle my mind from the splendor of absolute revelation. There it was again, the pragmatist inside me clawing to take control. Peters was right. He always was. Beneath the thrill, beneath the brilliant, impossible truth—it was too dangerous. The very knowledge of what we had found could tear the world apart—my hands trembled as they rested against the tablet, still clutching it like it was the Holy Grail. **Was Earth even supposed to know?**

I turned from the projections and caught Peters' gaze—his steady, unwavering resolve cemented against the churn of the universe. The awe that had filled my veins, the sense of *life*, drained slowly as the enormity of his words settled into every corner of my soul.

This was a discovery too monumental to share.

Peters' expression was no longer taut but hollow, drained of what little light had once flickered in his eyes. He knew, just as I did, that what we had now was no longer history or knowledge… it was what could break the fragile bones of humanity's ambition.

In the heavy silence that followed, we both felt the weight of it.

A slow pulse from the room itself—the artifacts—the relics responded one last time as though the moment of revelation itself were closing in on us, sealing the truth back beneath layers of stone and velvet darkness. History. Cold stone. Indifferent.

The walls returned to stillness. Their glow dimming gradually like a thousand stars winking out.

Peters tilted his head toward the exit, eyes never leaving the soft glow of what we had uncovered. My gaze lingered, fingers already feeling the tendrils of absence where awe once bloomed. But my hand moved against my chest, over the tablet, forcing it back down, forcibly pressing down on what had been *alive* beneath my grasp.

The room's breath quieted. The hum quieted. And the chamber… returned to the silence it had known for millennia.

Nothing but history remained.

21

The Shocking Truth

The chamber had fallen into a profound and breathless silence. The swirling projections, their celestial brilliance having faded into nothing more than faint memories, left the space hollow—stripped of the weighty revelations that had been woven through it mere moments before. The walls, so alive before, now seemed void—hushed, waiting, as though the room itself had closed its eyes in a long, eternal sleep.

I stood there, motionless, my breath shallow, feeling the ancient air settle back into place around me. The reverberations of that final pulse—the final flicker of cosmic energy—still rippled through me, embedded beneath my skin. The brass tablet was in my hands, solid and curiously heavy now that the energy it evoked had dissipated. Its surface, once warm, once humming with life, had gone cool, cold even, as if all the power it had held had retreated deep within, pulling back secrets it no longer intended to share.

My heart pounded, harder than it should have under the circumstances, as though my body were protesting the stillness. The adrenaline still surged under my skin, my fingers twitching, desperate to record, to jot down *everything*—here, now, before the weight of reality dragged it away from me like a dream dissipating in the cruel light of morning. My mind screamed with the need to preserve it, to tell it, to *shout* to the world of what I had seen and touched. My whole life— every instinct, every piece of study—had led to this moment.

But as those echoes faded back into the stone, as the silence deepened, thick as velvet, I began to feel the oppressive weight of the very history we had uncovered pressing in on me from all sides. It was no longer a dazzling discovery— it was a forbidden knowledge, dangerous in its potential. My heart moved from racing excitement to hollow fear.

My hand hovered over the brass tablet, brushing against its surface again, imploring it to spark back to life—to give me *something* to hold onto. It remained cold.

On the other side of the chamber, Peters moved more slowly now, his form a shadow against the dim remnants of the once-blazing glyphs. I could see the exhaustion in his stride—the way each step seemed burdened with the weight of more than just a battle, but of realization. His tall frame, usually so commanding, now seemed smaller, not in stature but in spirit, momentarily bowed by the magnitude of what we had learned. His face remained grim, his eyes hard as they scanned the blank, still walls, as though searching for something hidden within their depths. But this time, there was nothing left for either of us to see.

"We can't leave this behind," I blurted out. The words burst forth, tumbling from my lips almost of their own accord, driven by a wild surge of emotion, as if by simply speaking them aloud, they might lighten the immense weight of discovery. My voice rang out through the chamber, rebounding off the dead stone and pledging me deeper into uncertainty before it faded into the air. I swiveled toward Peters, desperate for affirmation, for something that might ground me in my overwhelming urge to *preserve* this truth.

Peters didn't respond immediately. He continued his slow, deliberate approach—each footfall as measured as the weight behind his eyes. When he finally stopped in front of me, his expression was unreadable, locked behind the familiar mask of hardened pragmatism I had come to realize was Peters at his most serious.

"You know what this means, don't you?" he said, his voice gravelly, worn. His words felt cold, sharp in the air, not just a question—but an accusation, one directed at the weight I sought to shoulder. He let the words sink in for a moment before continuing, adding a quiet but firm edge to his voice. "We can't share this. Not with the world. Not with anyone. This knowledge is dangerous."

I blinked, feeling heat rise in my chest—a slow burn of frustration that coursed through me, igniting old instincts. How could I abandon what we had just uncovered? Why should we?

"You don't understand—" I began, cutting off the rush of thoughts that warred within me. I met his gaze, my voice more intense, vibrating with emotion. "This is… this is everything! The answer to questions we didn't even know to ask. If the world knew—"

"If the world knew?" Peters growled, interrupting me, his voice heavy with scorn and raw disbelief. "You think they'd use it responsibly? You think they'd safeguard it? Think, Pym! The moment we *open* our mouths, the moment we *share* this—someone's going to come looking to use it." His hand clenched into a tight fist at his side, the other gesturing toward the lifeless walls around us. "You've seen what just happened—the lengths they'll go to. Do you want more people getting their hands on something they can't understand? The power to destroy…*everything.*"

The truth of his words landed with a brutal finality, their edge blunt and heavy. He wasn't pulling punches. He was speaking plainly—perhaps even more terrified than I realized. That pragmatism of his wasn't just a reaction to danger—it was what kept us alive. I inhaled, taking in his sharp words, feeling them swirl within me, cutting me deeper the longer I stayed silent.

Silence.

It wrapped itself around us now like iron chains, inescapable in its purpose. I could feel the chamber pressing closer, as if it too intended to stifle the knowledge I so wanted to scream to the world. Slowly, I lifted my hand again, brushing once more against the brass tablet, but it was no ignition of life this time. The glyphs had gone dark. Cold. Quiet. As quiet as Peters' grim stare.

I swallowed, refocusing my gaze. What could I say? What argument could possibly make sense when standing in the shadow of something that had come terrifyingly close to unraveling it all?

"We have to—" I huffed involuntarily, my voice raw and desperate. My hands pressed hard against the brass, as if there might be some further life in it, one final flicker of knowledge to impart. "We have to tell the Náiren, at least," I said, the urgency now quieter, yet no less fierce. "They need to know how close the Nazis came... What almost happened."

Peters let out a slow, tightening breath. His grizzled face softened for the briefest flicker of a moment. "Them, yes. *Only* them." He nodded once, then again, slowly, as if battling against his reflex for control. His eyes darkened as he held mine. "But no one else, Pym. Understand? No one."

The words settled in my mind, but it took longer for me to fully accept them. I wanted... God, I *wanted* to argue. I wanted to fight him on this, to convince him that this was too important to choke behind a dam of secrets. But as I stared into the worn lines of his harsh gaze, I understood. Peters wasn't just saying this to quiet me. He wasn't acting on fear alone. He meant it. His stance, his resolve—this was his truth. His *necessary* truth to protect the living from the destruction they unknowingly courted.

I hesitated, my fingers loosening their grip against the edge of the tablet. The chamber felt quiet again, nearly stifling in its cool, indifferent stillness. *Fine*, I thought, feeling the words gnaw at the inside of my throat. *Fine*, I could relent now— because Peters was right. Not the scientists, not the scholars, not the men who held power far beyond their comprehension. None of them could be trusted with what we had found.

"Fine," I said, the word coming out in a low, resigned mutter. But even still, beneath it all, my own determination flickered. I would tell the Náiren. And then we would decide.

I held the brass tablet closer to my chest, pressing its cool weight against me—both a reminder of this discovery and a burden for everything we were leaving behind. My thoughts twisted painfully back toward the stars projected overhead— the stars I would never again see.

We exchanged one final gaze. The look in Peters' eyes was hard and resolute—at peace with the decision. Perhaps as much peace as either of us could hope to find in this hell we had stumbled into. Then, with a stiff gesture, he turned away from the grand chamber, his steps leading toward the dark passage that would take us to the surface. But not before his eyes flicked up to the unseen gate, ever-vigilant, ever-forward.

I lingered a moment longer. My boots scuffed lightly on the stone as I turned in place, casting my gaze one last time across the hollowed remnants of an unimaginable history. The muted glyphs stared back—cold, indifferent stars resting in suspended quiet. I had uncovered so much. Yet the quiet gnawing voice in my head whispered—*What could I have shown? What could I have shared?* I closed my eyes and hoped—prayed—that I'd buried what should remain forgotten.

The room swallowed the moment whole, and I followed reluctantly in Peters' wake.

The climb back through the passage was long, the air cooler as we ascended, though heavier somehow, as if something followed behind us, whispering in the narrow dark. Our footsteps fell more softly than before, the overwhelming heat of battle no longer pushing us forward. But still, the weight of the truths we carried pressed in on us like a shadow—an invisible, suffocating burden.

Another rumble shimmied through the caverns, and my hand instinctively shot out, pressing against the cool wall for balance. It felt distant, as were my thoughts—spinning in wild, painful spirals. The Nazis—those men—how close had they come to unlocking it all? Too close. My stomach churned. The thought was unbearable.

The passage rose, leading us back toward hell.

As we emerged into the broken shells of the Nazi base, I blinked in the fading light, my eyes adjusting to the eerie scene before us. Scaffolding groaned under the weight of collapsed machinery, shattered beams hanging like broken limbs from a body that had lost its soul. And there, waiting in the center of it all, the Náiren watched in silence, their pale faces drawn and composed. Their inscrutable stares weighed heavily on my shoulders more than any ruin could.

Peters shared a glance with me, grave and worn, before stepping forward.

"There's... something you need to know," his voice was quiet, but the gravity was unmistakable.

***

The Náiren council hall was cast in an otherworldly glow, the soft luminescence from the walls rippling gently against the arches of the high, vaulted ceiling. Shadows played across the stone floor, thickening the silence into something palpable and weighty. Sitting before the assembled elders, Peters and I waited, our breath shallow, each intake of air feeling heavier than the last. The tension was suffocating, wrapping around both of us like an unrelenting vice, squeezing against the magnitude of what we had yet to share.

I held the brass tablet in my lap, my thumb tracing the cold glyphs that ran along its intricate surface. The symbols had gone dark—no longer pulsing with the energy I'd felt back in that Atlantean chamber. Now it was just a slab of metal, heavy with secrets and the awful burden of time. My chest was tight, each breath pushing against an invisible barrier lodged deep in my ribs. The knowledge we carried with us was too vast—too devastating—to contain much longer. And yet the silence stretched on, waiting to be broken.

Across the room, Elys, the Náiren leader, sat in quiet repose. His pale features remained impassive beneath the flowing strands of his silvery hair, but the light from the chamber bathed him in a faint glow, giving him the air of a figure drawn from myth—timeless, ancient. His eyes, calm and patient, flickered between me and Peters. Though his expression remained unreadable, there was no escaping the unspoken demand we felt in his gaze. He was waiting.

It wasn't unusual for the Náiren to be silent; much of their communication was subtle, mostly telepathic in nature. Their tranquility reverberated through the air, but today that tranquility felt expectant, maybe even brittle, like a crystal window that could shatter under the weight of a single breath. The other elders, seated in a semi-circle around us, exchanged furtive glances, their ageless faces betraying nothing—only the quiet flicker of their eyes reflecting the light of the hall.

I stared at the ground, sweat beading across my temple. The tablet was cold against my palm, and I gripped it tightly, hoping the feel of its edges would keep me tethered to reality. Somewhere deep within the cavernous expanse of the Earth's core, I could still feel its energy. That ancient power—alien, churning like a dream hidden beneath the bones of the world.

The silence pressed down harder, and finally, Peters spoke.

"We found something," he said flatly, his voice steady, each word carrying an edge but remaining level. The room didn't stir. Neither did Elys. The elders, gathered in their calm council, made no movement but continued to watch. If anything, there was a slight collective ripple—a disturbance in the stillness—like a breath collectively held.

Peters' gaze moved from Elys to the rest of the council. The weight of his words was meant to prepare them for the truth, readying them for the immense significance that we had to unload. "Something about the core," he continued. "About Atlantis. About all of you."

A murmur—a faint shifting of fabric, a rustle of robes—rippling across the assembled elders. Dismissive glances bent toward one another, though none dared yet to break the silence that Elys maintained. His gaze never left Peters or me. Calm, watchful—but not complacent.

"We thought the core was natural," Peters pressed on, his voice deepening, knuckles whitening against the worn leather of his gloves. "Like you did. Like the world does. A part of the Earth. But it's not." He paused deliberately, as if trying to choose the right words while bluntness did more work. "It's... alien."

I felt a tightening in my gut, a slight prickling beneath my skin as Peters' words landed. His directness was always unwavering, but here, in this setting, in this delicate moment, I feared it might tear open the silence like a wound, spilling everything in a flood beyond our control. Across the chamber, the gaze of the Náiren sharpened, and I saw it—just a flicker—the faintest narrowing in Elys' eyes. Far too subtle for most to notice, but it was there. The calm on his face held firm, but there was no mistaking the intensity gathering in its depths.

Peters hesitated for a fraction of an instant before continuing, his voice still carrying that certain, brutal practicality, as though he were laying hard truths one by one before the council like stones. Unmovable. Unchanging. "Your people… they came from the stars."

The air thickened at his words, but the quiet remained. I saw one or two elders exchange pointed glances, their pale lips tightening, the foundation beneath them—beneath their very identity—beginning to quake at what Peters had revealed. But still, Elys did not interrupt. His hands, long and slender, remained folded neatly in his lap. His ancient eyes, patient as ever, waited. Only the slightest shift forward, as if to focus more sharply on the words floating into the council.

"You're the descendants of an alien race that journeyed across the stars," Peters continued, his tone unwavering. "The core— the core we nearly lost—was once part of something far greater. It was a source of immense power… something crafted, not born of this Earth."

The gasps that followed were faint, barely audible, but they were there. Beneath the calm, measured exterior of occasional disbelief, the elders flinched as if struck by the sheer depth of this revelation. Some of them grasped it immediately—others traded wide-eyed looks of astonishment, clutching their hands tighter together. The gravity of Peters' words settled like sand sinking through water, slow yet inevitable, until there was no denying the truth spread before them.

I could feel the moment tipping precariously. My shoulders tightened, bracing for the moment when the room would break fully into understanding or defiance—or worse, denial. Elys, serene as ever, trained his gaze on Peters, but the weight behind his glance carried more urgency now, more purpose. The knowledge, the buried history of his people, shimmered beneath those ageless eyes like a tightly guarded flame.

But before the calm shattered and the tension gripped them all, I found my own voice.

"The Nazis almost unleashed it..." I blurted, louder than I intended, the tension rolling off my voice in a rush. My hands clenched the brass tablet tighter, my knuckles pale against the dark metal as anxiety rooted itself deep in my gut. "They came so close. If we hadn't stopped them—they would've destroyed everything. The core—whatever it is—it's not stable. It's part of something much larger... a starship... buried thousands of years ago."

For a moment, the council of Náiren froze. The stillness pressed deeper on the space, the air clawing at my throat with every breath I took. Elys didn't flinch. His eyes, laser-sharp through the calm, settled on me. They didn't blink, didn't flicker at the suddenness of my outburst. Instead, they pierced through the words I spilled—cool as a winter sea. They lingered on me, unwavering, as though Elys already knew. Perhaps that he had always known, but the words needed to be spoken aloud all the same.

"And you stopped them?" His voice floated into the silence, soft, patient, but there was an unmissable frisson of undercurrent laced around it—a subtle reading of something more than the surface of our actions. He was asking if we had won. But another question followed—the one hanging in the space between simply knowing and fully understanding—had we truly grasped what lay beyond this struggle, deep within ourselves?

Beside me, Peters nodded, his hand tapping lightly on his thigh, his body still thrumming with the aftermath of both battle and revelation. "We stopped them," he said firmly, though now, I could hear the slight wavering at the edges of his words. He paused, just for a breath, his eyes clouded—not with fear—but recognition. He had so often been the one who never wavered. But now… this was different.

"But…"

The word—they both knew what followed—hung in the air, locking all sound beneath its weight.

I took in a breath, shoulders stiffening as the words fumbled against my throat. "This… knowledge… It—it can't leave this place." I felt their eyes on me now—all of them. The judgment cutting deeper than the awe had moments before. The tablet seemed to grow heavier in my lap, the cold weight pressing into me like stone. How could I explain it—the madness and brilliance of discovery? The unspeakable danger behind the very thing I wanted to cherish, the thing that might change everything? "It's too dangerous. People… Humans…" The words caught, and I had to struggle to wrench them out of my chest. "We're not ready…"

There was a shiver in the air. The faintest tremor in the silence. I could feel the delicate threads of long-held wisdom unraveling within the room as the elders processed the weight of the knowledge—folding it into the centuries they had already lived, weaving it now into their bones. And there was something else: disappointment, subtle though it was, flashing just briefly within the deeper furrows of Elys' eyes. It stung. More than I had thought.

"You would keep this hidden?" Elys asked—his voice softened by something unreadable. Not anger—not reproach—but restraint. His face tilted ever so slightly, his delicate hands combining into a thoughtful pose. But behind the deliberate calm, I saw it—disappointment. He had expected more from us. The weary old prophet's quiet hope that we might be better than we were.

I tried to speak—tried to find something, anything, but the words wouldn't come. Instead, I found myself locked between the safe harbor Peters had drawn me into… and the storm I desperately wanted to embrace on the horizon.

Beside me, Peters rescued me from myself. His words rang clear but devastating, sharp with the edge of finality. "Yes," he answered bluntly, his voice unwavering, firm, as if sealing the conversation behind iron doors. "The world's not ready. Not for this."

The council did not stir at first. The air seemed to still, the ground itself refusing to shift. Slowly, though, I heard a faint rustling as the elders—one by one—exchanged long, solemn looks before nodding in unison. The finality of their gesture, the agreement shared between them, fell over me like a shroud, blanketing my protests before I could voice them. A silent covenant forged in that small, suffocating hall.

Elys, too, bowed his head, contemplative, though sadness followed the motion. His voice, when it finally reached us again, was no longer questioning, no longer searching—but resigned. "Then it must remain our secret." His words came softly. His eyes terribly kind, but impossibly distant. "The surface world… is not ready. This knowledge must stay beneath us." The glow from the chamber's walls dimmed as if nodding to his statement, a quiet understanding reflected in the solemn faces of each elder.

My mind blurred as every ounce of energy drained from me. Even as I sat there, I knew they were the words I'd needed to hear. But the buried part of me—the one searing under Peters' calm pragmatism—felt each syllable like nails to the heart. It was one thing to know the truth already. Another thing entirely to accept it, bound by another's declaration. My hands fell limp, my fingers curling weakly around the tablet.

Peters leaned forward, brushing absent dust from his sleeve. I could feel him next to me, his posture heavy, though his voice carried quiet strength. "It's done, Pym." His tone was final.

I glanced at him, but the sting pressed harder against my chest. I had always known it—he might have even been right. But as I lifted the brass tablet, that ache roared through my mind. The weight of history—answers now held in my hands—it was heavier than brass. It was… everything.

Quietly, automatically, I placed the tablet into Elys' outstretched hands—a handoff I never thought I'd make. Across the hall, the Náiren elders accepted it with silent reverence, their pale faces bent toward it, acknowledging the burden we shared—the knowledge that would remain hidden beneath the world's surface, known only to us.

I rose stiffly, though the motion was as weightless as it was against my will. Peters rose beside me, already facing forward, ready to emerge back into the ruins that awaited us. But as I cast one last, anxious glance back toward Elys, I couldn't stop the flicker of hope pulling at my chest—searching for reassurance.

Elys regarded me in silence for a moment before offering a gentle, sad smile that answered every question.

"We will keep your secret."

22

The Decision

The soft glow of the Náiren village filtered through the translucent walls of my quarters, a warm, diffused light that bathed everything in pale amber hues. It was a kind of light you would expect to see in dreams or distant memories, a wash of color recognizable yet elusive, as though it might slip through your fingers if you tried to touch it. I didn't risk moving through it just yet; instead, I let the serenity hold me, trying to match its calm, though my heart was anything but still.

I had been sitting here for what felt like hours, though how long, I couldn't say. Time had a tendency to blur here, in this tucked-away corner of the world—if "tucked away" was what you could call the hidden core of the Earth—and I found that trying to measure it felt strangely futile. I was adrift, not in the familiar sense of being lost on the surface, but tethered to a different kind of silence, one filled with the heavy weight of discovery and what followed it.

In front of me, resting on the smooth table that had been assigned to these chambers, sat the brass tablet, gleaming faintly in the village's ambient light. It lay flat, its surface cool and lifeless now, though it had not long ago pulsed with so much energy, so much knowledge, that my hands had trembled beneath its power. Now, it was cold—dead almost—but still it held a gravity that would not let me leave. As though the secrets it once shared still hummed beneath that inert surface, merely dormant for the moment.

I ran my hand over its familiar edge, feeling the grooves of the alien glyphs beneath my fingertips. Ancient Atlantean knowledge—far older, far deeper than even that title could encompass. Extraterrestrial. I could never forget the word Peters had spoken as we'd emerged from the tomb-like chamber hours earlier, our bodies thick with the weight of what we had learned. The Náiren weren't just lost descendants of a mythical empire. They were a fragment of something larger—something not of this world.

And, if Peters was correct—and he was always correct—we had to leave all of that behind.

My fingers stilled on the surface of the tablet as the memory of his voice echoed in my mind, that low growl undercut by the weight of responsibility he carried. His pragmatism had always stood in stark contrast to my idealism. But today… today those lines felt blurred. The conundrum before me, before us, was so vast, so bewildering, even I wasn't sure if I could bring myself to say the words I knew had to be said. Not without hesitation. Not this time.

As if responding to my thoughts, the door at the edge of my quarters slid open, and I felt rather than saw Peters enter. His presence was always unmistakable—a heavy force upon the space around him, filling it with energy, with potential for action, with his quiet intensity. He lingered in the doorway for just a moment, letting himself adjust to the atmosphere of the room, his silhouette casting a long shadow across the floor in the light behind him. The faint padding of his boots was barely audible against the soft floor as he stepped inside, but his movements were as deliberate as if he'd walked into a battlefield.

I didn't lift my eyes from the tablet. I didn't need to. Peters always carried himself with the same steady authority—a certainty about what had to be done. And after all these years, I had come to understand the rhythms of his silent communication. Without speaking, I already knew why he was here.

It still didn't make it easier.

"We're leaving," Peters said. His voice was decisive, heavy—a hammer falling onto an anvil, shaping the next step in our journey just as surely as it had shaped every decision thus far. The words, though expected, struck me deep. Unbidden, my chest tightened, squeezing like a fist. His voice carried something permanent this time. A finality that made the muscles in my shoulders tense as though bracing for the weight of it all to fall.

For a moment, I couldn't respond. My eyes stayed fixed

on the brass tablet, my fingers tracing the edges of those once-glowing glyphs. Every line, every symbol etched into its surface, carried the burden of what we'd uncovered—too much for any one person to know too much for the surface to comprehend. And now we were to leave it all behind. I felt each breath grow heavier, enveloped by the weight of the decision Peters had already made… the one I knew I had to accept.

One final time, I let my fingers brush over the cold brass before standing, the motion slow and deliberate, as though rising from a dream too sudden to fully comprehend but too real to forget. My eyes drifted to the window near the far wall, and I stepped toward it, feeling the gentle push of the warm evening air. Outside, the sounds of the Náiren village hummed faintly in the distance, carried on a breeze too light to resist, yet full of life. Voices, soft conversations mingling with distant laughter, the kind of peaceful murmurs that felt so alien now compared to the noise of the world we had left above.

Beyond the village streets, the great glowing sun—the inner sun of the Earth itself—hung impossibly in the distance, projecting soft light over everything, illuminating the world beneath the surface in a pale wash of eternal warmth. It beat steadily, like a massive heart, and for a moment, I tried to imagine how we could walk away from this. From all of this. The peace, the beauty, the incomprehensibility of it. Leaving it felt like letting go of a dream I hadn't had time to fully understand.

"How can we leave now?" I wanted to ask Peters, though I already knew the answer. How could the world outside take this truth and not break beneath it? We had been asked to carry secrets too great for anyone—secrets we could never share. And as my eyes lifted one more time to that impossible light hovering over the Náiren village, I accepted, deep in my chest, that this might be the last time I ever saw it.

Peters waited beside me, watching—ever vigilant, ever constant. I felt the gravity between us, unspoken, so thick that if I turned, I could see it flash across his face. But he let me have this moment, patient as a stone. Together, we both stared beyond the village, into the horizon, where that pale light bathed everything in silver-white serenity. And though he did not speak, I could feel his eyes tracing the distant ridge of the cavern above us, his sharp instincts always catching movement, even in places where stillness thrived. His jaw clenched just slightly, the line of his face carved in quiet resolve. He didn't need to say it aloud—we both understood the truth. The surface needed us more than this extraordinary world ever would.

"No, we can't stay here... can we?" The words escaped me softly, more rhetorical than I meant them but still carrying a prayer-like quality, as if longing for an impossible answer. I didn't even realize I had said them until they slipped past my lips, trembling.

I heard Peters shift slightly beside me, saw his sharp brow furrow just enough to betray the slightest quiver of emotion beneath that mask of controlled composure. "No," he answered. "We've done what we came here to do." His voice was steady, but there was something less rigid—quieter now, nearly gentle. "Now it's time to let their story stay buried."

I let out a slow breath, my head dipping in quiet acknowledgment, though the ache in my chest did not ease. He was right, of course. Logic had always been on his side when it came to decisions like this. But reason didn't soothe the pain of losing something so… magnificent. My hand instinctively drifted back toward the tablet lying on the table behind me, my fingers brushing the edges once more, seeking some last vestige of hope, though I knew there was none.

Peters, as always, was waiting for me to catch up.

"We'll start packing," he suggested, his tone matter-of-fact but gentler than it would have been on the surface. His pragmatism had a different quality down here—more grounded in a deliberate, careful understanding of what we'd uncovered. He wasn't rushing me. He wasn't pushing me to follow faster than I could process. He was simply waiting.

With a sharp exhale through my nose, I turned, stepping toward the table where our scattered belongings waited. Maps, sketches, notebooks, artifacts—small but significant pieces of this world's history—lay in neat piles, surrounded by the clutter of hastily scrawled documents and half-finished thoughts lingering on the edge of comprehension. There was too much here to leave behind, and yet… there was too much we couldn't take. Too much danger hidden within those illegible scrawls—too much knowledge that could break worlds rather than reshape them.

I began sorting, each item handled delicately, fingers tracing the edges as though afraid the weight of them might leave invisible marks on my skin.

Peters moved beside me, gathering what we had deemed safe to carry—those items that wouldn't tear humanity apart, the ones that simply whispered history instead of screaming it. He worked quickly, methodically, his eyes scanning every inch of the room with that usual meticulous attention to detail, making sure no lingering clues were left behind. Anything that could speak of the Náiren's greatest secret was hidden away—as though it had never existed. He moved toward a table where a single, dazzling piece of alien machinery sat—an intricate, quiet piece of technology we had vowed not to meddle with. Without hesitation, he wrapped it in fabric, tucking it carefully into a pack as if the temptation to understand it might be enough to undo everything.

I glanced across the table, my hands still resting lightly over an artifact marked with Atlantean glyphs, buried deep in my thoughts. Each symbol beckoned me, taunting me with the implications of what we'd uncovered—a language I had once been so certain would unlock the mysteries of the world now crowded my mind with secrets too dangerous to share. The weight of the decision pressed hard against my chest. And for a brief, flickering moment, I wondered—could we have done more? Could it have been different?

Peters' eyes caught mine across the room, his face resolute

but calm. There was no trace of hesitation behind his gaze—a soft nod conveyed all I needed. "We keep this quiet, Pym," he said softly, his voice a low rumble. A reaffirmation of what we both knew. "No one needs to know."

I nodded, not trusting myself to speak. Silently, I packed the final items into my bag, fingers still shaking with the weight of their meaning, the weight of their concealment. I couldn't keep my voice steady when it finally broke free. "The thought of never coming back…" I whispered, my voice cracking under the strain. Leaving not just this place, but the discovery—leaving a part of myself behind.

Peters appeared beside me, his hand firm and heavy on my shoulder, grounding me, pulling me back from the edge. "You'll never forget this," he said quietly, voice softer now. "But the world we came from isn't ready for this truth. We may never be."

The truth in his words anchored me more than I was willing to admit. As reluctant as I was, I knew he spoke not from fear, but from the necessary understanding that some knowledge had to stay hidden—buried, just like the world it belonged to.

With renewed determination, we both moved in silence to gather the last of our provisions. Peters ensured every pack was secured, every strap tied down, every remaining piece of our journey carefully concealed. It was efficient, meticulous—final. We made one last sweep of the room, checking and double-checking that nothing had been forgotten, that no trace remained of the discovery too dangerous to share.

As I cast one final glance at the tablet, resting beneath layers of fabric now, I felt the trembling reed of doubt give way beneath me, but the weight on my shoulders didn't lessen. It simply settled, heavier than before.

In silence, we prepared to leave the world behind.

***

The glowing sun chamber greeted us with a warmth that was both familiar and distant, a steady pulse in the heart of this hidden world that radiated a glow softer than the relentless heat that had once threatened to consume us. It wrapped around us now like a quiet farewell. There was something alive in this warmth—something sentient in the light cascading down in soft, ethereal waves, bathing the chamber in its all-encompassing glow. As Peters and I stepped forward cautiously, our footsteps echoed slightly across the smooth stone floor, absorbed quickly by the vastness around us.

The chamber hummed with a quiet serenity. I could feel its pulse beneath the smooth stone, deep within the Earth itself, like the steady heartbeat of a world that knew we were leaving. There was no malice here, no disappointment—just an understanding, quiet and profound. Beneath the calm shone a kind of finality that tugged at my chest. We were walking away, and the world beneath the Earth acknowledged it without bitterness. Something much older than us, something deep in the roots of this place, gave its blessing for our departure—but the weight of it still lingered.

My chest tightened as those palpable rhythms swelled thick in the air, and though the warmth was meant to be comforting, it only amplified what I already felt pressing down on my shoulders: the impossibility of leaving all of this behind.

That ever-present stream of light from the core bathed everything in a kind of quiet reverence, falling over the figures of the Náiren who waited near the far side of the chamber. They stood in stillness, no motion betraying their thoughts—save for the faint glint of light reflecting in their eyes.

Elys was there, at the forefront, waiting as though he belonged to the very stones beneath his feet, etched into the history surrounding him. His pale, ageless face was a canvas without emotion, but there was depth behind that calm—so much depth that it cut through the space between us with silent force. His eyes locked with mine before I could even fully approach, and without a single word, I felt every uncertainty swell up, gathering within my throat, pushing my breath back down inside me. I was no longer so sure if what I had to say could hold its ground before him.

Beside him, Lyra stood calmly, her presence softer, though no less weighted. The golden rim of light around her delicate figure gave her the appearance of something both gentle and grounded, like a stream flowing steadily, quietly—holding its strength beneath the surface. She didn't speak, didn't need to. Even in the silence of her gaze, I felt myself settle slightly, finding an ease that eluded me in the constant hum of thoughts spinning through my mind.

Elys was the first to step forward, breaking the small distance between our two groups. He moved fluidly, his robes whispering down the smooth stone as he approached, pausing just far enough to keep the space between us sacred but narrow enough to close the distance of understanding. He bowed his head slightly, every movement deliberate, conveying a greeting and farewell all at once—a gesture wrapped in acknowledgment of journeys both taken and left unfinished.

"Arthur Gordon Pym. Dirk Peters." His voice was soft, yet it rang through the chamber like a bell rung in memory, each syllable an echo that reached my very core. His words carried through the still air into our minds, not rushed, but as deliberate as everything Elys was—a constant presence. "You have walked among us as protectors. Our history, our future, now intertwines with your lives. We will not forget."

The weight of his words sat heavy in my chest, layering over the sadness already swelling there. We had walked through their world… but we had walked two paths. Theirs would remain as it always was—untouched by the madness that roiled above the surface, forever hidden from the hands that craved it. Ours was held in the chaos, in the noise, in the unceasing tumult of lives too greedy, too impatient to understand the history they would never know. Beneath Elys' words—I was certain—he understood that even more acutely than I did.

My throat tightened against the wave of sadness pressing upward, threatening to spill out uninvited. But I pushed it back down, though the act exhausted me, left me trembling at the edge of words I could never articulate. This place, these people—they would remain hidden from time. And as I stood there, staring into those pale, endless eyes, I knew that we would have to leave them behind.

Lyra approached next, her footsteps softer, but no less deliberate. Her smile was calm—in its way, strong, though there was no masking the kindness that radiated faintly from her gaze. Her presence eased the intensity, quieted the part of me that spun endlessly in circles, trying to reconcile everything we had seen, everything we would never share. There was a softness in her that Peters and I had needed more than either of us realized, though I felt her gaze linger on Peters with more intent.

She bowed gently toward him, acknowledging his leadership with a quiet respect. There was something about it, the way she moved—an understanding of the battles fought. Some quiet admiration for the part of Peters that had shielded those around him, even in the face of so much danger. Her eyes rested on him with a reverence that I had not seen from Peters before, and when she bowed, the small but deliberate movement carried more weight than any words she might have said.

Peters stood stiff for a moment, caught off guard by the show of emotion. He blinked, almost startled, his face betraying the briefest flicker of surprise—like he didn't quite know how to receive what was being offered to him. For a man so accustomed to conflict, to battle, this—an emotional gesture, an acknowledgment of his own quiet strength—was disarming. But Peters, in his usual manner, recovered quickly. Slowly, awkwardly, he returned the bow, as close to full humility as I had ever seen him. Something in him shifted after that, his posture softening ever so slightly as if the armor he carried—his constant vigilance—had finally relaxed under the weight of this simple acknowledgement.

The moment passed quickly, but the shift remained—that subtle change that still lingered between them, a quiet recognition of all that had transpired between us.

After a breathless silence, Peters and I moved further into the chamber, drawing closer to the core. It hung before us, hovering in the space like the glowing heart of the Earth, now duller than it had been in the clutches of rage days earlier. Its searing intensity had faded, but its presence still occupied every inch of the space around us. The faint pulse at its center—a steady hum now—served as a reminder of the vastness, the truth that we were leaving behind. Alive still, but hidden. Slumbering beneath the surface.

Its light was softer, easier on the eyes, but I could still feel it in my bones—an energy too vast, too overwhelming to completely comprehend. It wasn't finished yet, though it had quieted in the aftermath, content to rest. It pulsed beneath the surface of this hidden world. And as I stared into its subtle glow, feeling the slow beat of that ancient world cradled in the light before us, I understood that nothing above could see it again. Not ever.

The thought squeezed tight around my heart—an unbearable lump swelling in my throat. But I swallowed it down as best I could.

Elys stepped forward, reaching for something near his side, and my attention was torn away from the glow. His hand rose, outstretched, and resting delicately within his palm was a small medallion. Its surface was Náiren—marked and edged with intricate glyphs that seemed to flicker faintly, catching the light from the core behind him. It wasn't large, but there was something regal, timeless about it, like an ancient heirloom passed through generations. A memento, I knew at once—that would tie us to them, bound forever to the journey we had shared.

With solemn reverence, I accepted the medallion, feeling its cool weight settle into my palm like a piece of memory carefully delivered. When my fingers curled around its edge, I noticed how intimately it seemed to fit, as if it had always been intended for those who took this path—even if it led to silence.

"Take this memory with you," Elys said, his voice low, filled with the quiet depth of a world beyond anything I had known. "But remember, the truth you keep will protect more than just this world—it will protect your own."

His gaze softened ever so slightly. His eyes found not just mine but Peters', locking onto them with a piercing understanding that cut through the quiet, a reflection of what each of us was giving up to keep these worlds separate. His words carried the weight of sacrifice—ancient, eternal.

Peters met those ageless eyes squarely, standing firm yet slightly softer than usual, hands resting at his side. No words left his lips, only an unwavering nod—his final acknowledgment of what had been said, of the lives already sacrificed to protect this sanctuary. I watched him linger for just a moment longer by Elys' side, as if a deep, unspoken understanding passed once more between them before Peters turned away, beginning his final, wordless goodbye.

I remained rooted in place, my breath uneven as my eyes flickered toward Lyra, her calm presence radiating unwavering stillness. There was something in that tranquility—something unspoken between us that I couldn't quite define, but felt deeply in my chest. My voice, scarce as it was, escaped in a whisper, barely enough to carry through the space. "I will never forget you," I muttered, the words more for myself than for her, though her soft smile seemed to mirror back all the understanding I needed.

The Náiren elders remained silent as Peters and I moved slowly toward the edge of the chamber, toward the narrow passageway that would carry us upward—back to the surface world. I stopped once, my heart thrumming with the realization that this... this might be the last time I ever saw it.

All of it.

Peters noticed, pausing briefly ahead, his gaze finding mine with a look of quiet understanding. He didn't rush me. Didn't say anything. He felt it too, I knew it—though the weight of it always pressed differently on his silence. But that look was enough to push me forward.

Elys' parting words floated through the air behind me, gentle and final. "Go knowing that we remain."

With that, Peters pressed forward into the ascension, and I followed him, the heavy silence swallowing us whole.

23

The Ascent

We entered the passage tentatively, both of us caught between the atmospheric whisperings of the Náiren village behind us and the stretch of the unseen earth ahead. The ground beneath our boots was smooth but alive—subtle, nearly imperceptible vibrations pulsed beneath the rock, like the faint heartbeat of some distant thing, half-forgotten yet aware of its visitors. It wasn't a violent feeling, nor was it exactly welcoming. More than anything, it felt as though the cavern remembered our weight on it. Remembered every step we had taken before and now reacquainted itself, the occasional tremor of stone bowing underfoot. Not hostile—but sentient in its own subdued way.

I glanced at Peters, watching how his boots carried him forward, posture straight, eyes fixed ahead without betraying any hint of the tension that must have been boiling underneath. He had always moved like this in moments of quiet confrontation—deep in his own pool of practical thoughts, those turbulent storm clouds never quite showing on the surface unless roused. I could almost see him thinking beyond these walls, already performing whatever mental calculations a man like him required to survive the next inevitable challenge.

Ahead, the walls of the tunnel glistened, faint crystal sheen clinging to their surfaces. This was a new passage—strange and unseen, unfamiliar in its construction. Everything here was eerily still, as if untouched by the chaos and terror that had marked our descent. The smooth, crystalline walls bore no traces of the frantic violence we had left behind, no echoes of crumbling machinery or the titanic beasts that had pursued us. Whatever darkness had lurked in that other place was absent here—replaced by a quiet so deep, it felt both indifferent and oppressive. Just us—and the living stone at our feet.

The first stir of dissidence came soon after we set out.

The glow that had hummed throughout our time in this world, that comforting warmth that bathed the deeper parts of the village in soft golden light, inexplicably shifted. It wasn't immediate, nor was it threatening—not at first, at least—but as we ventured deeper into the tunnel behind the Náiren, the light overhead began to shimmer in strange ways. Faint beams, once consistent, flickered erratically, casting odd patterns against the crystalline walls. The warmth of it waned—for just a moment—replaced by a sharp, silvery hue that danced along the walls, giving the passage an otherworldly sheen.

The shift caused both of us to stop.

Peters slowed first, his sharp intake of breath telling me that whatever was happening, he had clocked it right away. Somewhere beyond his usual veneer of collected pragmatism, there was a flicker of unease in those narrowing eyes. For my part, I was already tilting closer to the tunnel wall before I quite knew what I was doing, my fingers unconsciously brushing against the crystalline surface. The texture was grainy but startlingly smooth beneath the tips of my fingers. Cool, like polished marble, yet humming with a deep kind of energy—a pulse I realized was syncing with the rhythm in my chest. Against my palm, I could feel the pressure inside my skull build ever so slightly, pressing faintly at my temples until it felt like distant thunder echoing through an unseen sky.

Groaning thunder that didn't exist—not in reality, but in whatever this place had become. A place where light turned from gold to silver without explanation. Where the weight of the air shifted against your lungs the deeper you moved. I resisted a shiver, though Peters seemed wholly unfazed. His broad back hadn't shifted a muscle beyond that brief, instinctive pause, the silhouette of him still layered against the faint walls.

"Do you feel that?" I murmured, my voice edging on the precipice of desperation. I wasn't talking solely about the walls anymore; I was talking about everything. This entire place stretched around us, pulling time and motion into its folds—but now it was shrinking, suffocating us under the weight of invisible forces I couldn't place. I brushed my fingers along the crystalline surface again, coaxing some thread of logic to surface. "The pressure... it's changing."

Peters remained quiet for a beat, his eyes narrowing. He broke away from his stillness with a huff, brushing past me with that same determined momentum that had driven him through everything we had faced thus far. "Eyes forward, Pym." His voice was gruff, practical—and just a smidge too sharp for it to be neutral. "We've only seen a preview of what this place can do."

I wanted to argue. I wanted to linger—to analyze the strange shift in the ambient warmth, the haunting dance of silver that had caught between the cracks of the rock—but Peters' words dragged me back to the present. The temperature, once bathed in the soothing warmth of the core, was beginning to drop quickly. My skin prickled at the sudden cold—frost forming along the edges of the smooth stone ahead of us. Clouds of breath puffed from Peters as he pushed forward, his hand gripping his jacket tighter against the bitter shift.

I followed.

Was it my imagination, or had the rhythmic pulse beneath our feet slowed? Cooled? The very air bit at my skin now, cold with a sharpness that twisted some primal section of my brain to stay alert, even as scientific curiosity fought to take precedence. For a moment—as impossible as it should have been—I noticed the rock walls shift beneath my peripheral. Fluid. Yes—fluid—the edges blurring, becoming less solid with every step we took forward. An ethereal glow chased us along the path, glowing phosphorescent tones that rippled in unison with each footfall. The lights flickered in brief, fluttering, vibrant hues, like neon veins jostled loose from the core itself.

We pushed through the strange oscillating waves of light, my breath catching between words—trying to make sense of it all. But another glance at Peters confirmed he'd made up his mind already. He pressed forward, his instincts trained solely on survival now, his eyes flicking toward the distant shadows while the light pulsed against the walls in unnatural displays.

Peters didn't halt until he noticed a far more worrying detail. He squinted into the stretching runway of tunnel ahead. The same path we'd started down minutes ago—it was strangely longer now. Narrower. Or was it smaller altogether? Time and space folded in on itself here, the walls on either side shifting inward, pressing down like collapsing ribs on a fragile chest only to expand again the next moment. I caught sight of it just a heartbeat later—standing still caused the space ahead to flatten—but moving forward elongated the stone ahead, bending reality as it stretched.

We traded glances. Part dread, part bewilderment.

Peters stood motionless for half a second too long before pressing onward. His jaw stiffened with frustration, the metallic scuff of his boot hitting the rock floor betraying his annoyance. I could sense that his sharp instincts—his usual barometer for impending disaster—were spinning wildly between every axis of this place. But it wasn't until I fumbled for my chronometer in the next breath that cold realization hit me. Full stop.

I glanced at the dial. And then again. Blinked incredulously.

"Peters," I stammered, half-choked on the words as I tried pulling breath back into a chest tight against unnatural realization. "It's… it's moving," I muttered, the edges of my voice raw in the sudden vacuum of static churning beneath us. My brows furrowed heavily, heart pounding as the pit formed in my gut. "We're moving through time."

He barely looked at me, stepping forward despite the dissonance we now teetered on. Beneath us, the world swayed. No longer solid in the way gravity dictated, the ground tugged my body between standing and falling. Peters sidestepped easily, his boots steady despite the disorienting shifts in space, but I could see the rising tension coiled within him. His breath fogged into the air again, forming spiraling clouds, betraying his unease.

Without turning, he grunted. "We keep moving. Focus on getting out. Not on… theories." His stance widened slightly, his boots scraping the floor with just enough friction to secure him. "Can't take risks here. Not until we're clear."

I swallowed hard. He was right, of course. We couldn't afford to lose focus now. But even standing still, my head swam with the implications, with the gnawing realization that this wasn't just a distortion of space. Time itself was slipping—bending between every blink of my eye, my pulse shifting in ways I couldn't fully comprehend. My heart thudded erratically against my chest—not simply from tension but from the cold, terrifying possibility that perhaps we were being spat out in and out of moments that bore no direction, no—no meaning.

"Time isn't linear here, Peters," I muttered, breathless. "None of this follows prediction—no logic. It bends—with us."

The tunnel narrowed further still. Every footstep carried us closer to its squeezing center. And yet, despite the pull dragging us deeper into whatever we'd broken free from, I could feel the weight of every muscle in Peters' body tense beside me. Ever-sensitive to unnatural shifts, he seemed to tighten his pacing. Too aware of the distortions lining every inch of this place. Through clenched teeth, in a voice taut with suspicion, he growled, "Whatever's waiting for us up top… it's not the world we left."

Between strained breaths, a sharp sound cut through the damp air.

Wailing gusts of air hit my cheek—like wind pouring through forgotten chasms too far beneath the earth for real wind to exist. The unsettling cry echoed in my ears, and as Peters' hand flashed toward his knife hilt, I froze. His palm was white-knuckled against the handle. Glancing back into the tunnel behind us, his neck strained toward the sound—his instincts screaming at us to run—but nothing in the dark hollow appeared except echoes.

The path tilted upward ahead, growing steeper. The air thinned, stretching tightly across my throat as though my lungs had forgotten how to draw oxygen. Each pull of air hit harder, my breath refusing to fill me the way it should. Was the tunnel trying to choke me? Or was it all in my mind?

Every bone fought against it.

Then, the ground itself shifted beneath. No more flickering light—just the faint, sickening sensation of slipping. My hand swung backward instinctively, eyes catching my own reflection in a glossy patch of jagged rock. But what I saw twisted my stomach a hundredfold worse than any slip of time.

My hand—older. For just a moment. Wrinkles? Age spots? Thick veins standing beneath papery skin flashed into my vision, searing against the gleaming stone. Then, as suddenly as it had formed—it snuffed itself out.

Gone.

My breath stammered—I had become something else. But only for an instant.

***

I was the first to emerge from the tunnel into the icy air. The cold hit me like a slap to the face—sharp, unrelenting, digging beneath my skin with the singular resolve of a predator that had waited far too long for its prey to return. For a moment,

I couldn't move. My boots crunched against the dry powder of frost, sinking ever so slightly into the layer of packed snow beneath, but the sensation was distant—muted. The Antarctic air filled my lungs, expanding inside me with a sharp ache, constricting my chest like a vise made from ice and iron. I gasped instinctively, each breath stabbing deep, and for a terrifying second, the world seemed to freeze with me—or perhaps, I with it.

The familiar sting of cold was expected, but this— **this**—felt wrong. The air no longer breathed the same indifferent chill I remembered from the maw of the Antarctic. No howling wind swept in across the horizon, no scathing gusts of frigid breath scraped across the tundra. Nothing moved. Nothing whispered. Not a single snowflake swirled around us. It was as though the land had forgotten what it meant to be alive.

Stillness. Frozen. And yet worse than frozen— *dead.*

"Damn it." I barely registered Peters' voice. The curse slipped through his clenched teeth like a hiss as he lifted his gloved hand to his ear, fingers trembling only to pinch uselessly at the lobe. It would've been lost in any other windstorm, but the world had gone quiet. Still. Too still. His eyes narrowed, blue and sharpened beneath the heavy hood that framed his angled face. The fabric fractured against the careless light.

There wasn't any sound.

"We're…" I faltered, blinking blindly. "…Back?"

Peters didn't say anything immediately. The instinct of survival kicked in first and took precedence over any mere acknowledgment of place or time. His body stiffened, every inch of him drawn tight as if he expected the ground itself to rear up and strike us—or worse, for someone lurking in the silence to fire the shot that broke it. His breath misted faintly in front of him, curling into nothingness before even reaching a second breath. A cold shiver briefly crossed his expression but vanished as soon as it had appeared. His hand was already on his holstered rifle, fingers curling near the clasp.

The ground beneath us was solid—ice packed with untold weight—but I could *feel* the emptiness beneath it. The cold didn't settle; it *burrowed*. We were standing on a surface that should be howling with wind, alive with the deafening rush of Antarctic air tearing through every crack and crevasse. Instead, it was crippled—silent. The very absence of noise was louder than any blizzard.

Peters noticed it first. He always did. His sharp eyes swept the expanse, cold, calculating, just as they always had under pressure, but this was different. A faint twitch in his brow, a tightening of the jaw. His gaze locked on the horizon, scanning. Something *out there*. He took another slow step forward, cold snow crunching beneath his boots—and then *he* froze. Immediately. That tension—the weight behind his military-honed reflexes—tightened like a coiled spring ready to snap. He wasn't breathing quite right, but I couldn't place why until my own breath caught in my throat and I lifted my eyes to follow his focus.

The horizon. We both stared.

And then, like an unraveling nightmare, I realized—I saw what he saw. The **contours**.

There—far beyond frozen ridges, broken like glass sculptures gone to ruin, stood jagged towers stretching pale fingers into the sky—grotesque shapes carved from ice, obliterated by years—**decades**—of wind, still standing sentinel-like, guarding a wasteland born not of nature but humanity. Stark shadows shifted in the bleached white expanse. Structures… ruins, *half-buried* beneath thick drifts of ice, eroded nearly to unrecognizable forms save their deadly symmetry. Years had hidden them from the world—time and snow conspiring to conceal the relics of something we thought we'd left behind. I blinked rapidly, my mind yanking me between disbelief and cold realization.

I fumbled for my chronometer, desperate for the small relic of our own time, something that would take this place and return it to familiarity. Something that would *tell me we still belonged here*. But the moment my fingers dug deep into the folds of my jacket—the instant I lifted the dial to stare at it—a sharp crack ran through the outer glass. The hands had stopped—the mechanized whirring broken, internal gears malfunctioning beyond repair.

I swallowed and tried to steady myself. Tried.

"We've… no, no." My words stumbled—rammed dead into the frozen air in front of me, disappearing into the silence.

My brain screamed against the thought, rejecting it outright. *Impossible*. This couldn't be right. Not this much time… not this abruptly— *not this way*.

But there was no time for denial. My eyes widened against the numbness crawling from the toes of my boots straight into my skull. The horizon was wrong. The haze—pale and wan— *wrong*. The *light was wrong*. I squeezed my eyes shut, trying to shake away the stillness likely clouding my senses, but it was no good.

Peters let out a half-choked sound—something like a rough inhalation, cut short at the moment of realization. "We're exposed." It wasn't fear. But there was a darkness stirring somewhere, something hard in his voice that made my skin tighten. The low sting of dread crept up my spine.

We were moving through a world we didn't recognize anymore—an era that had forgotten us. **Time didn't wait**.

The evidence was painfully, undeniably clear. We couldn't *unsee* what stood tall and frozen in the distance, their bones wrapped in the ice. Tattered ruins—shreds of old expedition sites, broken tents collapsed into sharp angles beneath mounds of frostbite and time long buried. Blackened skeletal reminders waving like ghostly specters from the past—forgotten remains of an age no longer our own. How many lay lost beneath? How many had never made it back?

A pang of sorrow twisted in my gut. But I couldn't answer it with names—only empty, foreboding *years*. The weathered remains of clocks long buried by tragedy, by nature's indifferent hand, now beckoned as distant warnings that this was *not our world.*

Peters had already taken another step forward, but his movement carried no weight of finality, only cold awareness— something shot through with creeping understanding.

And then, I saw the things that changed everything.

Metal. Rusted blades cutting through frozen arches, peppered with decay from untold winters. Half-obscured beneath thick drifts of snow, sharp, crude structures stood like monuments to history—forged through violence but drowned slowly by the weight of nature. Jagged spires of rust and iron, faces ossified in thick, hardened angles—no longer bright, no longer shining.

"War," Peters growled the word into the still air—barely audible but unmistakable. His teeth clenched tight, the suck of air flaring his nostrils. "We're walking back into it."

My chest constricted again—not from the cold, no, from something much worse— *loss.* The loss of—what? **How much? How many years?** I staggered backward, my hand squeezing involuntarily against the bottom of my jaw, fingers splayed in a futile attempt to stifle the bitter wave of panic hammering through me. My legs felt cold beneath me, prickling like needles jabbed viciously across exposed skin. I swayed. The weight of reality slammed hard into my ribs, crashing wave after wave of cold comprehension with it.

"Dear God," I whispered, the air choking in my lungs. "How long?"

"Whatever it was—" Peters clenched his fist tighter. His hand hovered near his rifle, fingers brushing lazily against the trigger as if merely touching the weapon would secure our survival. The rest of his body remained taut with dismal resolve. "Whatever it was that brought us here... We still have ground to cover—and fast."

It wasn't panicked; it wasn't hysterical. It was his simple solution: **get moving**. Survival always dictated the next action, and Peters' mind, so perfectly tuned to war, didn't dwell on *why* or *how*, only that we keep moving. That's what he did. **Move**. Forward.

But for me, staying upright had become a task of monumental focus. I could still feel it—the churn inside, that insidious pressure unraveling how much had shifted while we were gone. **How many decades lost?** My eyes burned—not from the cold, but from the sheer enormity of what we had re-entered.

The material world had spun too far on without us.

I might have collapsed entirely right there in the snow, my mind fraying under the weight of those fears—if not for Peters' rough hand on my arm, the sudden sharp yank that brought me back into my own body. "Focus, Pym," he growled through gritted teeth. His words were clipped, steady—determined not to let the world around us dig too deep into the psyche. "We don't know how far it's spread… or how long we've got."

With that, we pushed into the snow once more—toward the horizon, dark uncertainty coiling beneath our feet. Peters urged me forward; yet even his own steps slowed— calculating now, each one a grind in the unfamiliar terrain.

My breath rasped between my teeth, each pull doubling the ache flaring deep inside me. My toes curled numbly in my boots as the base of my spine screamed against the plodding, relentless cold, but I kept moving. Eyes down, stare ahead. Push.

The Antarctic stretched ahead at last, rolling in unending waves of bitter white and gray twilight. And then… there— far on the horizon, too faint at first. I squinted.

Smoke.

Something *moving fast*—something built, jet-black and sleek, thinning into jagged clouds scattering overhead. And then— past it—faint streams of *something vast* spiraled against the pale sky, too distant but visceral, unmistakably large.

Peters' focus snapped tight.

"War." His voice, dead-steady now, clenched so tight I could scarcely hear him over the rise of wind carried from whatever loomed.

He straightened his rifle.

"Whatever happened," Peters murmured—turning his gaze fully toward me for the first time—"we need answers. **And fast.**"

24

Burden of the Past

The Antarctic snow had a way of swallowing everything—light, sound, even hope—reducing the landscape into a vast, unyielding wasteland. Each step forward through the drifts was a battle in itself, our boots sinking deeper with every trudging move, the weight of our limbs heavy as though dragging stone. The biting cold gnawed its way past what fabric and skin could protect, chilling not just to the bone but deeper still—to where the mind begins to fray at the edges. I had lived through this cold before, but this… this was different. It felt personal this time.

Peters and I pressed on, silent but always so acutely aware of the meaning growing between us—the unspoken acknowledgment of all that had shifted, all we'd lost beneath the Earth. His eyes were fixed ahead, scanning the horizon with a hunter's efficiency, his movements fluid and controlled—always in step with the unforgiving rhythm of the elements. My own breath unfurled in great, pale clouds that twisted briefly in the air before vanishing as quickly as they had formed, devoured by the swirling wind. Every exhale seemed futile, stolen by the unyielding cold as soon as it left my body.

I moved with my head low, chin tucked inside the collar of my coat, but I couldn't keep myself from glancing upward, stealing looks toward the horizon despite my best efforts to steer clear of what awaited us.

And there it was, that smudge of gray-black on the far edge of what should have been pristine white—smoke, moving and shifting in icy currents, impossible to ignore. A dull ache had lodged itself behind my eyes, pulling my thoughts toward it, tugging me like a siren's call, though there was nothing soothing about the sight. No reason for hope. Just the shadows of something else lurking—coiled in that distant haze of war and destruction.

The first time I had spotted the rising smoke, it had been no more than a faint blur hanging low above the horizon, its details masked by distance and frostbite. But now, as we forced ourselves forward, step by frozen step, the smoke was growing clearer—darker—as if solidifying in form with each inch we gained. Thick columns twisted upward like arteries from the earth, veins clogged by the soot of man's desperate machines. There was something vile—almost alive—in the way the smoke spiraled up, each tendril winding inward on itself before bursting forth again in a violent dance against the steel-blue sky. The smoke wasn't passive; it wasn't drifting with the wind. It was violent, as if the land was bleeding out beneath the strain of whatever battle lay ahead.

Peters was squinting into that distant carnage now, head tilted ever so slightly, his brow low and furrowed. I could see it—how the weight of what lay before us was settling into him. His face had hardened even more than usual, the lines carved deeper into his weatherworn skin. There was no nostalgia in the way his eyes traced the horizon, no sentimentality to be found in those deep creases. No trace of the man who ached for the world we had left behind, wrapped in peace beneath the earth. This was something else—a bitter recognition of war. Peters had known conflict far too long to be anything but cold and calculating about its approach.

For a man like him, each whiff of smoke and the distant flicker of flames spoke of broken memories—of violence buried, then dug up again. He was always caught between revulsion and duty, between the man who had wanted to leave that part of him behind and the soldier who couldn't resist the call to arms.

I stumbled slightly, my boot catching in a drift. My instinct was to look at Peters, to search his face for some kind of reassurance, some flicker of insight, a reason we might still escape the madness searing its way toward us on the wind. But all I received back was that same hardened gaze, fixed forward—all his focus glued to the horizon, his expression as taut as ever. He was locked, prepared—but he hadn't forgotten me entirely. When his eyes finally slid sideways, he didn't fully engage. It was the brief acknowledgement of a man recognizing his burden. A moment of clarity before moving forward, alone, even as we traveled together.

"Two men back from the dead..." Peters' voice drifted low, rumbling from somewhere deep within the barrel of his chest. His words rode the wind, harsh against the silence but laced with a grim humor darker than the smoke above us. His eyes didn't leave the distant plumes, sharp and focused, betraying not even the subtlest tremor in his expression. "And stepping into another war."

His tone was biting—the kind of bitterness you weren't supposed to swallow. It circled in the air between us for a moment, drifting aimlessly like the vapor of our combined breaths while my mind tried to quiet itself. Tried to ignore the way his words echoed that same senseless spiral happening in my own skull. Two men thrown from one unspeakable place into another. We had crawled out from under the world... and here we were, world-shattered still.

I shuddered, though I wasn't sure if it was his words or the cold creeping deeper into my flesh. Maybe it was both.

For a breathless moment, my thoughts swam in the depths of the Náiren's world. In the glowing sun of the Earth's core—the eternal warmth that had soothed us and the knowledge that had broken through the surface of my mind like an ancient, forgotten sea sponge gasping for air. My body was here, back on this surface we couldn't recognize, yet my mind... my mind was still drowning beneath it all, searching grasplessly for some way to reconcile the distance between this reality and where we had left.

A strong gust of wind tore through me then, biting into my

chest and sinking sharp claws into my skin. But it wasn't just the cold; it was the smell it carried. I caught it the moment my breath stilled—faint at first, but unmistakable. Acrid, pungent—fuel-smoke, burning something I couldn't quite place, mixed with a faint trace of static electricity. My stomach twisted at that familiar tinge of burnt metal—of cordite—hanging in the air. As though the land itself had absorbed decades of violence and now bled it back into the wind. We were getting closer to whatever awaited us in the shadows of that smoke-laden storm ahead.

Peters' pace quickened beside me, his steps more intent now—each motion precise, cutting through the snow with greater purpose, though the wariness always remained. His instincts were pulling him forward, but cautiously. Every now and then, I would see his hand tighten on the strap of his rifle. He could sense it as keenly as I did. Something was rising from that horizon ahead of us—something dark, something inevitable. The dark shapes of machinery began to materialize, faint at first, but growing, massing rigid and angular against the horizon.

As the shapes grew clearer, my legs began to weaken. The cold and the snow fought back each step. I was fast running out of breath—my chest heaving, mouth open wide as my boots skidded over the ice. Every gain was met with a force ready to drag me back. But I couldn't stop—couldn't stop looking toward Peters. His steady frame urged me on, his limbs cutting a path for me to follow, even as my own mind fractured further. Every step carried me closer to… to what? The storm. The war I didn't understand. It festered and festered like a thing alive, pulling us closer as it ground the land beneath us into scorched ruin. The weight of time leaned into me, pressing from all angles, crushing harder with each breath I stole from the wind, and my resolve—already thin—began to crack under it.

We were nothing. Two men lost from time and place, flickering ghosts scrambling across a frozen hell. And I felt impossibly small in it all.

A low rumble coiled up through the snow, faint but unmistakable. Something stirred in the depths beneath us—an uneasy motion just far enough off to go unnoticed if not for the primal pricks of instinct alive in our bones. Both of us halted. Reflexes shared. Peters' hand instinctively hit the stock of his rifle, eyes scanning downward, flickering across the landscape with ferocity, trying to trace whatever disturbance had passed beneath us.

His gaze met mine for only a brief flash—hard and cold—as the wind carried a whisper of something darker still across its frigid breath.

***

The snow-laden wastes stretched out before us in a monochromatic void, devoid of any life, but ripe with brutal reminders of lives once controlled by forces far beyond themselves. I'd never seen the Antarctic like this before—so bleak, so suffocating, as though the very land had grown tired beneath my feet, curling in on itself under the weight of its own history. Here, beneath the pale, sickly light of an overcast sky, the expanse became more than just physical distance. It was temporal. We moved through vast cracks in time itself, caught between two realities, neither welcoming our return.

Peters stoically marched beside me, his exhaustion buried beneath years of gritted resolve. But even his bracing silence couldn't stave off the sense of being utterly out of place— of being relics ourselves. He hadn't said a word since we'd crested the last ridge and saw the black streak of smoke trailing in lazy spirals over the frozen horizon. Too much of him was locked in a kind of battle mode, suppressing everything but the immediate need to move, to survive.

Then I saw it—the scattered cluster of ruinous machinery lying just ahead, barely visible at first, the contours of metal and steel curling beneath layers of frost. Half-buried in the snow, they sat grotesquely, forgotten by time but never quite undone. My heart seized mid-beat, a sharp, involuntary reaction to what I saw unfolding before us. My boots slowed, faltering slightly, the weight of my legs suddenly doubled as if the gravity around us had increased.

"It's here," I whispered—though Peters had surely seen it first—his pace never slowing as he pressed forward with grim purpose.

The debris field sprawled out, a jagged mass of twisted remnants, frozen relics of a nightmare past. Time had strangled whatever life these machines once held. Bent limbs of metal protruded at odd angles, like the half-remembered skeleton of some long-dead beast, one the snow had claimed piece by piece. But, even in death, they held form. Nazi insignias, carved into rusted steel, jutted out, unfamiliar yet horrifyingly recognizable, sprouting from the broken frames like malignant growths. What was once bold, oppressive power had withered, turned inward during their cold decay—but it was never fully withered away. No. Those remnants… they *clung*.

As I approached, I saw the twisted remains of old carriages—futuristic weapons, machinery I couldn't name—all buckled under the weight of time and ice. Drifts of snow clung viciously to their frames, wrapping around these relics of war like a suffocating blanket. The edges curled inward, bent and fractured in surrender, rust having burrowed its way through the layers of steel, peeling back the stronger parts of metal like the dead skin of a long-forgotten corpse.

Time hadn't just gnawed on them; it had choked them into submission.

Peters advanced ahead, his boots grinding against the frozen crust of snow. I watched carefully as he crossed over toward what resembled the skeletal remains of a military machine, its once powerful treads now crusted over with ice. As he shifted his weight slightly, the ground gave way beneath him with a hollow crack—the thin veneer of snow covering it splintered outward, revealing what had been hidden just below. The exposed gears and spokes, now frozen fast together, twisted grotesquely under the ice, still too stubborn to fall apart completely. They were stuck in their own form of death—rusted but intact enough to tell us, unmistakably, what they were. I could almost hear the clanking, the roaring mechanisms that had fueled this frozen wasteland so many years ago. Still, Peters kept his hand poised on the rifle slung over his shoulder, eyes darting, the muscles of his jaw tight.

I stumbled nearer, my breath misting violently before my face as I caught sight of something darker, half-buried beneath the snow right at the periphery of my vision. A patch of cloth—frozen, stiff—the outline unmistakably that of a uniform. My stomach twisted. I knelt and brushed away the snow with trembling hands. There, beneath the brutal layer of frost, the Nazi regalia remained—decayed, but still there. The fabric had become stiff, hard as if time itself had rejected it, pressing down with the weight of endless winters. The once-bold insignia, gaudy eagles, and iron crosses were now faded to mere remnants of the past, echoes of a nightmare that would never fully fade. As my fingers closed around a crumpled armband, I could feel the brittle rot that had set into it, dead skin peeled away like dust. Time had punished them, surely, but... not enough. Not enough for what they'd done.

Peters stood tall behind me, looking over the ruin, his face grim beneath the weight of this discovery. And yet, there was no surprise in his countenance. If anything, there was a dark, bitter familiarity about him. He exhaled sharply through his teeth, a sound that came closer to a growl than a breath. "Time hasn't forgotten them," he muttered darkly, the words heavy with meaning, as though he was reminding himself of something unspoken. His boot nudged at something half-buried in the snow near his feet. He bent down, extracting the edge of a military map, frozen stiff. It unfurled with a brittle crack as he held it up to the light. Half-buried in a crate beside its owner—a soldier long since forgotten. His brow furrowed as his eyes scanned the crude markings, still clear despite frozen decay. Pinned locations—chillingly familiar—spotted across the map's surface.

I leaned closer—recognizing places familiar to our world's surface, and others... others I'd never seen before. Not even heard of. They were preparing for something, something far larger than just hiding down here. Planning.

"We were never meant to see this," I muttered, my voice trembling with the weight of the words as the reality settled heavier than the snow that lay over us. Peters didn't answer immediately. Instead, his cold eyes dropped down toward the twisted remnants of a machine near his feet—a broken mass of steel now rusting in the ice. For half a second, it sputtered—feeble, pathetic—as though the cold remnants of what once powered it struggled to return to life. A strange creaking groan escaped the machine, barely audible over the biting wind. But just as quickly as it stirred, life abandoned it again. The groan became a death rattle, collapsing inward under its own weight.

I had to tear my eyes away from the ruin before me—had to swallow hard against the rising bile in my throat. My breath hung visibly in the air, each exhale a reminder of how fragile this world had become—how fragile *we* were—cracks forming in the very fabric of the reality we stood within. Time wasn't just bending out here… it was disintegrating before us. The thought gnawed at my guts, churning with a sickly dread as the ground beneath me trembled.

And then it happened.

I hadn't been expecting it—not consciously. But the insignia on that rusted, forgotten machine—the twisted symbol of hatred and violence—twitched. No, not just twitched—shifted. I swore beneath my breath, scrambling back, eyes locked on it as it began to *curl*. The Nazi insignia—the angular symbols that curled into themselves painted so proudly across that metal frame—twisted itself like wax under flame, almost liquid in the way it folded inward. Turning, burrowing into itself—not with immediacy, but smoothly, subtly, until the once-familiar shape became an incoherent mess of strange, flowing lines. It felt conscious. Worse, it felt *intentional*.

A fragment of time's claws… distorting everything.

Peters growled again, louder this time. His eyes locked onto the shattered wings of a strange metallic structure, jutting up from the ridge of snow and jagged ice before us. Its design was like nothing we had ever seen, a ghostly remnant of some colossal machine, now broken and twisted by time and winter. The skeletal frame loomed, remnant of some desperate escape attempt that had failed catastrophically. The wings—their form twisted in bizarre patterns, as though they had been caught in motion mid-flight, frozen in time before their final destruction. The jagged, inhuman angles told a story of frantic escape and catastrophic failure—of lives torn away long before reason or recognition had time to intervene. Without fully understanding what these strange machines once were, it was clear: they signaled only defeat, despair solidified in steel and ice.

War. Betrayal. Ruined lives.

Peters glanced skyward, his shoulders rigid with tension. His eyes followed the faint shadows—military flying machines darting weakly overhead, represented only by the brief taint of war-darkened clouds. Far above all this… past and present converging in one trembling landscape. His hand twitched noticeably over his rifle, the hunter in him waiting for the impossibility of an attack while his mind clearly reasoned that battle was already here.

For me, the realization plunged like ice. We had climbed up from hell—emerged into a nightmare.

The world was *wrong*. From beneath us, the ground trembled once more as though *something*, something older and faster, bigger even than time's slow unraveling, prepared for its moment to emerge.

I couldn't shake the feeling. We had barely begun to understand it— our place, between the cracks in history—but worse forces were gathering, just beyond.

Peters, ever steady, finally spoke. "This? It's not finished…"

***

The horizon buckled beneath the weight of unspoken tragedy, its edges smearing together in strange, violent shades of black and gray, like the last desperate burst of breath from lungs that had gasped their final agonized breath long before we arrived. To the west, great plumes of smoke clawed their way upward, jagged fingers stretching cruelly to the heavens. It was as though the fabric of the world itself had come undone, riven by the relentless gnashing of human conflict—old and new—and what festered beneath it all. The Antarctic sky above, once blanketed in a motionless shroud of clouds, grew restless. Now, that shroud twisted and pulsed, turning black, as if a great storm were brewing against the horizon—one not of wind or weather, but something much darker, far more unnatural, swelling with every breath we took.

"Peters," I muttered, my voice catching in my throat as the weight of those distant flames cut across my soul, "are you…?"

"I see it," he shot back, his voice brisk but tight—no room for hesitation. His fingers tensed against his rifle's strap, every line of his body taut, like a hunter sighting a beast much larger than anticipated. His gaze never wavered off the distant carnage, but something in his tone was wrong— something darker than mere danger hung there.

We were close now—too close. The wreckage, half-submerged beneath decades of frost, stretched jagged across the desert of ice, relics frozen not just in place but in ambition, in failure. But more than the machines, more than the twisted skeletons of old weapons of war left to rot, it was the horizon— the unholy distortion of what should have been sky—that consumed the deepest part of my attention.

I stopped walking, forcing my legs to still themselves in the snow. My heart pounded sluggishly in my chest, not with the quick, erratic beat of panic, but with something more unnerving—a steady, oppressive rhythm, rising like the storm taking shape ahead. **That** was no longer just smoke. **That** was thrumming—alive. The horizon shivered. No, more than that: it **bent**, a twisted, angled reflection of itself crumbling piece by piece, as though the world was incapable of holding its own weight.

"What are we looking at?" My breath escaped in white, billowing puffs, barely audible over the icy stillness. But there was no mistaking it—not for either of us. The dark clouds held form now, pulsating out from the earth like some grotesque, mocking heartbeat. Not just clouds. Not just storm—but war memories wrenched loose from time, balled into a singular mass of fury and destruction. The horizon **rippled**, reality itself wavering, like the crescendo just before a scream of unimaginable pain.

Shadows flickered along the distant ridgelines, movements too fast to properly catch in the haze left behind. Peters' body tensed beside me, every inch of him coiled, ready to spring. "Stay low!" he barked, his voice suddenly sharp, almost feral. Without thinking, I dropped instinctively, sinking into the snow with a low crouch. The wind abruptly picked up, howling ferociously across the wasteland, tearing at my coat and driving wicked flakes of ice into my exposed skin like glass shards.

Peters scanned the distance, his narrowed eyes never leaving the chaotic, swirling mass beyond—a shape was beginning to take form within the storm. His jaw clenched, the firm line of his mouth a testament to his instincts fighting against what his eyes couldn't look away from. **Doom was coming**, and he knew it, even before I did—before either of us could assign an explanation.

And then the shape emerged.

I felt it in my chest first—an uncontrollable tightening, as though something thick and invisible had clasped its fist around my ribs and wouldn't let go, forcing the air from my lungs in a quick, harsh gasp. I stared, my fingers sinking deep into the frozen earth, prying against the pull that threatened to jerk me toward the storm. Something was moving—forming—becoming—inside that monstrous swirl of smoke. It wasn't mere machinery; it wasn't anything human could explain. The shape towered above the ruins and smoke, hazy and misshapen at first, movements shrouded by fog, by flame, and memory. But it didn't stay that way for long.

Peters reacted before I did, his rifle snapping upward to his shoulder, the barrel trained in perfect line with the creature that now loomed beyond. "Hell," he muttered, his voice barely audible over the shrieking winds. He bit back the rest of his words, his focus honed so intensely I could feel the vibrations of his pulse thrumming in the space between us. But his body language screamed it: something **immense** was standing before us, and it wasn't meant for human eyes.

It moved.

Not with human cadence, not with the predictable plodding of steel or iron or soldier's boots—but with the terrifying fluidity of something both alive and beyond life. Each shift in its grotesque outline unsettled the air in front of it, warping the horizon further, thrusting jagged lines into the veil between worlds—the seams of reality groaning under its presence. There were no edges, not really—just a mass of **shadow and smoke**, an assembly of war itself, wrapped in a terrible silence preceded only by the dull roar of an unstoppable storm.

My throat closed; no scream came. Just a desperate, empty sucking of air as though the figure before me drained all oxygen out of the sky. I could feel my body lurch backward, straining to escape, but there was **no impediment**. It moved as war had always moved: **inevitably**. There was no running. No escaping.

The figure was towering over us now—rising, impossibly tall—casting its frame against the sky like a funeral pyre whispered against the backdrop of time. Featureless. Ageless. Vast. I didn't need to remember it. I knew it. Knew every line of it, though nothing about it was clear. It was history. It was pain. It was every moment of conflict that had ever—**would ever**—shake the world. Here. Now. Endless, broken time given shape and form.

A shuttered breath forced itself free from my lungs, breaking loose in a panicked wheeze. But no matter how hard I pulled the air in, I couldn't speak. Couldn't scream. Peters didn't move either, his hyper-alert gaze glued to the shifting silhouette before us, his hands tight on the rifle, gripping—no, **clutching** against the growing unsteadiness of that figure's presence.

God. No **rifle** could stop this.

Peters' jaw twitched. He was analyzing, calculating, but the sheer enormity rippling from that space—it defied his mind, his instincts. Despite the enemy he saw, his mind rejected it. I could see it in how his hand dropped slightly, hesitating. Even Peters couldn't calculate a solution to something that **wasn't** supposed to be.

And me? I couldn't move. My legs buckled, no longer useful beneath me. I was on the cusp of understanding… yet each revelation hovered just out of reach, dissolving before I could grasp it.

And still, the figure **grew**.

It cast a jagged shadow over us, consuming the battlefield— not of weapons, or soldiers, or machine, but of war itself: **of time itself**. The **same** shadow I had seen those long, strange months ago—emanating from the mist, from the water, from the deep, unreal darkness at the edge of this Earth. An omen. A warning. And now?

Reality fractured further, splintering beneath our feet like soldiers' bones breaking in the cold. Something beyond us—beyond this **world**—had come.

It wasn't finished.

It wouldn't let us escape.

The shadow shifted.

It was no longer just a distant silhouette. The figure loomed now, taking shape against the desolate horizon, blotting out everything it touched. The ragged lines of smoke choked the sky, twisting like fingers grasping at the edges of the storm. It was as if history itself had gathered in great heaves, swelling against the frozen wasteland. The figure seemed to pull it toward itself, a magnet for the accumulation of time's most violent memories. Something vast, something old, something beyond comprehension was stepping into form, and the world beneath it trembled in response.

I couldn't look away.

My breath caught in my throat, hacking stale and sharp as the immensity of the thing pressed down on me—not physically, no—but in a way that felt worse. It was oppressive, inescapable, as though the air itself rebelled against my attempts to breathe. My chest tightened, and the cold gnawed at my lungs in the way cold does when it becomes more than a sensation—when it begins to crawl inside your very bones, seizing everything, eating you from the core. Every nerve within me screamed to flee, to run as fast as my legs could carry me. But my feet… my feet wouldn't move.

"Stop it—" The words slipped from my mouth, barely audible over the wind, my voice cracked and hollow. Panic. I was yelling, though to whom, I didn't know. The figure stood far beyond anything human, yet I addressed it all the same, hopelessly. I needed it to stop. Needed it to *not* be. As if by speaking, I could banish it, push it away, make it dissolve back into the mist of unreality where it belonged.

But it didn't stop.

It only loomed closer, more distinct with every pulse of the storm enveloping it.

It was too much. It was choking me. I squeezed my eyes shut but immediately pried them open again—I couldn't shut it out—and my breath came in short, rapid gasps. The cold seared behind my eyes and thudded against the sides of my skull. The air—the pressure—it just… kept pulling me down. My knees threatened to buckle, caught between the will to crumble and the need to stand against it.

It doesn't mean to crush me, but it will.

Next to me, Peters was silent, his eyes narrow beneath the brim of his fur-lined hood. His hand was steady even as the ground trembled beneath us. He gripped his rifle like a man gripping a lifeline. He wasn't accustomed to this kind of fear—not the abstract, metaphysical sort that squeezed at your brain, cracked your senses open, and left you drowning in the void. His fear was rooted in the physical—tangible. Something solid that he could face head-on, even in its most horrible, brutal forms. But this... this was different for him. And yet, despite the unknowable dread, Peters wasn't frozen.

His fingers tightened around the rifle, knuckles turning white as he forced his body into action. Old instincts returned, carved deep into him by years of war. The unknown demanded confrontation. Reflexes—so finely honed that they bypassed thought—took over. He had faced impossible odds before, stared into the face of death without flinching. Maybe nothing could prepare him for this, but Peters was nothing if not a fighter. His breath came fast, sharp against the ice-laden air, pooling into frantic clouds of steam that vanished as quickly as they formed. And with the practiced motion of a thousand battlefields, his finger inched toward the trigger.

I wanted to tell him to stop—to wait. But the words failed me.

The sky... God, even the sky above us was coming apart now. The storm had taken on a life of its own, not just raging but *fracturing*. I could see it—felt it too—a searing jolt of wrongness thrumming beneath my skin. The battlefield below, around us, seemed to bubble and shift, space itself pulsating as if it were being torn limb from limb, folding in on itself like images overwritten in haste. Shadowy figures— flickers of soldiers, past wars, uniforms I didn't recognize— appeared and vanished in rapid succession. Disjointed scenes from the carnage of human history melted together, ripped from whatever time they belonged to. Men charging blindly into battle, explosions erupting in a fractured haze of soundless chaos, swords clashing with no means or rhyme— all of it superimposed on the present.

It was like watching ghosts bleed into reality.

My heartbeat jittered to match the warping rhythm, my pulse lagging behind the rest of my body. I stumbled slightly as the ground beneath my boots tilted, a spasm running through the fabric of time itself. Beside me, Peters grunted— a low, frustrated sound—as if the disjointed vibrations in the air made his rifle twist in his grip. He wasn't sure if he could trust what he was seeing. Neither of us could. There was no sense to it. Only chaos. Only the constant pull backward, then forward—history splintered, breaking across our very skin.

"No... Don't." I managed to choke out. My voice felt like it was barely leaving my throat, but I had to try. Had to warn him. Peters couldn't see it.

He couldn't see what I could.

Everything—the figure, the battles, the storms—they were all connected. Continuations of themselves, yet outside of time, outside of reason. We weren't spectators. We were caught in it now, and if Peters lifted his rifle—if he tried to fight it—what would change? What would break?

But his eyes… He was too close now. Too far gone to hear it. His instincts had flared too brightly to just shut off. *Defend. Survive. Fight.*

He took half a step forward, his pulse surging beneath the weathered leather of his jacket's strap. He didn't speak, but the line of his shoulders, the newfound tautness in his stance, told me everything I needed to know. His calloused finger tensed against the rifle trigger as the figure grew taller, the storm overhead roaring into pure white fury.

It reared above us.

For an impossible moment, I saw the figure. Really saw it. It stood in full, sprawling majesty—a titanic silhouette of war and time and death itself—its cracked form bending into jagged edges, refracted by collapsing waves of history it now controlled, commanding at its whim. It was everything. And then

Snow.

Everything was swallowed in a suffocating, blinding rush of snow.

The wind howled into my bones as a massive gust hit us— obliterating everything in sheer white. Peters disappeared. The rifle. The horizon. Everything, gone in an instant.

I saw nothing. Knew nothing.

The world was white, and the figure—*taller*—stood hidden—forever—beyond the reach of any man.

My thoughts caught on the edge—fragmented. Distant. Had Peters fired?

I couldn't tell anymore.

"Amidst the storm, we stand…"
   The words echoed, trembling in my mind, unprompted.

"And the figure grows taller…
   forever looming…

forever out of reach."

About the Author

Jim LaFleur is a writer of short stories with surprising twists that will make you laugh, gasp, and think. He has a knack for creating memorable characters, witty dialogue, and unexpected endings that leave you wanting more. Jim also writes fiction and inspirational stories that explore the themes of courage, hope, and resilience. He is not the character from Lost, but he does enjoy watching the show and finding plot holes.